# Not Cast In Stone

Peter Georgiadis
Brigitte Bonnet

CIRCLE OF PENS
PUBLICATIONS LTD.

www.circleofpens.com

First Edition 2006 by
CIRCLE OF PENS PUBLICATIONS LTD.
www.circleofpens.com

ISBN 978-0-9552471-0-1
0-9552471-0-1

Cover and typeset by
Circle of Pens Publications Ltd. & Erik L. Lloyd


Printed and bound in Great Britain by
CPI Antony Rowe Ltd., Chippenham, Wiltshire

# Acknowledgements

Many thanks to Wenche Georgiadis who worked tirelessly researching the historical facts for this book.

Thanks also go to David Bartlett and Michael "Spider" Kelly whose knowledge of the Great War is without equal; that is why they are both included as characters within this tome.

Grateful appreciation goes to our friend Kenneth Wyatt who also provided inspiration with his natural wit.

We are also indebted to Sybille Chapman for her input regarding the German dialogues.

Acknowledgements with thanks to A P Watt Ltd on behalf of the Estate of Jocelyn Herbert and The Executors of Teresa E Perkins.

Though this book is a work of fiction, it uses many real historical episodes combined with actual names of individuals involved at the time. Most of the fictional characters are considered either friends or heros to the writers.

It has not been the authors' intentions to offend anyone.

# I

'This is going to be another soddin' long cold night!' Enrico sighed, absent-mindedly scratching himself: the lice were as active as ever, but the soldiers in the trenches had long become oblivious to their biting.  He leant heavily against the firestep, stomped his feet to work some circulation back into his frozen limbs, and glanced around.  What he had in front of him were coils of broken barbed wire laid mile upon mile in the hope of stopping a determined enemy from breaking through the lines, but now the wire was smashed after four endless years of destruction from bombardments.  Had he looked closely into no-man's-land, he would have seen the broken bodies of enemy and friend alike, lying in their dismembered and decaying state, oblivious to further onslaughts.  The landscape was nothing but fractured trees, rubble from demolished buildings, shell holes almost overlapping one another, many filled to the rim with the debris of war, or a soup of mud and water.  But Enrico, like all the other soldiers who manned this hell hole, had long forgotten what a real pleasure the country-side should be.  This was their home and they didn't like it, but they were used to it.  He overlooked most things except the need to keep his head well and truly below the parapet.

'Thank goodness for good old Matti!'  He smiled and stomped again and this time clapped his hands.  His childhood friend looked as cold as he felt, and was busy alternatively scratching various parts of his anatomy and slapping the top of his arms.

Enrico looked up at the night sky; it was heavy with clouds, but then huge gaps would appear showing the stars sparkling above. 'I wonder if there's any life up there… anyway, I'm too cold to give a shit.' Yet again he scratched, and this time managed to find one of the blighters, and crunched it between his thumb and his finger. As he looked around the sky the Milky Way emerged from yet another gap, looking for all the world like a faded milk stain on black cloth; but then another heavy cloud obscured those beautiful stars. His attention was brought quickly back down to earth as a German flare lit up all of no-man's-land. Instinctively he ducked behind the firestep and scratched again, shivered and wondered what tomorrow was going to bring them both. In their short lives, there had been very few times when the two lads had been apart; they were closer than brothers and had shared the horrors of the war together.

A particularly loud detonation interrupted his musings: a large German Howitzer shell had landed harmlessly not more than a hundred yards away. In spite of more than three years in battles, Enrico had never become used to the smell of rotting putrid flesh, stagnant water, or even the cordite from the shells. He ducked to avoid the falling debris and had to laugh when he heard Matti swear as the latter got hit by a clod of frozen foul earth. Further down their trench system a soldier called some obscenity across towards the German lines, some rifle fire was exchanged, but soon petered out. Occasional shelling happened well away from their sector, but that was more to just keep annoyed soldiers awake than seriously trying to kill anyone.

They were waiting for dawn to break, before making their way to the forward trench and machinegun dugouts, where they had to deliver orders to a Lieutenant Wilfred Owen: orders to attack enemy positions which seemed somewhat pointless, considering that Armistice was due to be signed anyway in a week's time. But these were orders from the top brass, Generals who thought they knew best, whose idea was to not let the Hun rest until that sacred piece of paper confirming the truce was signed, sealed and delivered.

As the night progressed and the cold intensified, sleep was out of the question. In order to forget his discomfort Enrico started to reminisce about early life with friend Matti.

"Matti, when we went to work on that famous day, did you ever imagine we would end up in a filthy trench, dodging muck and bullets? And here we are, looking as if we are surviving this bloody farce, and about to start our new lives!"

"*Pfff!*" snapped Matti, more from cold and tiredness than anything else. His attitude softened as the conversation carried on. "In some ways, I suppose we have been extremely lucky, not least of all because we've come through it together". This time Matti smiled at his friend, not that Enrico could see that sign of affection in the dark, but it was there anyway.

\* \* \* \* \*

"I was called that name by my folks because when we lived in Warsaw, Mum and Dad managed to go to the Opera House to hear the great Enrico Caruso singing an opera by Verdi. Mum fell in love with the great man and thought that having a son with that name would create some artistic ability within him."

At that, both the boys laughed heartily.

Matti still looked puzzled, as he had never heard of Verdi or Caruso.

"So, how did you come to be called Matti, which is after all, more than a bit girly?"

Matthew scowled at his friend, for being considered effeminate worried him. "And what's wrong with Matti?" he retorted sharply.

"Absolutely nothing!" laughed Enrico, as he threw his arm around his friend's shoulder and they quickened their step so as not to be late for their shift, which was starting at seven a.m., on this cold, frosty, grimy morning in January 1915. At first, the echoes of their hobnailed boots rattled around the cobbled terraced roads which led to the colliery. Each step was enhanced by the clatter of slamming doors and marching feet which quickly grew into an army, as the menfolk made their way to work.

"Brrrr, it's bloody cold!"

"You always feel the cold! If you carried around a bit of blubber like me, it would not seem so bad!" answered Matti.

"It's so dreary around here! Have you ever noticed how cold and depressing these houses look? There's absolutely no colour!" observed Enrico.

"That might have something to do with the fact that nobody can afford paint. It's hard enough to earn money just to pay rent, put food in your belly and clothes on your back!"

Having said this, Matti looked rather smug, thinking how clever it was to have worked this out for himself. Again, the friends quickened their step because today was Friday, and the boys looked forward to seeing their shift end, and getting into the queue of expectant workers to receive their pay packets. The siren sounded for the second and last time for this shift; they had five minutes to get through the iron portals, which were so grand in design that they just enhanced the dreariness and poverty of the surrounding streets and houses.

The ground was icy, the weather was cold, and the air was thick with coal dust and dirt, thick enough to eat. Yet the boys almost skipped with the anticipation of the day… *pay!*

It took three minutes from the clocking in to receive pick, helmet, and batteries, and to get into the first cage available. The descent was fast and always unnerving but the men could only think of getting the day over with. It was half a mile down to the first tunnel, then a walk of nearly a mile, sometimes crouched, sometimes erect, to the coal face. Enrico and Matti were young, they could get to the face quicker than most of the older men, and the two boys, being strong, were ready to swing their picks. It was the seam diggers that made the most money, and the danger and the dust seemed small problems against the possibility of earning a few coppers more.

"Matti, have you ever thought the reason it is so hot down here is because we are closer to the devil's fiery cauldron?" And at this moment Enrico poked both his index fingers into Matti's sides as if to give him a

4

ghostly scare. Matti looked around, and with the gloom of a sixty watt bulb lighting nothing but blackness of walls and ceiling, he could nearly believe that demons lurked in the shadows. He quickly lost the feeling, as he hastened his step and followed the lights which hung at hundred foot intervals. At least, this gave an idea of the direction to take!

It was ten minutes after Matti and Enrico had first wielded their picks at the face, that the other eight members of the Section, including Joe Cuddeley, known to his mates as "Old Cuddly" arrived. Cuddeley liked having these younger lads working with him as they could boost his bonus quite substantially. Seeing the boys already hard at work, filling the carts with freshly dug coal, the foreman smiled to himself. The work progressed well; all the men laboured with a will, picking at the face, shovelling into the carts, pushing full carts back, returning with empties, ready to repeat the whole thing over and over again. As the Section worked its way down the seam of coal, along came the team of proppers whose job was to fit pit props, so as to prevent cave-ins. The coal was good, the quality good enough for even the export trade. The management and investors were making vast profits thanks to the quality of the coal and the hard working talents of their men. Demand for coal, now that a war was on, had never been higher; money was there to be made.

It was eleven fifty-six in the morning when the foreman blew his whistle for the lunch break. Charlie Robbins, one of the team, laid back in the filth and grime, having just consumed his huge slice of bread and cheese; with a grin on his face, which couldn't be seen in the dark, he called out:

"Sing us a song, Caruso!"

"What shall I sing?"

"What about Tipperary?"

"It's a long way to Ti-pp-er-ary ..." sang Enrico, as always completely out of tune, with a voice that can only be described as bloody awful. It was so bad to the ears of the Section that they all finished off in the right key, not that Enrico ever got the message... "It's a long way to go". The laughter could have been heard through most of the shaft, had there been anybody else to hear it!

"Never mind singing out of tune!" chorused Jim Cole and Bill Watson. Silence befell the Section, as they drank their water and ate their food. Joe chirped in, a minute or two later, having just finished relieving himself against a pit prop: "Anybody got any news about the war?"

To this Bill Watson's ears pricked up. Bill was the oldest member of the Section at fifty one, with a razor sharp wit to match any youth, but a face and a body weathered and beaten into submission by years of hard slog and toil. He said in a sprightly tone: "My son came home on leave the other day. Some of the things he told me beggared belief, but one thing I must tell you about, though God knows whether it will ever get out. There was a truce on the front over Christmas!"

"D'you mean with Fritz?"

"I know it sounds crazy, but young Steve was telling me how, on Christmas Eve, they could see lights from the German trenches at about five o'clock, when darkness was falling, and some of the Germans had stuck a bloody Christmas tree which even had a candle or two alight on it in no-man's-land! Steve said that even the officers didn't know what to do and were shaken furthermore when they heard choruses of Silent Night in German and in English! Steve said: 'What the hell is this war all about? Fritz is just an ordinary bloke like us; why the buggery couldn't the officers and Generals see that?' " After a pause he added: "And you'll never believe what happened on Christmas day either! A German officer holding a white flag came in full view of our trenches asking for a truce! And d'you know what? Before the Fritz officer got his answer, there were men from both sides getting out of the trenches and up on to no-man's-land! Why, the buggers even started to swap cigarettes and exchange rum rations for German sausage! It wasn't long before one Tommy produced a football and before you knew it, a couple of hundred men did battle in a game of football! Nobody died *that* day."

"Right, boys, back to work! Enough of this bullshit! By the way, Bill, give best to the boy. When does he go back?"

"Seven whole days, and what's more we didn't even know he was going to get leave."

The prop workers had done their job well, and had moved on to another face. Work was hard and Joe mumbled under his breath a little ditty that he had known from his early school days… "Work is hard, pay is small; take your time, fuck'em all!" But of course to take one's time meant less bonus, so everybody worked as hard as they were able. About an hour had gone by, and the sweat was pouring profusely, mixed with coal dust, when a small but deep rumble was heard. Everybody stopped work. "What was that?" cried Matti.

Another rumble, this time louder, deeper and closer. "*Shit!*" This time there was no mistaking the voice of the worried foreman. "*That was close!*" No sooner had he got that sentence out that another rumble came but this time, bringing down a section of the roof which was behind them, and their only escape route. "Jesus Christ! We're done for!" It took several minutes before the dust settled and nerve endings stopped twitching. Finally, Joe took control of the situation and ordered everybody to take stock and account for themselves. Eight voices counted out, which, with Joe, made nine. "Who's missing?" cried Joe, but even as he said it he knew it was Bill Watson. "Look around you, where's Bill?" It only took a second before Matti chirped in with, "My God, here he is, under some rubble and a pit prop, which seems to be pinning his legs." The crew quickly gathered around the unconscious, half protruding shape of their friend Bill. "Is he alive?" asked Joe in a voice which was almost a whisper. Somebody bent and felt his wrist to see if there was a pulse. "I think he is". "Then with care, fellows, let's get him out." It took some time to remove the pit prop and rubble from Bill. They could see quite plainly that Bill's legs were broken and crushed, and were bleeding within. "Oh, crikey!" moaned Sam. "This could be serious!"

"Serious, serious for all of us!  At least Bill is unconscious!  How the hell are we going to get out?"

"Not only is our way out blocked, so too is our air flow… no air… no life!"

"Now, listen here," said Joe, "I won't have any talk like that!  Apart from everything else, it's my pay day; we're getting out of here!"  Very quickly they got Bill into a comfortable position and they noticed that he was beginning to move.

"Enrico, Matti, start pulling at that cave-in.  Start at the top, moving the spoil behind you, see if you can tell how bad this mess is?  After all, it was all very quick, so maybe it is just a small cave-in."  The boys clambered up the pile to the ceiling and lammed into the spoil with a will.  After a while they had dug a human size tunnel about ten feet into the fall.  Both lads were now starting to feel extremely tired from the exertion, plus the lack of clean air was beginning to take its toll.  Enrico was the first to crawl back out into the small space that held his friends.

"Joe!  Give me a breather, put someone else in there!" which was done by relieving Enrico with another, Sam Torridge, also a young man.

"Sam, get into Enrico's place and carry on and break through!"  Sam, being a slight but extremely strong young man, willingly obliged.  Enrico slumped to the ground next to his colleagues.

"Joe," he said, "do you really think we can get out of here?  I never heard anything that would make me believe people were digging from the other side to try and rescue us!"

"I won't have talk like that!" repeated Joe in a low but stern tone of voice.  "We are all getting out of here!"

A sudden moan drew their attention to the fact that Bill was regaining consciousness.  "Oooh!  Buggeration!  My legs hurt like hell!  What's happened?"

"We've had a fall-in.  You were the poor bugger that copped a packet.  But you're going to be all right.  You seem to have broken both your legs, but we got you out from under it all and things are never as bad as they appear! We'll make it, don't you fret!" But in his thoughts he wondered. As time went, so did the air. The boys had stopped digging, as it had become too much; with each shovelful of spoil they moved, the pain in their chests had started to become unbearable. It was Matti who crawled out first, having now reached around fifteen feet into the fall.

"Joe," he said, "enough is enough, I've had it!" A short time later Sam followed suit. Nobody was going to go back into the tunnel. A gloom had descended, as dark as the blackness of the walls and ceiling, with the realisation that this could quite well be their last hours on God's earth. Breathing became harder and more laboured. Each man seemed resigned to his fate. Sleep seemed the best way to go, and a quiet, peaceful snoring sound started to gently roll around their tomb.

It was the foreman Joe Cuddeley who first realised he was not dead: in his subconscious he could smell what he thought was clean country air, he could feel the wind whistling through his hair. He tried to make sense of this sensation. "This can't be right," he thought, as he then heard noises which to him sounded like the mooing of cows and the bleating of sheep. "Am I crazy or am I dead in Heaven?" he wondered. He suddenly understood the sounds he heard were in fact rescuers who had broken through. With this realisation and with a grin on his face he murmured: "Boys, I said we'd make it out of here! And we have!"

In fact, since the industrial revolution had started and mining had become the major industry, this area around Darwen and Blackburn had become prone to cave-ins within coalmines, causing minor earthquakes. Collieries had long since developed highly trained engineers and workers who in an instant could organise a rescue team. Collingbrook mine was no exception, so when the cave-in occurred, within a short space of time, a team was assembled and sent to the face.

Bill was the first to be removed from that black airless hole, but soon all the miners were up top; in spite of the dark and the smog, like in

Joe's dream, they felt they were in pure country air.

Back in the washroom, all except Bill who had now been taken to hospital were laughing and joking as if nothing had happened and this was the end of a normal day's shift. "Pay time!" exclaimed Joe as he wiped his grubby hands on an even grubbier cloth hanging next to the gutter which constituted the urinal. The men and boys lined up and waited for their names to be called.

"Lokowski, your pay. Enrico, you get one pound four shillings and tuppence ha'penny. Don't spend it all in one pub!"

Enrico pocketed the money readily, smiled at Matti, looked at Joe and promptly threw up.

"Blimey! Anybody would think you'd never been in a cave-in before!"

Nervous laughter came from all of them, as they started to realise how close to the brink fate had taken them. Matti lifted the gloom, "Enrico, I think it's time for a drink!"

As they made their way to the exit, Lord Collingbrook, the owner, walked from his office to greet the men.

"I am glad to see you are all fine." Then he added, but in a very dismissive way, "I suppose it's down to the pub for you lot!"

Joe and his fellow workers could hardly disguise their disgust at these casual remarks.

"What does he think we are, a horde of bloody drunkards?" remarked Joe under his breath. As no recompense had been offered, not even the standing of one drink by the owner, the men dispersed to wend their way home. As the Section passed through the gates, the few worried-looking women who had gathered at the sound of the first siren quickly disbanded when realising that their husbands were not involved. As point of fact it had been a minor incident. Only Matti and Enrico were going to have what they thought was a well deserved drink. The two boys walked the small distance to the "Red Lion" public house with the hope of being taken for two eighteen year olds. As the mist and darkness enveloped them a gloomy silence came over Enrico. The rhythm of their boots on the cobbles punctuated his thoughts. Somehow the events of the day activated a melancholy within him, and he started to reminisce about earlier troubles that had brought his father and himself to their present situation.

Enrico 'Caruso' Lokowski was born in Warsaw, Poland in 1898. Born to a middle class family in a leafy suburb, he was the only adored child of Stefan and Marie. Stefan had inherited a thriving family hardware business, and his way with figures had even further improved an already comfortable existence for the family. But the troubles in Europe had always loomed high in the mind of Stefan. There never seemed to have been a time when nations were at peace with one another. This always spilt into ethnic problems. There seemed to be only one solution for the Lokowskis' future security because this no longer seemed possible in Europe. The only logical thing to do, like millions of Europeans before, was to emigrate to the USA. It appeared almost as a whim to Marie, when, one Friday afternoon, Stefan came home from work to inform his wife that he had obtained a good price for the business and was therefore taking the family to their new home and a safer way of life in Pittsburgh, America. The house, being a detached and well maintained home, was very quickly sold and brought a good price. Stefan realised that they had enough money to travel to America in style, and decided to take the family down through Europe by train, crossing over to England on the ferry, and travelling to Liverpool, where they could get a more luxurious liner to the USA. There was enough money for the family to settle into a comfortable existence once arriving at their destination. As he did not believe in letters of credit, Stefan spent several weeks organising the changing of his money into US Dollars and English Pounds. There was enough to fill a rather large suitcase with banknotes.

Having had an eventless journey, they arrived in Dover on January 22nd 1901. This was a black day for the British Empire. Queen Victoria, England's longest reigning monarch had finally succumbed to the mourning of her Prince Albert and old age. It was also three years to the day that young Enrico had been born. The whole country was in mourning; shops and businesses had closed out of respect, and it became a nightmare for Stefan, wife and child to get to Liverpool. With a skeleton service now operating, they eventually caught a train from Dover to Waterloo. As nothing seemed to be open, it made more sense to carry on and go direct to Liverpool. Luckily for them, they managed to procure three tickets on the overnight post train. Uncomfortable, slow, but reliable. Reaching Liverpool the next day, still with the country in a state of shock, they were lucky enough to find a large family room in the Station Hotel where the three of them sank into a deep luxurious restful sleep. Stefan woke up the next morning refreshed and with a feeling of exuberance:

"My dear wife, now that the first part of our journey has been successfully completed we should explore this city! I shall put our suitcases in the wardrobe and lock the door. Anyway, my dear, everybody knows the British are an honourable, honest people. Let's enjoy ourselves!" It was a cold, blustery morning; rain was in the air, but it did not dampen his enthusiasm. The New World beckoned, along with the new life.

Liverpool is not a pretty city, but no-one can say it is not interesting. The grime of industry marked everything equally, and, like most industrial cities, you did not breathe the air, you ate it! They decided to stroll down to the harbour area as just, maybe, they could glimpse their steamer, the Cunard's liner, Campania. Though they had booked their tickets in Warsaw, they had to pay for them in cash within two days of the sailing. They were going in style! No steerage for them! A state room on the starboard side! The town was full of bewildered people, having just lost their queen; it was as if the whole country was suspended in time. People seemed to be milling around aimlessly. The only places that were open were the Chinese restaurants and the brothels, where the working girls were always kept busy. At least the sailors seemed to have a purpose!

The Campania was in! There she stood, all six hundred and twenty feet of her! Even Marie looked on with a pride, as if she and Stefan owned this twin-screw twenty-two knot Cunard liner.

"Darling," said Marie, at last with a smile on her face, "when I look on this wonderful ship, I start to believe!" She put her arm through his and nestled in close. At this, young Enrico sensed a rare moment of joy, and wished to be lifted high into his mother's arms as if to share it. It had been a long wait to see his mother smile and he was not going to lose this time of elation. As it now was early afternoon, hunger pangs overtook them.

"Let's try one of these Chinese restaurants Liverpool is so famous for!" suggested Stefan. So they made their way to the closest, half decent looking establishment they could find. Stefan's and Marie's English was broken, but it was not as bad as the Chinese waiter's who was trying to serve them! One sailor was heard to say to his lady friend: "Blimey! Talk about the blind leading the blind!" which led to more than a little laughter throughout the restaurant. In the end, the only way the family was going to be fed was by pointing at various dishes.

They had enjoyed their first day in Liverpool; grimy, gloomy, cold and rainy Liverpool had not dampened their spirits. After all, the sun never stopped shining in America! As the day progressed Enrico started to get tetchy from tiredness; too many new experiences for one three year old who now needed, more than anything, to sleep. The family, gorged with new sensations but wearied from their efforts, made their way back to the hotel. They were greeted by the doorman with a hearty "Good evening, Mr. and Mrs. Lokowski!" as he opened the door for them to pass through. They walked across the deep red carpet and were given their key by a Liverpool lass.

The sight that greeted them, as they opened their bedroom door, was one which would stay in the memory of all of them for the rest of their lives: everything was tipped upside down. Clothes and bed linen lay everywhere. Stefan's first thought was to check the room. Surely this was not their room! Realisation came with a jolt. Marie and Enrico stood like statues, erect and marble-faced in the doorway. Stefan's next reaction was to run to the wardrobe with a hope that it might still be locked. Sickness welled in his gullet, as he quickly established the fact that they might well be ruined.

"Marie," he called, "get the manager, quickly! Hurry, woman!"

It seemed an eternity until Marie returned with the manager.

"We are thieved!" cried Stefan to the middle-aged, rather rotund man. The manager who was sweating profusely, and mopping his brow with a huge handkerchief, said in return:

"What have you done to the room?"

"We have been thieved! It's all gone, everything!"

There was something in the way the manager spoke which showed to Stefan that either the man was a fool who did not understand him, or did not believe what he had said.

"Please! Get police!"

"Yes, Sir, I'll get the police," as he again wiped his brow with the kerchief. He did not seem to feel a sense of urgency, though, as he walked away far too leisurely for Stefan's taste.

A lone policeman, led by the manager, eventually arrived to find Stefan trying to console Marie, who was sitting on the bed, sobbing with her head in her hands. This had also become too much for young Enrico, who could be seen curled up in an armchair close to the window, sound asleep.

"So, Sir, how can I help?" inquired the police constable.

It took several minutes for Stefan, in his broken English, to explain that everything they had in the world had been stolen that very day. Again, it seemed that, like the manager, this officer seemed almost bemused and not very sympathetic, almost unbelieving. Stefan somehow managed to ask if any investigation was going to be undertaken. But to his horror, the constable produced a notebook, sat down, and asked for their names and addresses, which seemed totally ludicrous as they no longer had an address. All that happened was that the constable just took down a lot of irrelevant information. It was only when mention was made of the suitcase containing all the money that the policeman's ears pricked up.

"We have nothing, now,"

"Does that mean you cannot pay the bill, Sir?" asked the manager, still busy wiping perspiration from his beleaguered brow.

"Of course not! Not until I get money back!"

The manager frowned, took the police constable aside, and spoke to him out of earshot.

"I tell you, Bill," he said quietly. "I don't believe a word of it! They are just bloody foreigners trying it on!" The police constable cupped his chin in his right hand, resting his elbow in his left hand and leant heavily on his left leg, sighed deeply and said:

"You could be right, Charlie; who would ever have thought up the idea of stealing from this man a day after the queen has just died? There is something rather fishy about all of this."

Within twenty minutes the Lokowski family had collected whatever few items of clothing that were left on the floor, been allowed to wrap them in some brown paper tied with a piece of string, and were discharged into the cold evening. Marie was overcome with grief, and with grief comes cold; leaning heavily against a gas streetlight by the roadside she started to tremble uncontrollably.

"Please, Marie, I need you to be strong now. What the hell are we to do? Remember, it's not just us, we have a child!"

"Oh, God! Oh, God!" she mumbled, but hardly seemed to hear him.

"God! Of course, the church! They must help!"

Though neither of them was devout, being erstwhile Catholics, all three of them had been christened. At this moment Stefan noticed the police constable emerge from the hotel. He called him over.

"Please, we need help."

"You need locking up," replied the police constable, now smelling of a very large whisky. "Wasting police time is a serious offence, and technically you could be charged with stealing from the hotel, so I suggest you move along, while I still feel in a good mood."

"Wait!" said Stefan. "Where is a near catholic church? Please help!"

"Going to pray for forgiveness, eh? Bit late for that! But there is a church just three streets away down yonder on the left, and may God help you!"

Unknown to Stefan and Marie, the Station Hotel, as grand as it was, had a notorious reputation for stealing from foreigners. Who knows if the manager and the policeman were even in collusion?

They found the church, and though it was cold, it was at least open and dry. By now Marie was in a state of stupor, and Stefan had to look after her and Enrico. After what seemed an eternity, but in fact only an hour, along came the sprightly young Father Lyon, who had been seconded from Marseille in France.

"Mon Dieu!" started Father Lyon, seeing the well dressed, but obviously distressed trio huddled together on the front pew. "What has happened to you?"

Stefan was equally startled by the approach of this very young French priest.

"Father, please help us!"

Hearing the strongly accented English, the priest asked:

"Parlez-vous Français?"

"Non... Sprechen Sie Deutsch?" queried Stefan, with a wistful look of hope in his eyes.

"Ja," said the priest.

'Thank the Lord!', thought Stefan, 'Finally someone will understand us!'

The priest listened intently to the family's tale of woe and felt a Christian urge to help in some way. First things first, though, "Come back to the presbytery with me. I will get the housekeeper to prepare some hot soup, and make up a bed for the three of you. It won't be luxury, but it will be dry and warm." Then as an afterthought, he said: "This will give us more time to consider the situation."

Bowing and crossing himself at the altar, young Father Lyon thus took charge of the Lokowski family.

Having eaten gratefully — as sometimes eating can relax the various burdens of guilt which now hung heavily upon Stefan's head — he glanced wistfully at his woeful-looking wife and at Enrico who was now sound asleep in her arms. The dark thoughts that were swirling around in his head made him feel desperate and alone.

"I think it is time you all went to bed," said Father Lyon in a compassionate tone. The family retired to their makeshift bedroom, but only Enrico was going to sleep. Having spent most of the night pacing the floorboards of their room, Stefan too, fell into a deep unconscious sleep in the very early hours; only Marie lay in the bed, hardly daring to move, still in a total state of shock.

"Tell me, Father," asked Stefan, toying with his bread and butter, "do you think we will ever get our money or our goods back? It was all we had in the whole world."

"One would like to give hope, my son," replied Father Lyon, "but as you are in a desperate plight, reality would seem the best answer I can give, so I think it must be no. I suggest that you contact any relatives that you might have, and ask for help to get you out of this present situation."

"I had thought of that, Father, and I will do it, this very day."

"In the meantime, my son, you and your family are welcome to stay here for some days. Maybe you can repay the church with helping around the house and garden."

The priest walked behind Stefan who was still sitting, toying with his breakfast, and placed both his hands on the older man's shoulders. This young priest understood all the anguish that he was going through; it was as if he was trying to draw the poison out of Stefan and into himself.

"And what of Marie, how is she?"

"Father, I am worried. I've never seen Marie in such a depressed state. I feel as if I have brought her and Enrico to hell and ruin, and she can't take it."

Marie had indeed fallen into a deep depression. She was not a well woman anyway, having had recurring bouts of tuberculosis, hence the reason for just the one child in their marriage.

"Then we will let Marie spend time in bed. You, my son, must spend the day writing letters and caring for your child. My housekeeper, Mrs. Miller, will look in from time to time on your wife and try to be of some help."

Father Lyon was as good as his word. He allowed the family to stay, showing that Christian charity was not dead in this part of Liverpool, even though it took a young French priest to demonstrate it. As the weeks went by, the state of Marie's mind worsened and her physical strength ebbed away. Though Stefan had received no replies from relatives, he had got used to the situation, helping here and there within the house and church, even taking on the role of accounts keeper, as money and maths had always been his strong points.

The weeks merged into months. Marie's condition had never improved. By the beginning of August, the local doctor had been called, and had warned Stefan to prepare himself for the worst. The irony of it all was that Marie gave her last breath at twelve a.m. on the ninth of August 1902, just as the new King Edward VII was having the crown of England and Empire placed on his head. Father Lyon had been wonderful throughout their sojourn, and though he had expected them to stay but a few days, had enjoyed the company of Stefan, and even accepted the disruption brought about by young Enrico. The funeral had been a quiet and dignified affair, graced by the attendance of a few of the local parishioners, who, over the last months had got to know Stefan Lokowski and his terrible troubles. Father Lyon had presided over a wake at the presbytery for Marie and officiated at the funeral. That night the two men got very drunk on two bottles of Irish whiskey, kindly donated by one of the parishioners. It was in this condition that Stefan came to the realisation of what he must do.

The next day, armed with a letter of recommendation written by Father Lyon clutched in his hand, Stefan went to see the manager of a newly opened Woolworth shop to seek employment as an accountant. Maybe the Lokowski luck was changing: he was awarded the post of assistant accountant with the grand salary of one pound two shillings and sixpence a week.

And indeed their luck had changed: in June 1903 he was made chief accountant with a substantial rise in salary. It was time for them to find their own way in the world. Though Father Lyon had never once asked them to leave, Stefan knew the moment had come. He had saved a little money, and was able to now buy, with the help of a bank loan, a small two-bedroomed terraced house in Tranmere. This was to be their home for the next ten years, until Enrico left school and was to find employment at the age of fifteen.

That September, Enrico had his first day in primary school. The day had not gone well; when in the playground talking to some young girls a slightly bigger boy had come up to him and kicked him in the shin. The pain was severe, but he showed no fear: swinging wildly with both arms, he hit the boy full on the nose, causing it to gush with blood. Of course, it was this blow that the teacher saw, and not the build-up to it. The teacher dragged him by his ear, not listening to any of Enrico's protestations, straight to the headmaster:

"I will not tolerate any rowdy behaviour. I don't care if this is your first day at school. You will learn that the headmaster's word is law."

With that, the headmaster walked to the cupboard and withdrew a long thin cane. "Bend over," and Enrico felt he had no alternative but to oblige.

"Touch your toes!" *Thwapp! Thwapp!* Tears welled in his eyes, but not for the first time in his life he suppressed any sobbing sounds.

There were many occasions during which Enrico was to experience the displeasure of this master, but the years passed, and at the age of eleven, he had moved to senior school.

Though loved by his father, he really needed the guiding hand of a mother, and had become artful and cheeky. Enrico's yearly school reports would always state: 'Like most boys, Enrico could do better, if he only applied himself.' But secretly, the headmaster admired this troubled youth. Mr. Cluff always liked boys with spirit, and no one could deny that young Enrico had spirit. He was pushed, banged, thumped, and generally bullied by bigger boys, but he never kowtowed to any of them, and would often go home with a bloodied nose, having tried hard to administer such to the offender. But Mr. Cluff's greatest admiration, if admiration be the right word, was when Enrico tried to stop an older boy from beating a newcomer, one Matthew Dumbridge. The headmaster was watching from his window. His policy was generally — let boys be boys. Enrico ploughed into the bully, and yet again, received a bloodied nose, but he also received the lifelong friendship of Matthew 'Matti' Dumbridge.

Enrico grew tall, wiry and strong as the school years progressed; he never became a scholar, but excelled in boxing and football. After all, what more could a young man want in life? On the other hand, Matti was to become slightly rotund from his love of too much bread and dripping. His naïve looks may also have derived from the fact that he too, was not academic. He tried boxing because his mate Enrico boxed, but he only seemed to get black eyes and bloody noses.

The day eventually came when children put down their school books and take up the mantle of adult work. Enrico and Matti had long decided that whatever work was offered and paid reasonably well, they would do it as long as they were together.

On the last day of school, an opportunity presented itself, when a representative of Collingbrook mine came recruiting.

"We need strong boys with strong backs!" said the man. "If you work hard, you will be well paid. Mining can be a career for life!" Enrico and Matti exchanged a glance, and their future fate was sealed there and then. A few days holidaying in Darwen, just outside Blackburn, where Lord Collingbrook's highly productive coalmines were situated, allowed the boys to find temporary digs. The mine itself was in a blackened area South of Darwen, but close to Turton Moor. The extremes were not lost on the boys, with the filth of the coalmining town contrasting with the clean fresh air and open countryside of the moor which would be their playground in the coming months. The winds tended to be prevailing northerly, which had always kept the town grimy, but the moor clean.

A week later, at the tender age of fifteen, the two boys went to do their first shift, starting at seven in the morning and not finishing until six at night. Meanwhile, back in Tranmere, Stefan was faring badly. Since Enrico's departure he had become melancholy with loneliness; he had never found another companion like Marie. Enrico had been the light of his life after her death. At least once a week, he would visit his friend Father Lyon, and together they would drink heartily and discuss the problems of the day. But gradually, he started to become dependent on alcohol. The more he drank the more melancholy he became.

The boys progressed well in their work, and as months turned into the first year, nobody who would have known them from their schooldays would recognise them now: they had developed into strong young men. Hard work had made them both muscular, and they were popular with their working Section as their enthusiasm brought bigger bonuses for all of them.

All these thoughts and more flashed through Enrico's mind in seconds, as the two boys walked along the cobblestones. He was jolted back to reality when his right foot scuffed a loose stone. "You a'right?" asked Matti, gripping his arm to stop him falling.

"Oh, just remembering…"

Though the Red Lion was only five hundred yards from the gates of the colliery, it had seemed an eternity, but at last the dusty, smoke-dulled light of the public bar loomed into view.

"What's it be, boys?" asked the bartender.

"I'll have a pint of mild and bitter," said Matti.

"Make that two!"

The bar was not seething, but there must have been eight other miners all drinking heavily, trying to clear the dust of a day's work from their throats. Putting down his empty glass, one miner called over to Enrico:

"I heard there was a cave-in today. D'you boys know anything about it?"

"Sure do", said Matti, quickly finishing his first pint, and pointing in the way of the barman for a refill. "We were in the middle of it. One of our mates got his legs crushed, but he's alive. But I have to admit I thought we were goners."

At this he picked up his second pint and gulped lovingly at it. It was not long before both the boys were feeling extremely light-headed, what with the excitement of the day and the several pints of beer. One of the men standing at the door called out to his friends in the bar, as if giving a warning: "Hey, boys, here comes Sally Atlas. My God, she's got a wonderful pair of tits!"

She entered the bar, with her long hair flowing down her back and though she wore a dark overcoat, the front was undone just enough to show deep cleavage, which she knew always turned men's heads. Sally was twenty-two years old, living with her widowed father; she was admired for her voluptuous figure and though she was stepping out with the local policeman, thirty-five year old bachelor Angus Higgins, she loved men, and flirted whenever she could.

Producing an empty ewer from under her overcoat, she smiled at everybody and called out: "Fill this up for Dad, please, Sydney!"

"Take your turn, girl, there's others before you!"

Sally walked slowly to the bar, making sure that all the men could get their eyes filled with her delights. She came up next to Enrico, placed the empty jug on the counter, turned to her left and looked deep into Enrico's eyes, enjoying the fact that he had gone bright red.

"I've seen you around before," she said.

"Well, I... I've seen you too, on several occasions," he stammered back.

Most of the bar fell about laughing at the nervous way Enrico had reacted.

"We've got a live virgin, here," said one of the miners, and he was not referring to Sally!

Matti was struck dumb by the sight of this buxom beauty, also creating howls of laughter from the drinkers as his mouth dropped open, and his eyes boggled. Sally was enjoying her moment; she already had the boys in the palm of her hand, and she had been there but a second or two.

"What a nice pair you are!" and at this her hand had slipped down and clutched at Enrico's testicles. The men were now crying with laughter.

"What the hell! What do you think you are doing, you slut?"

The laughter stopped immediately; Sally turned sharply to the door, letting go of the hapless Enrico, and saw to her horror the threatening shape of her uniformed boyfriend. An enraged Angus Higgins strode quickly to the bar, and in one swoop almost lifted Sally off her feet with a slap to her face.

"What the hell are you doing?", cried Enrico. "She's only a woman!" — as if nobody could tell! To this the angered police constable grabbed at Enrico, saying: "And don't think you are getting away with this!"

Swinging wildly, his fist contacted with the side of Enrico's face, knocking him to the ground. It was a glancing blow that did more hurt to his pride than spoil the features of his face. As Higgins turned back to the girl who was by now sobbing profusely, he leapt to his feet and charged at the back of the policeman, knocking him heavily into the bar, and making him fall hard on the sawdust strewn floor.

"I'll kill you for this, you little bastard," said Higgins, and as he got to one knee, he started to draw his truncheon. In the melee, his helmet had come off, and was resting on the bar, next to the empty ewer.

Matti, all this time, had been standing there with his mouth open, as if in a trance. But seeing the policeman pulling out his truncheon and threatening to actually kill his friend, without a moment's thought, Matti grabbed a pint bottle from the counter, and brought it down heavily on P.C. Angus Higgins' head. Higgins fell to the ground. For a moment, there was complete silence… nobody in the bar moved, until one of the miners said to the general assembly: "Jesus! I think he has done him in!"

Then the crowd gathered around Higgins and turned him over. His eyes were wide open.

"Oh, my God," said Sally. "He's dead!"

"Christ, boys!" somebody said. "You'll hang for this! You must get away, and quick!"

As the bystanders realised the horror of what had happened, the Red Lion emptied speedily, and the two lads also moved into the street. The gloom of the night closed in around them. Everything that had taken place seemed but a dream, yet reality told them they had to escape, and fast!

"Matti, we have to leave, and we must leave *now*," said Enrico. "The police will come soon, and it won't take them too long to find out who we are and where we live. I reckon we just about got time to go to the digs, pick up what we need, retrieve our money from under the mattress, and then we can make our way to Blackburn and get the overnight post train to London where we can disappear."

Quietly and resolutely, this strategy was carried out.

# II

In the early dawn of the next day, Matti and Enrico alighted from the post train from Blackburn. Yet another grey, cold, drizzly day. It was not the sort of rain where you cannot see a hand in front of you, but a misty haze of cold, clammy wet, that got through all your clothing and onto your skin. Soon both the boys were soaking and miserable. Their flight from Darwen had been fearful but uneventful. They had hurriedly left a note for the landlady, thanking her for her kindness, stating that work was taking them to Glasgow. This subterfuge, they hoped, would fool the police into believing they had gone north instead of south. They walked across moorlands as far as they could, aware that it was unlikely that anybody would follow them. Yet the evening mist swirling around each boulder and tor, gave them the impression that the ghost of Higgins was already pursuing them. When they got to the station at Blackburn, they had just a few minutes to wait before the train left for London. But those minutes seemed like hours. Everywhere they looked, it seemed that a policeman was lurking. An officer was by the toilets, another one by the ticket booth, and yet more by the entrances to the platforms. Were they there waiting for them?

"We can get onto the line just up the road there, make our way back onto the far end of the platform and get onto the train. With luck no one will see us," said a very nervy, subdued Enrico. A few minutes later the boys had managed to get around the road, over the railway fence, and clutching their few belongings, they made their way onto the line and back to the platform. Furtively, with trepidation, they boarded the train. It left on time, much to the relief of both lads. Now they felt they could snatch some sleep and relax, at least between each station. The post train was a slow, unwieldy, lumbering steam train which had been in service since the late 1870s, carrying at least thirty-odd years of grime and oil. But like all heavy steam trains of the 19th century, it worked well, if but slowly. It stopped at every station they came to. Each stop represented a few minutes of extreme nervousness for the two lads who kept looking carefully out of the window to see if the police were boarding the train at all. But all they ever witnessed was the loading and the unloading of the post and various goods. One thing caught the eye of Matti, and he remarked:

"Every station has about half a dozen posters of Lord Kitchener pointing and saying 'Your Country Needs You'. Maybe that's what we should do!"

"Come on, Matti, wake up! People die in wars; they promised it would be over by Christmas, and that's already turned out to be a load of *shite!*"

The train arrived at Euston, at around six thirty in the morning, just as the gloom of dawn was fighting to break through the weather and the grime. As they left the train they held back, waiting to see if they could leave the platform without trouble. There had only been possibly another eight people on the train, and it did not take very long for the platform to empty of the few passengers, post and goods. The duo looked very carefully before coming up the empty platform. But it was clear, and they could walk out, having not once been approached by any railway staff, which was just as well, as they had never bought tickets!

London is a vast metropolis, big enough for any wanted people to disappear in. They walked, like all newcomers, unknowingly, to the heart of the city, that being Trafalgar Square. Everywhere they looked was an exciting new sight, but the first thing that struck them was the amount of uniformed young men: Army, Navy, and even young flyers from the Royal Flying Corps. Everywhere, posters of Kitchener, pointing accusingly, demanding one's attention, hung on walls, lampposts and hoardings. There seemed to be a mass of people, gathering at the lions, by the great pillar supporting Lord Nelson. This surprised Matti and Enrico, as it was still only eight-thirty in the morning. From out of the throng, a very elderly army officer was helped onto the platform that supports the column and the lions. He looked every part the nineteenth century cavalry officer that he was. His bushy handlebar moustache, which age had made grey and wiry, sagged down under the weight of the damp, making him look very much a caricature. He wore tartan breeches and a flared tunic with the entire attendant belting and buckling, even sporting a side arm. His proudly displayed medals made one wonder if he had fought in every campaign since Claudius had conquered Britain. He must have been eighty-odd years of age, yet he stood erect and commanding. He was handed a megaphone which he brought to his mouth and said, in a rather high-pitched voice, somewhat surprising for his age:

"I am Major-General Sir Hubert Alexander of the Household Cavalry, retired. Men, we are in the worst crisis since that little social climber Napoléon thought of conquering the world. This small insurrection that we thought would be over by Christmas has turned into a very dangerous state of war. The Kaiser, that upstart, and his hordes of coal-scuttle-helmeted soldiers have to be stopped!" At this point the hubbub from the crowd turned into howls of laughter, along with arm waving and cheering.

"Our boys who numbered around a hundred thousand met the full onslaught of three million Germans at Mons in Northern France. As you know, this was August of last year, and our gallant B.E.F. was pushed into a retreat. But being British, did we panic? Of course not!" he said, raising his hand in salute, thus raising more howls of approval.

"Why, we allowed them to push us back almost to Paris. But we knew this would stretch their supply lines to breaking point, which it did!" More howls from the crowd.

"Then we took our stand, and we stopped them dead. We knew we were better than the Hun! Now it was our turn to drive forward, and for Fritz to retreat." More cheering and waving from the crowd.

"I can tell you, men, there was a big battle at the river Marne, but again we crossed and pushed forward, driving the enemy before us."

At this point, it was noticed that a recruitment table was being set up, and that a kindly, smiling — which seemed a bit of a contradiction in terms — very stout, middle-aged sergeant was trying to encourage young men to come forward and sign their names for the duration, and accept the King's shilling. The line very quickly formed for this.

"I won't dally with words; like Lord Kitchener says, your country needs you! Anyway, this is the adventure of a lifetime! This is your chance, not just to serve your King and Country, but to show what mettle you are made of! Your children and grandchildren will one day say... tell me, what did you do in the Great War?"

As he spoke, more onlookers gathered, amongst which were several middle-class ladies in their finery. They would go up to young men, asking if they were going to join, and if the answer was in the negative, handed them a white feather, which brought laughter and derision from the enlisted men, and scowls of shame from those holding the feather. One thing that Major-General Sir Hubert Alexander had failed to remark on, was the fact that, now the Germans were building trenches all the way from the Alps of Switzerland to Ostend in Belgium, the British and the French had to do the same thing to the South of the German lines. Sometimes no-man's-land was hundreds of yards to possibly a mile across, in other areas the gap could be as little as ten yards.

Again the wily old General neglected to explain about the shelling; his speech was on a need-to-know basis. He rambled on about how wicked the Kaiser was, and how wonderful King George V, Britain and its Empire were, and how we had gone to war to protect little Belgium. He ended with a glorious finale saying...

"Once we have broken through the enemy lines," he puffed out his chest, "the cavalry will finish the job."

A crescendo of cheering, and more than a little mocking laughter, as the old boy strutted on his blackened granite dais, fingering his drooping moustache, looking more like a male pigeon courting its mate, greeted this pomposity.

As he raised his right hand to the heavens, looking up as if expectant of a bolt of lightning to appear through the clouds, his last parting words were:

"How can any man not want to do his duty?"

His speech had worked its wiles; the thin trickle of boys and men putting their name to the register started to turn into a torrent, the men jostling each other in their eagerness to chase the Hun.

Enrico and Matti had stood on the periphery of the crowd, having never experienced any such gathering before. They were overwhelmed, their eyes bulging with the excitement of the moment. Matti broke the silence between them:

"Christ, Enrico, I've just realised we haven't eaten anything since yesterday! I'm bloody starving!"

Picking up their bundles, off they went in search of sustenance. Once replete, feeling came back into their bodies. The lousy winter weather, along with the troubles of the previous day seemed to melt thanks to the warm glow that was in their bellies.

"I think we ought to find somewhere to stay for the night."

"Good idea," answered Enrico.

"It will have to be cheap and quiet, so that our money can go further, at least until we get jobs."

The boys had been walking in the general direction of Parliament Square, when out of the gloom, came their first sight of St. James's Palace and Big Ben. As they came closer they were astounded by the amount of cars that were going in and out of the Parliament buildings. They thought it best to go to the south side of the river, as this was all too grand and expensive looking. They strolled across Westminster Bridge to Lambeth and for the first time, spied the mighty Thames. Half-way across, they leant heavily on the parapet of the bridge, looking eastwards as the tide ebbed at a fast rate.

"My God!" said Enrico, "what *don't* they throw in their river!"

Indeed, as the boys watched, it seemed to them that most of the flotsam and jetsam of the world rushed by in the water.

"Blimey!" said Matti, "you won't get me swimming in that!"

The boys instinctively turned left on the Lambeth side, and strolled for another hour, until they reached Southwark. Here, many ships from all over the world were having their cargo discharged, while mid-river, other ships were moored on buoys, awaiting their place at a wharf. Everywhere was hustle and bustle, lorries coming and going, cars to-ing and fro-ing, horse and carts and people on bicycles, all going around in some form of organised chaos. All these sights and sounds were new and exciting to the senses of our pair. Turning in from the river, they came across Tooley Street and in one of the terraced houses a sign could be seen that was a feast to their eyes:

### -Bed and Board for Gentlemen-

"Keep your fingers crossed, Matti, this could be just what we are looking for!"

An elderly man answered their knock at the door and peered at them through very thick-lensed glasses; he was wearing two parts of a three-piece black pin-striped suit and a fob watch and chain in his waistcoat pocket. Everything was rather threadbare and well used, but it reminded one there had been better times.

"Yes?" he said, squinting squarely at them. "What can I do for you?"

"The sign says bed and board. Can you help?"

"I think we can, we have one last room," the old man lied, for the reality was that no-one else was staying there, and had not for some weeks.

"D'you want to come and see a room?"

"Please!" returned both boys at the same time. He led them to a back room on the first floor where everything had seen better days. The room had a large bed which the boys would have to share; the windows were grimy and looked out onto a yard littered with all sorts of debris. The wallpaper, which had once been victorianly grand, was now starting to peel through condensation and cold.

"If you like it, you get breakfast of an egg, two slices of bread and a mug of tea; and at night 'er indoors makes a wonderful meal, why, sometimes we even has fish and chips! All this luxury for seven bob a week!"

"We'll take it," said Matti, much to the annoyance of Enrico, who would like to have kicked him in the shin to stop him there and then.

"In advance, please, boys!" the old man said with his hand held out in expectation.

They counted out fourteen shillings of their remaining funds, leaving them with the grand total of three pounds, eight shillings, seven pence and three farthings: a grand sum that could keep them both for several weeks, if they were prudent with their spending. The old man held the money to within four inches of his eyes to check the amount given and, as he left through the door, he said over his shoulder:

"The washroom is down the passage on the left, there, and the kazi is in the yard, but make sure you let us know if the bucket is full!"

He then added, walking down the stairs, "Breakfast is at seven o'clock sharp!"

Enrico closed the door with a heavier than casual bang.

"What the fuck have you got us into?" Enrico enquired of Matti. "This is a shit hole!"

"Look," said Matti, "I've used my head, here." To this, Enrico's head came up in astonishment. "This place is ideal: nobody will look for us here, and as for that old codger, he's half blind anyway! Nobody will suspect!"

Later that night, it was agreed that they would have a drink down the pub. The boys found themselves walking up to London Bridge, and turned left into Borough High Street, and just a hundred yards down on the left, they came to this wonderful Elizabethan court-yard that housed the George Inn. It was teeming with life, and it was the noise that drew them into this charming enclave. Immediately the boys felt at home and relaxed. After a couple of pints of beer and a cheese sandwich each, they felt ready to tackle the world again, at least after a night's sleep!

They lit the gas lamp in their bedroom, pulled back the bedclothes, and to their horror, discovered little black objects flitting around on their sheets. Matti immediately knew what to do; having been brought up with five older brothers, he had experienced bedbugs before. He gently placed the blanket back over the scurrying insects, put his finger to his mouth and went: "*Shhhh!*", and quietly whispered to Enrico:

"I know what to do." He tiptoed to the bathroom, and then came back again with a wet piece of soap in his hand.

"When I say lift, Enrico, pull the blanket back quickly!"

Each boy on either side of the bed prepared themselves.

"Now!" he exclaimed. The blanket was thrown off the bed, and at least ten bugs could be seen scattering in the light of the gas lamp. *Whap! Whap, whap, whap, whap!*

A delighted Matti, grinning from ear to ear, held the soap high for his friend to see, and there, all the bedbugs were stuck fast! Enrico almost squealed with delight, but then calmed down and said:

"But they are the ones we can see! What about the others?"

"Well, as the great bard said: yer pays your money, yer takes your chance!"

Enrico had a fitful night's sleep, dreaming of being eaten alive by millions of bugs, whilst Matti dreamed only of his early life and his family left behind, now maybe for ever?

Matthew Dumbridge was born at home in a two up-two down terraced house in Woodstock Lane, Tranmere, in the early hours of April 1st 1898. His father, John Senior, was a wood turner in the local furniture-making factory, close to his beloved 'Tranmere Rovers F.C.', and his mother, Stella had worked in service until the arrival of her sons. Matthew, very quickly became Matti to his family and friends; his oldest brother was one William Dumbridge, born in 1880, but he had already joined the army when Matti was born. William served with the Royal Artillery and was in the first wave of the British Expeditionary Force to fight at Mons in 1914. He had risen to the grand rank of Corporal. His second brother, John, born in 1882 and named after their father, had joined the Royal Engineers at the turn of the twentieth Century. He too, fought with the B.E.F. at Mons, and had also become a Corporal. The third brother was Steven, born in 1885. He did not join the army until both his brothers had come back from serving in South Africa, at the end of the Boer War, in 1902. His mother, Stella, had forbidden him to enlist for fear of exposing yet another one of her sons during the troubles. In 1903, he joined his brother John in the Royal Engineers. Like his other brothers, he too, fought at Mons. The last brother was Alan, born in 1887. He had joined the Cavalry in 1910, and was the only brother to make Sergeant. Though at Mons, the cavalry were kept at the back of the line, not being used, except when German skirmishes broke through it during the long retreat of the B.E.F. Alan's company was used for quick raids, on advancing German troops in a form of cut and run tactics.

Matti dreamed of his brothers even though he knew none of them very well. He dreamed of Christmasses and family reunions that never seemed to happen. Stella had always dreaded the idea of Matti also enlisting, and so was extremely happy when the friendship truly developed between her youngest son and Enrico Lokowski. Even the danger of going down the mines seemed a small price to pay to keep her son close to hand. Matti had never become academic: because of being spoilt by his mother and father he had never pushed himself at school. His blond hair and blue eyes gave him a certain innocence which endeared him to all around. He had never taken to the sporting life, much to the chagrin of his father, whose only real dream was for Matti to be centre forward at Tranmere Rovers. The fact is, that too many slices of bread and dripping, and the odd steak and kidney pie or three, had made him a rather rotund fourteen stone young man! But Matti carried his weight well; even though he was only five foot eight, it made him look cuddly in the eyes of the opposite sex. Though having never had a girlfriend, he was well aware, and enjoyed, the fact that women found him attractive. He had never in his life experienced sex, but with four older brothers, he knew everything there was to know at a very early age in life, and yearned for the day when he would experience his first lady friend. Wet dreams were one thing, but nothing in his mind was going to compensate for the real thing!

Matti slept heavily, moving a great deal from side to side. His eyelids flickered as yet another dream flashed though his mind. Enrico, on the other hand, having spent the night in a dazed stupor, believing that every part of his anatomy was being bitten into, and every drop of his blood was being sucked from his defenceless body, yearned for the break of dawn to end his troubled night. The boys woke to the sound of clattering on the stairs and in the kitchen. Roused, but not completely *compos mentis*, Enrico turned towards Matti, and tried to focus his encrusted, sleep-filled eyes to see whether Matti was awake.

"Matti," Enrico said quietly, "you awake?"

"How could anybody have slept through that bloody noise?" answered Matti. "I have not slept a wink all night."

"For a man who has not slept, you made a hell of a blooming noise!" At this Enrico pushed his feet out of the bed, and onto the floor; leaning forward with his head almost between his knees, he tried hard to waken himself. Mumbling under his breath, and scratching his left calf with his right hand, he said:

"I think every bug in the house got me!" The truth is imagination can sometimes play terrible tricks, for he was swollen in many parts of his body, not from bug bites, but from the incessant scratching which he had subconsciously done throughout the darkness.

Matti, on the other hand, slowly pushed himself upright, pulled the covers around his shoulders, made a *"Brrrrr!"* sound, closed his eyes again, and thought 'just another couple of hours, please!'

"If we want breakfast," exclaimed a now wide awake Enrico, "we'd better get down there in the next few minutes! I'm going for a quick wash and shave, and I suggest you get out of bed and get dressed!"

Within ten minutes both the boys had done their ablutions, and were sitting expectantly at the dining room table. Matti eyed the room casually, and remarked quietly to his friend:

"Seen better days!"

This simple sentence summed up the whole establishment, along with the owner and his wife. While the lads were sitting there, a fusee mantel clock, perched on the sideboard, chimed out seven times. As if the chimes were a signal, in glided a very old and large landlady with a tray of breakfast. This was gorged within thirty seconds of it hitting the table by the duo, neither of them giving time for the food to hit the throat on the way down to the stomach! It relieved something, but the lads knew they would be buying food very quickly once outside. A melancholy, not unknown to both, came upon them. They started to think of their misfortunes, which had brought them to this sorry state. Tears welled in Matti's eyes, as he thought of the shame that would now be heaped upon the Dumbridge family. He could see his mother's gasps of horror, being told that her youngest son was a murderer. A killer of a policeman, as if it could possibly be worse! He knew, as did Enrico, that this would almost certainly lead to the gallows. At Matti's loud shuddering, his friend Enrico placed a hand on his arm and said in a whisper: "I don't know how, but things will be all right!"

"But it's the shame! How could Mum and Dad really understand what happened?"

"That bastard asked for it! It was him who provoked the trouble, not us!"

"But no-one will ever believe that! He was a copper, for Christ's sakes!"

There was a pause, while the boys pondered this. Finally Enrico said, "Look, it's Sunday, let's get out of here; we'll get a paper, and see if anything is written about us."

A few minutes later, the old man who owned the establishment came into the dining room, looking for all the world like an over-aged, well worn nineteen Century would-be gentleman, who was never going to quite make it, wearing clothes that had been stylish in their time, but now showed the ravages of time and spilt food.

" 'Ello, boys! So what are you up to, today?" And without waiting for an answer, he continued:

"Looking for work, or enlisting?"

Again, before the boys could even answer, he added further "You'm both from up North, ain't you?"

Enrico was the first to interject with:

"We used to live up North, but moved down some time ago," giving no further clues.

"Oh, is that how it is?" said the old man, looking more than a little puzzled.

"Why, you ain't even giving me your names!" At this, Matti rose to his feet, Enrico followed suit, and, heading for the door casually stated: "We'll give you all the details you need when we come back this afternoon."

"Alright, then, but don't come back drunk! The old girl just don't like mopping up uva people's vomit!" and as he finished his sentence, he chuckled to himself. Looking very disdainfully at one another they left the boarding house.

"Thank God, it's not raining and I do believe the sun is shining, albeit that it's not reaching the ground!" To this Matti laughed.

"That's better! We must try and cheer ourselves up a bit."

"First things first," said Matti. "Let's get that newspaper!"

The boys walked up to London Bridge Station in the knowledge that there would be a newspaper seller somewhere on the concourse. Everywhere was busy; people, like the day before, were briskly going about their business.

"Blimey, Enrico! This place never sleeps! Back home, it being Sunday, you were either in church or bed."

Enrico nodded in agreement, as he was nearly trampled underfoot by the throng of people. The noise of train whistles, of ships' sirens and general hubbub of traffic just overwhelmed and amazed the two lads. They bought their paper, and nearly destroyed it in their haste to scan the pages for news of the murder.

"Well, I can't see anything about it!"

Matti had a puzzled expression, and then commented:

"Maybe the police are keeping it quiet for a bit, while they are looking for us. Anyway, I don't know about you, but I am still hungry. There's a taxi booth over there, let's grab something to eat and another mug of tea! Then we can read the paper more thoroughly."

Enrico eagerly agreed to this, as he, too, still felt pangs of hunger. As they stood by the stall, eating their cheese and pickle sandwiches, and swilling their mugs of hot tea, they both read very carefully through each page. Nothing! In the distance, they started to hear the refrains of "Pack up your troubles in your old kitbag" being played very jauntily from a marching brass band. The sound was coming from north of the river, heading south across London Bridge. And even with the noise of London around them, gradually they began to make out the words of the song. The louder it got, the more interested the boys became, and soon the London Rifle Brigade, with its band leading, came into view, from across

*37*

the river. There must have been only sixty bandsmen, but the noise of the band, and the marching, singing voices of the regiment behind, soon overwhelmed all other sounds.

*Pack up your troubles in your old kitbag,*
*And smile, boys, smile*
*Though you've a Lucifer to light your fag,*
*Smile, boys, all the while*
*What's the use of worrying*
*It never was worthwhile*
*So, pack up your troubles in your old kitbag*
*And smile, smile, smile.*

The sound of five hundred men marching and singing at the same time was a very moving experience. Men and women cheered and waved, dogs barked excitedly, even the London pigeon seemed to be enjoying the occasion, swirling around in the air above the soldiers, and every now and again, dropping a little message of approval to the people below! The boys were mesmerised by all of this; they had never seen or heard anything like it; they loved it!

"What a fantastic place London is!" Enrico said, as the marching band finally drifted into the distance.

"I tell you what: let's take a stroll over to Hyde Park. I've heard it's a very beautiful place with always something going on."

He turned to one of the taxi drivers who was also supping his mug of tea,

"Tell me, mate, is it far for us to walk to Hyde Park?"

"It'll take you about forty-five minutes, but only about ten by taxi!"

Enrico quickly interjected with:

"We can't afford the fare!"

"In that case" said the smiling cabbie, "go across London Bridge, turn left, walk along the river until you come to the Houses of Parliament, turn right, making your way to St. James Park, go round the right hand side of Buckingham Palace, walk on for another half a mile, and there, to behold, will be the wonders of Hyde Park."

The cabbie winked and nodded at the boys, as they set off on their walk.

"One thing about London," thought Enrico, "there's so many people around, there's bound to be someone to help us if we get lost!"

They did not get lost, but it took them nearly three hours, to finally reach their destination. There had been so many interesting sights to see, and sounds to hear, that time just drifted on. This was turning into a special day for the boys; they were enjoying every aspect of their rambling, each turn revealing a new sight to see, a new experience. They made their way through a mass of walking civilians and soldiers alike, also having to dodge out of the way of cavalrymen, exercising their charges around the park. Matti thought immediately of his brother Alan, and pride swelled up within him, as he watched the soldiers canter by in all their finery. Soon they were at the Serpentine, and the sun had finally broken through the pollution of London.

"Good Lord" remarked Enrico, "if I had not seen it, I would not have believed it! Look at all those people!" for there, in the middle of the lake, on this cold but bright January Sunday, were lots of men and women rowing around. It truly amazed the boys that everywhere something was happening. After all, this was winter, and winter at war, to boot. On the north side of the lake, about a hundred yards from the edge, could be seen many soldiers, with their trousers and braces just covering a white woolly vest. Some were exercising in sequence to a Sergeant's bark; some were drilling, in close order. Masses of people looked on, as if watching a circus in performance. The boys walked slowly to the north side of the park, and could see several men and women standing above the crowd that had gathered, waving fists and arms in the air, and mouthing sounds that were totally inaudible. As they approached, the silent mouthing turned into a mumble, then into a medley of various orations. The crowd either jeered or cheered, depending on what was being said, and by whom. There was a lady of very upper middle class, talking with an assurance that was showing a lifetime of ordering people about. She was extolling the virtues of abstinence from alcohol, and trying to instil a moral code that brought the fear of God right into your face. There might have been a hundred or so people listening to her, but more than half were jeering and laughing at her. But did the heckling disturb her? Oh no! Her crusade lifted her high above the sounds of the crowd. She was on a plane that to some people could only have been induced by the smoking of opium. The next speaker they came across was a man of middle age, very thin and wiry, but again, of obvious middle class, who, much to the amazement and horror of his smaller gathering, had been talking about the war, and how wrong it was for Britain to be involved in what was, after all, a European conflict. There was an undercurrent of murmuring, which turned into a hiss, when the speaker in fact started to praise the Kaiser, reminding the listeners that if they loved their King, they should appreciate the Kaiser, his cousin. At this point, a rather large dollop of dog's excrement, which had been picked up and thrown with the aid of a stick, landed smack in the centre of his face.

" 'Ere's a turd for a shit like you!"

A policeman nearby, having seen and heard all that had happened purposefully turned to the woman preaching abstinence. A few seconds later, the luckless speaker, chased by a few irate listeners was racing across the park, not to be seen again that day! There must have been half a dozen other speakers, all pontificating on various subject matters, all being heckled by a crowd of people, urging one another on to more outrageous acts of disruption. The two young lads enjoyed the banter of Hyde Park Corner, experiencing for the first time in their young lives the eccentricities of people whom they had always thought of as their betters, expounding on subjects that must have meant something to them, but meant nothing to Enrico or Matti. Gradually pushing their way through the throng, they decided to make their way lazily down Park Lane; again the *clump-clump-clump* of marching feet could be heard, and a brigade of soldiers in full uniform with rifles on shoulders came marching past at quick step.

"Left... left... left-right-left!" sang out a very short rotund Sergeant-Major, with his swagger stick tucked neatly under his left arm, and his hand holding the end of the said stick; a picture of precision. The friends were much impressed by the speed and smartness of these soldiers, and were greatly amused at a collection of little boys and dogs that tried to copy the marching, following closely behind.

The two lads drifted gently in the general direction that the marching soldiers had taken; it was when they approached Buckingham Palace that Matti turned to Enrico, saying:

"The sun is starting to go down, and I don't know about you, matey, but I'm starving!"

Enrico laughed, and retorted in a jocular voice:

"I should have known you'd be the first to feel you have a hole in your belly!" but his own stomach agreed with Matti. There were still plenty of people around, and quite a crowd had gathered at the gate of the palace, looking up at the balcony, as if expecting their King to come and greet them. It was not until the boys had passed Charing Cross station that they found a little fish and chip bar.

"Blimey," said Matti, pointing towards the lights of the bar, and taking in the aroma of Fish and Chips. "And I thought these Southerners weren't civilised! Seems they are after all! Fish and Chips, just what the doctor ordered!"

"Two large cod, and an a'penth of chips, please!"

The boys put oodles of salt and vinegar onto their greasy looking mass, which had been heaped onto the previous week's Daily Sketch. The hot grease drew out the ink from the soggy pages, adding yet different flavours to the whole concoction! They ate while walking, as it was now getting dark and they had to find their way back to Tooley Street. Following alongside the Thames, Enrico smacked his lips together, licked them, wiped his face with his sleeve, threw the empty rolled up paper into the river, looked at Matti, and with a contented grin, said:

"It's been a bloody exciting, fun day! I can't remember when I have enjoyed myself more," to which Matti, pressing the last of his chips into his mouth agreed with his friend, at the same time managing to spit bits of chips everywhere. By the time they reached London Bridge, it was now quite dark, and a yellow, grimy smog had descended again, filling the gap that the sun had tried to penetrate. As they entered Tooley Street, the noise of the river and the railway seemed very eerie, as they could only be heard and not seen through the gloom. They got within fifty feet of their boarding house before Enrico came to an abrupt halt, putting his left hand out across Matti's chest to stop him. He pushed Matti to the side of the railings, and said in an urgent whisper: "Matti, that's a police car outside!"

Enrico's eyes were good, and he had been able to detect the vehicle. At that moment, the door of the house opened, shining a pallid light down onto the car, showing that a police constable was sitting in the driving seat. A police officer came out of the door, accompanied by another man in a long, brown raincoat, which nearly reached the ground, and a brown trilby hat. Stopping on the threshold, before taking the few steps down to the pavement and to the car, one of the policemen shouted back, and the boys heard the sounds they had been dreading:

"So, if you see these two men, please let us know quickly. There might even be a reward in it for you!"

Enrico's heart stopped. Even in the gloom, he could see that Matti's rotund, red face had now turned to chalky white.

"Jesus Christ, they've gotten on to us even quicker than I thought they would!"

At this, they stepped back a few paces, and quietly crossed over to the other side of the road. Matti was shaking very badly. He could feel the rough hemp being placed around his neck, and in a quivering, almost sobbing voice, said:

"We've got to get out of here, real quick, we can't get back there! All our things, we're going to lose them!"

"At least we've got our money, Matti, they haven't got us yet!"

What the boys would not have known is that the two policemen were in fact looking for two Portuguese sailors who had jumped ship, and it was quite common that the shipping line would offer a reward for their apprehension. Without any rhyme or reason, the boys instinctively made their way south. Within an hour they were halfway down the Walworth Road, a dark and dreary road, which seemed rather menacing to the duo. They quickened their pace, and before long, had crossed over Peckham Road, into Denmark Hill. It was now well after nine at night, the fog was laying thick upon the ground, and Enrico, who was starting to feel the cold, turned to Matti, saying: "We must find somewhere to shelter."

As the area had now obviously turned from down-at-hill into more prosperous, they felt they must keep going, or run the risk of looking suspicious. It was not until after midnight that they were aware of a huge building looming out of the night.

"My God! This is huge, and it all seems to be glass!"

Indeed it was huge; the two friends had stumbled almost blindly into the Crystal Palace. Lights were shining from within, and through the rather dirty and steamed up glass, they could still make out the opulence and wealth of a time gone by. Palm trees grew to great heights, lily ponds were glistening in the dullish electric light shining upon them. They could even see the occasional movement of large golden yellowish fish.

It was late; now extremely tired, hungry and thirsty, they knew they needed to sleep.

"It looks as if this whole area is a park; let's see if there is somewhere we can snatch some sleep."

Matti nodded in agreement, feeling too dejected to answer with words. Moving quietly, they walked around the back of the palace, and through the ornate, classically styled gardens, making their way downhill into the park proper. After a few minutes, they came across a large lake, and as they started to stroll around, suddenly stopped in horror, as a huge Iguanodon loomed out of the mist before them. They had come across the Victorian life-size models of prehistoric monsters. Next to the Iguanodon, a Tyrannosaurus Rex reared up, mouth agape, revealing sharp teeth ready to pounce in a threatening posture. At this point, the path they were walking on was just a small jump away from the island that the creatures had been erected on.

"Follow me, Matti," and with that, Enrico leapt the small gap onto the island. It was not so easy for Matti, who felt he needed a long run at it, but once over, they started to explore. There were lots of prehistoric animals, and the boys walked from one to another in wonderment. When they came to the Iguanodon, Matti looked under its tail, as if to discover the gender of the creature.

"Hey, look here!" There, before them, hidden from the general public, was a hole, big enough for a man to crawl in.

"Enrico, you still got those matches?"

Matti put his head inside and struck a match.

"Perfect, this'll do us!" He scrambled in, and Enrico could just see the glow of yet another match being struck. It was big enough for both the boys to lay in what was the stomach of the creature. There was a lot of animal detritus, which they moved out of the way, so as not to get too dirty. Both now very tired, they lay down, back to back, so as to maximise body heat.

"No farting, Matti!" A little giggle came, with also an expulsion of gas from Matti's rear end.

"God, you are disgusting!" to which they both giggled, releasing a bit of the tension they had been under since leaving the boarding house. They were cold, but they were dry, and they slept, if but fitfully…

Not knowing what time it was, but being aware that dawn would soon be chasing across the heavens, Enrico nudged Matti, and said: "We should get out of here, before the park gets used. Somehow, we need to find somewhere to wash and tidy up."

He could feel a coat of velvet upon his tongue and teeth, and he knew by the way that Matti pulled away from him that dragon breath was coming from his mouth as he spoke. They crawled out of their hidey-hole, and retraced their steps back to the jumping point, then made their way back up the hill to the front entrance to Crystal Palace.

"Stand still a minute, Matti, I'll run my fingers through your hair to slicken it down, and you can do the same for me. We don't want to stand out!"

After a few minutes the boys found themselves at the junction of Anerley Hill and Church Road. Here they came to an omnibus-and-tram terminal and there, to their great relief, was a stall, selling food and hot drinks.

"Please, Enrico, let's eat something! It will bring us back to life!"

"Two mugs of tea, lots of sugar, and two very thick bacon sandwiches, please!" Matti said with a grin on his face, to the man behind the counter, who in his white overalls, had been staring blankly into the distance in a trance-like state while wiping his greasy hands on a badly stained towel. Brought back to life with a start, he answered:

"Oh, sorry, did not see you! Coming up straight away!"

Dawn now came upon them rather suddenly, and looking around they realised it was going to be a nice day, as the fog had lifted, and the sun was making a determined effort to break through. The hot tea brought colour and life back to the boys and they started to notice that the roads had become busy. Though the traffic had been there all the time, it took the revitalising qualities of sustenance to make them aware of their surroundings. People were to-ing and fro-ing, making their way to their places of work. Other customers had collected at the booth, but nobody took any great interest in the unkempt pair having their breakfast.

"Enrico, I don't know about you, mate, but I need a dump, plus a good wash."

They finished their food, and Enrico leaned over the bar to the man who had served them:

"Tell me, friend, is there a bathhouse close by?"

The man thought for a few seconds:

"If you catch the number 12a tram that goes to Catford, it will take you past Bell Green. There, on the corner, is a bath house. You can get everything you need there," he said, looking at them, rather suspecting that they were runaways, who wanted to join up.

Twenty minutes later, the boys found themselves at the entrance to the bath house.

"Damn!" said Enrico, reading the notice that stated it did not open until nine a.m.

"Never mind!" coaxed Matti. "We can spend the next forty minutes looking to buy a couple of shavers and toothbrushes." This the boys did.

They came back to find it still was not open, and sitting on a bench outside watched the world go by. Enrico was the first to break the silence that now hung between them:

"Matti, there's only one thing we can do that makes any sense!"

"What's that?"

"We have to get out of the country, and I think the only way we can do that is to enlist!"

Matti sat there, brought his left leg up, balancing it on the edge of the bench, placing his chin on his knee, and without opening his lips, mumbled: "*Mmmmmm...*". The doors of the baths opened, and the two friends were going to be the first customers of the day. They walked up to the pay booth to find an old lady who virtually spread to all four corners of the booth, being so obese.

"Two baths, please," said Enrico, handing over the few coppers that it cost to change from a scruffy, smelly pair into something that was a little more acceptable. The boys had cubicles next to one another, and as they lay in their individual baths, deeply filled with piping hot water, both yet again, and not for the last time, dwelt upon their fate.

"Right, you two!" a voice said, accompanied by a banging on the doors of each of their cubicles, "You've been in there for more than an hour, and that's more than we usually allow. Time for you both to get on with your business!"

Once again, outside the red-bricked establishment, the friends decided to walk in the direction the tram had taken after leaving them. They came to a railway station, the boldly stated Catford Bridge.

"So, it looks as if we've reached Catford!" exclaimed Matti. The sun shone down brightly onto them; it was not hot, in fact, it was almost frosty cold, but it was bright, and sunshine induces a feeling of optimism. The traffic was extraordinarily busy, but as the boys turned into Bromley Road, yet another military band was heard, and there, in the distance, could be seen the tail end of what had probably been a large troop of soldiers, marching through the gate into the barracks.

"Well," said Matti, "is this as good a place as any?" as he looked at Enrico, and pointed half-heartedly at the now closing iron gates of the barracks building.

The two boys, looking clean, but dishevelled, with muddied boots and rather dirty clothing approached one of the motionless sentries who were guarding the barracks.

"Excuse me, Sir," said Enrico.

"I'm not a Sir, boy; I'm a Private in this man's army. So what d'you want?"

"We want to enlist," replied Enrico in a totally confused manner, not knowing quite how to address this soldier, but after a second or two, ended with: "er, Private!"

The soldier turned and looked at an open door leading to a small room. "Sergeant!"

"Yes! What d' you want?" came a very gruff throaty retort.

"Two lads 'ere want to join up!"

The Sergeant appeared at the door, a very smart soldier of about forty years of age, who obviously had kept himself in prime condition.

"Yes, boys! So you want to join up?"

Then without waiting for an answer, added:

"Come on through, let's talk it over!"

The boys were led into a darkish room that sported one little window with bars on it, a desk that the Sergeant sat at, and a bench on the opposite wall with clothes hooks festooned with various oilskin rain attire hanging from the hooks, making it impossible for anyone to sit comfortably on the bench, not that the boys were asked to sit!

"You realise, boys, that this is a Territorial Army Barracks? That means you probably won't have to go abroad, more likely to be on home guard duties?" At this both the boys started, and Matti said:

"But we are volunteering to go overseas!"

"Then, laddie-o, we probably ain't the right ones for you!"

"Well, er…Sergeant…" Being again embarrassed by not knowing the correct form of address, "Can you tell us where we can go to join the proper army?"

"This is the proper army, son. It's just that we also hold down jobs outside of the army. We are likes volunteers, so to say," said the Sergeant, puffing his chest out, and holding his chin high with pride. "Well, boys, you might still be in luck. What about the London Northern Rifle Brigade? Do you fancy that?" but before the boys could answer, added a further: "I've a truck going over to their barracks in Finsbury. Would you like to go over?"

And the answer came:

"Yes, Sergeant. I think that would suit us fine!"

The truck, with a working party of engineers going there to clear the drains, which the influx of hundreds of new recruits had quickly filled, took the two lads along. It arrived in the early afternoon, with all the men having been thoroughly shaken around in this old military lorry, with its solid tyres and rigid suspension.

The Corporal, who was in charge of the men, and had also driven the lorry, smiled at the boys when they arrived, and said to them: "Well, lads, this could be the start of your big adventure!"

To which the four other soldiers almost choked with laughter, and as the Corporal led the two boys to the duty Sergeant, a high pitched voice teased: "You'll be sorry!"

They were led to another anteroom, again dimly lit, but warm with the glow of a coal brazier. The Sergeant was sitting at his desk, with his name plate proudly pushed forward for the entire world to see: "Sergeant Michael Kelly"

"Sergeant!" said the Corporal, coming to attention, "I've brought these 'ere two young lads over from Catford. They want to enlist in the London Northern Rifle Brigade." The Sergeant acknowledged the Corporal, and with a rather disdainful smile, looked at the boys. He turned to Matti:

"How old are you?"

"Seventeen, Sergeant."

"Right, boy, see that lorry you came over 'ere in? I want you to walk to it, smarten quickly, walk around it three times, and come back 'ere when you are eighteen!"

Then he turned to Enrico: "Your age?"

"Eighteen, Sergeant."

At this point the penny dropped, and Matti marched smartly round the lorry three times, and came back into the office, to be greeted by the Sergeant saying: "How old are you, boy?"

"Eighteen, Sir"

"Don't call me Sir. I'm not an officer," he barked, which brought both the boys to attention. "See these three stripes? That puts me in charge of the 'hole army!"

At this the Corporal backed away, as if to get his men down to the work they had come for, and as a passing remark said:

"Well, I'll leave them in your capable hands, Sir! er…Sergeant!" Smirking to himself, he went to find his men.

"Right, then! So you want to take the King's shilling?"

But before they could answer, he added in a gruff voice "My name is *Sergeant* Kelly, also known as 'Spider' Kelly, but don't ever let me hear *you* say that! You will address me at all times as Sergeant. You will stand to attention, feet together, shoulders back, stomach in, chest out, with your hands down by your side, fist clenched and the thumb following the seam of your trousers. Is that understood?"

"Yes, Sergeant!" they replied in unison, trying hard to stand as the Sergeant had ordered.

"Right!" he said. "Before you get your money, you must fill out this form, which will contract you for either the duration of the war, or your deaths, whichever comes first! So," he added, "names?"

The boys paused, not quite knowing what to say for fear that giving their correct names might lead to them being discovered by the police.

"Name?" he barked again, looking at Enrico who had nearly jumped out of his skin.

"Enrico Caruso," he replied, biting his lip, as he had wished to say something else.

"Caruso? Are you pulling my leg, boy?"

"No, Sir, er… Sergeant. My mother wanted me to be an opera singer." The Sergeant, shaking his head, as if in disbelief, wrote this on the form.

"Date of birth?"

"22nd of January '97" he replied, more calmly, now knowing how to lie.

"D'you have an address?"

"No, Sergeant, we came from up North."

"Any next of kin?"

"No, Sergeant."

"I'll fill in an address 'ere to suit."

Then handing Enrico the scratchy pen that was spilling ink everywhere, he ordered:

"Sign there!"

This duly done, a metal moneybox was opened, and a newly minted shilling was passed from the Sergeant to Enrico.

"Welcome to the London Northern Rifle Brigade!"

Enrico tried to be nice by saying:

"I'm sure I'm going to enjoy being in the Brigade, Sergeant", but the Sergeant screamed back:

"You ain't 'ere to enjoy it. You're 'ere to do your duty, and if you want to get on with me, you'll be smart and quick at everything!"

Then turning to Matti: "What's your name?"

Again, being caught by the bark, he replied:

"Dumbridge, Sergeant."

"First name?"

"Matti, Sergeant."

"What sort of name is Matti?"

But Matti was now regaining his composure. "Matti is the name my mum and dad gave me," thinking it be better than Matthew, again as if to try and fool any snooping policeman, not giving them any intelligence to work out the difference!

"Date of birth?"

"April 1st '97, Sergeant."

"Well at least that fits! You look like a bloody April fool!"

Having also discovered that Matti had no next of kin that he was prepared to admit to, nor any address, Sergeant Kelly agreed to do an address similar to Enrico's. Matti signed his name, and like his friend, received the King's shilling.

"Right!" barked Sergeant Kelly. Both the boys straightened to attention yet again.

"Have you anywhere to stay tonight?"

"No, Sergeant."

"Well, we have a spare cell in the glass house that you boys can use for the night!" and chuckling to himself, added:

"I promise not to lock the door on you both, when I've finished reading your bedtime story! If you go through there," pointing to another door, "and across the hall to the furthest door on the left, that's the canteen. Tell the Section Cook Sergeant Kelly said it's all right for you to be fed. Then I suggest that you clean up your clothes and shoes, and have a real early night, because it might be the last decent night's sleep you'll get for a while! Tomorrow, we will try and get you kitted out; you'll have a few weeks here, learning basic training, then, along with all the rest of the new recruits, and yours truly 'ere, we'll be going to our camp for proper training."

"Where will that be, Sergeant?" asked Enrico.

"That's for me to know, and for you to find out, when I'm ready to tell you!"

As the boys walked across the hall to the canteen, Matti whispered in Enrico's ear: "What a bastard!"

# III

Sleep came quickly and soundly. Guns could have been fired, there could have been a party going on in the cell, they would not have been disturbed by anything! The pressures that had come to them in such an abrupt fashion vanished in dreamless oblivion. They were clean, dry, fed and warm, the right combination for deep undisturbed rest.

That is, until six in the morning when the reveille sounded. The shock waves were instantaneous, bringing them to the real world in a hurry.

"Crikey, what's that racket?" exclaimed Enrico. But before any answer came, the cell door burst open and in stepped the duty Corporal.

"Up, now! Get washed and dressed, clean up this mess and get over to the cookhouse for duties. You have twenty minutes. Time to start earning your keep". As quickly as he came, he went! Dressed? Dressed in what? All they had were the clothes that they came in.

Enrico was wearing the suit that had been bought for him as he left school. The trousers had been lengthened as and when needed by taking the turn-ups down; the jacket was now beginning to strain at the seams as he had grown taller. The three piece suit was made from a blackish-grey rough woollen cloth; even when it was new it looked old! And now, it was without question threadbare and in urgent need of cleaning. He wore a collarless white shirt that reeked of perspiration, and was stained with body grime. His shoes were heavy and cumbersome, but they fitted well, and his feet were strong from wearing them.

He had a vaguely exotic appearance which set him apart from other youngsters. He was tallish, thin, with deep-set eyes, giving him an air of serious concentration; his black, shiny, wavy hair and sallow skin showed off prominent cheekbones in a bony face. A square locket containing a memento from his mother hung from the chain around his neck. He did not really remember her, but acutely felt a need for her presence, and in a way, this gave rise to a protective attitude which manifested itself in his caring approach to Matti.

Matti, on the other hand, was a true Anglo-Saxon in his appearance: cherubic looking, with a rather girlish, petit nose, and a twinkle in his eyes which denoted the bon vivant, fostered by the extravagant love from his parents. He was the surprise packet that came eleven years after his nearest brother!

His attire, like Enrico's, had seen better days. He wore grey threadbare slacks, more suited for summer weather than cold winters, held up by a broad leather belt buckled on the last eye, and still straining hard, a thick woolly vest that buttoned right up to the throat, a white and blue striped shirt, again with the collar off, open at the neck, showing his rather absurd looking vest underneath. His jacket, which was a little too big for him, having been his father's, was made from black mottled corduroy now made smooth with age. It had two leather elbow patches, both almost entirely worn through. His whole appearance was more than a little absurd in style. His shoes were too large for him, and the toes had newspaper to fill the excess space. He too, had very strong healthy feet. He sported in his left trouser pocket, the only one left that could hold things without them falling down his trouser leg, the most disgusting looking handkerchief, which had obviously been used to wipe every nose in Collingbrook mine! When he produced it for use, any luckless person watching would turn away and wince. Why he never had it cleaned, God only knows! Having lost the pocket of the right hand side, Matti had never been bothered, as this gave him an excellent chance to play pocket billiards, or just have a good old fashioned scratch.

Having dressed and cleaned themselves as best they could, they very quickly tidied the cell that had been their haven for the night. They found the duty Corporal, who led them to the cookhouse for their first experience of fatigues. They were greeted by the cook, Sergeant Glencross, whose rather rotund exterior showed a man who had enjoyed sampling his own culinary creations over many years. He was a jolly man, until he was annoyed, when he became the epitome of a bully. What annoyed him most was when Privates would stare at the very large mole which he sported between his nose and his upper lip. The trouble was that all Privates looked at this protuberance! Thus Sergeant Glencross seemed always in a foul temper.

"Right, boys! Stand erect when I speak to you!" which was duly done.

"Names?"

"Enrico Caruso, Sergeant."

"Matti Dumbridge, Sergeant."

Turning to Matti, he ordered:

"Right, Private, I want you to slice up all those loaves over there and you…" now turning to Enrico,

"You're gonna slap margarine on them, but thinly, mark you! What we've got has to go a long way!" Now noticing that the boys were looking at his upper lip, he screamed:

"Now! Jump to it!"

As seven a.m. chimed from the main canteen clock, a trickle which soon turned into a flood of new recruits, flowed eagerly into the canteen adjoining the cook house. The regular kitchen staff, along with the cook, stood in line, ready to serve the new soldiers. There were lashings of fried eggs, bacon, fried bread and porridge, and as each man went along the line you would hear: "Egg," "Bacon," "Bread," then if the soldier was not quick enough, the porridge was slopped on top of the whole glutinous mass. A voice bellowed out, quickly bringing everything to a halt:

"Get your food. Eat smartly, tidy everything after you, and be ready for your first parade in the square at eight sharp! Woe betides anybody slacking!" thus barked Sergeant Kelly. It was strange that with around a hundred men, all rushing around, trying to have their first breakfast, how really quiet they were. Fear of the unknown closes the mouth, except for the intake of sustenance.

Matti and Enrico were also allowed to get their food and join the gathering. Eight o'clock struck, but already, the canteen had emptied, everybody milling around on the parade ground in a dazed bewildered state. Sergeant Kelly appeared as the last chime struck the clock.

"Right, men. Make four lines from left to right." The panic that ensued would have made any bystanders roll around on the floor in laughter; this was more like "Keystone Cops" as opposed to military drilling! Eventually, after several minutes, four wavy looking lines were formed. Kelly, walking to the left side of the men, barked:

"Put your right arm out, touching the shoulder of the man next to you and look to your left and right, making sure that your line is straight. Not you, you fool!" he said to the man at the end of the line, and then turning to the next line, he said to the first man:

"Come up close behind this man", which was duly done.

"Now, one stride back, as you were, boy! A stride is a long step, not a mamby-pamby hop as you just did! This is a man's army, and don't you forget it!"

Fear was in the faces of all of them. Soon all four lines were more or less straight, and the Sergeant walked to the middle of the front.

"Right, you scruffy buggers! When I talk to you, you stand to attention, you don't look at me, you looks straight ahead, you don't look left or right, you looks straight ahead, you don't look up or down at your feet, you looks straight ahead. Is that under bloody stood?"

Nobody dared say a word, so, in an even louder voice Kelly screamed: "Understood? You will answer Yes, Sergeant all together!"

The answer came, in a very subdued manner, and certainly not said as one.

"Speak up! I can't hear you!"

As one, the roar came back:

"Yes, Sergeant!" one poor lad added: "Kelly" at the end and the Sergeant glared balefully at him.

"Boys, lads, men, you have joined the London Northern Rifle Brigade. You are no longer boys or lads. From now on, men is what you is! Firstly you are going for a haircut to get rid of the mop, and the pets that are living inside it, then for a medical, and after the M.O. has made sure that you have not got a social disease, and that you can hear me, and actually see down the end of a rifle, you will come back here for drill practice. You will be given your kit, you will be given a bunk, and you are gonna be thankful for all of God's blessings that are being bestowed on you."

To this, there was a smirk from the four corporals who were there to help Sergeant Kelly.

"No one said you could slouch, stand to attention! When I says to each row in turn, turn left, you will do that, when I says march off with the Corporal, you will do that! Corporal!"

"Sergeant!" Corporal Harrington stiffened to attention, awaiting the order to take the first line of men to the barber, then to the M.O. In the first row Enrico and Matti stood side by side, looking straight ahead. The order came "Left turn!" then from the Corporal came:

"By the left, quick march!" followed quickly by:

"Left, left, left right left!"

The men dutifully followed, but hardly in any great military precision. The barber was a genius; over many years of destroying hairstyles, he could cut a man's hair in about two minutes, which sometimes could be a painful experience! They were then marched into a room that looked to all the world like a church hall, as it even had stained windows. It was a big room, and more or less in the middle, there were two tables, one table with rubber gloves and various hospital items and at the other sat two white coated orderlies, whose sole purpose was to get the names and the various information that the doctor would pass. The men were brought into one line, again to stand to attention, and wait for the M.O.'s address.

"Men, I am Doctor Bennett. My rank is Major. You will at all times address me as Sir. Should we ever have reason to pass one another, and you are in uniform, you will salute me, as befitting any officer."

He was an elderly man, who had been in the army since leaving medical school. He had experienced many military campaigns, and watched many young soldiers come and go in the name of King and Country.

"Without losing your places, strip to the buff, and drop your clothes behind you."

The sight of these men, naked, was not a pretty one. This display of nude men did not conjure up a painting by the Flemish master, Rubens. The sight that confronted the M.O. and the orderlies was one of sagging shoulders, rounded backs, fat and thin tummies, lumpy or skinny legs, a general, unhealthy array of bodies, but the M.O. was inured to this.

He went to the first man in line:

"Name?" which was duly given. He turned to the nearest orderly: "Give this man a serial number."

The orderly, who had written the name, spoke without looking up: "F853711."

The M.O. turned back:

"Open your mouth and put out your tongue." He then added after a pause, as if speaking to no-one in particular:

"Furred. Brush your tongue when you clean your teeth! Your mouth harbours many germs; you must be vigilant at all times, for germs, like the Hun are your enemy!" which was written down by the orderly. "Let's see your teeth! Not bad, though you've had some removed. Let me look in your ears. Fine. Have you had any social diseases? Gonorrhoea? Syphillis?"

"No, Sir" came the answer, in a rather hurt tone.

"Can you see that poster over on the wall? Read the top line!"

There was a long pause before the man answered almost in a whisper:

"I can see it, Sir, honest, but I can't read!"

"Right!"

At this, the M.O. put a rubber glove on his right hand, asked the man to open his legs, and he squeezed his testicles. To this he said "Cough!" The man coughed.

Major Bennett said to all the men:

"You are being given a serial number. Remember it for ever." Then turning to the man he had examined:

"Get dressed, and return to the parade ground. You are A1!"

It took approximately two hours to examine all 86 men; all were passed A1, though many were possibly very unfit, but they were not going to stay like that for long. For the first time in these young men's lives, they were going to get copious amounts of good food, and masses of healthy exercise. Minds and bodies were most definitely going to improve! At least until they got to the front!

The rest of the day was spent standing to attention, standing at ease, forming four lines, turning left, turning right, quick-marching around the parade ground. Towards the end of the day, having only had a break of fifteen minutes for a sandwich lunch and the proverbial mug of tea, with something quite new to most of the men, sugar, the men were already starting to understand the concept of drill, and though excruciatingly tired, all felt a little smug from thinking they now knew it all. It was four o'clock, and getting quite dark, when Sergeant Kelly brought them to a halt, facing the front again.

"The Corporals will now take each Section to get your kit; you will love your kit as if it was your mother, you will kiss and caress it, keeping it smart and clean at all times." Not for the last time, the Corporals were to smirk at the sarcastic way the Sergeant addressed the men.

"After you have your kit, you'll be allotted a barracks room and a bunk. At six o'clock sharp, now in your military attire, at least *looking* like soldiers, you will present yourselves at the canteen for supper, for which you will all be very *grateful*", he said, leaning forward and emphasising the word grateful.

Matti kept close to Enrico at all times, making sure that whatever they were assigned to, they would be assigned together. He marched next to him, he did press ups next to him, he sat next to him in the canteen, and now he made sure he had the next bunk in the barracks. A Corporal was assigned to be in charge of each Section, and generally there was a Section of not more than sixteen recruits, but needs must, and as the recruiting had become more intense, Sections were getting bigger. Hence there were twenty-two in Corporal Harrington's Section.

It had been a full day, and the evening meal had been consumed eagerly by these foot weary, tired but contented soldiers. Having even been allowed to have seconds, they had eaten every morsel that had been prepared for them. Sergeant Glencross and his kitchen staff sat back with the satisfaction of knowing a job well done. He lit up a Woodbine and turned to the orderly next to him:

"Get four of those rough recruits, two can do the washing and wiping up, and two can wash the floors and clean all the utensils." With that, he flicked ash onto an empty plate.

Corporal Harrington's Section drifted back to their dormitory in dribs and drabs, some smoking, some talking, some quiet, but all replete, and more than a little exhausted. The Corporal was waiting, somewhat impatiently, for his men to return.

"Right, let's be having you. Stand by your beds. You have to make everything sparkle. I am going to show you how to keep your lockers, your kit and your bed. These barracks must shine."

"But, Corporal," came the voice of a rather plump Jewish lad, called Maurice Bechstein, "we've been hard at it all day. Surely we deserve a break!" To which there was a general hubbub of agreement.

Harrington put his hands in the air with frustration.

"You have to learn, and you have to learn bloody quick, that when a superior officer, including Corporals, gives you a command, you jump to it!"

Then looking more sternly at them, he concluded:

"Discipline is everything, no matter what one says, we have to work as a team. The General orders the Sergeant, who orders me, and I order you, and you jump to it! Remember, one little bullet can kill you! It's up to me to teach you how to save your own skins, and that means discipline from the off. So, now, watch me, because I hope to have to tell you only once; I'm going to show you now how to blancko your boots so well, you'll be able to see what the guy in front of you has had for breakfast. That's the sort of shine we expect! I'm going to show you how to make your bed, so tight that if you drop a penny on it, it will bounce. I'm going to show you how to lay out your kit, so that if the King himself comes to inspect you, he will go away thinking you are the smartest soldiers in this 'ere army! All this is going to take time, and we don't have time; that's why, me sweet young laddies, we are going to work now!"

Corporal Harrington was as good as his word; he showed them how to get the best results possible to please the chain of command. It was quite late at night before the Corporal gave permission for everybody to sink between the sheets. His parting words, before turning out the lights were "You'll be up at six, and we will have a kit inspection by seven o'clock. If it goes well, you will have breakfast, and still be on parade by eight. If it goes badly, forget breakfast, you will be working to get it right."

And he meant *right*.

"Sweet dreams, and remember all you have learnt! And don't forget, if one is wrong, all are wrong! We help one another."

Lights went out, troubled and weary minds started to unwind. Everybody went quiet and asleep in minutes. They slept the sleep of babies, or of men who had now put their faith in the army; troubles became other peoples' troubles.

NCOs and officers now spent time in their messes enjoying a quiet drink, playing cards, or philosophising with peer group about which way the war was evolving. To the outsider the barracks itself could be likened to a children's scout camp, with the officers now benevolently watching over their sleeping young charges. Sadly, this was far from the truth.

Five thirty came; lights blazed on within the dormitories. Corporal Harrington, fully awake and dressed, was walking down the aisle between the beds, banging two empty saucepans. Startled young men sprang to their feet, and those who did not were soon rocketed out of their beds onto the floor, with their bedding and clothing on top of them!

"Blimey, Corporal!" said Thomas Hill, "I don't remember hearing reveille!"

"What's your name, boy?"

"Thomas Hill, Corp!"

"I am Corporal to you! And as you think you're a bit of a wag, your name is going to be 'Hillbilly' from now on!" and that's what it became.

"Right, Hillbilly, the reason you did not hear reveille is because it has not gone yet. I'm doing you a special favour. At seven o'clock you have your first dormitory and kit inspection. Today, it's just Sergeant Kelly, tomorrow, it will be an officer."

Boys were standing and getting themselves together; some were wearing just underwear, others, pyjamas, and one boy, who must have come from a very well-to-do background, was sporting very fancy silk nightwear. Another boy close to the exit door was completely in the buff; he had his hand covering his wedding tackle, with his knees together and slightly bent, feeling very embarrassed and looking shamefaced. The Corporal turned to him:

"Name?"

"Stanley White, Corporal."

"You are now Whitey Boy."

Then turning to the silk attire:

"Name?"

"Martin Riddle, Corporal."

"That's easy! You are Jimmy, as in Jimmy Riddle!" This last remark did not go unnoticed by the rest of the Section, who laughed heartily. Martin Riddle now went bright red.

"Where are you from, Jimmy?"

"I live in Gloucester Road, Kensington, with my mother and father, Corporal."

"Are you still at school?"

"No, Corporal. I worked in my father's law office, and it is Father who wanted me to join up, Corporal."

"I'm surprised you did not go to officer training!"

"Father thought it was better to start at the bottom and work one's way up, Corporal."

"Enough of this crap! You've got ten minutes to get washed, dressed and back in here, and you must shave every single day, whether you shave or not!"

A scramble for the latrines ensued, followed by a rush towards the washroom, and somehow they all managed to appear just as reveille blared out. That had given Corporal Harrington a chance to sit back on the only chair in the dormitory; leaning dangerously back against the wall he drew heavily on a Woodbine. As his charges reappeared, he blew one final smoke ring, dropped the butt on the wooden floor, and with his mirror-clean boots stubbed it out.

"Right, remember what I said last night? We are all for one and one for all! Make your beds like I showed you, get your kit tidy, like I showed you, and if you see your neighbour in difficulty, help him, because he might be there to save your life one day. When you've done all that, sweep the floor, clean the lights, clean the windows, and make everything sparkle."

Busy bodies started to move in a more organised way. Things got done; the dormitory began to look like a manicured hospital ward. The Corporal re-entered, with just twenty minutes to go before inspection.

"First appearances…not bad!"

He then ran his fingers across the window sill:

"This is not done!  There's dust!"

He dropped a penny on various beds, and if it did not bounce, they had to be re-made.  Eventually he said:

"Well, let's hope for the best!  You have five more minutes, and I suggest that you use them to make your shoes shine with a mirror finish. Remember, breakfast depends on it!  One last thing, when Sergeant Kelly comes through the door stand to attention at the end of your bed, and look straight ahead, never talk, unless you are spoken to."

Seven o'clock came, and like a genie appearing from the end of a bottle, in burst Sergeant Kelly.

The Corporal stood to attention, and shouted:

"By your beds, 'ten-shun!"

Sergeant Kelly looked very carefully at everything; the first bed he came to "Blanket not tight enough!" turning the cot over, spilling bedding and kit all over the floor.

"Corporal, take that man's name!"

"Name?"

"Brian Baxter, Corporal!"

The Sergeant moved on.  At Richard Allen's locker, he found a minute amount of dust, tipped the locker over, spilling its contents over the floor.  Looking to the Corporal:

"That man's name?"

"Name?"

"Richard Allen, Corporal!"

Sergeant Kelly smirked inwardly.  'I've the buggers right where I want them!' he thought.

At approximately twenty past seven, he turned at the door; to the expectant men, still standing at attention, eyes front, and winking at the Corporal, he said in a loud, gruff voice:

"This is not the worse mess I've seen today, and as I am a kindly, loving soul at heart, you can have breakfast!" But he added very quickly: "But clear up this bloody mess first! Next time, any names taken will be on a charge." With that he was gone.

The Corporal relaxed his stance.

"Right, stand at ease, men. Let's get this mess tidied up, and go and eat."

Breakfast was a rushed affair, but nevertheless extremely welcome. Parade sprang at them, sharp at eight o'clock, and there was an hour's physical training with the PT Sergeant, followed immediately by drill and more drill. In the afternoon, Sergeant Kelly appeared, and stood the four Sections to attention.

"Men!" he barked, "We are now going to present you with your own special life saver. It is a Short Magazine Lee Enfield rifle, which has a 303 calibre, a ten round magazine, and has a killing range through human flesh of two thousand yards. You will learn how to knock a fly out of the sky with it. You can be in a position to light the enemy's cigarette with a single shot. At close range, a bullet will even penetrate up to an inch of steel. This rifle, from now on is your God: you will keep it clean at all times, you will learn how to take it apart, and reassemble it, even in the dark. If I ever see anybody misusing their rifle, whether it be by accident, or by design as a joke, or whatever, that person or persons will do, I promise you, at least one week in the glass house with no pay! Where your God SMLE is concerned, there are no jokes! On the shooting range, you will have targets at one hundred yards, five hundred yards, and even a thousand yards. I want there to be bull's-eye scores on all and everyone. In time, you will learn how to fire up to twenty-five or more rounds a minute, knowing that at least fifteen of them will be accurate. This weapon will surely save your life. You will sign for each weapon, and you will learn your own weapon's serial number by heart."

He then looked at the Corporals, and said in a quieter tone: "Take your men, get their rifles and bayonets, assign a couple of men to get the rifle racks as well, take them back to their dormitories, and show them how they work."

Two weeks of drilling, long marches, sometimes with heavy packs, but always carrying their rifle, changed the men from footsore boys to highly tuned, fit young soldiers. The thin boys had generally put on weight, and the plump ones had turned fat into muscle. Matti had lost a lot of his rounded features, and had become more angular. They were now the fittest they had ever been in their lives; even the smokers amongst them, seemed to be able to breathe deeper. A twenty mile route march was becoming a comparatively easy exercise for all the young soldiers.

On the thirteenth of February, Colonel McBride advised all his officers and NCOs that on the twenty-first of February 1915, there would be a Battalion target competition to see if there were any potential snipers within the Battalion. It would take two days, and they would all be billeted in tents at Hythe Gunnery and Rifle Range in Kent. When the news drifted into Corporal Harrington's Section there was a buzz of excitement. Having been working hard over the past couple of weeks on their rifle practice, the Section knew that the best rifleman amongst them was Jimmy Riddle. Martin had grown up, having spent many October days with his father and mother shooting grouse in Scotland. The SMLE had very quickly become an extension of his right arm. He had even managed to score twenty hits a minute at five hundred yards, which even to Sergeant Kelly had seemed quite incredible.

After supper, back in the dormitory, Corporal Harrington's Section was sitting around, busy cleaning their rifles and kit, and talking quietly amongst themselves.

Whitey Boy turned to Enrico: "So, what do you think of this competition? Does anybody here, other than Jimmy, have a chance of making a name for the Section?"

"Don't look at me, I am lucky if I can hit the brick shit house!" which caused a ripple of laughter among those who were eavesdropping.

"Matti, are you gonna be a hit by making a hit?", again more laughter.

"I don't know, I'm a little nervous of being seen to be good. I can kill Fritz, if I have to, at a distance, knowing he is trying to kill me, but as a sniper?"

To this Matti shuddered: "I really don't think that's me! I much prefer the idea," he added, "of being a bomber. Give me a satchel full of Mills bombs, and I might be all right." He concluded with: "I was lousy at sport, but now I wish I played cricket, because, the way I throw those bombs makes me believe I could have been a good bowler!"

This caused a general: "Oh, yeah?" of derision.

The consensus of opinion within the Section was that there was only one potential marksman, Private Martin 'Jimmy' Riddle, but he had his own ideas.

Over the next eight days, inspections became an every day formality, and were generally passed with flying colours by all Sections. Drilling had become a highly organised exercise, and the four Sections were now capable of performing even the most complex form of ceremonial drill. A smart soldier was no longer an individual; he was part of a homogenous entity: a Section working together with precision, like a very fine Swiss watch. Practice on the rifle range was a daily occurrence, and even Enrico was managing to fire between fifteen and twenty-five aimed shots a minute — not that he always hit the target!

They were now very quickly becoming the King's soldiers, who were going to be of use, and hopefully not a liability. On the morning of the twentieth, six bone-shaking lorries appeared in the parade ground. Breakfast was hurried, equipment that was not needed was stowed away, dormitories cleaned and shined, and men were eager to have a couple of days away from the barracks.

"Sunny Hythe!" said Enrico, slinging his rifle over the left shoulder of his great coat, and throwing his right arm around Matti's shoulder.

"Matti, my boy, this will be our first holiday! Hythe by the sea! In sunny February!" and he led him towards the awaiting transport. It was by the sea, but it was not sunny; it was extremely cold, with a sharp north easterly wind, coming straight from Siberia. It was carrying particles of snow, which were annoying, but not settling. These army trucks were noisy and extremely uncomfortable. The benches in the back were solid oak, and with the rigid suspension, and the solid tyres, travelling any sort of distance became a bit of a nightmare. Apart from the buffeting that they got when they went over a bump or cobblestones, which had been known to throw men to the floor, sometimes even break bones, the rocking from side to side would also often bring on a state of nausea. They drove in convoy across London, and much to the horror of both Matti and Enrico, they crossed over London Bridge, passing Tooley Street. Both boys instinctively went white, and heads shrunk into great coats. They need not have bothered, of course, as they were not the same boys that had left to sign up only a month ago, forgetting that nobody could see in the back of the lorry, anyway. But they felt happier when they realised they were past the Elephant and Castle, heading eastwards along the Old Kent Road.

It took five hours, from Finsbury Barracks to the old Cinque Port firing range at Hythe. No stops for sustenance or relief, so by the time they got there, there was a lot of soldiers rushing to undo their fly buttons and extricate their members, partaking in a very relieving expulsion of bodily fluids!

They were very relieved to have relieved themselves!

The men were gathered together into the normal four lines; Sergeant Kelly ordered that firstly they should stow their kit in the tents allotted to them by each Section's Corporal, then chow! And with a warning tone in his voice, Sergeant Kelly reminded them:

"Your rifle goes with you everywhere, even if you have to have a shit, you take it in there! Anybody without a rifle is on a charge."

This said he dismissed the Section.

It was an extremely cold night, and the temperature had not really risen above freezing. The ground was frozen solid, so whatever the men did, they could not get warm. Dawn could not come too soon for them, and when reveille trumpeted itself in the grey of the morning, nobody was asleep, and nobody needed to be woken. Soldiers of all shapes and sizes, including young and old, roused themselves grumbling about the conditions.

"What the hell are we doing here on a day like to-day?" exclaimed Matti, as he pulled off cold covers to find it was even colder without them over him. "This is real miserable; I wish we were back at barracks." Matti and Enrico had shared a bell tent with three other members of their Section: Jimmy Riddle, John Hutton and John Smyth. Jimmy was the oldest by several years, and because of the rather posh way he spoke the others had looked to him as a natural leader. They got dressed as quickly as they could, nearly knocking the tent over in the desperation to get into something warm, though of course nothing was warm. John Smyth had hung his trousers up onto the centre pole only to find them frozen solid. This at least cheered up the others as he struggled to get his legs into them. "This is a real nightmare, I've never ever known anything like this," said John Hutton, shaking from head to toe. "I reckon it must be well below zero." In fact it was a couple of degrees above, but when you get cold everything seems even worse. As the Section assembled itself, there was a grey glint appearing from the east to show that a new day was dawning. A hot breakfast of porridge, followed by an hour's Physical Training brought all of the battalion back to life. Daylight struggled to emerge, showing a brittle misty hoar, which left the shingled ground sharp and cold; yet the upper air had now cleared, so that the soldiers could look in an easterly direction towards the top of the Downs, with the lower reaches still in a hazy mist. The battalion was brought together for parade and inspection. Colonel McBride and his staff walked up and down the lines, mostly with an air of indifference. Having ascended a dais, he addressed the men.

"Men, it is an extremely cold day, but it is even colder on the Western front, so you can think of this as a trial period. We want to find marksmen. Marksmen will get an extra two shillings a week in their pay, so, men, it's got to be worth having a go for!" he then turned to the Lieutenant, who turned to the Sergeant, who marched the men off to the various areas for the trials to begin. Corporal Harrington had his men on the five hundred yard range, and was expecting very good things, especially from Martin Riddle, but Martin had already decided that having grown quite fond of the rest of the Section, he did not wish to be removed. The whole Section did reasonably well, but Martin's efforts left a lot to be desired. The Corporal was handed the score cards, and then handed them onto Sergeant Kelly:

"Riddle, what the fuck is all this?" said the Sergeant, throwing the score card at him. You ain't fooling anybody, boy!"

"Stand to attention when the Sergeant talks to you!" screamed Corporal Harrington.

"We were expecting great things of you, and you have flunked it!"

"Why have you done that, Private Riddle?" interjected the Corporal with a hand on his forehead, giving an air of a person in great pain.

"Well, Corporal…"

"Talk to me, not the Corporal!" said Sergeant Kelly.

"Well, Sergeant, I'm not sure what you mean by flunking it."

"Don't take us for fools, boy! You might not want to be known as a great marksman, because you missed the bull's-eye and the inner ring, but your mistake is that you made up a perfect clip of shots off to the left."

"Sergeant, I just don't want to be removed from the Section! Over these last few weeks I have made some very good friends, and with all due respect, it was the Corporal and yourself, who on all occasions emphasised how important it is for a Section to work together as a team. I know I can shoot a rifle, but I'm not sure I could creep around with the sole intention of killing someone, especially if they are not aware of me being there, and they are not trying to kill me."

"Why, you conchie bastard!" shouted the irate Sergeant, who had to be almost restrained by a very worried Corporal.

"No, Sergeant, I am not a conscientious objector, and I am quite prepared to do my duty, I just don't see myself as an assassin."

This remark left both Corporal Harrington and Sergeant Kelly a little dumbstruck. They were not quite sure how to handle this situation. The veins in Kelly's temple had been throbbing, and looked for all the world like purple rivers on a map. But he started to visibly control himself, and with a tone of reason, he concluded the inquisition by saying:

"Look, boy, do your very best, show the Battalion that our Section has something special about it. You cannot be made to become a sniper, and I think you will possibly have a good protective influence on the Section." Then he added, almost to himself in a sarcastic tone, "If you live that long!"

The day stayed cold and crisp, and though there was no snow, the frost on the ground tended to swirl around in the cold light breeze. The Sections all did their various shooting trials, and the day eventually reached its conclusion. From the Colonel's point of view, the day had been a success: he had found twenty-four marksmen, who were keen and eager to become snipers. They had been seduced by the prospect of the extra pay, and an easier time, which was to be later revealed as being far from the truth. After the final parade, the Battalion was dispatched back to its various barracks. Sergeant Kelly's men returned to Finsbury at about three in the morning; they were dismissed, and allowed to sleep for the few hours left until reveille.

The weeks went by quickly. The boys had many duties to perform, with drilling and shooting being the top priorities. All soldiers had to do extra duties in their period at Finsbury; guard duty was especially despised, because, though they were given guns, they were given no ammunition, and there had been one incident, one very foggy night, when the sentries on the gate were badly shaken by some Irish accented voices calling out for the English to leave Ireland. And when they challenged "Who goes there?" the answer came in the guise of a Chinese firecracker, which banged and hopped all over the road, putting the wind up the duty sentries who thought they were under fire, and therefore called out the guard. This left the camp in a state of high alert until daylight came, showing the remains of a firecracker on the cobbled roadway outside the main gate.

Often the recruits were allowed short leave breaks, as most of the men from Finsbury barracks had lived nearby. Enrico and Matti never had anywhere to go, wishing to stay within the confines of the barracks for fear of being recognised. They thought a great deal of the families they had left behind, but never knew how to make any contact for fear the police might intercept any attempts they made.

Winter started to turn into the blossom of spring: longer and warmer days, with the thrust of spring flowers and tree buds showing that a new season had approached, more birds singing and nesting, totally oblivious to humanity's farce on the Western front.

It was the last Sunday of April, and the Battalion had just finished the obligatory church parade, when Colonel McBride spoke to the men.

"Men, you will be happy to know that your time here at Finsbury has ended! There is no more leave, and all letters home will be censored, so anything you write must be handed to the Lieutenant of your Section. Anybody breaking these rules will be severely punished. Tomorrow, we will be leaving as a Battalion, soon to be going to France. You will be going first to Newhaven for a few days, there to be ferried across to Calais. We will be at a big camp site, at Friston, and there will be several long route marches with full kit. For the remainder of this day, you must clean up these barracks, ready for the next intake. You have all worked hard these last few months, and I can honestly say that I am proud to lead you."

The next morning, all the recruits were fully kitted and ready for the journey to Newhaven. The lorries appeared, just after breakfast, with the usual military punctuality. As the men loaded their kit and climbed aboard, many looked back wistfully at this red brick edifice that they had called home for the last four months, and wondered as the streets passed by, whether they would ever be returning to Old London Town.

On arriving at Newhaven, on a beautiful warm sunny Monday afternoon, all were surprised to see that the town was almost completely taken over by the military; very few civilians still lived there, only those working for the various armed forces. It had a feeling of being a ghost town in parts, with many houses, shops and pubs boarded up, awaiting better days. The stores that were being loaded onto the ships were like mountains on the side of the docks; trains filled all the lines with the coming and going of goods, horses and men alike. The first shock that came was seeing the lines of hospital trains, almost as long as one could see. A hospital ship was moored at the quayside, and what seemed like a nest of ants was scurrying in and out of that ship, and into the trains.

"Jesus!" said Barry Knight, to the rest of the men in the lorry, but no-one in particular. "Is this what we've got to look forward to: a holiday in sunny France followed by a restful time on that there cruise ship?" Nervous laughter answered him, but it did make them all wonder.

The convoy passed through the town, making its way east towards Friston, this beautiful valley, nestling peacefully in the South Downs Way, alongside the meandering Cuckmere river. In better times, a wonderful pleasure spot for the bird watcher and the rambler, today the valley had become a tented city. All the soldiers were in a state of awe, at first struck by the beauty of the countryside with the wild flowers giving off a heady scent, and the yellow gorse shimmering in the sunlight, as if setting the Downs on fire, and then to become amazed by the thousands of tents, lined up like newly planted trees .As the lorries wound their way down into the confines of this new encampment, they began to notice the thousands of other soldiers, busily doing as they were told, some doing PT, others drill; more were kitted out for long route marches, and to their surprised pleasure, they even noticed some men lazily catching the sun, lying by the bank of the river.

"Matti, I think we've come to a holiday camp!"

All in the lorry laughed at Enrico's remark. All the Battalion were in high spirits when they were disgorged from the lorries. Corporals rallied their Sections, Sergeants gathered their Companies, and officers arranged the Battalion. Once again, in a rather tired and croaky voice, Colonel McBride spoke to his men:

"You'll be assigned tents, watch your gear, as there are thieves about, and if you lose your rifle, for whatever reason, field punishment will be administered. If you look over to your left, you will see that such is already happening to that worthless dolt yonder."

All the men craned their necks, wondering what the Colonel was talking about, and to their horror, they could see a soldier who had been stripped to the waist, and had been tied, spread-eagled to a large cannon wheel, there to be left for twenty-four hours.

"'Tenshun!" came the bellow of the Sergeant-Major. "Nobody has given you permission to shuffle about, listen to what your Colonel has to say!"

"Once you have settled in, you can have chow, and more or less do what you want, except for those who have been given duties. Nobody, and I emphasize nobody, will be allowed to leave this camp." Turning to the Sergeant-major, the Colonel concluded:

"Sergeant-Major, dismiss the men!"

Enrico and Matti were given a tent, along with William 'Scotty' Scott, Robert 'Bob' Gregg, and Harold 'Harry' Gimson. They settled in quickly, and sporting their rifles on their shoulders, they went exploring. They walked to the edge of the beach, looking out on to the deep glistening blue of the English Channel. April had been a warm and sunny month, and along with the rebirth of spring, the young men were glad to be alive. It was Bob Gregg, who first dared that they should take their shoes and socks off, and go paddling. The excitement of being free to do this was wonderful for them; they were all laughing and joking, pushing one another in the sand, and playing tag. They went into the sea, and like little five year old girls, immediately rushed out again, squealing.

"Crikey O'Riley!" stammered Harry Gimson, the only other north countryman in their Section. "That's bloody cold!"

The next morning reveille came early: it was just before dawn, at five thirty in the morning, when the whole Battalion mustered for its first parade. The only water for washing and shaving had been extremely cold, and more than a few chins sported the nicks of a bad shave. The men were brought to attention, and as dawn broke, a sight from bygone days appeared, like a ghost in the mist: there, on a white stallion, was the caricature figure of a nineteenth century cavalry officer. It was Colonel McBride, followed closely by his Adjutant, Major Tyler-Latham, riding a piebald.

The Colonel was a rather weedy, tall man, with a very small greying 'tache under his nose. He was wearing a dress suit, more fitting for a royal ceremonial occasion than a parade of soldiers. His sword, in its scabbard, clanged rather noisily against his right boot and stirrup. Even Sergeant Kelly and the Corporals looked on in awe. Without dismounting, the two nineteenth century officers traversed the lines of erect soldiers. The Colonel's sunken cheekbones almost filled out with pride, as he looked at this well turned out collection of soldiers.

"Men," he said, as he pulled up the reins of his stallion. Getting the horse to stand still was not easy, so whoever the horse faced, the Colonel addressed. "Today, we are going on a little hike, and you will have to take your complete kit; it won't be long, just twenty-four hours."

To which the whole Brigade's shoulders sagged visibly.

"Make sure you have plenty of iron rations, and that your water flask is topped to the brim. You will have a very quick breakfast, and we will be on our way, whether you are finished or not, by 07.45 hours."

As now the horse was facing entirely the other way from the men which made the Colonel address a line of tents, he then ordered the Sergeant to dismiss the troops, and be prepared for the route march.

At 07.45 sharp the whole Battalion was in a column of four, and stretched for several hundred yards. With his full pack and rifle slung over his shoulder, each man carried a considerable weight. Again the Colonel appeared on his mount with the Adjutant in tow.

"Sergeant,"

"Sir!" screamed the Sergeant.

"Make an about face, and let's get under way. Nice steady rhythm, and for the time being, let's try and keep some semblance of formation."

"Sir! About…turn!"

The first mile or so was a gentle incline up the South Down going west; they were at the top of the Down, looking out to sea. In the foreground, the whole area was fortified with massive guns. The beach areas seemed deserted, except for the frolicking of gulls between the barbed wire and the sea. They had walked all the way to Rottingdean before they left the ridge to turn inland. In front of them lay yet another beautiful valley, which they were to follow for the next few miles. Once down into the valley, farm workers and cows in the fields stopped what they were doing to watch the sight of two officers on horseback and a thousand men walking in step behind. Sergeant Kelly barked at Enrico:

"Caruso!"

"Yes? Sergeant!"

"Get a song going: We're here because we're here!"

"Yes, Sergeant!"

After a long pause and a whispered: "One, two, three, four!" Enrico started to sing: "*We're here, because we're here, because we're here, because we're here…*"

This was sung in his normal out of tune voice, to the refrains of 'Auld Lang Syne'. This was speedily taken up by the rest of the Battalion, this time singing more or less in tune. For probably the first time since enlisting, Enrico noticed Sergeant Kelly smile broadly, and when the refrain ended, heard him say in a jokey voice, loud enough for most of the men around Enrico to hear:

"Blimey, Caruso, how did you get your name?"

By the time the column had reached the windmill on the Old

Roman Road, just outside Burgess Hill, it stretched for over a mile. The Colonel brought the men to a halt within the confines of the old mill, much to the horror of the local populace, as they watched men doing what men must do against trees, bushes and sides of buildings.

"Sergeant!"

"Sir!" said Sergeant Kelly, as he brought his feet together and saluted.

"Half an hour's break for the stragglers to catch up, and to take on water and eat some rations!"

Onward they marched, now fortified, with again a new spring in their step. Songs were now coming fast and furious; this helped to keep spirits high, and by the time they reached Ringmer, they had covered approximately twenty-five miles, and night was starting to close in. The pace had now slackened off, and ranks had been broken; weary, tired feet with many men starting to limp with blisters, kept going towards Hailsham. There was a ford across the Cuckmere at Horsebridge, and the men delighted, even in the dead of night, in splashing themselves with the cool, refreshing water. Now turning south, and most definitely showing signs of wear and tear, they made their way through Polegate to Eastbourne. As they approached the Martello tower, which shone in the moonlight like a beacon for them, they were all happy to see that an army canteen was there to administer hot soup and strong tea. Then came the hardest part of the journey: the last five miles were over Beachy Head, which seemed like scaling the north face of the Eiger during winter to these foot-weary soldiers, but only two hours more, and they could make out the entrance to Friston Camp. As the last man came across the parade ground, dawn only too quickly came from the East. The Colonel dismissed the men, saying they could sleep until ten o'clock, and the afternoon would be spent running over an assault course, again in full kit, and working on bayonet practice. But few heard, as brains were numb, and bodies drained. Everybody fell into a dreamless sleep, only to be awoken occasionally by noises from the rest of the camp.

The week was spent in tough combat training conditions, and not one soldier thought of Friston as a holiday camp, or of Colonel McBride as a friendly out of time gentleman.

None too soon, came the first Monday in May, and the London Northern Rifle Brigade was to cross over from Newhaven to Calais. What under normal circumstances would have been a three hour journey, actually took six, as the troop transport and its escort zigzagged through minefields on a very set course to Calais. It was while out at sea, that some of the troops became aware of a distant rumble, like continuous thunder. It was Sergeant Kelly, on the deck, smoking a cigarette and talking to the Corporals around him, who first realised what it was. Turning to Sergeant Glencross and Corporal Harrington, he informed them in a knowing voice:

"That'll be the German guns. I've heard they have huge siege guns, some even stationed in Ostend."

The ship docked at Calais at approximately sun-up, and as the men disembarked, the first horrors of war were there to be smelt, heard and seen. The smell was a sweet smell of corruption, mixed with the odour of disinfectant, and there was the ever present smell of cordite and petrol. The first thing the men saw was lines and lines of hospital trains, and ambulances, plus a long line of feet sticking from under a huge tarpaulin. As they walked from the ship, Matti grabbed Enrico:

"My God! They are all dead!"

Even though they were more than fifty miles away from the nearest action, distant rumblings of individual cannons could be heard and the skyline would occasionally light up, giving all too briefly a feeling of instant daybreak. Again the dock was crammed with stores; there seemed to be enough food to feed the world, and enough ammunition to blow it up. Captain Fritten was waiting by the dock gate for the Battalion to arrive. He explained to the NCOs that they would be catching a train to take them inland off Dunkerque, where they would be spending the next two or three weeks, honing their trench skills in yet more training. As the idea of travelling now on a train seemed a nicer prospect than being thrown from side to side within a ship, with men in some cases leaking from both ends of their bodies at the same time, spirits started to improve. That was until they saw the train, a long line of cattle trucks with one late nineteenth century third class carriage thrown in for good measure! The men were herded into the cattle trucks, like many soldiers before them. The NCOs and officers took the only carriage. The train stood there, ready to leave, the engine chuffing contentedly, but it did not move. Four hours went by, before the train finally pulled out of the siding. Fortunately for the men, the sliding doors to the cattle truck had not been closed, so that, as the bucket got filled within the carriage, it could be emptied through the open doorway. Woe betides any luckless soldier who might have been leaning out of a truck downwind!

They had only gone a matter of four or five miles when the train was herded into yet another siding, this time to allow an ammunition train to pass by on its way to the front, then to allow a hospital train to go by from the front.

Again, it was a beautiful day, and had there been plenty of food and drink, one could be assured that the men would have enjoyed the journey, but as rations had mainly been used on the transporter, and even water bottles had been emptied with no chance of a refill, things were becoming more than a little miserable. Heads were dropping as the time went on.

Once the train finally left the outskirts of Dunkerque, it turned in the direction of Lille, but it terminated at the small town of Mont des Cats.

Mont des Cats was famed for its monastery and the black beer the monks made. There had been a serious skirmish between the British Cavalry and the Uhlans, which are the German equivalent. This was one of the first contacts between both of the armies' mounted men. It happened in the winter of 1914, when the Cavalry just stumbled onto a small group of German Lancers. The British rushed forward catching the unlucky enemy drinking water from the local well. Before the Uhlans could really take in what had occurred, one of their group was lanced, and several others killed from rifle fire. One of those unfortunates was Prince Maximilian von Hesse, nephew of the Kaiser. He was later buried within the confines of the Monastery. One of the strange but all too often reoccurring coincidences that took place during the war was the fact that Alan Dumbridge had fought in that skirmish, and that was completely unknown to Matti. He had not distinguished himself, but he had survived his first death struggle.

Very weary troops then had to march about two miles north to a system of trenches which were going to become their training ground for the next three weeks. All the way from Calais, they had been surprised to see lush, clean countryside, farmers working the fields, animals grazing them, all totally oblivious to the raging guns. The farmers never stopped, even to watch a side show of two planes in deadly combat overhead, this being the first time that the battalion had become truly aware of a life-and-death struggle.

Their time in these trenches was well spent. Lectures on warfare became a daily occurrence. They learnt how to fire trench mortars, a very dangerous weapon, sometimes worse for the firer than the fired upon: they had a tendency to explode before the loader got clear. Some of them became very adept in the art of Mills bombing. They spent long hours carrying tools of war, such as barbed wire, ammunition, A-frames for the building of the trenches, and duck boards for walking within them. Their routine was two days in the trench, which would include guard duty, trench raids, fixing the barbed wire during the night hours and of course, firing on the enemy. Two days were then spent behind the lines, but doing the manual work, such as the building of new trench systems, and carrying essentials up to the front. The next two days after that, was for recovery, with of course added further training, not to forget drill and kit inspections. Sleep, forget it! It became something that one just dreamed about, and there was no time for dreaming either.

Sleeping in the trenches! The men would expect to snatch at odd moments, either sitting or lying on a spare place, more often than not the fire step. They very quickly learnt that to be caught sleeping on duty could, and on many occasions did, mean the firing squad. Never let yourself be in that situation. Toiletry was always a problem: soldiers just squatted over a board in a designated place within the trench. You had always to find time to shave and keep clean. This was of course hard, but woe betides you if an officer made a sudden inspection and you didn't come up to scratch.

Matti and Enrico were now finding out how tough this man's army really was.

It was in the third and final week that the accident happened. The training had gone well, at least the soldiers themselves thought so. They were now doing a mock defence of the trench at night from a raiding party of make believe Germans. Rifles were firing at a rapid rate, and then someone suggested that they start throwing Mills bombs at the enemy. One got dropped within the group before it could be thrown. Two men lost their lives and two more had their legs blown off. This was just a few yards from Matti and Enrico who were on the next firing step. A whistle was blown, the firing stopped. All that could be heard were the screams of the two soldiers who were missing their limbs. Enrico rushed past another stunned soldier only to fall over one of the legs still in its trouser leg and puttee, sporting a very clean boot. When he saw what he had done, the next thing to do was to promptly throw up his dinner. The shock of seeing screaming men and limbs was almost too much for many of them. How soon they were going to get used to it! Enrico was helped away from the area and the injured were quickly taken to hospital; then after a time, they would be sent back to Blighty. Their war was over, but it was going to be hard to tell their grandchildren what they had done in the Great War. The dead just disappeared.

Actually, this happened a great deal of times in training, and though unfortunate for the victims, it was thought of by many officers as a fine lesson for new recruits to see and be aware of the dangers that were going to confront them.

The men got regular parcels from home, but were rarely allowed to write back, and that only after strict censorship had been enforced. But it was a parcel from Barry Knight's parents that aroused the real interest. Apart from the normal Woodbines, matches, tea and coffee, his parcel contained birthday cake from his younger sister. The cake was quickly shared and eaten, but it was what it was wrapped in that caused a big stir. It was enclosed in several pages of the Daily Mirror dated May 9th 1915. The headlines were… "Lusitania Sunk - Many Dead". The story went on to tell how this unarmed liner, on its way from New York to Southampton, had been torpedoed by a German U-boat on May 7th. Hundreds, including many famous people had drowned. The American government was furious with Germany for allowing such an outrage to happen, and called upon the world to condemn this atrocity, and view it as a war crime. This would soon have a profound effect on the men, one that was to be far reaching. They all stared at this cutting, saying nothing, all more than a little stunned. Finally the silence was broken by Corporal Harrington, who with glazed eyes just whispered, "Well, boys, now you know why we're fighting."

All the time the guns rumbled on in the not too far distance.

# IV

May 23rd 1915 came and the London Northern Rifle Brigade were now preparing for their first tour of front line duty. All those months of hard work, were they going to pay off? Very soon they would know! There was not a soldier amongst them that was not the fittest he had ever been in his short life: plenty of good food, plus health giving exercise had seen to that. Bodies were hardy, muscles trim, strength at its apex. These boys carried loads on their backs of up to one hundred pounds, plus their guns. They could do this for hours at a time, without suffering from total exhaustion.

Now at the train halt again, they waited for the engine to take them close to the front line; this was it!

"Not again!" laughed Enrico to Matti and anybody else who might be listening. "More bloody cattle trucks for us!"

They piled into their waiting trucks, checking to see if it was the same train that had brought them here; it was not. These trucks had straw in them, as if it was going to be a long journey, yet the front was only about twenty or so miles away. What the men didn't know was that these trucks had just delivered a few hundred horses up the line, and now it was the turn of men.

"For crying out loud!" exclaimed Jimmy Riddle, "there is horse shit everywhere!"

"God, I hope this isn't going to be a long trip, or I can see myself adding my load onto the floor as well," said Matti.

Men and equipment were hurriedly loaded, and then without much of a fuss, the aging blackened 0-4-0 pulled its human cargo off to war.

It was not long before they were again shunted into a siding to allow a fast ambulance train to speed its way towards the coast and safety. It seemed like hours before they resumed their journey, but in fact it was just about thirty minutes. It was a beautiful day, with the sun shining, and not a cloud in the sky.

"I think it is time to break out some rations," said Matti. "What time is it? We left about nine o'clock this morning, and it seems like hours. Anyone got the time?"

"Nearly half past ten," answered one of the other soldiers who were sharing these comfortable quarters! Before anybody could say or do another thing, the train jerked noisily to a stop. There had been an explosion, completely unheard by the soldiers inside the creaking, lumbering train. Many men fell over, bringing others down with them. More than a little mayhem ensued. The train had come to a complete stop, still on the main line.

"What the fuck is going on here?" shouted one John Smyth, as he picked himself up off the floor and tried to wipe horse droppings from his clothing. Enrico and Matti looked through the open doorway of their cattle truck to see that the officers and NCOs were now walking up to the engine. The driver had stopped, as he had seen the explosion, and it had been close to the rails. When they walked to the small crater, moulded into a nice round hole, they saw that the rail had buckled somewhat, making further progress in that mode of travel unlikely for many hours. Nothing would be coming or going on this line until the offending rail was replaced.

"This is the end of the line for us," stated one of the officers, "better unload the troops, it is still going to be a long march".

It was Sergeant Kelly who first started organising the men from the now useless train.

"Out of there! At the double! Bring all your equipment. We are going for a stroll."

Men spilt from the cattle trucks like water from a ewer. No order was maintained. All the soldiering was going straight out the window.

"Get your bloody selves together, quickly. There'll be trouble for anybody slacking, you have my word on it!" screamed Kelly. "Get your arses down on terra firma", again followed by a frantic "Quickly!" His chest heaved, veins nearly detached themselves from his neck, his whole face was the darkest shade of crimson, and he was fit to bust. Men tried to form into some sort of order, but to no avail. It was while this melee was doing its rounds that one bright spark said out loud. "Look, up there! Two planes having a dog fight!" Men paused in what they had been trying to do, and stood around in groups, eyes to the heavens. "Wow, they *are* in a dog fight!" said Enrico. "The triplane is a German, and he looks to be getting a pasting from the other flier."

"I think the other is a Frenchy," interjected Whitey Boy. No one could blame the men for looking skywards, as all the officers and NCOs were doing the same. *Rat, tat, tat, tat, tat…* The sound of machine guns could just be heard from above. "This is better than watching the flicks," said Matti to Enrico.

It was after a few seconds that an officer shouted for the men to take cover.

"Get under the train," shouted Corporal Harrington to his Section.

"Oh, Jesus, what on earth has happened to Baxter?" cried Enrico. There, lying in a heap on the ground was Brian Baxter; a pool of blood was collecting around him, leaking from a hole in his head. It was Sergeant Toomey, an elderly Sergeant who had been in the army for what seemed most of his life, but had never been out of Blighty before, never seeing any action other than the odd skirmish down the "Thomas Beckett" in the Old Kent Road, on Friday and Saturday nights, who got to Baxter first. "Blimey, I am quite sure he is stone dead," said the now much shaken Sergeant. In fact Brian twitched a couple of times as nerves started to die within the shell of his lifeless body, but he was for sure the first casualty of war that these men had seen. "Get under that train," screamed an officer at all the soldiers. "Why haven't we been issued with steel helmets yet?"

Poor Brian Baxter was extremely unlucky. No plane was aiming at him personally. The pilots were too busy trying to shoot one another down to notice a luckless group of untried soldiers. He had died, either from the German or the French pilot's hand by accident. Bullets had been flying everywhere. When spent, they fall to the ground. And in this case, one had fallen straight through Baxter's head. It was soon noticed that there were bullet holes in many places, but only one casualty. In future days, this would come to be considered a good day. One dead… got off lightly!

After what seemed an eternity, but was in fact just a few minutes, the planes ducked and dived out of view of the Battalion. Sergeant Kelly ordered the men on their feet again. Baxter was put to the side where burial squads could deal with him. The Adjutant made many notes in a large diary his Batman was carrying, concerning the first death, time, place and circumstances. All the men looked poignantly at their fallen comrade as they marched past in the direction of the guns. As they progressed, for once all equal, as all officers, NCOs and men had to walk, because there were no trucks, no horses, just shanks's ponies, it was noticeable how green and lush the countryside was, as well as flat. There seemed to be very little high ground. They were now in Flanders, where flat is flat, and it goes on for miles. After an hour of walking in the bright warm sunshine, heavy loads were starting to slow men up.

"Sergeant!" called Colonel McBride, "give the men a twenty minute break." Sagging shoulders, along with the bodies that supported them slumped to the ground, very gratefully. The Colonel, realising that the men were extremely upset through losing a friend, decided on a few choice words.

"Men, we are all unhappy about the loss of…?" then turning to his Adjutant.

"Private Baxter, sir."

"Private Baxter," he repeated as if he had always known, "but this is dangerous country. From now on you must look out for yourself and your friends". Then he added with a slight cough in his voice, "Let Baxter's death be a lesson to all of us. Never take your eyes off the enemy". All gathered there looked at one another in a puzzled way. What the hell was he talking about, how do you see a bullet coming, such a load of codswallop, was the general consensus of opinion. But forget the rubbish, the rest did men good. When they got to their feet again, it was with a certain spring, at least for the next couple of hours.

"Caruso!"

"Yes, Sergeant."

"Sing us a song, lad".

Under his breath came... "One, two, three." Then at full throttle and completely off key... "It's a long way to Tipp-er-ary, it's a long way to go, it's a long way to Tipp-er-ary, to the sweetest girl I know..." Then in unison and more or less in tune, "Good bye, Picc-ad-illy, good bye, Leicester Square, it's a long, long way to Tipp-er-ary, but my heart's right there..." It didn't go unnoticed how many grave sites there were as they walked. 'So strange,' thought Enrico as he walked and sang the next verse of the song. 'If it wasn't for the graves and the military presence, one would never guess there is a war on.' He was forgetting the guns now getting closer. How quickly people get used to all manner of noises and difficulties! The further north they got, the more shell and bomb craters they passed, many of them filled with water and litter. Every now and again, they came across the occasional ruined building, spewing its paraphernalia of every day life, like the disembowelled carcass of a prehistoric animal.

Several more hours of marching with the odd intermittent rest period elapsed before a sign said in English:

**Welcome to Poperinge.**
**The soldier's holiday home from home!**

Poperinge was a small Flemish town, with many medieval period houses along with the odd 19th Century dwelling places that neither flattered nor disgraced the town. It was their first serious sights of war since leaving the train for their epic walk, with all the armaments, ammunition dumps and soldiers about. Soldiers stood around, or were busily working at some task or another, as the Battalion now marched in step into the main square of the town.

"Halt!" screamed Sergeant Kelly. "Right turn! Stand at ease! Easy". Kelly turned towards Colonel McBride, who was walking towards him.

"Men, we will be staying here overnight, unless we are ordered otherwise. We are now going to arrange billets for you. Keep your rifle with you at all times. You can explore the town, but do not, and I repeat, *do not*, leave the town for any reason. Muster here tomorrow morning at seven sharp. Sergeant, keep the men at ease until I return, then assign billets and dismiss them."

"Sir!" answered Kelly, bringing his right foot sharply down to attention.

An hour later the men were billeted; most had washed and groomed, and were looking to see what Poperinge had to offer.

The main square was a fine example of a Flemish medieval market town. The square was cobblestoned, whereas most of the streets leading into it were just mud roads, which even on this beautiful spring day, were wet through from the long winter and all the unnaturally heavy use by military vehicles and horses. They had not been designed for this. Some of the shops and dwellings had panes of glass missing from their frames; this was due to shells from the German artillery that occasionally fell within the town's confines. There had been some buildings that had been burnt out through the shelling, but on the whole they had not suffered too badly. Some townspeople had moved away in panic at a possible invasion by the Hun, but most had stayed, either to farm the land or more likely to make a pretty penny from the Tommies that frequented it in times of rest from the front and trenches.

Enrico and Matti walked the town, happy to be allowed to roam without the fear of Police arresting them upon recognition. No one knew them here. At least until they turned into a street that had a ruined mill standing rather forlornly in its dilapidated state. As they ambled up the roadway leading to the mill, Matti spied some Cavalry soldiers, all grooming their horses. He stopped dead in his tracks; tears welled up in his eyes, which did not go unnoticed by his lifelong friend. "What's up?" enquired Enrico in a concerned way, seeing that he was shedding tears. Matti just stood there, then pointed to one of the Cavalry men, a Sergeant. Enrico did not understand at all, until the man he was pointing at looked up, saw him and cried out. "Matthew! What the hell are you doing here"? It was Matti's brother Alan. All the soldiers watched in fascination as two brothers came together in a hug of affection. There were tears from both of them, and also from Enrico, who kept them secret, but felt the sadness of knowing he was not going to be able to see his family.

"So what are you doing here? Why on earth did you enlist, aren't you still too young anyway?" Matti tried to explain, leaving out the death of the policeman. Enrico was introduced to Alan, who was at least happier for knowing that Matti had such a very good friend that seemed to be looking out for him.

"Jesus Christ! What a fool you are, getting into this mess when you really didn't have to!"

"The trouble is," said Matti, "we did have to come here. I haven't told you the whole story and I cannot, but trust me when I say we had to come." Alan thought that meant they had come out of love for King and Country, and was frowning deeply when Matti added "We have been in a little trouble with the law, I cannot tell you about it, but I didn't want Mum or Dad to know anything about the problems, so enlisting seemed the obvious way of getting out of the country. In fact, I would prefer it if you write and tell them that you have met me, but to keep it under their hats!

By all means tell them that I am in good health and spirits, and I will write myself before long, I promise."

"Well I'm sorry mate, but you really should write to them yourself. There is no excuse for putting Ma and Pa through misery. I have some paper, so write now and I will send your note with my own letter, and as I'm a Sergeant it won't get censored." Alan suggested that the three of them go to a local estaminet, where they could get ham and eggs, tea or coffee, and all that just for a few coppers. They walked back into the centre of town, Alan with his arm around Matti's shoulders. "I don't care what you have done, boy, it's good to see you." They all laughed happily as if drunk with alcohol, but in this case they were intoxicated with the pleasure of the reunion. They had their eggs and bacon, along with fried bread, cheese, and oodles of hot strong tea. Matti wrote his letter, explaining some things and asking for discretion from his parents. If they wanted to write back, they had only to write via Alan, and with a little luck it might reach him. Of course, there was no chance, as it was unlikely that the brothers would ever come in contact again, at least not until the end of the war. This had been a minor miracle, not likely to be repeated! "How are William, John and Steven, have you heard anything from them?" enquired Matti.

"You haven't heard, then? Of course not, no-one has been able to get you these last few months." Alan's face sagged under the weight of knowledge. Tears again welled into his eyes. "William has been posted missing, presumed dead."

"No!" said Matti, "How and where?"

"It was at the battle of Neuve Chapelle. They were crossing a river, over a bloody rope walkway, though for Christ's sakes, why? He was carrying a load when he slipped into the water. Even if he hadn't drowned, he certainly would have died from exposure as it was early March of this year and the weather was bloody freezing. I guess it would have been quick, that's all. And think what Mum and Dad were thinking with you disappearing to boot? Christ, they have had a real miserable time of it these last few months. Let's hope your letter cheers them up some?"

There was a long silence while all three of them took in the significance of what had been said. It had been so heart warming to meet Alan again after so long, but now, Matti was in a gloom for the loss of William. He really hadn't known big brother William, but blood is blood after all. After a while Alan ordered three beers, and things started to cheer up again. "Do you have a girlfriend?" enquired Alan, with expectation in his voice.

"No." was the quick reply. "You?"

"Well as a matter of fact, I do. Her name is Sarah, Sarah Buckley. I met her last time I was on leave and we have been walking out ever since. I intend to ask for her hand next time I get home. It is time I got married and started a family, one of us must!" Matti smiled, put his hand on his brother's arm. "I am pleased for you, Alan. Be happy." The way Alan smiled in that knowing way, Matti knew he was going to be just that.

Time passed quickly; it was getting dark and a lighting curfew was imposed at sun down: black curtains were draped everywhere to stop any light shining through. It was in case enemy planes were flying overhead. Let's not help them, was the idea, though if a plane was flying after dark it was more in danger than the populace below. Landing in the dark was a nightmare, one that often caused terrible crashes.

Soon it was time to part. Enrico and Matti knew that they had to rise early for inspection: time to get some sleep. Alan too, would have to make tracks: he had left his horse with a friend who had either bedded the animals down for the night, back at the billet, or would still be waiting at the mill. He hoped the first thought was the right one!

Enrico watched at a short distance away, as the two brothers embraced for what might be the last time, and noticed tears streaming down their faces. He felt his own eyes watering in empathy. 'Emotions,' thought Enrico, 'who needs them?' He turned his back on them, cleared his throat, using that as an excuse to wipe his eyes. As they walked back quietly together to their billet, the flashes from the big guns could be seen like impressive fireworks displays. Matti slept fitfully that night and though extremely tired, next morning was eager to get up and do something positive. At six in the morning, they woke and prepared themselves; the sun was breaking through the mist of the morning with a bright red ruddy glow, showing once again that it would be a cloudless kind of day, with spring warmth. Much to the amusement of other soldiers that were milling about, they were made to drill, and then had a kit inspection. Again the Colonel called the men to listen to his words.

"Men, we are still not going up the line today, so there will be exercising and drill, which will take up the morning. This afternoon you are again free to please yourselves. But I need a Section for special detail for tomorrow morning. And the volunteers have been Corporal Harrington's Section."

'Volunteer, who volunteered us?' wondered Matti and Enrico, knowing darn well that their Section had just been picked at random. 'What do they want us for? What special duties?' The day was busy; everybody was glad not to be going up the line as the guns seemed to have got louder. There had been several dog fights in the air, though it was hard to tell who had come off best. They watched in morbid fascination when one plane came down several miles away in flames. "Matti, look at that!" said Enrico, pointing to the plane blazing and falling in a spiral to the ground. "Blimey, that poor bastard never stood a chance! Either he was shot dead or he burnt to death on the way down!"

"Was it a Hun or a Tommy?" enquired Matti. "Couldn't tell, too far away." They had only been within the danger zone two days, but how quickly they were getting used to the idea of death. Matti lost interest in the dog fight and wondered if Alan was still around. They made enquiries, but to no avail. When troops move, nobody is willing to talk, even if they know where they might have gone to. Careless talk costs lives: this is one of the adages that had been drummed into all soldiers' heads. Only give name, rank and serial number: anybody might be a spy! Of course, nobody really took any of it seriously, but you just got used to saying nothing.

That night they bumped into Corporal Harrington in the estaminet where he was drinking rather heavily. "Hello, Corp," said Matti. "Can we join you for a drink?"

"If you buy the drinks, you can sit with me," came back a drunken sharp retort.

"Three beers, please." Holding three fingers up so that he could be understood. "Tell me, Corp, what are these special duties tomorrow morning that have kept us here?"

"Oh, you will know soon enough. And you ain't going to like it, not one bit you ain't."

"Come on, Corp, give us a clue?"

"Sod off, and be on the square for five thirty in the morning. Fully washed and ready for these 'ere specials. Sleep tight, my little beauties." And with that, he dismissed them even though they had bought the drinks and were hoping for some company. Corporal Harrington then sunk all three beers as quickly as if it had been one. He was now as drunk as the proverbial skunk! As the boys walked back to their billet, Enrico said "Blimey, how is he going to manage, whatever it is, with the head he will have in the morning?"

Five o'clock came; they arose from their beds, washed, shaved and tidied themselves ready for action. By five thirty, the whole Section was parading on the square. Corporal Harrington was there, looking like a new pin. Enrico looked at Matti, "Crikey, how does he do it?"

"Enrico, if I tucked away what that man drinks, I would be dead as anything."

"Attention," called the Corporal. "You have all been wondering what these special duties are. You might even be wondering why we are here so early, without any breakfast. Well, sadly we have a special duty to perform: we are to be witnesses at an execution." There was an audible gasp from the Section. "No one will be allowed off this, so don't ask. You will stand where put, don't close your eyes, watch everything. I don't know who the poor bugger is, or what he has done to deserve to die, we just must be there." There were several unhappy looking soldiers. It was Bob Gregg who plucked up the courage to speak first.

"Why us, Corp?"

"Just because, that's all. No special reason, but soldiers must have other soldiers to witness a fair death, as if you care when you are being lined up!" With that, Corporal Harrington brought them to attention, and marched them around the back of the town hall to where the prison cell was. As they went past the cell, they could hear a padre giving the condemned soldier his last rites. They were led into a small quadrangle, and then brought to attention again. Nobody spoke to them. There, against the far wall was a post. Bullet holes were peppering the wall all around it. Already some members of the Section were feeling very queasy. "Stand firm, lads," whispered Harrington, in a more understanding tone than usual. "You cannot help this poor sod, the best you can do is stay strong for him." A little while later the soldier was brought out. He was gently sobbing. He didn't break down; it was a sob of sadness, maybe of wasted life? He was tied to the post and blindfolded. Very quickly a firing squad was marched out. The Captain in charge of the execution read out the charge and verdict.

"Private Peters, for cowardice in the face of the enemy, for leaving your post and returning to your own trench system without permission while leaving your rifle to be taken by the enemy, the court martial has found you guilty and sentenced you to be shot by firing squad; this is to be carried out now."

Before anyone could even blink, the Section Sergeant called the squad to order. "Take aim... fire!" *Bang!* Ten rifles blasted out as one. The poor unfortunate folded like a rag doll. The Captain drew his pistol and waited for the MO to say whether he was dead or not... dead indeed.

The Captain reholstered his weapon, and smartly walked away. Next the firing squad was dismissed. Then Corporal Harrington turned the Section and marched them back to the square. "Well done, men. Not an easy thing to witness. But remember one thing, he didn't suffer, all over in a mo..." With that, he dismissed the Section and told them to have breakfast and muster back there for parade and inspection at eight thirty sharp.

"How can one eat breakfast after that?" said Matti, who always thought about his stomach before most other things.

"Well, we are seeing army life, that's for sure," quipped Enrico, trying hard to be funny and relieve the gloomy atmosphere. Nobody saw it as a joke; none of them actually knew the man, but they could still relate to him as a human being. They just moved away to quietly mull things over.

It seemed funny that the sun still shone, soldiers still did their chores and the citizens of Poperinge went about their normal daily lives as if nothing had happened. Yet a man, just an ordinary man, possibly with a wife and family, and a life to live, for just one second of panic, had ended up shot, with the stigma of this execution hanging over his entire family for the rest of their lives. These thoughts ran through the whole Section as they too went on to make their way through this war.

As they mustered for parade at eight thirty, one small Section of the Battalion were feeling somewhat subdued. No one made jokes and they were left to their own devices. That morning they just went through the motions.

"Men," called Colonel McBride, "We will be moving out of here in just two hours, so go and get your gear and come back as soon as ready. We have quite a walk ahead of us."

As they moved through the streets of Poperinge towards their goal, Ypres or Wipers to most Tommies, they all became more aware of the damage of German shelling. They also started to pass many graveyards. Crosses in neat little rows, showing exactly what they had to look forward to. Soon they stumbled upon a hospital sorting station, and they weren't short of business! And of course right outside, were more little crosses to show that doctors cannot cure all ills. The closer they got to Ypres, the louder the war got. Cavalry passed by at a gallop. Artillery was being drawn this way and that, sometimes with horse power, often with steam tractors. Huge guns, best used for siege were being positioned. Eighteen pounders charged by, dragging their full limbers, pulled by four horses. These could be sent almost anywhere and would be ready to fire upon the enemy within a minute or two. Stores of all sorts lined the road on either side. Most were being carried and sorted by Chinese labourers, sporting their normal loose fitting outfit, and rarely in any form of shoes. Indian soldiers were displaying wonderfully coloured turbans, some on horseback, some marching, others standing around a camp fire, cooking some rice and whatever they could scrounge. Soldiers of all nations started to appear as if from nowhere; most seemed to be working with a purpose. And with every step, the guns got louder…

It was about one o'clock in the afternoon when they were halted for chow. This meant taking out a can of Bully Beef, and tucking into it straight from the tin. Water was passed around, though some of the cleverer ones had filled their canteens with some alcohol, purchased in Poperinge. Wine or spirit could have a very beneficial effect to weary bodies, though one had to be really careful that an officer didn't realise that it was not water.

Whilst they were sitting by the side of the road, a Section of the Royal Naval Division, commanded by one Lieutenant Herbert, came up and joined with the Rifle Brigade, as they too needed a rest and maybe a little sustenance. Lieutenant Herbert had recognised a friendly face from his past. It was the Adjutant, Major Tyler-Latham. They had not met since university days. They were smiling and laughing together, with Tyler-

Latham in fine fettle. He then went to speak to Colonel McBride, who nodded in agreement. Sergeant Kelly was called over, who in turn having heard the request, went up to Corporal Harrington. He smiled, looked at his Section and said, "Boys, have I got a nice little job for you all!"

It was Lieutenant Herbert who addressed Harrington's Section. "Right then. You have been seconded to my Platoon for the next few days. My Sergeant will supply you with ammunition, keep it, and your rifle with you at all times. We are going up the line to a system of trenches which are patrolled by a unit of Algerian troops."

As he finished this sentence there was a ripple of laughter from some within the Battalion who knew of the Algerians' reputation for being slovenly and filthy.

Several thousand Algerians had been drafted to fight on the Western front. Their baggy bluey-grey pantaloons and their red waistcoats and greatcoats which, had they been black, would have been more suited for French waiters in Parisian cafes, gave them a very peasant-like appearance, but then, they *were* peasants. These soldiers found the army, with its meagre pay and poor food, a better prospect than working arid and overused fields as farmers. The guns and ammunition that were issued to them would have been better suited for 19th Century war, not this massacre that was occurring in Flanders Fields.

Lieutenant Herbert gathered his men, along with Corporal Harrington's Section for the long trek. They had stopped in the small village of Vlamertinge; it had once been a very prosperous market garden town, but was now mainly ruins, and within those ruins, many stores were hidden as well as the billets of men who scurried around like rats in a sewer. They marched to several depots to pick up all the equipment they were going to need, and for Harrington's Section a special treat was in store: steel helmets were on issue for them. Ypres, or the ruins of Ypres, now clearly came into view: smoke could be seen drifting skywards as buildings were set alight by the spasmodic shelling from the German artillery. Now, as they walked, the real horror, chaos and waste of war was to be seen everywhere: continuous shell holes, almost joining one another like a giant jigsaw puzzle, wrecked vehicles of all kinds, some still smoking, smashed guns, with dead horses bloated in the sun, legs sticking out, making them look more like toppled statues than the real thing. As the men now followed the path north-easterly, along a cart track, they came to another field dressing station called Essex Farm, built beside Ypres Canal. As they approached this heavily banked area, all the men were told to keep low, and "don't speak!" as they were now close enough to be caught by enemy small arms fire. Every available space outside the dressing station that did not have the detritus of war was being used as a burial area, with masses of crosses to be seen. Even the graves were not safe, though, as heavy artillery fire had, over the past months, disgorged some of the putrefying corpses, scattering bits of human remains everywhere. All the men that had hands free, held them over their mouths and noses, for the stench of corrupted flesh, disinfectant, stagnant water, and cordite was everywhere. There was just a hint of a new smell, too: chlorine…

On the twenty-second of April 1915, the Germans set a new precedent of dastardliness in warfare. Without any warning, they opened hundred of cylinders of chlorine gas which drifted over the French colonial trenches, the very trenches that Lieutenant Herbert's Platoons were making for. The gas had killed hundreds, and panicked even more into fleeing, and as the fleeing Algerians passed the Canadian trench system, many could be heard screaming the words: "*Gas! Gas!*" It was extremely lucky for the Canadian troops that one of their number was a chemist, and as this now dispersing green cloud came within smelling distance, he quickly realised that it was indeed chlorine. The word went out, along all the trench system that if you urinate over a handkerchief, or rag, and hold the said contents over your mouth and nose, the ammonia within one's pee would help neutralise the effects of the chlorine.

The Germans themselves had failed to appreciate the real potential of gas and did not advance in strength, so that what gains they did make were quickly lost to the Algerian and French troops who swiftly recovered their lost positions once the gas had cleared.

The Allies condemned Germany for this new weapon, but immediately started in the making of their own gas shells and bombs.

The Platoons gathered close under the protective thick concrete walls of the nearby hospital shelter; many were squatting, with their loads by their side, lighting cigarettes, and drinking copious amounts of water. Lieutenant Herbert was making his way to one of the steel-door entrances when it opened before him, and out into the late afternoon sunlight came the very tired figure of Surgeon John McCrae. He was attired in a long, white smock, coat and trousers, which were covered with human blood all down the front. He had on a close fitting white cap, which covered all his hair. His eyes were drawn, and his skin seemed lined beyond his age. As Lieutenant Herbert approached him, the overworked Surgeon put his right hand in the small of his back, and stretched back, yawning, and waved his arms several times in a propeller-like fashion, so as to keep himself awake. Lieutenant Herbert came up before McCrae, stood to a rather slovenly attention, and gave a very feeble salute, which prompted just a nod of the head in return.

"Sir, I brought some supplies for you. Where would you like them?"

A gesturing of the right hand from McCrae showed exactly in which direction the men should take the supplies. This was duly done, and now the men could redistribute the rest of the supplies they were taking to their own trenches more evenly. Herbert and McCrae both leaned heavily against the concrete wall.

"Cigarette, Sir?"

"Thanks."

"Tell me, Sir, how on earth can you face all this death and suffering? We only see it in passing; you live, eat and breathe it twenty-four hours a day!"

McCrae drew on his cigarette deeply and gazed lazily at the shadows lengthening as the sun was now starting to set.

"I find some kind of solace in writing poetry. I love poetry, as I love music, and the good use of words can have the same effect as a Beethoven Symphony. What about you?"

"Me, Sir? Yes, I love poetry too, but I like to write more with wit and irony, as opposed to beauty."

The men chatted for a long time, before McCrae was collected by an orderly to prepare for yet another operation on a wounded soldier. They stood erect, looking at one another closely, and it was McCrae who, smiling, held out a hand as a gesture of goodwill.

"Goodbye, Lieutenant. Thanks for the supplies, and good luck to you. Visit anytime, but make sure it's on the outside!" With that passing remark, he went back into the dimly lit operating room, and the heavy steel door was once again closed, keeping out sunlight and fresh air. Herbert turned to his Sergeant and told the men that as soon as it was dark, they would cross the canal, over a flimsy pontoon bridge, and camp quietly on the other bank. Darkness came very speedily, and with the darkness came the cold. Clouds were gathering, and what had been a perfectly sunny day, started to have the look of a wet night. The Lieutenant was thankful for the clouds, as they dimmed the bright full moon that had first appeared. They were now completely within the range of all the fire power that the Kaiser's army could throw at them.

"Men, we are going to cross over the pontoon to the other side." As he said this, a German flare rocketed into the air, lighting everything as in daylight.

"That's useful! Now we can see!" he spoke quietly to the men. "See those ruined buildings about a hundred yards from the canal, on that little buff? We will camp in and around there tonight. We will drift across in groups of six at a time; there will be no talking, and no smoking. Stay in the shadows at all times, and if another flare goes up, drop to the ground, or stand completely still. Then in the morning, we will be only a matter of a few yards to the start of the trench system that we will be going to. No fires tonight, and though I've said it before, no cigarettes. The German artillery has this whole area marked like a grid system; they can lay a shell in at any point that they wish. Once again, they must not know we are here."

By this time, everybody was a little edgy and jumpy, but this was a mission, and orders are orders, so in groups of six at a time they went across. A couple of shells were indeed fired, but not at them. Fritz was firing at something unknown to Lieutenant Herbert, away to his left, probably at the Algerians themselves.

It rained heavily that night, and nobody got any sleep. Guards were posted, but it made no difference, as nobody was looking for them. The next morning was colder, and though it had stopped raining, there was that feel of drizzle in the air, a drizzle that went through all your clothing and on to your skin, making you feel cold and miserable. They crawled, carrying their loads the few yards to the start of the trench system, and then it was a walk of approximately a third of a mile through the zigzagging trench to the main frontline, where the bedraggled Algerians were waiting to be relieved. Mud, and excreta were everywhere; the smell of human waste hung, worse than anything they had smelt before. Though there were no corpses in the trenches, they had not buried their dead, preferring to throw them over the parapet, where it became out of sight, out of mind. Lieutenant Herbert soon found his counterpart, Lieutenant Ahmed, who saluted and said in perfect English: "Am I glad to see you!"

Sentries were speedily established, and a machine gunner crawled to a very wet and slimy forward position to set up his Lewis gun. No sooner had the Algerians departed than Herbert ordered his men to start to clean up the human waste that was prevalent everywhere. Buckets were found and issued to scoop out the rainwater and urine alike, and discharge it over the parapet. It was no more than fifteen to twenty minutes into this operation that along came a full blown English General, with his entourage in tow.

'What and who the Hell is this?' wondered Lieutenant Herbert, but he jumped to attention, saluting smartly. The General was in a terrible rage; he spat out at Lieutenant Herbert the following:

"I am General Shute, I have come down to inspect these trenches, and visit my men in a good will gesture. I have never in my life seen such disgusting trenches! All this filth is hardly becoming of the British Army!"

He raged on, and on, hardly pausing to take breath. General Shute was an old Cavalry officer, who had distinguished himself at the siege of Mafeking in the Boer war. He was an old man then, and now he was ancient. What was he doing in this twentieth century war that had no resemblance to anything he would have known, or could imagine? And on this cold, May morning in 1915, what was he doing inspecting frontline fighting trenches? All this time, Lieutenant Herbert had stood to attention, and tried to defend himself from the verbal onslaught. And all this time, he was stopped from saying one word. When General Shute finally stopped spitting blood with his venom, he ordered his Adjutant to get every name in the Platoons and informed that they would all be on a charge. This said, the General and his collection promptly about-faced and marched off.

"Sir," said Corporal Harrington to the still seething, erect Lieutenant, "tell me, what was all that shit about?"

Herbert looked at him, relaxed visibly, slapped the Corporal on the shoulder, and replied: "Buggered if I know! And who the Hell is General Shute when he's at home?"

Both men laughed heartily, leading the way for all the bemused onlookers to relieve their tension with a good laugh.

"Men, for God's sakes, let's clean up this mess at a will, and Corporal and I will get a brew going, and hustle up some form of breakfast for you."

Lieutenant Herbert was a very humane, extraordinarily funny man, who was much loved by his men, and though he had joined the navy to go to sea, seasickness was such a bad problem, almost to the extent that he felt ill getting into a warm bath, that ships had very quickly become out of the question; hence the reason for him being a soldier in the navy on land! The men worked at a hearty pace, and soon had some semblance of 'respectability', if that were possible, back in the life of the trench. The smell was still there, but at least you did not have to look at it! The Corporal and Lieutenant Herbert had made a sort of stew that looked almost as bad as the mess that the men had cleared, but tasted infinitely better, and did them more good! It was while he was in his covered dugout, having a hot mug of tea, that the latter composed the following poem to celebrate this momentous start to the day. A huge roar of laughter came from the mouth of Corporal Harrington, as he read the verses over the shoulder of Lieutenant Herbert:

"Sir, please, let me show this to the men, as I am sure it will be greatly appreciated for the work of genius it is." At this remark they both chuckled. Corporal Harrington took the paper given, and handed it to the first man he saw, which happened to be Enrico.

"Caruso, read this, and pass it on." A big grin of pleasure was clearly visible on Harrington's face. Every few minutes, bursts of laughter could be heard erupting further and further along the trench, as the poem got passed from man to man.

*The General inspecting the trenches*
*Exclaimed with a horrified shout,*
*'I refuse to command a Division*
*Which leaves its excreta about.'*

*But nobody took any notice,*
*No one was prepared to refute,*
*That the presence of shit was congenial*

*Compared with the presence of Shute.*

*And certain responsible critics*
*Made haste to reply to his words*
*Observing that his staff advisers*
*Consisted entirely of turds.*

*For shit may be shot at odd corners*
*And paper supplied there to suit,*
*But a shit would be shot without mourners*
*If somebody shot that shit Shute.*

Hot food, a good laugh: these are the little things that can bring moments of complete joy to a soldier. Standing on a firing step, constantly watching for an enemy that you cannot see, even though he might be just a few yards away, is soul destroying. But the food and poem from Lieutenant Herbert had been a great restorative, or as the old adage says… "Just what the Doctor ordered!"

Lieutenant Herbert was a fine psychologist: he had always known how to get the best from men under him, he never stood on ceremony; as long as men did their duty, he really didn't expect more from them. They were familiar with him as he was with them. These troops were no exception: they loved him, and would follow him to hell and back if asked. But the responsibility hung heavy on his shoulders, and he was ageing fast, with heavy lines and drooping sad-looking eyes. In fact he was just thirty years of age, but he now looked as if he was in his forties.

The drizzle that was in the air dissipated and the sun broke through. Now it became easier for the men to go about the business, the business of war. Some of the soldiers, and this now included the Section under Corporal Harrington, were on the fire step, ready and waiting for the attack that might come at any moment. This is always a huge strain on soldiers, waiting there, maybe for a sniper's bullet to get them, or a wiz-bang to explode overhead showering them with hundreds of red hot lead balls, of which just one is liable to kill them. And what if the enemy charge? They know that they have only about thirty bullets for their rifle, maybe a further six or seven Mills bombs. Maybe the ammunition carrier might be shot dead before they can be re-armed. Maybe they will have to fix their bayonet and be prepared to thrust it into the enemy as he stands with his eyes wide with terror. These thoughts and many others went through the minds of the soldiers. What about the trenches further along, manned by other units? How would they cope? Maybe the enemy would overrun them, and come along the trench system to their area? Unless the mind is kept busy, the devil gets into it.

Lieutenant Herbert noted that the time was two in the afternoon and changed the guards. He knew the worst job was to be on point in a small dugout with the Lewis gun. The advance machine gunners were always the first to die in a battle as they were the nearest to the charging enemy, and furthermore it didn't take a genius to realise that a Lewis gun must be eliminated quickly for the sake of the onrushing troops. Harrington's Section were holding up well, this being their first day under fire, even though a shot had not been sent or received in anger, yet! But indeed their blood pressure was high, like all the soldiers' on both sides. Each man knew for sure that the entire German army was there just to kill him. Harrington was handling himself well, but he had become aware of a tic in his right eye, all the time annoying him, and since leaving Essex Farm his right hand had started to shake ever so slightly, quite unnoticed by other people but obvious to the Corporal. Each man carried his own cross which he must bear in the best way he could.

Lieutenant Herbert knew all these things and more. But their tour of duty was going to be only two days in the trenches, plus the two nights, and they were the worse. He would somehow keep his men from harm. 'Don't fire unless fired upon. Live and let live.' Hardly what General Sir

John Denton Pinkstone French, then commander-in-chief of the British forces, or his soon-to-be successor General Sir Douglas Haig, whose idea of fighting in this war seemed to be, 'if we lose one million, but the enemy lose one million and one men…we win', had in mind. Lieutenant Herbert was a thousand miles below in rank, and he just happened to care about his fellow men's lives, *all* men, friend or foe. Herbert was a humanitarian, whose attitude towards this war was one of 'let's get it over with, as quickly as possible. Don't waste lives!'

There had been some local shelling from both sides that day, but nothing near Herbert's trench system. Eyes were nevertheless being kept alert; you never could tell what the other side would do. The guns around Ypres were starting to blaze, making the ground shake. Maybe something big was happening on some other sector? Herbert called all the NCOs into the dugout. "I really have no clue what is happening, but alert all the men that something might be on the cards, keep them all on their toes. Anybody off duty asleep, wake them and give them a task, or put them on the firing line. We don't want to give Jerry the idea though, that we are imminently going on the offensive ourselves. Let's try and keep the status quo." This was agreed, with no argument from anyone.

About an hour went by, with nothing coming from the opposition, which pleased all. The guns at Ypres started to fade with more spasmodic firing, and men visibly relaxed, tension draining from tired, weary faces. No one had slept for the last thirty-six hours, and it showed. Guards were changed again and again. Soon shadows were forming and as they lengthened the tension started to mount again.

"I have a gut feeling about tonight," said Lieutenant Herbert to Corporal Harrington and two other NCOs that happened to be there with him. "I want the guard doubled, plus extra men out on point. Give out plenty of ammunition, and allow only one in four to sleep at any time. Understood?" he snapped, testily.

"Yes, sir," came the reply.

Darkness arrived, and so did the dread. The night was extremely dark with the moon completely obliterated by the heavy rain clouds that had appeared. 'This is good as well as bad,' thought the Lieutenant. Good because if it rained heavily, it was unlikely that a raid would occur. Bad, because the darkness gave way to the basest of man's fears and fear creates nerves which in turn lead to mistakes. It was shortly after midnight that a sentry came running to the Lieutenant. "Sir, when the last German flare went up, I am sure I saw a few soldiers crawling across no-man's-land. Maybe four or five, but I really don't think I was mistaken." Herbert again called the NCOs to hand. "I said I had a gut feeling. Well, I think we are in for some trouble. But let's get there first. Harrington, are any of your men up to a spot of fun in no-man's-land?"

"Well, sir, you know they are untried, but I have two who might just fit the bill: Privates Caruso and Dumbridge. They stick together like glue, and just might come through for you and themselves."

"Get them."

Eight men all told were gathered quickly, with only the duo from Harrington's Section. Herbert addressed them.

"Get your guns loaded, and fix bayonets, men. Sergeant Martin will be taking you on a small stroll; nothing much to worry about. No, that's rubbish; there is plenty to worry about. There are German soldiers out there, possibly coming this way on a trench raid. I want you to go out there and stop them. If you can, use your knives and bayonets, the less noise the better. If possible, bring back prisoners: that always pleases HQ." Then he added in a burst of energy, "Sergeant, take them beyond the Lewis gun; you all had better crawl, blacken faces, and create an ambush. Most of all stay alive and return."

"Sir, thank you, Sir. Men, do as the officer says." They blackened up, went onto a special area known to the Sergeant where they could climb over the firing step without being seen, through a cut in the barbed wire, and out into the craters, filth, dead, and wreckage of battles gone by. He spoke to the men around him in a subdued quiet voice, just loud enough to be heard by them all. "Keep your heads down as much as you can. If a flare goes up, keep absolutely still, as a statue. Watch out for bumping into anything that will make a noise. Watch out for the craters, some are full of water. If anyone is hit by enemy fire, but is able to return, make your way back. If not, we will get you back ourselves, no one is being left out there. If we get prisoners, gag them and keep them quiet with the fear of death. Keep your rifles shouldered and don't lose them, remember it can be a serious offence to lose one's weapon. This is going to be a job for bayonets and knives like the officer said. Let's go, and God help us all."

"Amen to that," came an unexpected reply.

They crawled from shell hole to shell hole. It sounded to them as if they were making the noise of a Symphony Orchestra tuning up, but in fact could not really be heard by anyone back in their lines. The rain was coming down, but not in torrents, just yet another cold drizzle that made them all shake so badly that they could no longer tell whether it was cold or fear. They passed by the Lewis guns and their gunners, who were all wide awake and very, very jumpy.

"Good luck," came a whisper from one of the gunners.

On they crawled. Another flare went up; luckily for the men they were then in a largish crater, big enough for all of them to be on the lip and not be seen. The Sergeant was the first to stiffen with tension. 'There they are, crawling towards us, only six of them and nine of us. Seems like good odds.' thought Martin. "Get four of you over to that crater, there, see it? When they come between us, we will have them from both sides. No noise, let's do this without Fritz knowing," he said, pointing to another large hole not more than ten feet away to their left. "Curly, take Caruso and his sidekick, plus another. Go! Wait! Now!"

The four of them moved in a jerky but fast crawl to the crater pointed at. As they crawled, Enrico could smell something extremely sweet. He put his hand forward to reach the rim of the crater; it was then that he realised that he was in fact crawling across the putrefying remains of what had once been a living, breathing human being just like himself. The poor departed creature's guts, had trailed along with Enrico as he crawled. For once his sensitive stomach was controlled, much to his own amazement, and he did not heave up his last meal. But the smell was now all over him. 'Christ, this is shit awful,' he thought, shaking with dread and fear. The four were now in place, and waited silently. 'These poor bloody Germans don't know what's going to hit them. What is that smell, has Caruso crapped himself?' thought Sergeant Martin. But there was no time for another thought: here they came. They all had their knives out, or in Enrico's case, his bayonet. "Now," rang a distinct whisper. From both craters, men spilled into one another, knives and bayonets swished back and forth. Enrico's bayonet crashed down and into flesh. He heard a deep moan, and felt a body shudder from under him. Immediately Enrico felt the horror of what he had just done. Tears forced their way up and out of his eyes. He lay there shaking with fear and excitement, and was overwhelmed at the realisation that he had killed his first human! This was almost too much for him. He just lay there as if he was also dead. Four of the Germans were dead; two more were wounded but able to be taken back as prisoners.

There of course had been considerable noise, but neither side knew what had gone on, so it seemed reasonable to not make any more noise or trouble by firing into the no-man's-land. None of the British were wounded; in fact all the others except Enrico were now in extremely high spirits. 'We might even get medals,' thought Sergeant Martin, as he helped drag the luckless Germans back to British lines. They had to nearly drag Enrico too, as he was in a terrible state, shaking almost from head to toe. But they kept him slightly behind, as no one could stand the smell.

After what seemed an eternity, they reached their own lines to be greeted with pats on the backs from all assembled; all except Enrico, who was now led away to wash off all the human remains and get rid of the worst of the smell. The two prisoners were there on show. Lieutenant Herbert always allowed the showing off of prisoners, as it was a good way to show the men that the Huns were not supermen, just young ordinary fellows like themselves. They could be defeated. This was good for all the men's morale.

The two Germans were terrified, and stood there shaking with fear; they were also in some pain as they both carried wounds from the knives, but luckily for them, it was not wounds that threatened their lives, as the cuts were superficial and only in their arms. Their fear stemmed from the knowledge that their future was not guaranteed. They now thought of home, and especially of their Mothers. 'What is going to happen to us?' was their collective thought. They could not speak any English, so they understood nothing that was being said to them. A cigarette was passed around, then to the Germans too. This eased their fears a great deal, and they relaxed, tensions being released and heart rates slowing down. The Sergeant ordered that Matti and another search them. Their pockets were emptied. There were no hidden weapons or any papers that could be useful to HQ. Their only reason for coming across had obviously been to spy out the British trenches. And maybe capture a soldier or two themselves to take back to their lines for interrogation. If it had not been for their own flares, they might have succeeded.

The moment that stirred up the trouble was when a medallion was found on each of them. The Germans would not have known that this medal which had been struck in Berlin and sent to them by their parents would become a serious cause for worry. In fact, had they been captured by any unit other than the Royal Naval Division, things might have been different. The medallions were handed to Lieutenant Herbert. He looked at them and began to get extremely angry. The two Germans were completely mystified by the reaction that was rapidly developing. Again they started to get worried, and once more began to shake badly. The medals were passed from soldier to soldier within the RND, and they all reacted strongly. The situation was fast getting out of hand. The two Germans were sobbing uncontrollably as they realised their future was now looking extremely precarious. "What is going on?" asked Corporal Harrington, to anyone. He then looked at Lieutenant Herbert. "Sir, what is all this about?"

"Look at the medals!" came the reply in an extraordinary show of anger, which even startled the Corporal. He took the medallion and looked. Then he understood.

The medallion had a carved relief picture of a ship being sunk, and on the reverse side, people waiting to enter hell. That ship was the "Lusitania". This medal had been struck the same day the liner had been torpedoed. Which indicated that the ship had been a target all along, and this must have been a planned operation, not the accident that had been portrayed to the world by the German government; otherwise how could this medal have been produced so quickly?

The men were all baying for blood. Lieutenant Herbert's only way out was to get the prisoners back through the lines, and taken to HQ. They had to leave straight away, as he didn't think he could keep the lid on the kettle for much longer. "Sergeant Martin!"

"Sir."

"Take two men and lead these two Germans back along the line to HQ, and make sure that they don't escape."

"Sir! Jones, Harding! Get your rifles and bring them along," he said, pointing to the two prisoners.

They had only been gone about ten minutes when two muffled explosions were heard by all. Another five minutes went by, when Martin and the two men returned wiping their hands and laughing. "Sergeant, what happened?" asked a more subdued Herbert, but knowing exactly what the answer would be.

"Sir, the prisoners tried to overpower us," stated Martin with a broad grin on his face. "Fought like devils they did, Sir!" and this indeed seemed strange to all, as they had had their hands tied behind their backs. "Tried to run off, Sir, so we lobbed a couple of grenades after them."

"They have joined their mates in hell!" explained Private Jones, who too had a broad grin on his face. There was a general clapping of approval from the members of the RND, but Corporal Harrington and his Section stood listening in dumb horror.

Men went back to their posts, honour satisfied. Lieutenant Herbert's wrinkles deepened.

It was not long before a token firing of trench mortars came over from the German lines, as realisation dawned that their raiding party was not going to be returning.

Nobody got hurt as all the mortars fell short, but it certainly put the fear of God into them all. "What had they been a party to?"

The men were all put back into their positions, waiting alertly as anything could happen. The machine gunners were replaced with new men, guards came off duty, and others went on. If you got the chance, you slept, but sleeping in the rain is not easy, no matter how tired you are. The ambush party were informed that the rest of the night was their own. Most went straight to a fire step, found some form of cover, and tried desperately to snatch some rest. Enrico however, was in a bad way, feeling now very feverish from the fretting that had befallen him after the stabbing. He sank into a corner of the trench, brought his knees up to his chin and waited for daylight and relief from the nightmares that were going on in his head. But he was not alone, Matti came to offer his bottle of water; as it was rejected, the only thing he could do was to sit opposite, upwind, just being there for his friend.

Still the rain drizzled down, making everyone low and depressed. 'The only good aspect about this weather, is that it is just as miserable in the German trenches too,' thought Lieutenant Herbert, as he wrote the report in the candle light of his dugout; this report had to be presented at the end of each tour of duty to HQ, when they were relieved by the next batch of troops, who were to occupy this place of filth and death. The night passed without any more incidents. Dawn broke through the gloom of men's souls with sunshine.

How easy it is to forget the happenings of the past night in bright clear sunlight. Even Corporal Harrington, not known for his love of the beautiful things of nature, saw some poppies growing on the top side of the parapet. He smiled to himself, as he wondered what they might taste like. Breakfast came and went. Bully Beef straight from the tin was the order of the day. "Don't even light a small fire to brew some tea; cold water only." This meant washing and shaving in cold water too. Still, rules are rules, so all did their ablutions as best they could. "The German trenches must not be aware of anything going on here: that means quiet; if you must smoke, make it close to the ground, so that the smoke would disperse before it could be seen." In other words, this was typical army life, in time of war. All they had to do was get through this day, then back to HQ, where they would have two more days of hard work, then hopefully another two days of rest in Poperinge.

It was about ten in the morning when once again the big guns in Ypres opened up on the Germans.

Ypres had been a really beautiful small city. It had never been taken by the enemy, only passed through by some Uhlans during the early part of the war. It had become the Verdun of Britain, Verdun being France's city that the nation was almost prepared to fight to the last man for. And very nearly did. Ypres became a symbol for that sort of steadfast bullish arrogance that would take men to their deaths by the hundreds of thousands during this, 'The Great War, The War To End All Wars.' It was also the sort of action that could inspire men to victory.

Ypres was a salient in the British lines. A salient is a huge bulge in the line of trenches, the line that stretched all the way from the Alps in

Switzerland to Ostend, the Belgian port which backs onto the English Channel. The trouble with this bulging salient was that it was built on low ground, with no high points at all. The Germans held all the high ground, and could, and did, fire into any part of Ypres from any Section held by them outside the salient. Ypres was fast becoming just one huge pile of rubble. It had had the most beautiful medieval buildings found anywhere in Flanders. And the two most prized edifices were the Cathedral, and a famous Cloth Hall, which for several hundred years had been the major trading centre for cloth in all the Low Lands. Both these buildings were now just a mass of tangled metal, and broken masonry. There were very few dwellings still in an undamaged state, and what was left was being targeted by the German artillery on a daily basis.

Now being fired upon, the Germans thought it time to respond in kind. So massive shelling appeared in all sectors of the trenches around the bulge of Ypres.

'Welcome to Wipers,' thought Matti. He had carried off his duties well during the ambush, and felt no qualms about the possibility of having to kill again. No, he felt for once in charge of the situation, more than a little smug: his destiny was surely well and truly in his own hands. But seeing the sorry state that Enrico was in, he tried very hard to comfort his mate. "Come on, Enrico," he chirped, "this is not like you. Nothing frightens you, I know that; apart from your stink, we all think you did really well out there," pointing to nowhere in particular. Enrico warmed to life, as his friend was there for him. "You know…I killed one of them out there!" His voice broke ever so slightly.

"We know you did, but if you hadn't got him, he would have hell like, got you. You did only what you had to do. Forget it, for I'm guessing he won't be the last, by any stretch of the imagination."

"Take cover!" The voice no sooner spoke than a loud whining sound came over, then·an ear-splitting bang rocked the two lads from their day dreaming. The shelling was starting in their Section now. Metal and earth fell to the ground, showering everybody. The rain of steel came in strong and fast. 'Is this an attack?' pondered Lieutenant Herbert. His position in a covered dugout was a little more secure than the men's outside. Their only real defence was to press their bodies close to the walls of the trench, or huddle on the floor. The Lieutenant's dugout was about six feet deeper than the bottom of the trench they all occupied, and it was covered by a corrugated metal roof, that had been covered by earth. Fine for overhead shell, but a direct hit would bring the whole structure down, smothering the occupants that might be cowering inside. The noise of the shells bursting outside was a little muffled, making the artillery attack seem further away, but nevertheless, Herbert crouched in the corner bringing the small table that he did his work on, close up to him, so it might give some extra form of protection. Like all soldiers, Herbert being no exception, he was terrified of this sudden bombardment, and tried to take his mind off what was happening by thinking of home and his new bride and the children he hoped to have one day, when this crazy war was at an end.

Just as suddenly as it had started, it stopped. There was immediate confusion as the soldiers all rushed to their firing positions waiting for the attack.

Herbert too, drew his pistol from its home in the holster and got to the nearest position. "Wait for it!" he yelled down the line for all to hear. "They might start shelling again, or this might be an attack. Do not, I repeat, do not fire, until I, or Sergeant Martin gives the command!" They waited and waited; nothing happened, and after about half an hour the stand down was called, much to the relief of all and sundry. A count was taken to see if there had been any casualties. Fifty men had gone with Herbert on this little jaunt, and he wanted, as always, to take those fifty back with him. "Martin," he called out.

"Sir,"

"Anybody......?" But before he could finish the sentence, Sergeant

Martin pre-empted his question.

"Sir, we have two casualties. One Private Georgio, who I'm afraid is dead, the other is Private Richard Allen from Corporal Harrington's Section. He has a serious wound in his head from a shell fragment. The medical orderly is there with him now…But I think he is a goner too, Sir."

"Shit, shit, shit. I thought we might get away with a quiet spell on this tour of duty," said Herbert, probably to himself, or to anyone that could hear; he didn't care either way. Sadly Richard Allen did die, about forty minutes after the shelling had ended. Had he lived, for sure he would have been a vegetable, as parts of his brain had oozed out of his skull along with the blood. Neither of the men could have felt a thing.

The rest of the day passed quietly, though the tension was there to be felt by one and all. Men were quiet, few words were spoken: nobody knew what to talk about. Both Lieutenant Herbert and Corporal Harrington spent time in the dugout completing the Platoon's report for HQ to read. Though two dead! A drop in the ocean! The report, like most reports, would be glanced at as a formality, then filed and forgotten.

Night took over from day. Nobody slept. All nerves were tense. Fingers played nervously on rifle triggers. Many men stood on the firing step watching over no-man's-land, dreading the thought that there might be another trench raid from the Germans. Herbert sent out more men to assist the Lewis gunners. All waited, and waited. It was a long and cold night and the moon now on the wane shone as brightly as it was able to, not worrying if it was lighting the Central Powers or the Allies. This was a very impartial moon. It had no Kaiser or King, huffing and puffing sending it out to war!

Morning came, and none too soon. Nothing had happened, though there had been two or three false alarms which had frightened all assembled. There had been the occasional firing from trenches around theirs, but no trouble in their sector. As the morning sun shone on the waste ground between the Hun and the Tommy, steam started to rise, along with the temperature. Hearts began to lift again. Very weary men, some who had had no sleep since this adventure had begun, tried to unwind. Sagging eyelids showed the real effect that these days and nights had had on them all. 'Time over,' thought Herbert. 'Let the relief be quick, please Lord.' Corporal Harrington and his men were extremely sad as the body of Private Allen was lifted as gently as possible over the parapet along with Private Georgio. 'Would they ever get a proper burial?' thought the Corporal.

Breakfast was had, yet again, as best they could; again Bully Beef. The general thought being… 'If I never see or eat another can of Bully Beef, it will be too soon!' But that didn't apply to Matti. He tucked into his can with a relish. "God, man, one would think you have never eaten the stuff before. Aren't you sick of it yet?" said Enrico, with a little sparkle of humour in his tone of voice.

"I love it. If anybody doesn't want their can, give them to me please…" Before the sentence was finished, half empty cans came zooming in Matti's direction. "Take it easy. You will finish the job Fritz tried to do last night", rebuked Matti with his arms held up to his face, trying not to be hit by the offending missiles. This brought about a very welcome round of laughter, which finally lifted the gloom from these weary warriors.

They busied themselves by tidying up the trench, filling in parts that had collapsed under the bombardment, generally making good for the next relief who were coming there. The relief arrived at about nine in the morning, as men had now done their work, and had gone some way to make themselves presentable. Time for Herbert's and Harrington's men to retrace their steps, except this time they would be in the cover of trench systems all the way back into Ypres. No reason to go via Essex Farm again. They gathered their belongings together, and started the couple of miles it was to the centre.

"Good luck, and watch out tonight, the Hun has been on the prowl!" said Lieutenant Herbert to his Irish counterpart whose men, being from the Ulster Rifles had already taken up their positions. These were extremely well disciplined soldiers, who were used to fighting, especially one another. The remark back baffled Herbert though. "Have you heard any digging, while you have been patrolling here?"

"What sort of digging?"

"There are rumours that the Germans are digging tunnels under our lines again." They parted with a hand shake. The men walked back grateful that the two nights were over, and that they had survived the experience. The column of men was long and weary in its step. Behind the slowly drifting men, the lone figure of Private Enrico Caruso Lokowski could be seen, about five paces behind the next man. No one wanted him upwind of themselves.

All the time the guns around Ypres made their presence known...

# V

They finally made their way into Ypres. So *this* was the famous Wipers that Harrington's men had heard so much about, from their lectures during training! They arrived just in time to get to a canteen that had been set up, situated close to the old ruined Cloth Hall. It was just slightly out of sight from any viewing gunners from outside the salient, so therefore moderately safe from trouble. 'Hot sweet tea, soup, buns, bread and butter, wow! This is heaven, could anything make life better?' was the general thought. The men's revival was almost instantaneous. They had come alive again. Lieutenant Herbert now had to find the HQ, while Corporal Harrington had to find out where the London Northern Rifles were.

Ypres, even in ruins, was a big place: they could be anywhere. One thing was for sure though... 'Let's not find them too quickly!' This was the warmest day so far; it was going to be a very restorative time, if only they could spend a little of that time relaxing. "Listen to me, men," said a yawning Corporal Harrington to his charges. "I'm going with the Lieutenant to HQ. I shall find out where the rest of our battalion is. Stay here, don't wander off. If shelling should start, make sure that you all stay close to one another, but out of sight, and get into some ruins. I have no idea how long I shall be, but until I get back, Jimmy Riddle is in overall command, so for God's sake do as he says." The Lieutenant thanked the men for their help, and added that they would be mentioned at HQ for their stoicism under fire. When they made to stand to attention, Herbert laughed and waved them back down. "Relax, you have all earned it." With that, Corporal Harrington and the Lieutenant, along with his whole Platoon, casually sloped off. "What a nice chap that Lieutenant is! Treated us like a real gent!" commented Bob Gregg to Hill Billy. "You ain't wrong there," was the chorus from many quarters. Enrico looked at Matti. "What about a little wandering? As long as we keep out of the way of officers, we might be lucky and find an estaminet."

"Could be fun... But I really think we must get a bath first and a change of clothes. I still can't think of having you close by with that smell." Lying in the sun getting warm again? Maybe a good long sleep? That's what Matti really wanted.

Enrico agreed that a bath was the order of the day, as he had taken to scratching various areas around his body, and that probably meant lice. As he turned back towards his friend, all that greeted him was a low heavy breathing. Matti was spread out by the side of the Cloth Hall, facing towards the rubble of the Town Hall, sound asleep.

Traffic was starting to make its presence known, with the clatter of horse hooves upon what remained of cobblestones: guns, being pulled this way and that, marching men going to and fro from the front line trenches. The noise was deafening, but not to Matti and most of his Section. Enrico left them there: that bath seemed like a very good idea. But where to look? He retraced his steps to the canteen. "Where can I get a bath?" he asked the orderly working there.

"There is a building, not far from here...it used to be a slaughter house...I think they have put up a temporary shed and a tent to combine as wash house and laundry room?" Smiles and a nod were exchanged, and Enrico made his way there. Sure enough, when he finally found the place, there were now two temporary sheds which replaced the rubble of the abattoir; they managed to get running water pumped up from a deep well. There was a queue extending at least thirty soldiers long, all waiting to de-louse with a scalding hot bath, and at the same time kill the lice by steaming their clothes while they bathed. It was a spiritual occasion for Enrico, pleasure poured from every pore of his body, along with the dirt and grime. At last he got rid of the smell of decomposing bodies, which had hung so miserably upon him. He reclined in a huge vat of really hot water. There were five other soldiers in there too. The fact that there was possibly a quarter of an inch of scum floating on top of the liquid did not matter one iota to any of them. The heat of the bath was somniferous, and on three separate occasions, he nearly drowned, as his head sank under the water. Each time he came up, coughing and spluttering, only for his eyes to get so heavy again he could not keep them open, and the whole procedure would reoccur. Eventually, a very far off distant voice, starting to get louder, with every syllable bringing him back into the land of the living pierced the fog of his exhaustion: "Get the hell out of there, you've had too long! The officers want their turn. Quick, man, at the double!" screamed a Sergeant, who was obviously in charge of the bath house.

When Enrico arrived back at the Cloth Hall, it was to find only Matti waiting for him.

"God, you look and smell much better!" said Matti.

"Where is everybody?"

"Gone to find food. Probably over at the canteen, if it's still there. Let's go and find them as well. Anyway, I'm starving!" exclaimed Matti.

Over at the canteen indeed, Harrington and the Section were already tucking into nourishment. As the duo appeared, Harrington approached them.

"Right, fellows, I've found out where the Battalion is; they are billeted at a place called White Sheet. To get there, we have to find somewhere called the Lille Gate, and it's maybe half a mile outside of Ypres. But as they don't know when to expect us, I thought we'd make our way up tomorrow morning, as we've all had a baptism of fire!", spitting bits of cheese and bread in the lads' general direction as he spoke.

That night, the Section found shelter further back into Ypres, almost on the road to Poperinge. Luckily for them, a large barn presented itself, and most of the tiles were on the roof, making it nearly weatherproof. In the field outside, there were six dead cows, in various states of decomposition. But the wind forced the smell in the opposite direction, making this barn a real haven: they lit a fire, they had hay to lie on, and they were cosy and warm. This had been a day to bring the stuff of life back into weary bodies with sagging hearts and minds.

"Rise and shine, it's seven. Get that fire stoked, get a brew going, get washed and shaved, an' then let's get going!" urged Corporal Harrington in a light-hearted way.

It was not until about ten a.m. that the Section, having found the Lille Gate made its way to the depot and billeting area called White Sheet, where they hoped they would find Sergeant Kelly and the Battalion.

Normal trench duties were resumed. How quickly all these young soldiers had become veterans! With the loss of several of their comrades through stupidity, carelessness or just plain bad luck, the men knuckled under, and learnt how to survive: 'Soldiers don't put their head above the firing line, soldiers don't run across open land without cover...' to do so certainly brought on a fusillade meaning almost certain death. Amateurs were turning into professionals; if injury or death occurred, it happened because of bad luck; the number was on the bullet.

Life in the trenches was one long round of tedium with ninety-nine per cent boredom, one per cent terrifying excitement. Though the days on the firing line had extreme moments of terror, especially when trench raids would occur, or if a sniper was sent out, generally it was more conducive to bringing on a sleep mode. If any soldier should be caught asleep on duty, his life might well be at risk from the firing squad.

One of the most dangerous jobs was to be a bomber. This was a man who would creep out into the night, armed with a bagful of Mills bombs. These men were often sent out to neutralise a particularly annoying machine gun nest. If caught by the Germans, they were often summarily executed. The bombers were given insignia to wear, but when it became apparent that Fritz did not think too kindly of them, these were torn off and discarded.

The boredom also extended to the two days back from the firing line, when it was the task of the soldiers to carry out supplies. This could mean a man having to carry equipment of up to a hundredweight for a mile or more. The fatigue this caused was excruciating, but also it had its dangers. Men fell off duckboards, often into shell holes filled with water and mud, and the mud was like glue, and would often draw them down into a slow, cold, miserable death. Another dangerous period was when they took rolls of barbed wire up to the front on moonless nights, and it would be their task to go over the top to start stringing out the wire. In the early days of the war, the wire was strung out on metal poles, which were banged into the ground with wooden mallets; this would inevitably lead to a German flare going up, and the wire party being killed or injured, because they had been heard. But by May 1915, they were using a screw-like post, in which men could push a handle through the top, and turn it into the ground like a corkscrew. Though still dangerous, it was a heck of a lot safer than what had preceded it. There were supposed to be two days of rest and relaxation; this now sadly rarely happened: the death rate had become so high that men could not be spared for rest periods. Subsequently this caused a dreadful slump in the whole Allied army's morale.

When they did get a chance for breaks, it usually meant a couple of days in Poperinge, and the soldiers were always happy to see the well known figure of Padre Philip 'Tubby' Clayton. This was a man who endeared himself from the Private to the General, with his tireless devotion to the men who were fighting. 'Tubby' Clayton, as he was popularly known, would often travel to the front in a motorcycle and sidecar with a portable harmonium, and he would administer succour and comfort to his flock. He would often be seen on the firing line at the beginning of a major battle, and of course, was there for the burials afterwards. During this period in 1915, 'Tubby' Clayton was also in charge of a rest house named after its founder, Talbot. There, soldiers would never be refused entry, and they could find temporary respite from the war with food, warm beds, and often the odd concert party or two. Whether you were religious or not, Talbot House became home from home.

The London Northern Rifle Brigade had fared quite well in the casualty stakes; since their formation they had lost fourteen dead and five wounded, of which all five were sent home. One particularly nasty incident concerned Sergeant Mere who had been shot by a German sniper, while going on patrol from the billets at White Sheet. Seeing the Sergeant, lying there with his knees crumpled to his chest, and face into the ground, with a pool of blood gathering around the now still body, spooked some of the men with him very badly, and one of them, a Private Peters, had dropped his load, and ran for the safety of the billet. Unfortunately for Peters, he did not stop at the billet, but ran and ran, throwing away his gun, and helmet. As he stumbled through Lille Gate, he was immediately arrested by two burly military policemen. He was speaking total gibberish, his eyes blazed a fiery red and he had a look of madness about him. Nobody heard of him again, until notice was posted that had been shot by firing squad. This saddened many of the troops who had known him, as Peters had been a friendly, gentle soul, and had always done his duty well.

Months passed, and rumours abounded of a new push that was going to be made to break the stalemate. There was even talk of a second front coming down from the north by invading neutral Holland, but talk is cheap, and though there is an element of truth within some rumours, the only truth here was that there was going to be another push.

It had been a hot, sunny day, and Enrico and Matti were finally having a well deserved break in Poperinge. They had gone to Talbot House to see a musical review. It had been a little too dull for the boys' taste, and they had broken away early to go for a couple of beers in an estaminet.

"Do you feel like me, Matti?" enquired Enrico. "I am so sick and tired of this continuous drudgery that we have to endure. Surely there is something else we can do? Maybe even get a transfer to something else?"

"Chum, if I knew a way of getting out of what we are doing, I'd be two streets ahead of you!"

Leaning back on his chair, he took a deep gulp from his lukewarm beer. While they had been quietly talking, neither had noticed a rather ragged young Belgian girl drifting into the bar. It was only when Matti stuck a hand up for the waiter that they noticed her. She must have been no more than sixteen years of age, and though she was ragged in appearance, her skin was extremely clean. Matti smiled in her direction, while again asking for the two beers. This gesture seemed to prompt the young girl to come to their table. Without giving a chance for the two boys to stand up through good manners, she had already grabbed a chair, and sat there between them, as if she had known them for years.

"Please, you buy food and drink to me, give me a little of money, and I give you what you want," she said to the two astonished lads. This was the first time that they had seriously been approached by a girl; they had not even thought in terms of women since the tragedy back in Darwen, and though she was young and ill-kempt, there was a certain attractiveness that made the blood pound within the boys.

"What's your name?" Enrico almost stammered the words.

"Eugénie," she answered.

"Are you really hungry?"

"Yes, very."

With this, Enrico summoned the waiter for three plates of ham, eggs and potatoes. All this time, Matti had sat there, looking directly into this young girl's face, with his mouth agape. Finally he summoned up the courage to ask.

"You will give us what we want? How much money?"

"Enough to buy food for tomorrow."

Matti dropped his gaze from the young girl, sidled his chair up to Enrico, and nearly spat into his ear:

"Blimey, Enrico! We've got to do it!"

The food came, and was greedily ingested by Eugénie; so consuming and intense was her appetite that the boys gave the remains of their portions to her too. All three had yet another beer, but this beer had not been enough to stop the swelling that had appeared between the boys' legs, which had become so hard that when they stood up, it was going to be a very obvious protrusion.

"Where do you live?" asked Matti.

"Reningelst."

"Can we go back to your house? Don't you have any family living there?" enquired Enrico.

"No, not at all. My father and my mother dead, killed by Germans. Just me and my young sister, Annette. She is only twelve, too young for soldiers."

"Matti, let's take her behind the ruined windmill."

"Hope I can last that long!"

Enrico then turned to the young girl, smiling broadly; he pressed into her hand enough coinage for the sisters to have food for a week. They paid the bill, and made their way to the windmill. All three of them stood on the grass that was now growing inside the mill, looking at one another. The boys did not have a clue as to what to do next. It had to come from Eugénie.

"Who is first?" she asked. Again the boys looked at one another.

"You first," she said, pointing at Enrico.

She lay on the ground, and pulled her loose-fitting, rather dirty woollen skirt up to reveal a black mass of female puberty. She did not wear knickers because she could not afford to replace the old ones that had fallen to pieces. The boys' eyes bulged, as they looked on, almost drooling, at the thin line of pink flesh that parted, showing very clearly an extended clitoris, which swelled in size ever so slightly the wider she opened her legs. At this moment Enrico was not sure that he could wait any longer, so without further ado, he dropped his trousers to his ankles with rather soiled underwear following. His member stood erect, more at attention than he had ever been as a soldier! Still not knowing really what to do, he waited until she beckoned him to mount her. He got to his knees, showing clearly the scratches and bruises of the toil and labouring that they had been doing. He was almost panting, when Eugénie opened herself up to him and said: "Do it now!" As he entered her, the shock of the warmth of her body made his head spin. He tried to kiss her lips, but was rejected when she said: "No kissing." He thrust in and out of her at such a fast rate that his whole being exploded in less than thirty seconds, though he himself thought that it had been for hours. At first he just lay in a heap on her, so utterly exhausted that had not Matti coughed loudly and said: " Come on, it's my turn!" that otherwise he would have fallen asleep. What an experience! His first moment of passion! Sometimes during the night he had relieved himself with his right hand, thinking of girls, but generally sex had not entered his life.

Now Matti had dropped his trousers. The bruising was there again to be seen, but this time on more rounded flesh. He could hardly contain himself, and as soon as Enrico was on one knee and rising, Matti rushed to fill the void that Enrico had left. Eugénie stiffened visibly with a little pain, as Matti had been too quick in mounting, taking in some pubic hairs with his penis. Though Matti must have felt it too, he was not going to be delayed by any little discomfort. This was his moment of glory, and he was determined to enjoy it. Like Enrico before him, his passion exploded in no more than a dozen or so thrusts and white semen spurted from him like water from a fireman's hose. Eugénie had been expecting much, much more from the boys, not knowing that this had been their first time. For her this had been just a job of work, like the six men before on that day. She had felt no pleasure, and at her tender young age, she felt rather repulsed by the bad breath and sweaty, hairy bodies of the male gender. But needs must…

As the trio dressed and straightened their attire, Enrico asked the young girl: "Tell me, how old are you anyway?"

"Fifteen," was the reply.

Matti interjected with:

"Will we ever see you again?" To which she frowned, curled her lips, and shrugged her shoulders.

"Bullets are flying and shells are exploding everywhere, planes are shooting at us all the time, we could be dead tomorrow," stated Enrico, and the only response was another shrug of the shoulders followed by:

"C'est la vie!"

With this, Eugénie turned and strolled away. The day might not be over for her, maybe she would be able to earn some more money. The boys just stood there, looking at one another, grinning widely, whilst the guns of Ypres went on spasmodically firing.

As the two friends strolled back to Talbot House, there was something different about them. They could die for their Country, but they could not vote. They had always been boys, not men. Twenty-one was when you became a man, getting the proverbial key to the door. At twenty-one, the World was open to you, whereas at seventeen, you were still a boy, or at least made to think so. But sex had changed things. Sex is something that men do, not boys. 'We are men,' they thought jubilantly, both carrying smug smiles upon their faces.

"Boy, I enjoyed that. I could have gone on for hours," lied Enrico. His lie was the lie of all men that have just made a conquest over women. It did not matter to either of them that they had had to pay for their pleasure. It did not even cross their minds that the girl was almost a child, and underage. They were men now, and everybody was going to know it.

That night, while lying in the bunk beds at Talbot House, they talked over the day's experiences with much rejoicing. After all, they had done this lady a great favour, hadn't they?

Just before sleep came, Matti said to Enrico: "What we talked about this evening, before we met... what's her name? Are you serious about wanting to get out of the Battalion?"

"Absolutely!"

"Well, did you hear what Sergeant Kelly was saying about an officer chap looking for miners?  Somebody called Empire Jack?  Never heard of him myself, and never really gave it a thought until now, but if it's true, what say we apply?  It could get us off these awful fatigues?"

"Christ, man, are you mad?" came a sharp reply, "I never want to go underground again.  Anyway, we cannot admit to be miners, connections might be made?"

"If you say so.  Good night.  Please Lord, let me dream of women, and the other thing." Too late; Enrico was already snoring gently.

Soon August came, without any break in the routine.  Two days in the trench, two days with trench fatigues, then maybe an odd day of rest, though usually not.

There had been no push, no battles, just the fact that at any time Fritz could send you your number, and what is more you hardly ever saw him.

Most of the German casualties came from the terrible infestation of rats that ate the dead.  For some unknown reason, German troops fared worse with the nasty diseases that came via the rats.  When the guns fired, the rats would instinctively run up the incline to the German trenches.  That is not to say that the Tommies did not have them too: thousands of them.  But everyday would be a rat killing day.  Air guns were supplied, which didn't make any noise.  Often, within a day's rat hunting, you could fill a large fifty gallon petrol drum with them, and then set fire to the whole kit and caboodle.  The main problem with the rats was twofold.  First, they had almost lost their fear of man, and their bites were nasty.  It only was really the artillery that moved them out of the British trenches, usually in a crazed fashion.  Secondly, they carried fleas, and it is the fleas that carry the seriously dangerous diseases.  They had become so fat, gorging on human flesh that they were like a new species of rodent, just as big as most cats.

The other major problem was the lice.  All soldiers, friend or foe, fought a continuous battle against the onslaught of lice. They got everywhere. A good hot bath would do the trick. Clean clothes, and always steam what you last had on. But the very next day, you had them back. It was a war that the soldier never won.

It was August 14th, while doing a routine tour of trench duty that word came through that there was to be a trench raid, to capture a few Hun soldiers for interrogation. HQ wanted information as to what the enemy were expecting the Allies to do in the coming weeks. As if maybe, a German Private would be privy to any of the Officers' secrets?! Enrico and Matti were to take two others from Harrington's Section across no-man's-land, penetrate the German trench without being seen, very quietly capture some prisoners, bring them back, and get them to HQ, then report back to the Section Sergeant for further duties.

"Are they mad?" thought Enrico. "This is a moonlit night; and there's at least a quarter of a mile to get to the enemy trenches. Find a gap in the wire, get through into their trenches, capture the enemy without any noise, and get back again? This is indeed, insane. What stupid idiot thought this one up?"

Enrico took complete control, only because he thought that anybody else would be more likely to get them into serious trouble. Enrico had now gained a great deal of confidence while serving in the army. He picked Bob Gregg and Hill Billy to go with Matti and himself. They were given pistols, instead of rifles: easier to carry. Banging rifles against the debris out there could only help the enemy. Noise must kept to the minimum. They also carried several Mills bombs each, plus knives and clubs.

Darkness seemed never to come. The four of them just hung around in the trench, getting more and more nervous. Eventually Sergeant Kelly appeared, reiterated their objectives, wished them good luck, and then sent them on their way. His last words in parting were: "Don't forget the password!"

The four of them scrambled over the fire step and into their own barbed wire. They knew only too well where the small tunnel-like groove was, to crawl through, and then out and onwards to enemy trenches. They had only gone about ten yards, when a volley of machine gun fire raked past to their right, from the German lines.

'Oh Christ,' thought Enrico, 'they must know we're here!' But as quickly as it started, it stopped again. "Matti!" whispered Enrico, "take Hill Billy further round to the left, then keep parallel to us; at least you will be able to see us, and not get lost. I'm sure the whole German army plus the Kaiser is up there watching us right now."

A small nervous giggle emerged from Matti, which indicated that he understood and would concur. All four now crawled across no-man's-land, dodging from shell hole to shell hole. Fortunately, it had been a dry summer so far, so most of the shell holes were hard and dry. One hole that Enrico and Bob crawled into had a skull staring right at them. That didn't worry them, it was the huge rat that crawled out of its mouth, that got them shaking. "Crikey, Enrico, is that how we're going to end up?" asked Bob in a low murmuring tone.

"Shut up, stop talking. You will give our position away." Enrico glared really hard at Bob, who immediately shut up and ducked down below the rim of the crater. It had taken them more than an hour, and they had only got maybe a third of the way. A flare went up. All froze. A mortar from the enemy lines crashed into no-man's-land, about one hundred yards to their left. 'They know we're here all right,' thought Enrico, but kept his thoughts to himself. There was a scratching sound, just in the next hole. "Blimey, that's one of them waiting for us!" Both Bob and himself stiffened, and waited for the thrust of steel or the bangs of rifle fire... nothing; but then another scratch. He nudged Bob, drew his pistol. They both leapt into the hole with the noise. "Nothing! No Germans! Nothing!" A more relieved Enrico sat back into the crater and sat right on top of a rotting corpse. 'Not again, please Lord, not again,' he thought; too late, to expect help from the Almighty. There he was, sitting astride what had once been a German infantry man; and he was having the last laugh, by oozing his remaining bodily fluids all over Enrico. Then, as if to make matters worse, a huge rat scurried across the shell hole right over his feet. "*Shit*", he said under his breath. By now he was panting, sweating and shaking all at the same time. The smell was awful, enough to make Bob retch and nearly throw up. "God," he whispered, "you smell like after you came back from our first tour of duty!" Matti and Hill Billy had fared no better. They had both stumbled into the dead and rotting remains of yesterday's heroes. They had crawled into bits of wire, bomb fragments, glass, bricks, just about everything one could find on a battlefield. All four of them were feeling the effects of cuts and bruises, added to the filth that now covered their tunics, and permeated every pore of their bodies.

Another hour went by. They were now close to the German wire. Luckily for all four of them, they again slithered into a deep shell hole, just as another flare went up. 'They are laughing at us,' thought Bob, 'they know exactly where we are.' As they closed in on the wire, they spied the lights of many small fires that were in the German lines. This light could never be seen from the British trenches. 'They are cooking. Blimey, they have heat, and comforts. Hot food, what I wouldn't give for a hot meal!' thought Matti. As usual, all fear passed from Matti, at the thought of sustenance.

"Give me the wire cutters!" said Enrico to Matti, in a whisper, right into his ear. Enrico looked along the line of wire for a place they could cut, and where no light was coming from the trench. "Look, just to my right. There is a break in the wire. There, see it?" Again in Matti's ear. "Let's try there."

They quietly crawled into position, got under the first wire without having to cut it, got through the break, which Enrico had pointed out, then came up against a depth of eight feet of wire, that would mostly have to be cut.

They started to cut. "Christ oh Riley," said Matti under his breath. "They must hear this row." *Click... click... click*, went the cutters. To the quartet, it sounded like an express train travelling down the line, as the wire seemed to ping loudly. 'I know, just as soon as we pop our heads over their parapet, they will be waiting with presents for us,' thought Hill Billy, who was shaking in an almost uncontrollable state of fear. They were now through the wire. "Matti, stay behind here to guide us out. You two, come with me." This was not a request, it was an order. Even though Enrico was at least four years younger than Hill Billy or Bob, they knew that he was the natural leader. Enrico crept, now on all fours to the top, looked over and could see nothing. He waved the others over to his position. "We can wait here for maybe a minute or two, and see if anybody will come along, and then we can grab him."

They waited, and they waited. At last, after an hour, they heard footsteps coming. It was a good eight foot drop to the bottom of the trench, so if they were to pounce on anyone they must not miss, or it would be them who'd be the prisoners. The steps got closer and closer. They could hear a soldier coming as he was whistling some unknown tune. Just as the luckless soldier appeared before them, Enrico jumped. He hit the German square in the face with his boot. The whistling German stopped dead in his tracks. He fell to the floor with a thud, then two more thuds came, as the others followed Enrico's example. The man was out cold, with maybe a broken jaw to add to his troubles. The three of them looked around. "Wire up three Mills bombs, across the trench, just over there," said Enrico to the other two. It took a minute to set the booby traps that the hand grenades had now become. They were ready to lift the still body of the German onto the parapet. He seemed to weigh a ton, being a rather large man, probably in his late forties. This done, they climbed back up themselves; then came the slow and painful attempts to drag the still lifeless body of the Hun. After about half an hour they had retraced their way back through the wire. Just on the other side the German started to come round.

"Now, why couldn't he have woken before we had to drag him!" exclaimed Enrico under his breath to the other three. They gagged him and he was made to crawl along with them. Another hour went by, when *Bang! Bang! Bang!* All hell was let loose. Some other Germans had finally walked into the trip wires of the Mills bombs. Flares went up. Machine guns started to rake the British lines. Mortars went off. The five of them crawled into a large shell hole. Even the German was cooperating with all this going on! "Maybe setting those traps was not such a good idea?" said Enrico, as they all cowered in the cover.

"Enrico, how are we going to make it back to our lines now?" said Matti.

"We can't stay here forever, not if we are *alive* anyway!" exclaimed Hill Billy, more than a little nervously. The German could only stare wide eyed. He was thinking now about his wife and his son, who had also been called to service in the Kaiser's army. He was hoping so much to meet him again, and now he would never see any of them. He lay there, tears now welling in his eyes, knowing he could no longer control his bowels: he was on his way to the toilet when he got jumped upon.

The three of them looked at one another then the German. "Jesus! As if there weren't enough smells upon us four! I do believe our friend Fritz 'ere has done a rather smelly shite in his pants." This remark had come from Hill Billy, but acknowledgement came from the other three. Another star shell went up, lighting up the whole area with white light so bright, that it gave great long shadows to everything.

"Time to go! We can hop from hole to hole," said Enrico. "With this sort of light, we might have a chance." They dragged the German once again, hole after hole. The shelling was now coming from the German artillery, though it was more of a gesture than the real thing. But the shells were landing all over the place, even in the British trenches. More flares, more machine gun fire. Each step took the five of them closer to home, and friendly lines. It was nearly dawn when the British wire was in front of them. They found their way back into the area that they could crawl under. "Who goes there?" demanded the harsh voice of the sentry.

"Bloody hell! What's the password?" Enrico asked the other three. "Silent night," answered Matti. "Oh yes, thanks; Silent night!" he called out loud enough to be heard, he hoped. A German mortar landed not more than ten feet away from them, on their left side. All five of them scrambled through the wire, and then came to the edge of the trench to find the smiling face of Jimmy Riddle shining brightly up at them. "Help the prisoner down. Right, you three after him," said Enrico. Just as Bob Gregg was about to clamber over, a series of whining sounds reverberated, along with the thuds heralding the bullets hitting the ground around them. A small gasp that could be clearly heard stopped Enrico in his tracks. He noticed that Bob had gone into the trench, so he followed suit. But, as he landed on the fire step, he and the others noticed that Bob had fallen straight through onto the duck boards.

"Bob, up you get! Are you all right?" No answer. Enrico moved slowly to his friend, knowing but wishing otherwise, that Robert Gregg was no more.

"Oh no!" he nearly cried out, as the others crowded around, to see the last twitches of Bob's body, as it gave up the ghost. "I really hope this is going to be worth Bob's life."

Sergeant Kelly greeted them. "Well done, men!" This was praise indeed, coming from 'Spider' Kelly. "I'll see to it that you get some sort of recognition for this night's work." The prisoner was taken off to HQ. They had what they wanted.

A bath, a hot meal and a sleep, that now, was the order of the day. But no such order came. Back the four of them went, to the fire step. It turned out that two Germans had been killed by the booby traps. There was also one other sentry, on the British side, that had been killed by the German shelling, and never to forget, Bob. Two all: a draw in anybody's eyes. The local shelling had now stopped, with just the occasional machine gun or rifle fire. Dawn had come, the weather was breaking. Clouds were coming fast along with a warm wind. 'Why couldn't we've had the clouds last night?' thought Enrico, as he stared down the sights of his Lee Enfield 303 rifle into no-man's-land. Other men nearby moved away. What an awful smell!

Having spent a wet blustery morning looking across waste land, land that was going to take many years before it would be arable again, the Battalion had a visit from the Adjutant, Major Tyler-Latham. "Sergeant Kelly!"

"Sir!"

"Bring me the four men who brought back the prisoner," said the Major in a mild manner. The three of them appeared in a wet haggard state. They stood to attention before the officer.

"Where is the fourth?" he enquired.

"Dead, Sir, probably underground by now!"

"Sorry, I didn't know. Which of you is Enrico Caruso?"

"Sir, that would be me."

"Congratulations, you have been mentioned for your work, and it has been decided that you are to be made up to Corporal!"

"Oh, right, Sir...thank you," came the less than enthusiastic retort. All three saluted the officer, and Enrico was handed his stripes. Just as the Adjutant was about to turn and go, Enrico stopped him in his tracks, asking, "Please, Sir, was the prisoner of any use?"

"Well, I guess you have a right to know. He was the chief cook for the men. Knew nothing about anything, and we believe he was telling the truth. So, to really answer your question, he is a complete waste of time. But you did well anyway." He then turned and walked away, leaving three, now soaking, cold men, looking at the trench duckboards. He didn't notice the tears that were being shed by the men for a good friend they had just lost, and for what? Nothing! Absolutely nothing!

It is hard to imagine the destruction that the shelling was causing, not just to buildings, but the very land itself. Buildings can be rebuilt. Even the drainage of the land could be rebuilt; but what about the land itself? Heavy metals, raining down, polluting every acre, every hectare, every square mile; gas, seeping into the very fibre of the soil. Chlorine, mustard and something that combined many deadly poisons, which a real bright spark had called Yprerite, oozed everywhere. All life was dying, not just human. And the carnage of death was to be seen everywhere. Bodies lay in no-man's-land, unburied for many months at a time. This had brought the rats, and in their turn the rats brought disease. Dead horses and cattle hardly ever got moved, just gradually rotted away. Because Flanders is so low lying, being in some places below sea level, water stagnated where it fell. This caused terrible flooding, mainly in the British sectors, as the Germans knew what they were doing when they had fought for the high ground. The German trenches stayed comparatively dry, they just pumped the water out and over the parapet, watching it run down into the British lines. The rotting corpses, lying out in the battle zones, would just disappear, being sucked under the mud, then to reappear, either by natural causes, or by being blown skywards from yet another shell. The stench was almost a sweet heady scent, which hung to one's clothing, penetrating through and into the skin. The local folk knew when a soldier returned from the front, just by his smell. It was everywhere. If this war was ever going to end, it would be a hundred years before nature took control again. But then, nature is patient, time is on its side.

The very next day when Harrington's Section stood down from their frontline duty, all the Battalion was brought in for special orders. Their trench system was then re-manned by others soldiers from another Battalion. Each Sergeant was given his orders, which in turn were passed onto the men.

"You will collect all your gear, and I mean right now! You will all muster back here for immediate transportation to another location which will become apparent, when, and only when, we get there. There are no letters home, at least for the time being. Clean up quickly and be back here within one hour from now. Dismissed!"

It was now Corporal Caruso's job to make sure that the men did just as they were told. 'Here we go again. No food, no sleep, work, work, work. Maybe mining is not such a bad idea!' thought Enrico to himself.

The journey was once again by lorries. It took nearly six hours of bumping around muddy, potholed roads before they reached their destination, which in fact, was no further than thirty miles away from Ypres. The Germans had soon become aware of the troop movement, and started to send over some big boys to say good bye to them, in a very unfriendly manner. One shell hit another Battalion's lorry, which just blew apart killing all inside, and wounding many on the lorry behind; and this too, caught fire when the petrol tanks ruptured. The lorries passed by this appalling mess, and men could only watch, as their friends were being burnt alive as the second lorry was trying to disgorge its unlucky load. The screams that could clearly be heard by one and all put the fear of God into all of them. Anyone who heard and saw this tragic event would never forget it.

Their destination was a small town called Hazebrouck. It had been nearly completely taken over by the military, and the civilians that remained were there, more or less, just employed to help service the forces. By the time they arrived, it was time for a late meal. The confusion was extreme. Nobody seemed to know where anybody else was meant to be. The logistics of sorting this melee out took some doing. But time helped to get just about everyone under canvas, and hot food inside them. They were all there for training. 'So, it was true, there was going to be a push!' This time, it was going to get the Hun really on the move. The army would break through the enemy lines; where, they could only speculate. The so-called pundits were everywhere. They heard this from the Corp, or the Sarge, or some Officer or someone in high office. "Believe me… I know what I am talking about!"

This sort of remark and a thousand others went around the camp, like wild fire. Soldiers got completely bored with hearing about the latest place of attack. If there had been German spies there, they would have been so confused that the entire German population would have been needed to defend the areas that the Allies were going to be attacking from.

Life in Hazebrouck became like life in any other sector of the army. Work, drill, lectures, gun practice, new weapons to try out, and one last little detail, that worried most of those who underwent the experience, "Gas mask drill." Respirators were now standard issue: gas was now a matter of fact. "You must carry your gas mask at all times." This was the new order of the day. Men would feel terribly claustrophobic in the new head gear. Also it restricted the vision: you had to turn your head from side to side, all the time, so as to get an overall picture of what was around you. Doing hand to hand combat with bayonets became daily practice, to make sure that when, and if it happened, you could cope. But for most men, the thought of sticking a blade into flesh was almost too much to bear. To shoot another soldier from a long distance, knowing he might be shooting at you, that was one thing, but to tackle someone at close quarters, bayonet against bayonet, that didn't bear thinking about.

Killing is never an easy thing to do. Young men joined the army, more or less for the excitement, and to get the chance for a better life, regular meals and money. It was always simple to talk in Blighty about how one was going to chase the Hun from France and Belgium, all the way back to Berlin; it soon became clear that it was going to be a very long and protracted conflict. And the top brass knew it was going to be a costly one in human life. So when the young men enlisted for the duration, only to find that it would not be over by Christmas as they thought, and that in fact it was not quite the glorious event that had been promised, thousands of them then became disillusioned, almost to the point of rebellion, which is exactly what happened in France, and to a lesser degree in Germany, within their navy. For most people, killing is hard and you need a real reason for doing such a thing, not the hogwash that had been handed to you, by your so-called betters. At the end of each day, when you looked at the enemy, he was young and just as naïve as you.

It was a sad fact that old men ruled the World, the Army, the Church, and just about everything else. Generals took charge of organising battles, which would have been more suited to the plains of a specific country, so that the Cavalry could charge through, in a glorious formation of colour and splendour. How could old men understand about trench life, mud, rats, lice, disease, but most of all the artillery and the machine gun, not forgetting gas, flamethrowers, and grenades, planes strafing and raking the trenches with machine guns and bombing them with high explosives? These were all twentieth century devices; and *they* were all nineteenth century soldiers, with nineteenth century ideas. The two did not mix at all.

It was the Kaiser himself, talking about the British forces, who called them 'That Contemptible Little Army,' 'An Army of Lions, Led by Donkeys.' He was not wrong, but sadly, he hadn't looked too closely at his own army either, all brave young men fighting for causes that had no meaning in a progressively modernising world. They were just young men, fighting for their Kaiser, with exactly the same thought as the Allies… "God Is On Our Side."

This was the world that Enrico and Matti had come into.

One of the hardest tasks that befell the troops at Hazebrouck was the new trench systems that they had to dig. Nearly all the trenches on the Western front connected, so that wherever a person was, he could traverse through the trenches to almost anywhere, without leaving, or raising his head above the system he was in. Now the powers that be wanted the men to dig sap lines. Saps, as they were known, were trenches that would be dug, just like the knight of old would have done; when they set siege to a castle, they dug a trench so that arrows could not hit them, then a tunnel to undermine the fortress. For this they would at first use props, which shored up the whole edifice, then set fire to them, and as the props crumbled, so would the castle they were supporting. That at least was the theory. But in the Hazebrouck area, they wanted the trenches to go out into no-man's-land, and then come up near the enemy, so the troops could rush to the enemy trenches, making it easier to overwhelm them.

But still nobody really knew where the push was going to be from.

The training became more and more intense, with the young soldiers working from early morning until late at night, with very few breaks. None of their hardships were helped by the weather: since their arrival, it had rained almost continuously. On the 18th September, they were finally told where and when the push was going to happen. They were going to the front that very day, and it was going to take place at the mining town of Loos, in France. "Your training will not have been for nothing. First you will be digging out new trenches into no-man's-land, and these will be the jumping-off points. The bombardment has already started, and will carry on until the actual day of the attack. The attack will start with a few thousand gas shells being fired into the enemy trenches. You will follow them. With all the shelling that will have gone on, and the Chlorine gas, there will be no one left there to fight, they will all be dead." These were the profound words, which turned out to be ironical indeed, uttered to all the Battalions, just before they left for Loos.

The battle of Loos was a plan that had been devised by General Joffre, with the intention that the British should take further command of the trench system, thus linking more or less completely to the river Somme from the Channel. The plan was to be a combined operation with the French pushing north from the Champagne and also jointly attacking with the British in Artois. The idea was to cut a wedge in German lines to allow the cavalry to sweep through. Joffre himself believed emphatically that this was the battle that was going to end the war. Meanwhile, General Haig had toured the area of operations and was horrified to see how exposed the ground was to German machine guns. When he confronted Joffre, the latter refused to alter the plan in any way, believing entirely in his own rhetoric. The arrogance of Joffre, convinced that there was divine help on his side, prevented him from seeing — and one wonders if he cared anyway — any forthcoming potential massacre. Lord Kitchener made a special visit to Sir John French, then Commander in chief of the B.E.F., and pleaded with him that co-operation with the French was essential, even though it was expected that there may be many casualties. General Haig, realising that this battle could be a disaster on a wide front, devised a plan in two parts. Firstly, a wide front would only be used if the weather conditions were favourable for the deployment of Chlorine gas. This was to be used for the first time by the Allies.

Secondly, if the wind did not permit the use of gas, a two division assault would be made in a narrow front. It was eventually agreed between the British and the French that because of the fear of the German machine guns, Allied shelling would start on the original attack date of the 8th of September, building up to a crescendo for the revised attack date of the 25th with the idea of neutralising the enemy trenches, but most of all, their machine gun nests. The serious bombardment would be carried out from the 21st September, with the combined use of a hundred and ten heavy guns, and eighty-four smaller calibre guns and howitzers, then continuing day and night until the actual assault on the 25th. It was also agreed that the whole combined attack front would be smothered in smoke to hide the advancing troops. At the same time as the smoke, the gas shells were to be fired, and hundreds of gas cylinders would have their valves opened. The whole point was to create panic and mayhem within the lines of the Hun. What the Allies failed to know, was that the front line trenches, constructed upon the slopes overlooking the plains that would be traversed by combined Allied troops, were easily evacuated if shelled upon. Indeed there was a deeper and more heavily constructed system of fortified trenches behind the buff of the hills, unseen to the Allies, which could hold all the defending Central Powers troops. As the shelling became fiercer, the majority of the troops plus the vital machine guns could evacuate to the stronger fortifications.

Loos is situated in the Artois region, and is famed for its coalmines, slag heaps and wasteland: a perfect place for defending, a lousy one for attacking. The British lines ran from North to South, skirting the road from Vermelles in the British sector to Hulluch on the German side. The Germans had had much time to build heavy fortified redoubts, with the most famous being Hohenzollern behind which was a huge slag heap, and as this towered high, it became a very good vantage point for the German machine guns and lookouts. There were many quarries and mineshafts; winding gear and mine buildings loomed everywhere. The Germans had built large defences on the Hulluch Road around pylons, which fed the mines.

It was to this that two Divisions which included the London Northern Rifle Brigade were now being sent.

"Blimey, Matti!" said Enrico, "pure bloody luxury!" As the Battalion assembled, their transport appeared, and to everybody's excitement, it was to be the London omnibuses, which had been released for military duties. The men got quite boyish in behaviour as these hard, rickety, open topped vehicles came driving up to them.

"Clamber in, let's get on as quickly as possible!" shouted an already angry Sergeant Kelly to all and sundry around him. Immediately the open top part was filled, as if this was a gay summer excursion that they were all going on. The men acted as if they were children, quickly squabbling about who should be sitting next to whom. But then, in many ways they were children, children going off to play a very deadly game.

It was not long before all the NCOs had a job on their hands, settling down their charges, so that the buses could get under way. "My God, what a bunch of namby-pambies! I thought we were going to be here all day before the little dears would settle," stated a now dazed Kelly shaking his head from side to side, much to the amusement of his fellow NCOs. But soon enough the buses were on their way. They rattled and shook as they hit ruts and cobblestones. This soon started to have a dramatic effect on a large number of the troops, who sat on topside of the omnibuses. More than a few had their heads over the sides losing their breakfast, then last night's dinner, then everything. They looked and felt like a bunch of sailors who had drunk too much and where now going around Cape Horn, backwards. On several occasions, buses came to a stop, one behind the other as the leading bus would break down, or run out of petrol, or just give up for a rest. Soldiers would have to get out and push the offending vehicle off the road to await repairs or more fuel. Many of the men were now starting to wonder if they or their friends would survive, or be wounded, after this forthcoming battle; their thoughts soon turned to home and loved ones; it was such a long time since last seeing their family or friends. Would they ever see them again? Could they take a wound without disgracing themselves? 'Please Lord, if I should be shot, either let me die quickly, or make me a man so that I can endure the pain without crying like a baby.' One thing the journey did, was to make the entire troops gradually become pensive and withdrawn, dwelling hard on what was to come. For most of them, this was the first time in a battle, maybe their last, too?

It took just over four hours of uncomfortable solid-wheeled driving before they reached their destination, a small village called Maroc which they understood was about a ten miles walk to the front line trenches. Canteens were everywhere, many hosted by the Voluntary Aid Detachments. These were women who volunteered for working in hospitals or canteens, but close to the front lines. Often these brave young women were of very high birth: more than one Lady or Baroness worked cleaning wounded men, or just gave comfort or succour. Sometimes they worked as long as eighteen-hour shifts, day in and day out.

It was while Corporals Harrington and Caruso were standing, having a hot brew by one of these canteens that Private John Hutton asked for a song from Enrico. "What do you want?" Enrico replied with a smile on his face, knowing this was all going to be a big wind-up for a laugh. " 'The Rose of No-Man's-Land', please, Corp," said Hutton, giving a knowing wink to his mates, who were standing around. Enrico was never slow to enjoy a joke, even if it was against him. So he started…

*"I've seen some beautiful flowers,*
*Grow in life's garden fair,*
*I've spent some wonderful*
*Hours, lost in their fragrance rare,*
*But I have found another,*
*Wondrous beyond compare."*

As usual, sung at least a quarter of a tone flat, with a range of just a couple of notes! But this time, it didn't bring the normal laughter, but a swell of sound from one and all in the chorus.

*"There's a Rose that grows in 'No-man's-land'*
*And it's wonderful to see,*
*Tho' it's sprayed with tears,*
*It will live for years,*
*In my garden of memory.*
*It's the one red rose the soldier knows,*
*It's the work of the Master's hand;*
*In the War's great curse,*
*Stood the Red Cross Nurse,*
*She's the Rose of 'No-man's-land."*

Gradually, work stopped; Privates, NCOs and Officers were affected by the song. The singing started to make men very emotional. So with the soldiers all standing, as in a trance, they started to take up the second verse. The sound turned into a heavenly chorus of triumph; for those few minutes

145

all the men were at peace with humanity around them, just singing at the top of their voices in the best possible way, all the time thinking of what was to come, then of home and families.

> *Out in the Heavenly splendour,*
> *Down to the trail of woe,*
> *God in his mercy has sent her,*
> *Cheering the world below.*
> *We call her 'Rose of Heaven'*
> *We've learned to love her so,*

Once again ending with the chorus…

> *There's a rose that grows in 'No-man's-land'*
> *And it's wonderful to see,*
> *Tho' it's sprayed with tears,*
> *It will last for years,*
> *In my garden of memory.*
> *It's the one red rose the soldier knows,*
> *It's the work of the Master's hand;*
> *In the War's great curse,*
> *Stood the Red Cross Nurse,*
> *She's the rose of 'No man's land'.*

Then as quickly as the singing started, it stopped, a few men clapping, some wiping the odd tear from their eyes, and after an embarrassed self-conscious moment or two, everybody got on with whatever tasks that had been given to them.

How soon a person gets hardened to various noises, around and about. It was as if the guns just did not exist; they knew it was going to be dangerous, if a shell had your name or number on it. So men learnt to live with this din and danger, even sleeping through a barrage, quite unaware that it had happened. But there they were, and it was obvious to all, if they stopped and listened, that the guns were now getting much louder: a huge crescendo was building up. The guns were trying hard to knock out the German barbed wire: blow it to smithereens, break it up into small pieces, or just move it to another place, out of the way of the forthcoming attacking forces. What good would it be to have neutralised the enemy in their front line trenches, if your troops could not cross through the wire to actually occupy the trench?

The guns themselves were part of the trouble. There were not really enough heavy pieces of artillery to cover the miles of the attacking front. Ammunition was still scarce, so rounds had to be rationed. Some of the guns had been firing just a few dozen rounds every day. Many of the lighter calibre fifteen-pounder guns were last used in the Boer War, and really didn't have much relevance in this sort of conflict. So, were the guns doing what was asked of them? Was the wire being cut?

The gas cylinders were now up on the front line trenches, ready for the off, if the wind was right on the 25th. To keep the whole gas attack hidden from the Hun, the top brass changed the name of gas to the *accessory*.

"So when is this 'ere attack going to 'appen?" enquired Maurice Bechstein to Corporal Harrington. Bechstein was a real cockney Jew boy, who had signed up just to get away from his Father, who was a Rabbi from Silvertown in the East end of London, very near to the docks.

"Real soon, so don't you go wandering off looking for a synagogue!"

"Corp, don't be a schmutter all your life! What would I want with one of them? Didn't I just get the 'ell out of one of those places? I 'ad all that rubbish crammed down me voice box all me bleedin' life, ain't I?"

"You might be glad of God before this lot's over?"

"Not a chance, it's all pony and trap." And with that he walked away, with the Corporal wondering, really what was he talking about?

The next few days were spent carrying the paraphernalia of war, either up to the front line, or loading such stuff onto the waiting lorries. There were just thousands of men from so many Battalions there in Maroc, and very soon they would all be traversing the few miles that hung between them and life or death.

Occasionally the German guns returned fire. They knew roughly where the troops would be; it did not take a genius to look on a map and work out where the billets were, then with the help of the spotter planes marking where the shells landed, they soon got the range. Buildings were systematically being blown to rubble. There were casualties, but not so many. It was really more for keeping the troops morale low, and prevent them from organising themselves, from doing what needed to be done; just keep them tired and on their toes awaiting the next packet.

At least the weather had cleared; there was a little wind, but no rain, though the ground was still muddy from past rain and excessive feet and vehicle use. Shell holes were generally without water, but not all. Shell holes with clay bottoms tended to fill with water and stay full.

So, finally the big day had come! This was the day that the Allied army was going to push Fritz back to Berlin. Haig and Joffre were going to get their afternoon aperitif with the Kaiser, and it would not be drinking Schnapps, no Sir, he would be made to drink Pink Gins like any other Gentleman!

The day of the 24th had gone quietly for Enrico and Matti; they had slept in late, or at least tried to. But in the night they had both fretted about the next morning, wondering how they would both fare in the coming carnage? They arose at seven thirty, just in time to get some bread, with something that resembled scrambled eggs, thrown on top. It tasted bitter, the tea tasted bitter. No matter how much sugar they applied, it still tasted bitter. After a couple of mouthfuls of food, and a mug of over-sweetened tea, they just didn't feel in the mood for anything else. Matti was the first to break the gloom that had gathered like dark thunder clouds.

"Enrico, please, let's stick close to one another."

"Of course, it goes without saying. Anyway, someone's got to look after you. I am more frightened of the wrath of your Mother than the Hun across the way. So, old pal, it's you an' me all the way down the line."

The day went slowly for everyone, though one would hazard a guess that many wished this day would never end. But nine o'clock in the evening came, and the Battalion was called to muster. This was the allotted time to make their way to the front line, and whatever destiny had in store for them. There were no omnibuses to take them; this evening it was going to be a hard moonless walk, and ten miles of it. They had to be in the front line trench ready for the off, not later than three in the morning. Ten miles in six hours, should under normal circumstances be easy. But these circumstances were far from normal. It would be dark; in the dark they could come off the road, fall into old shell holes. Added to this, they were carrying a full pack, their rifle and maybe some extra ammunition, or Mills bombs. They might be part of a team of machine gunners, in which case they had also to help carry the gun, and they were heavy. So, for a night hike on worn-out mud tracks full of shell holes, wet and tired, carrying a load that would have been hard work for a few hundred yards, it becomes obvious why the men needed the six hours.

The shelling from the Allies was so loud it could easily burst an ear drum or two. Apart from the noise, they could feel the ground shake under the concussion.

'Are we walking into the jaws of hell? Is this what I lived to do? Why, oh why, do I feel as if I am going to shit myself? Think of something else! If I ran for it, could it be possible to get back to England without being caught? If I got caught, would they shoot me? Left, right, left, right…That's it, think of a song!' All this was going around in Enrico's mind as he put one foot in front of the other, closely following the soldier in front.

"Sergeant Kelly."

"Corporal Caruso, what d'you want?"

"Shall I sing a song for the men?"

"Good idea! that is if anyone can hear you above the din of these guns!"

'Right, what shall it be?' thought Enrico, then he knew.

*"Three German Officers crossed the line, parlez-vous.*
*Three German Officers crossed the line, parlez-vous.*
*Three German Officers crossed the line,*
*To fuck the women and drink the wine,*
*Inky pinkie parlez-vous."*

He sang loud, and for once, almost in tune, but this time there was no response, nobody felt like joining in. So after the second verse, his voice drifted away into the nothing gloom that hung over everybody.

There was a cool breeze in the air, which made Colonel McBride turn to his Adjutant saying, "if this wind turns, and they let the gas go, we are all in trouble. I really rather hope it is not used."

"I've been thinking much the same, Sir…Look, Sir, I can see the flashes of our guns; we must be near the Artillery firing dugouts?"

"Every step takes us nearer," said McBride.

Though Colonel McBride and his Adjutant were walking to the front with the men, they had been ordered to go to the control dugout. Top brass didn't want Majors or Colonels risking their lives going over the top. Their jobs were to plan, not to do what had been planned. Going over the top was for Captains, Lieutenants, NCOs and mainly Privates. There were plenty of them, so it didn't matter quite so much if a few thousand lost their lives or were injured in any way. Life was cheap!

Soon they had passed the gasping guns. Many men walked past with any free hand clasped over an ear. For the untrained, it was a painful affair being near big noisy guns. Even though the nearest was about sixty yards away, when a round was fired you could feel the concussion in the air, and it was a very unpleasant feeling. The guns behind them meant they had only one more mile to the start of the trench systems, then another two miles to their jumping off position. They would be there in plenty of time. Colonel McBride sent good wishes to his men through the NCOs. "I want to see them all in one piece when we reach and take the enemy trenches." This was conveyed through a word of mouth, Chinese whisper-style, which meant by the time the sentence reached the last man, it came out as something like…"There'll be just one piece of us when we reach the German trenches!"

As they approached the trench system, they where now mixed with many Battalions, all finding their way to the various jumping off points. The London Northern Rifle Brigade had to make its way south, as the plans were that they were to join with the 21st Division and the 47th Division, to take the village of Loos itself. Once the bombardment stopped and the Chlorine was discharged, they were to proceed at a walk, more or less in formation and towards Loos, in which all the defenders would be dead, or happy to capitulate, or so went the plan! Once in the labyrinth of trenches, making their way to the jumping point, they came across a traffic jam that took some defining, not of cars or lorries, but seething humans, in their thousands, everybody seemingly in a confused state of anxiety; Sergeants screaming at Corporals, who in turn were screaming at Privates, but gradually, men got to their place within the framework of this confusion. Sergeant Kelly, sweating profusely, gathered his other NCOs around him.

"Right, you know the drill. Harrington, Caruso, you take your Section on the left flank, Sprite, Collins, right flank. I don't care what the orders have been, break ranks and use the cover that there will be out there. Keep alive and on your toes; this is not going to be a picnic, so use the shell holes for cover when you have to. Caruso, make sure that a ration of rum is issued to each man, Dumbridge and Riddle can help you. Don't let anyone drink too much, either. A drunken soldier will be a serious danger to us, more than the enemy. This is our first test in battle, let's come out as heroes, never be a disgrace to the Battalion, and never, ever let your men down. Any questions?"

"Sergeant, why are the Germans not shelling back?" asked Enrico.

"That's one of the things that bothers me; I suspect troubles are just about to come, and in the shape of large calibres. Right, if nothing else, I will see you all in Loos." Then with a rare touch of gentleness, "God's speed!"

The rum ration had been doled out, all had partaken. Nerves were high and on edge, some soldiers were praying to themselves, some openly. "God, help me through this day." "From now on I will be a changed man, if I live through this day!" "Our Father, who art in heaven, hallowed be Thy name..." These and a thousand others were winging their way heavenwards. Many men stood quietly just thinking of home, and Mother.

There were three sap trenches leading out into no-man's-land from where McBride's Battalion was entrenched, three that would take them into... what? They led out approximately two hundred yards, some parts as tunnels, some parts open, but all three coming gradually up to the surface and exposure.

Young Officers and NCOs checked and rechecked watches. Whistles would soon blow.

'We will soon be fighting, or dead!' thought Kelly, as he lifted his whistle to his lips.

The guns seemed to quicken pace. The huge roaring shells whistled and sang, as they shot overhead and into the enemy trenches. Surely, nothing could survive this bombardment; surely, the wire would be torn apart.

To the north of the battlefield where the 9th Division was going to attack the Hohenzollern redoubt, the erect figures of General Haig and his aides were seen entering the trench system. He turned to his ADC, Major

Alan Fletcher, saying the fateful words: "Light me a cigarette!" He held that cigarette slightly above the parapet, and noted that the smoke drifted in a leisurely north-easterly direction. 'Was this acceptable?' thought Haig, as he looked at his watch, noting that it was 05.00 hours. Again he held that cigarette above the parapet, and turning to Fletcher, he asked with a worried frown upon his face: "Do we discharge the accessory?" but without waiting for a reply, he gritted his teeth, turned on his heels, moved away with the entourage following in close procession, with the words: "Accessory to be discharged at all cost." These words were to ring in the ears of many soldiers, long after the war would end. At 05.50 hours, his plan was realised. The gas was released, and the emissions continued, on and off for the next forty minutes. The first problem to be encountered was that there was not enough Chlorine gas for a continuous flow, so smoke shells had to be dropped into no-man's-land to fool the enemy.

Sergeant Kelly looked at his watch: 05.30 hours. "Right, pass the word: respirators on, now!" Gradually, this order was complied with, and *there* was this sight of thousands of men, looking and sounding for all the world like a swarm of strange alien beings, with the appalling wheezing sound that came from the inhaling and exhaling. Those that had not worked it out before soon understood what the word accessory meant. Just over the parapet in small individual dugouts came the hissing of the released Chlorine gas. It swirled in the air, and drifted into no-man's-land, but not as quickly as the officers had expected or wanted. There was even some that was starting to drift back into their own trenches, and along with the noise of the war could be heard the occasional screaming of the luckless men who, for whatever reason, could or would not wear their gas masks. In many cases, the fatalities that followed were also caused by faulty respirators, inducing a panic that usually ended in the poor soldier's death. 'Men dying from our own hands, this cannot be right!' was a thought that was generally spreading through the men. What was also spreading was the green cloud, drifting backwards and forwards in no-man's-land, as the wind changed sides continuously. All this went on until 06.00, when the mighty roar of the guns just ceased; everybody's ears rang. Now they could hear that ringing in the silence. What was worse, the thunder of the guns, or the silent swirling deadly mist which was in front of them in no-man's-land?

06.00 hours. Whistles started to blow all the way from Givenchy in the north to the most southerly point of the attack, a line of eight miles. Sergeant Kelly's whistle blew with the others, and in a voice muffled by the respirator, he said: "Good luck, men. See you in Loos!"

The crowding soldiers congested the sap trenches, which led into the unknown of no-man's-land. All along the trench system could be heard the sound of men yelling with excitement and pent-up aggression. "Kill the Hun!" was the common shout. The silence that had followed the ending of the artillery barrage was now replaced by a distant rattling sound, as German machine guns opened up. As men surged forward down the sap trench, the momentum of moving bodies was like the river Severn bore in spring time; once set in motion, impossible to stop. As the first men reached the end of the sap, and their heads and bodies appeared above ground like the last Day of Judgment when the earth and seas shall give up all their dead, then a nearer rattling sound was heard.

*Thwap…thwap…thwap!* Resurrection had ended early. Men just fell forward, as pieces of lead the size of a farthing tore huge holes into their bodies. The trouble was, as the first soldiers fell, either killed or wounded, the momentum of those following caused them to trip and fall over their luckless comrades, so even before the men got out of the trenches, they were being slaughtered. On seeing a Lieutenant in front of him crumple up and fall forward into already fallen victims, Sergeant Kelly knew he must take control quickly.

"Stop, stop!" he screamed through his respirator. The men around him, seeing the melee that was occurring in front stopped and got others to stop. Still bullets were hitting the men, so they ducked behind the now seething mass of dead and wounded.

*154*

Poking his head slightly above, he surveyed the panorama in front. Their trouble had been that the smoke and gas had cleared too quickly, and to make matters worse, the Germans had witnessed from their position of high ground that these trenches were being dug, and had secreted machine gun posts in various strategic locations, where they could do the worst damage.

"Caruso, Riddle, come here quickly! You see that small mound of earth about five hundred yards to the left of centre? Then look, men, close to the two tree stumps protruding from the ground. Can you see it?"

"Yes, Sarge, I think I can," said Riddle.

"Well, that's the bugger that's getting us. We will wait a minute, because the gas is drifting across, and when we are obscured, we'll spread out and run from shell hole to shell hole. Riddle, you are the best shot; it's your task to get close enough to knock them out. Caruso, you keep close to Riddle, and keep an eye out for any other little nests to deal with. Understood?"

"Yes, Sarge!", came both the replies.

"Right, the smoke is coming across… wait a mo', go!" and out they went, Dumbridge following in every footstep that his friend left. Now that the way was obscured with fog and gas, men spilled all along the line onto the battlefield.

But the Germans had not been wasting the weeks preceding the attack: big guns and reserve men had been brought forward; they had purposely refrained from firing the artillery, except in token, keeping it as much a secret as possible, so that the effect of surprise was maximised. A cacophony of noise started to erupt from behind the German reserve trenches, as the various calibre pieces opened their bombardment. Shells began to rain down, in no particular order within no-man's-land, killing and maiming as they went. Then came a barrage of shrapnel shells, which would burst, maybe as low as fifty feet above the heads of the attacking forces, showering them with balls of red hot lead which would hit them at speeds of up to five hundred miles an hour. These balls could pass through anything: steel helmets, flesh and bone meant nothing. It was a carnage developing upon biblical proportions; everywhere along the eight mile stretch were soldiers, either dead or writhing about in the agony of death throes. Rivers of blood and gore began to form, as bodies emptied of their life juices.

With all this storm of steel and machine gunfire, there were men who did make it across that desert of death, and would shelter in the comparative safety of shell holes. Half an hour had gone by since the whistle blew, and already hundreds upon hundreds of men lay dead or dying.

Enrico, Matti, Jimmy and several others from Harrington's section had managed, through more luck than judgement, to get within one hundred yards of the first machine gun that was giving them hell. They seemed at this point to be unnoticed by the enemy and took full advantage of this fact to reassess their objectives. Enrico had once again taken complete control, and as they crouched in the shell hole, the men gathered around awaiting the orders.

Barry Knight, crouching next to Enrico, put his hand on Enrico's left knee, and staring at him with wide, bloodshot eyes, in a trembling voice said: "What shall we do? How the hell are we going to get out of here?"

All the others looked on at Enrico, expectantly.

"First," said Enrico, "pull yourself together, Barry. And that goes for the rest of you, too."

Bullets and shells were flying everywhere, and at last, the English machine gunners were opening up, and making their presence felt.

"Jimmy, come here. Let's both look over the top towards their machine gunners. I think the first is about fifty or a hundred yards away on our left, and I don't think they know we're here." They looked over the top of the crater, and there, they could see the three shapes of the German machine gunners in their small dugout, firing continuously ahead of them onto the oncoming Allied lines. One was firing, one was feeding the gun with the belt of bullets, and the third had binoculars to his eyes, and was spotting for the soldier firing. Enrico whispered to Jimmy: "You take the firer, and get him if you can in his head, I'll get the loader, then you finish off the spotter. You tell me when."

Jimmy very carefully brought his gun to bear over the brim of the crater, adjusting the sights for the guessed range, licked his trigger finger, and took careful aim.

"Are you ready?"

"Yes."

*Bang! Bang!*

The gunner slumped forward onto his machine gun, his helmet almost completely knocked off his head. Fortunately for Enrico, he caught the loader in the arm; with the pain he stood up and was in turn caught by some English machine gun fire; he was spun like a top, gushing blood everywhere. The third German hardly had time to lower his binoculars, when Jimmy shot him full in the face, taking out the whole of the back of his head.

"Jimmy Riddle, you are a bloody genius!" This lifted the tension greatly within the shell hole, and Matti turned to John Smyth to say: "Blimey, you'll never believe what keeps going through my mind!"

"Well, what does? I always thought nothing!" retorted John, with his head almost completely facing to the ground, his hands holding his helmet on, as if the wind was going to blow it off, and his bum sticking into the air as a nice target for any German to aim at. Matti then declared with a nervous giggle: "I was wondering how many goals Patsy Gallacher scored last week for Celtic. I could not think of anything else."

"Yes, it's crazy! I wonder if they'll win the Championship again this year, and I was also thinking about how it's time they gave us some leave."

Tension was beginning to settle for a minute or two, and they became aware that many more friendly troops were rushing past. Other machine gun nests had been knocked out, and though the carnage was appalling, the push was still going in the right direction. They could see now that they were quite close to the German front line trench; they could also see that though there was huge damage to the earthworks within the trench system, there seemed to be very little damage to the wire. This was going to be yet another major problem.

"Right, men, follow me," said Enrico, and to a man, they did. They ran zigzagging for about twenty more yards, bullets zinging past their ears, shells bursting on all sides. Enrico was the first to jump into a very large crater, so big that he could stand up in it without being seen. Matti and Jimmy followed suit, but just as Smyth was about to jump in, a ricocheting bullet hit him in the calf of his right leg. It was almost a spent bullet, as luck would have it, so though he bled quite profusely, it was not a Blighty wound, or even an injury that would end his army career, but it was enough to end his time in the 'Battle of Loos'. They noted that the gas had cleared, having done more damage to their own troops than the enemy, and Enrico gave the order: "You can remove the respirators, but for Christ's sakes, don't lose them".

He quickly turned to John Smyth who was lying at the bottom of the crater, cursing the Germans, while rocking to and fro, holding his injured calf: "Bastards, fucking bastards!" The profanities helped him from doing what he really wanted to do, and that was cry. Enrico took some gauze from his own pack and slapped it on to the offending wound.

"Is it real bad? Do you need an injection? Do you think you can crawl back under your own steam?" The answer came as: "No... no... yes." Enrico then turned to Jimmy and they started to scale the side of the crater closest to the German line. They could make out quite distinctly that there was a great deal of German movement coming from the trench. Heads and guns bobbing up and down all the time; he called down for everybody to take position on the rim of the crater. "I want three bombs at least, and we throw them into the German trenches one after another, then while the confusion is going on, we'll move to the crater on our right," then to John Smyth, he

158

added: "Crawl up to the other side now, wait for the bombing to start, then crawl as quick as you can from crater to crater, retracing your steps, then wait for nightfall before going back to the English lines."

Looking towards the German lines all the men had removed three Mills bombs from their pack.

"Right," said Enrico through gritted teeth, "there's no time like the present." And he concluded by throwing his first grenade with: "Let 'em have it!" Bombs rained in on the packed German trench; there were so many men crammed in, awaiting orders for a counter attack, that when these grenades came crashing in on them, they were stuck there like sardines in a can. Those that were not killed or wounded by grenade fragments were being trampled by men trying to escape the onslaught. This gave very valuable time for the British to get up to the wire in their sector, and for Enrico to get into yet another shell hole with his team. All the time, Matti stuck to him like glue. The whole bombardment that had rained down upon the eight miles of German trenches and wire had done very little to disturb this offending barb, but for Enrico, luck was on their side, for yet another huge shell had come down at some time over the wire. Though it had not actually cut the wire, or broken through, the crater that it made undermined it, so that they could creep into the crater, and crawl under the wire. They were now on top of the German parapet, and one small step from gaining their first part of German-held territory. Taking yet more Mills bombs from his pack, he indicated by pointing and miming that another three per man should be dropped forthwith into various sections of this trench.

The screaming was intense, as the explosions of the bombs did their work. On this, Enrico ordered: "Fix bayonets! Then follow me!" Jumping down into the trench, he did what he hoped he would never have to do again: he stuck his bayonet into human flesh. As dead and dying Germans lay in the bottom of the trench, caught by the grenades, the ones still looking menacing were quickly dispatched. As the rest of his team jumped down with him, he said quietly: "You three, go to the right, Matti and the rest of us go to the left. Shoot everybody; we can't take prisoners, finish them. Back here in an hour, and keep a sharp eye out not to be fired on by our own boys."

Enrico and the others trod over the dead and fatally injured enemy soldiers. Bits of human anatomy were plastered on all parts of the trench; the occasional low moan could be heard, but generally it was just the sighing sounds from gasses escaping out of the bodies as they settled. Picking up a box of stick grenades, which had been meant for them, they went forward along the trench, Jimmy and Matti taking the point with their guns ready to be discharged into any German who appeared. They only went about ten yards, when the trench turned left, then right, then right again, then left and so on, in a castellated fashion. At each turn, they peered carefully around the corner, expecting to be fired upon, but there, on the fire step, was only one German in a firing position; it was obvious to them that he too, had joined his ancestors in Valhalla. It seemed their Mills bombs and the English machine guns had done a good job of work on this stretch of the German trench. But as they went, yet another corner appeared, and this time they could hear the firing of German rifles. Enrico peered around the bend to see six German infantry soldiers, firing round after round. Handing Matti two German stick grenades, he indicated that they should both throw them at the same time. The noise was much louder than their normal Mills bombs, and it did a thorough job on the six Germans. Only two were writhing with any life left in them, and they were quickly dispatched, with sharpened best Sheffield steel. Looking around the next corner, Enrico was relieved to see that other English troops had now jumped into the enemy trenches, finishing off the occupants.

"Whoa! We're English, too!" one of the soldiers came up to Enrico with a huge grin on his face.

"Blimey, mate, I don't remember when I've had a better time!" said the man, grabbing and shaking Enrico's right hand enthusiastically. As

Enrico turned to retrace his steps back to the point where the team were to meet, he was pleased to note that there was no tremor in his hands: 'I really haven't been afraid! Strange, I thought I would be!'

When getting back to the meeting point, he was even happier, not only to see that the others had returned safe and sound, having scored a few hits, but also that Sergeant Kelly, Corporal Harrington and dozens more had found their way there, too.

"Good work, Caruso! You've held your end up well! Keep this sort of work up, and things will happen for you, my boy!"

"Sergeant," answered a startled Enrico, having never heard a more complimentary sentence uttered by the loathed 'Spider' Kelly.

Overall, the day had been costly, but from the Battalion's point of view, targets were well on their way to being met. Members of the 15th Division were now storming into the German trench to help swell the thin line of men that had first taken it. Kelly turned to Enrico and Harrington, and said: "It's about one mile roughly due east of our present position to the village of Loos. It should be quite open ground, and the 15th Division are going to make a feigned attack on Hill 70, but will cut around the back to stop any retreating Hun. Our job is to take it from the front; first thing is to knock out any machine gun we see, but I repeat, but we are in no position to take enemy prisoners, so make sure your first bullet finishes them." As he spoke, more and more stragglers appeared over the enemy trench. Enrico called out: "Has anybody seen John Smyth?"

"Yes, Corp. He was on a stretcher, being taken back to the line."

"Good, that's one less to worry about!" said Enrico.

"Share out the ammunition and the bombs," said Kelly to half a dozen young soldiers, dragging along the wooden cases filled with these bounteous gifts. Everybody took their fill.

"Right, men, over we go again. Stay low and keep cover as best you can; look out for your mate, but most of all look out for yourself!"

"Matti, for goodness sake, put the bully beef down, and let's get over this trench and away!"

Matti mumbled incoherent words under his breath, spitting bits of food everywhere. Three minutes later the German trench was vacated by the first wave of attackers, and the second wave was now making its way forward to occupy that trench. The shelling from the German artillery was still very heavy, and it was later estimated that out of the thirty thousand attacking troops, there were eight thousand who were either killed, injured or missing.

As the Battalion reformed itself, there in the distance, could be seen the smoking ruins of the village of Loos. To the left, already several hundred yards away, was the main body of the 15th Division, heading in the general direction of Hill 70, mopping up the Germans as they went. Kelly ordered the men to spread out and move forward, which they did cautiously. They had gone no more than a hundred yards when a machine gun, halfway between them and the village opened fire upon them.

"Take cover, men!" ordered Kelly, but too late for William Scott, known to his friends as Scotty. He was walking close to Matti, and Matti was just about to talk to him, when he witnessed what looked like a bolt of lightning going into the front of his friend's belly, and coming out of the back in a flame of blood and gore. It was as if everything was in slow motion for Matti; he stood there, watching Scotty, as a startled expression came across his face. His arms and legs both slowly came forward, and his back arched deeply. The rifle he had been carrying seemed to hang in the air, as the now bloodied, lifeless body of William noiselessly crumpled to the ground. This had all seemed so bizarre to Matti, taking several minutes, when in truth, it was over in a second. He knelt by his friend, and felt for a pulse, knowing that there would not be one. Silence ended, the reality of speed returned, and Matti could hear the zinging of bullets all around him, and the far off words:

"For Christ's sakes, Matti, get your bloody head down!"

Blood now flowing once again normally through his veins, he

charged for cover, and how the bullets missed him, God only knew.

"Riddle, where are you?" cried Kelly, with his face shoved into earth.

"Just behind you, Sarge," came a softer reply.

"Did you see where it came from?"

"Yes, Sarge."

"Do you think you can get it?"

"Yes, Sarge," he answered as he passed Kelly into long grass, with his gun already pointing in the right direction. The men were now returning rapid fire, having taken cover, in the general direction of the machine guns, and while this duel was going on, Matti, Enrico, and Jimmy kept creeping forward. Eventually, they were less than one hundred yards from the offending weapon, and Enrico indicated that they should traverse to the right, all the time looking for a good position to fire upon the gunners. With the hundreds of rounds that had poured both ways, you would have thought everybody on both sides would be dead, but luck had kept everybody from being hit. The machine gun stopped firing, while yet another belt was loaded into the gun, and the three of them noted precisely where the enemy were, thanks to a gush of steam that rose from the machine gun, when one of the Germans had emptied his water flask on to the weapon to try and cool it down.

"What do you think, Jimmy? Can you get him?"

*Bang!* Jimmy had been one jump ahead, and seeing an easy target, he seized his chance. The loader fell backwards, clutching at his throat, as the bullet tore through his windpipe. The other German looked totally surprised, and realising that he was about to die tried to surrender by putting his hands up. As he stood with his hands raised, there was a volley of fire from the rest of the men which took him apart. There had been another German there, and he ran in the direction of the village, zigzagging, but only managed about fifty feet before another shot from Jimmy brought him down with such a thump that he skidded along on his stomach for a good ten feet. Again the dwindling Battalion picked itself up, and moved in the direction of their goal.   There were many skirmishes before they reached the first dwelling place; some had been costly for the London Northern Rifle Brigade, all had been costly for the enemy.

The sun was just starting to go down, leaving great shadows from the attackers, but making them hard to be seen by their foe.  They must take this village; it should have been taken hours ago, but they could not stop before Fritz had vacated the premises.

"Fix bayonets! Gather round, men." Now very close to the first house, but out of sight of any enemy guns, Kelly told his men the rules of the new game:

"We are going to divide into four groups: the first two groups to take a house on either side, and as that attack goes on, the other two groups start on the next two houses, and so on, until every German has been eliminated.  Use Mills bombs, and when we go in, easier to use bayonets, or pistols if you've got them, but try not to have to use your rifle for shooting, as ricocheting bullets could be a bad thing for all of us."

Four groups were quickly formed, Kelly taking the first, Enrico and Matti the second, Harrington the third, and Riddle the fourth.  Pins were drawn, bombs thrown through the buildings' windows.  Screams of terror and pain could be heard, but not by the two groups who rushed in through the doors to finish what they had started, and so the process went on into the next houses.  Inside Enrico's house, they came upon two dead Germans, but could distinctly hear the sounds of feet moving across floorboards upstairs. Enrico was reluctant to send men up the stairs, as almost certainly a machine gun was set up, waiting for them, and the angle made it impossible to throw a grenade up.  So indicating silently, he gestured for the men to aim up at the ceiling.  A fusillade riddled the ceiling and the floor above, and after hundreds of 303 bullets were discharged, Enrico raised his arm for silence.  It was noted that blood had started to seep through some of these holes.  There was also a terrible creaking sound, which meant only one thing.

"Christ, men! Out of here, quick!"

None too soon, men spilled out of windows and doorways, just in time, as the whole floor above crashed down. Two bodies, machine guns, furniture, food and wine fell to the floor below. Matti, almost in tears with nervous laughter turned to Enrico and said: "Do you think we went for a touch of overkill there?"

The first four houses had been easy to take through the element of surprise, but from then on, the foe knew it was fighting for its very existence. Hand to hand combat took place in every building, and many of Enrico's friends and colleagues never made it through that night. But eventually, as the night wore on, the enemy wore out. Those who did not die within the buildings or the surrounding areas were finished off by members of the 15th Division, who were lying in wait for any fleeing foe.

Men sat around, with tired, dark, sunken eyes, some shaking with fear, others grinning with delight. They had taken their objective, albeit hours later than expected. Many had not slept now for nearly forty-eight hours, and fatigue took its toll on everybody. The dead were taken outside, and covered; the injuries were dressed as well as could be expected under the circumstances. Enrico and Matti were sitting in a room with their backs to the wall, Enrico with his hand held out again, thinking to himself: 'I'm getting through this with no real fear; I have no shakes, maybe I'm indestructible.' Matti was too busy to give any thought to anything, as with great danger to himself he had 'liberated' from the hands of the dastardly Hun a decent bottle of hock, some salami, and some pumpernickel, with which he was happily indulging himself. Sergeant Kelly appointed guards around the perimeter of the village, with a change every two hours. The rest of the night, apart from guard duty, the soldiers were allowed to get some well earned sleep. That was until the German Artillery decided it was time to give a wake up call.

*Boom, boom, boom, boom!*

Shells of all sizes started exploding all around the village, then in amongst the houses themselves. The effect was devastating to the defenders.

From deep sleep, to instant arousal. Enrico awoke with a start, still in the dream where he was home in bed with his Father reading a Polish story to him...Where was he? What were all those explosions? Then he remembered! Just before the wall fell in on him, there was a deafening crash, and his last thoughts were of Dad: 'What has happened to you? Do you know what has become of me? Do you love me or hate me, for the disgrace I have brought to the Lokowski family name?' Then blackness...

Shells rained in from all over the place. The panic that ensued was a spectacle to behold. Men not knowing what to do, or where to go, scurried from house to house. It was the strong voice of Sergeant Kelly that could be heard even above the roar and crashing of shell, bringing them to their senses.

"To cover, dig yourself into the ground. Don't stay in the buildings, if they go, you go too." Weary men scrambled into fox holes that the Germans had vacated, pressing themselves close to the walls or ground. Shells were exploding everywhere; other soldiers, from the 15th Division, were also taking cover around the area of Loos, as they too were taking a huge pounding. This was the time for men to pray, as each and every shell had somebody's number on it. The German Artillery must have been prepared for this, because the accuracy of the firing was startling. Men were being blown to pieces, and there was nothing that they could do to retaliate, just lie there and take what was coming. John Hutton and Barry Knight were digging like crazy in the hole that they had found.

'Must get deeper into this hole,' was their common thought. But as much dirt as they threw out, twice as much was being blown back in by the explosions.

Just on the south side of Loos is a little and very old churchyard with graves. Many of these graves had lain undisturbed for several centuries. Now they were being blown completely to heaven or hell. Sergeant Kelly had taken refuge in an old shell hole along with two Privates from the 15th, Corporal Harrington and a Major Turner, who was cowering and sobbing uncontrollably, crying out at the top of his voice, "No, not me, I am too young to die, not like this, please, Lord!" Over and over again, he was chanting this theme. Kelly looked at Harrington, and without a word being spoken between them, Harrington lifted the head of the Major, put his tin helmet on straight, then Kelly hit him full in the jaw with an uppercut that just put him out like a light. The two Privates looked at one another, then noticing that Kelly and Harrington where staring hard at them, turned away, having seen nothing.

Kelly turned again to the graveyard. "Look at that!" said Kelly to Harrington. "My God, was that a coffin going through the air?" Harrington replied in wonderment: "Look, another one!" Shells were thundering in on the graveyard. Personal safety became a secondary matter, with the fascination of seeing flying coffins and bones of long-dead people doing their dances through the sky. Even stranger was that it was a full moon, and every now and then a coffin would be silhouetted against the moon, giving a very spooky effect. All that the scene needed was the music of Wagner's 'Ride of the Valkyrie,' and they would have thought that this really was indeed judgement day. A shell exploded much nearer, bringing them back to their senses, and they put their heads once again close to the earth. Kelly was brought back to his paternal role once again when he saw the feet of a soldier run past, and heard the unmistakable babble of Matti Dumbridge. He was just tearing around, not knowing where to go or what to do, shells bursting all around, yet he didn't seem to be getting hit by fragments. "Dumbridge, you bloody fool. Get over here with us: you will be killed for sure. Get here now, that's an order!" Matti stopped in his tracks, wondering where the shouting came from. "Over here, you idiot!" Matti thankfully clambered into the hole with them, looked around and saw the Major lying flat on the ground, sleeping like a baby. "Don't ask," was all he got to his unspoken question.

"Where is Caruso?" Kelly asked him.

"Sergeant, I really haven't a clue. I went out of that building," pointing to a pile of rubble, "to have a dump, when this lot started. I think Enrico might still be trapped inside."

"Well if he is, he is done for!"

"No, Sarge, he will be all right, you'll see."

Daylight came, but no end to the bombardment. Men now realised that this was never a sudden revenge attack by the Hun, but an organised plan that had now been put into perfect operation. 'Clever bastards, those Jerries,' were the thoughts that came thick and fast, from the men that had time to think at all.

This incredible fusillade of very accurate heavy gun firing just was not giving up; it was coming down on the whole of the British lines, especially the areas the Germans had once occupied; it was if the Hun had allowed the Allies to take the trenches, just to give them a false sense of security, and then hit them with everything when their guard was down. Well, it had worked well, whatever the plan had been. The British lines were in total confusion.

Sergeant Kelly watched in horror, as a shrapnel shell burst above the dugout just a few yards away from his own. He knew that the occupants were three men from Harrington's section, and it was so very unlikely that any of them would have survived. In fact, the three men were Maurice Bechstein, Harold 'Harry' Gimson, and one Thomas 'Hill Billy' Hill. Harry Gimson never felt a thing: it was all over in the blink of an eye. Hot lead entered his head and shoulders killing him instantly. Hill Billy was more fortunate as he was just hit with lead in the left arm and through his right foot. This hurt like hell, but biting his wrist stopped him from completely folding up. Little Jew boy Beckstein was lying flat at the time of the explosion, and didn't even know that it was overhead, until Harry fell over him and warm blood started to soak through his clothing. Then he heard the muffled cries from Hill Billy, and knew that something very bad had taken place.

"What 'appened?" he asked Hill Billy, but there was no answer, as Thomas was desperately trying not to cry out loud, and he was also trying very hard to control his bowels, which felt as if they were going to burst at any moment. Anyway it was fast becoming obvious to Maurice exactly what had just occurred. Moving his friend Harry very gently off his own body, he tried to open his pack to get a dressing to aid Thomas. "Blimey, my pack is on fire!" Sure enough, smoke, then flames started to find their way out of the pack. Scrambling madly to open it, he realised there was among other things live ammunition in there, waiting to overheat and explode. "Ol' Je'ovah, 'elp me open this bleedin' bag. There's Mill bombs and ova nasty little buggers in there." After what seemed an eternity, but in fact was a second or two, he managed to open the bag. A flame was dancing about and he put his hand into it to find the explosives. 'Shit, shit, shit, that hurts,' he thought to himself, but succeeded in retrieving the bombs and bullets, and threw them into a safer area, where, if they went off, they would probably hurt no one. When he put out the small but nasty flames he managed to find the offending item that had started this problem. A jagged piece of metal, still quite hot from the explosion, was the culprit. It was a lucky chance that he had gone to his bag, for if the shrapnel shells had not killed them, the exploding Mills Bombs would certainly have finished the job. 'I'll keep that as a souvenir. It might be a lucky omen.' He managed to dress all of Hill Billy's wounds, who, as the pain increased, was falling in and out of consciousness. It was at this moment that he heard calling from the next dugout. "Anybody left alive in there?" It was the unmistakable voice of Sergeant Kelly, and for once it warmed the cockles of young Maurice Bechstein's heart. "Sarge! Me an' 'ill Billy is alright, poor ol' 'arry 'as bought it, I'm sorry to say!"

'Gimson, that's a shame, nice boy. Glad the other two are alright though,' thought Kelly, and then added. "Are you both unhurt?"

"I am, Sarge. But poor ol' 'ill Billy is in a poorish state: got it in the arm and through 'is foot. 'E's unconscious now, but I fink 'e'll be right as ninepence soon enough."

Yet another shell crashed earthwards with a loud roar, bringing the war very quickly back to any who might have forgotten about it. Matti was worried about his friend Enrico. 'Where are you, me old mate?' he was thinking. 'Stay alive! I'll come and get you, and that's a promise.'

Matti rummaged around in a pack that was lying on the floor of the dugout. He found what he wanted, and taking his bayonet out, he opened a can of Bully Beef. "How can you eat at a time like this?" asked Kelly, then as he looked at the open pack: "Who the fuck gave you permission to enter my pack?"

"Sorry, Sergeant, I really wasn't thinking, but eating is the only way I can keep calm. I didn't realise it was your pack. Do you want the rest of the tin?"

"No, I bloody don't, not after your grubby digits have been all over it. Didn't you say you had been to the bog for a dump? Did you wash the shit off them?" But he didn't wait for an answer, as another big blast occurred a few yards away. And even through this, Matti ate almost happily.

There was yet again a huge explosion, then many little spasmodic bangs followed; a shell had hit a mortar dump resulting in all the ammunition going off as it heated up. 'This was meant for the Germans, not us', thought Kelly.

There was a long groan coming from the bottom of Kelly's dugout. They had completely forgotten Major Turner who was now starting to come around.

"What happened to me?"

"I hit you Major, for which I am sorry, but you were losing it quite badly. Are you alright now?"

"You hit me, Sergeant? I don't remember that; no, I was knocked out by the concussion of an exploding shell. And to answer the other question, I am now fine. So what is the situation?"

"Sir, we are having the stuffing knocked out of us, and we cannot do anything to hit back."

"Have you sent runners back to HQ, telling them of the situation?"

"No, Sir, it's been a matter of staying alive."

"Well, it's time we got someone back there, and I mean now, Sergeant."

"I will call some men over; you can brief them, Sir."

"Are there any other surviving Officers around this sector?"

"Sir, to be honest I haven't a clue; I didn't even know you were here until we jumped into the dugout. Shall I get the men, Sir?"

Turner stroked his jaw and moved it from side to side. 'Christ, I must have acted like a complete coward and fool!' were his mortified thoughts.

Kelly turned to the two soldiers that were cowering inside the dugout with him.

"Names?" he barked.

"Andrews, Sarge,"

"Squibble, Sarge."

"Who? Oh, never mind! Right, listen to the Officer."

"Right, men, I want you both to make your way back up the valley, get to what was the German lines, cross over the old no-man's-land, and find General Merlin's HQ. Tell him what the situation is here, and ask him 'Are we to hold out or retreat if things get worse?' I will sign this piece of paper so that you can hand it to him, or his ADC; obviously we will expect you back within a few hours."

'That is so unrealistic, maybe my wallop really stirred his brain up?' thought Kelly.

The two men prepared themselves for the long run back to HQ. Both were sweating profusely from being more than a little terrified. Squibble turned to Andrews, smiled in an unconvincing manner, and said. "Ready, Ted? Then let's do this stupid thing." They were over the rim of the dugout before Major Turner could remonstrate about their insubordination. Kelly watched as they sped from shell hole to dugout, from dugout to rubble, and so on up the valley. Soon they were out of sight of Kelly and the others, but not the Germans. The Germans had spotters everywhere. They were also using the new radios that they had, to contact their own headquarters. Two were watching the runners gaining distance up the valley, a valley that was almost a complete grid system for the Artillery. All the spotters had to do was inform the guns where a target would be in a given moment. This they did, in the case of Squibble and Andrews. The first shell was all that was needed. It hit between the two, as they started their climb up towards the old German lines. The next fifteen shells were in the area of overkill.

As the two boys ran, panting and gasping, they knew their chances of making it were slim; they had zigzagged for some time, but fatigue had overtaken them, and panting and holding their aching sides, as they both had stitches, bending forward so as to get their breath back, they first heard the sound. At least Squibble did. He knew that whine when he heard it. He squeezed his eyes shut, and made two fists, knowing that this was going to be it for them both. The first shell hit just four feet away from them, slightly ahead. They didn't feel a thing. The next shells kept blowing bits of them skywards, up and down, up and down. Soon there was nothing to distinguish what human remains were, from good honest earth. But now it really didn't matter, at least as far as they were concerned.

The emphasis of firing moved from Loos to Hill 70. This was a lucky breather for Loos, and the surviving defenders had a chance to make good use of it. It was Matti, thinking of his friend, who asked the first question.

"Sir, can I look in the rubble there for my friend, Corporal Caruso?"

"Caruso, was he named after the famous tenor?"

Matti seized his chance.

"Yes, Sir, he was. Can I try and help him? I know he's not dead."

"Yes, please help yourself. We cannot let a good tenor go, can we?" joked the Major sarcastically. Matti leapt over the top of the dugout and charged over to the pile of rubble where Enrico was buried. He scrabbled desperately at the pile, and kept calling out: "Enrico, come on, Enrico, I know you are fine, shout back, you cretin!" No sound other than his own breathing could be heard. He pulled off more bricks, called again, listened, and then called again. After an hour had gone by, and the shelling had not returned to this sector, Matti had moved a large amount of bricks. He was starting to lose hope. Bechstein came over to assist, having helped to put aside the dead body of his friend, ready for burial; the medics had started to patch up Hill Billy, who once more had lost consciousness. "You fink 'e still alive?" asked Maurice.

"Don't talk, dig," came the sharp reply. So they both dug. It was not long before the attention of both Sergeant Kelly and Corporal Harrington settled on this scrambling duo.

"Enough is enough! He must be dead!" shouted Kelly over to the boys hard at work. Matti, for the first time, lost his temper with a superior.

"Instead of giving me grief, why don't both of you come and help?"

Harrington looked at Kelly. "Well, maybe we should." So they did. Thirty more minutes went by, when Matti, calling once again, heard what he thought was a moan. "I told you he'd be alive! You can't kill old Caruso that easily with a shell!"

Five minutes later, they had him out of there. He had been unconscious all through the bombardment: even when further shells fell amongst the existing rubble, he was out for the count. The wall had come down bringing a wardrobe with it. Enrico's good luck manifested itself in the fact that the doors of the wardrobe had been blown open, and therefore sheltered him from falling masonry. So there he was, snug as a bug in a rug, except, if Matti had not decided to look, he would have been buried there alive. As the house fell in on itself, Enrico was entombed. But his friend had always believed that he was indestructible, now here was the living proof.

Truly, the two boys thought they were now supermen.

But Enrico had not come out of this completely unscathed: his arm was broken, quite cleanly, but nevertheless broken. That would mean treatment when and if they got back to their own lines. A medic came up to help Enrico, but the pain made him become unconscious yet again.

"What a wimp!" laughed Maurice, and everyone joined in, more through nervous excitement than really finding his quip funny.

Distant guns began to roar; this time it was the British Artillery firing on the German lines, but more to the point, they had found the German big guns, and had zeroed in on them. This hopefully would give a well earned respite to the Allies in the defence of their gains. Wounded were gathered up, and medics were working overtime to stop blood flows, and ease pain. There was no chance of doing any operations as there were absolutely no facilities or equipment, since none had survived the bombardment. The wounded had to be got back past the old lines, to aid stations that were already set up and able to help. It became a matter of urgency; men were dying from wounds that could have been healed. The next major problem was that of the dead. There were hundreds of them scattered, literally all over the village and surrounding area.

"Sergeant, get burial details to start digging trenches for the use of graves. I need any information as to who has died, for the Battalion diary," said Major Turner, addressing Sergeant Kelly and four other NCOs who had come to the Major for their orders. "Call in all Officers around here for a meeting. We need a quick plan of action!"

"Yes, Sir, right away," was the instant reply. Soldiers were drifting into Loos from all over the area. This seemed to be the main gathering place; at least there was cover amongst the ruined buildings. Smoke was floating skyward from several fires that the shelling had produced. The scene was one of disorganised chaos, with very little purpose to any soldier's movements. But that had to change, and extremely quickly: the Hun didn't send out a calling card, he just came. Officers were ordering slit trenches to be dug, for the manning of machine gunners; these were placed all around the perimeter of the village. Men were posted far away, towards the enemy

174

lines; they were the first warning if an attack was to happen. Allied planes had been circling overhead, also assessing the situation, and there had been two serious dog-fights, which had caused the death of one German and his plane, and serious damage to another. At least Britain was winning the war in the air.

It was nightfall of the 28th, when the force guarding Loos was ready to receive the enemy, should they decide on a visit. This was also the moment to get the seriously wounded back to the old lines. Many medics and doctors had now managed to find their way to the besieged Loos, and were busying themselves trying to help all those that needed it. Some soldiers were past help, and they were gently put aside so that the doctors and medics could concentrate on those who had a realistic chance of survival. They had even managed to get some ambulances through the lines, and were now busily filling them for evacuation. The walking wounded were to make their own way back as best they could. That is what Enrico had to do, and he was happy to do it: for once he felt mortal: it was time to get out of this battle. His arm throbbed like hell, but his spirits were high, but so was his temperature and this gave some cause for alarm to the doctor who had packed his arm in a splint.

"Are you all right for this trek? It's a bit of a distance, and you really don't want to be caught in no-man's-land. If you wait a day or two, there might be transport for you." "Doctor, I appreciate what you are saying, but I can walk and it might take time, but I will get there, see if I don't!" What he hadn't told the doctor was that he didn't want to stay another minute there, so, bad as walking might be, it was infinitely better than staying and maybe being caught in another storm of steel. Enrico, after being freed from his tomb, had got Matti to find his rifle, which he now slung casually around his shoulder. A flask of water was given and some cans of food, most being apple jam and also the famous Bully Beef, not that there was any way of telling, as there were no labels left on the tins.

There was a steady procession of men and vehicles, going from

West to East, and vice versa; supplies were being brought in, wounded taken out. Occasionally, a German gun would make everybody duck into a fox hole, but for the time being, this was not considered a problem. Enrico and four others, who also had minor wounds, started the long hike back to the aid station. It was a slightly cold and damp night; the clouds were now obscuring the moon, and as the five of them trod wearily westwards, a certain relief fell upon them all. The general feeling was 'we may be in pain, but at least we are out of that!' There was constant traffic of lorries bringing in supplies of ammunition and food. Though where they would be stored, was surely going to be a problem, as most of the village was overlooked by the enemy.

The pain in Enrico's arm increased tenfold, when he stumbled over some rubble, and instinctively brought his arm out to save the fall. None of the walking wounded were faring well, as injuries were exacerbated by the lack of sleep and the tiredness induced by the long trek. They all knew that it would be safer to reach the aid station before dawn, as it had seemed to them and everybody else that the enemy was yet again gathering its thoughts, and preparing for the next onslaught. It was very late, almost twelve o'clock when they reached the old German lines; the devastation within these trenches, with the dead lying everywhere, was horrific to see, and the old, now familiar sweet smell of corruption was permeating the air. By now, Enrico was in the throes of a high fever, and each step was like walking through knee-deep treacle; though he was managing to put one foot in front of the other, he now lagged many yards behind the group.

"Can we stop? I need to drink some water, and I really must have a rest," said a shaky, slightly stuttering Enrico to the four men who were awaiting his presence on the rim of the captured trench. Reluctantly, the other four agreed to this request. Enrico sat down heavily, with his feet just dangling into the trench.

There was a flash and a glare of light that lit up the night sky from the German lines; the light kept dimming and brightening, and about five seconds after the first brilliant flash, came the rumble of the explosions, followed by the shock wave which, though not powerful, rippled past like a sudden breeze.

"Crikey, that must be a German ammunition dump going up! I certainly would not like to be around that at the moment!" but Enrico could barely glance up. He took a long gulp of water; this helped, and brought a little life back into that sunken, ashen face.

"Listen, could one of you open one of these cans for me? I'm not hungry, but I feel I ought to eat something, just to keep me going."

One of the men, having two hands that were quite capable of succeeding in this task, took a can and opened it with the use of a bayonet. It was a can of pears. Slurping the sugary syrup, and pulling a pear out with his remaining hand, he felt his spirits begin to rise.

"Right, come on! We don't want to stop here all night. The ghosts of these dead Germans," he said laughingly, "won't be happy to see us here!"

The night sky was still ablaze, though now much dimmer, and the rumble of exploding armaments could be distinctly heard even above the roar of the big guns, when the wind changed its course. Intermittent shelling from both sides was still having a very lethal effect. The five of them crossed over the trench, stumbling heavily on the corpses that lay everywhere. None of the five was startled, as disturbed rats scurried from their interrupted dinner. How quickly this had been taken as part of the norm! They were only one mile from their jumping off positions, but to Enrico, it could have been a thousand. As they walked across the old no-man's-land, cursing as they tripped over debris, human remains, and general detritus, the mile turned out to be several miles, as they had to zigzag their way around barbed wire and shell holes. By the half way point, Enrico had fallen back by several hundred yards, and was in a bit of a desperate situation. It had obviously become every man for himself and the other four were just thinking of their own salvation. Finally, Enrico could take no more, and sank in despair into a small, but dry shell hole. He then lost consciousness.

*Boom…boom…boom. Rat-t-t-t-t-t-t.* The noise brought life back into a now warming Enrico. The sun had risen, and was extremely bright, directing its full brilliance onto Enrico's face. His unconsciousness had given his body time to completely relax, and now he was feeling almost wholly *compos mentis*.

'What is that booming noise?' he wondered, and the more the bangs and booming went on, the more he came back to reality. He managed to turn himself over onto his knees, and peered over the rim of the crater. The Germans had started their bombardment again, and this time, it was concentrated on their old trench line. Their shells were doing much more damage to the trench than the Allied shells had managed in a week of shelling. Men were yet again being slaughtered in their hundreds. Enrico lay there, in dumb fascination, as shells would hit directly into the trench, lifting enemy and Allied bodies alike high into the air. To Enrico, this was without doubt, 'Dante's Inferno', and though it sickened him to the core, he was unable to take his eyes off this horrific spectacle. He even realised that he could see, on occasions, the same bodies losing parts, being blown to Kingdom come.

It was not long before he surmised that this was developing into a creeping barrage, and he had better get out of there, somehow. With great difficulty, and now using his own rifle as a walking stick, he trudged yet again towards the safety of his own lines. He had managed no more than one hundred yards when he stumbled yet again, but in this case for the last time. He was still unconscious when he was found, in the late afternoon, by two stretcher bearers, and was finally taken to the safety of the aid station.

# VI

The ambulance taking Enrico to the hospital in Hazebrouch had a perilous journey, trying to dodge the various shell holes and avoiding the convoys of armament snaking to the front; he was quickly seen by a doctor and was deemed unlikely to live. He was then placed in a ward which was known as the "Ward of no Return". Generally those who entered only came out in a box. Enrico had an extremely high fever, and the doctors thought that this had created an infection within his broken and very swollen arm. He did not regain consciousness for a week, with the fever going up and down, really confusing the medical staff. A well-meaning but very young doctor suggested that it might help his condition if the arm was amputated, but the general consensus of opinion was to wait and see.

Fortunately, on that seventh day of hospitalisation Enrico became aware of his surroundings. A VAD nurse was the first to realise it, when he mumbled a request for water, and something to eat. As he had lasted so long in the dying ward, there had been a book running as to the time and day of his death; all the medical staff had become immensely fascinated to see how long it would be before he gave up the ghost. Ten centimes was bet by most doctors and nurses, the nearest to the time of death would get all the money, which worked out to be nearly ten francs. As nobody bet on him recovering, it was unanimously decided that the money be awarded to Enrico, much to his amazement! But this bet had probably saved his life, as it had kept the entire hospital on their toes fussing and caring about him, probably more than they normally would have. After recovering from his deep coma, he started the process of healing within himself. He realised that the more he applied himself, the quicker he would recover. Like most people, Enrico had a natural fear of hospitals and doctors. His arm started to knit well thanks to the improved nourishment he received, and he was told at this rate he would be back with the Battalion within a few weeks. 'But while you're here, enjoy the moments that you have; you will soon be able to fire that gun again, and then it's back to the war.' This was the thought that passed through his brain, making him shudder to the bone. He need not have worried quite so much, as the doctor in charge was a Belgian civilian who only sent soldiers back to their Battalions when he thought they were fit enough, or when a military doctor overruled him, which did happen from time to time. But in Enrico's case, it was not so much the broken arm, for that would mend, it was the fever, which had been extremely serious, and they knew he would be weak, and weak bodies tend to have recurring problems. "Let us make sure he is truly over the worst of his problem!" was what the doctor had written on Enrico's chart, and he only had to look at that to reassure himself, but Enrico being Enrico, never thought of doing anything quite so easy.

'But what of Matti?' thought Enrico, 'He saved my life by digging me out, I must find out something about the battle? Whether he is alive or dead, whether any of the section is still alive?'

Enrico asked around the new ward that he had been placed into, having survived the "Ward of no Return"; he approached wounded men in their beds that might have fought on that front, asking if they had any news. None had heard of Sergeant Kelly nor Corporal Harrington, but most of all, nobody had any news to tell of his dear friend Matti Dumbridge. So many men, so many battles, such a huge army, how could anyone keep in touch with anyone else?

Enrico had been very lucky: many problems could have befallen him, and instead he was fortunate enough to get transferred directly to a civilian hospital. It could have been far worse. Often wounded men just lay in no-man's-land for days, either dying of what could have been cured, or waiting so long that whatever injury had befallen them became far worse. He might have been taken to a field dressing station, which might have assessed his wounds as being trivial, dressed them and just sent him for recovery still within the Battalion which, with his extreme fever, would probably have proved fatal within a short time. He might have been fortunate, and been sent from the field dressing station to a half way hospital; there he would have had better treatment, but still might have been sent back too early, as the urgent need for beds was just enormous. But, had he survived that experience, he might have been sent back to a hospital far behind the lines or even back home to England. Had that happened, it might have taken days, which maybe he did not have, because of the infection. So, all in all, Enrico had been extremely lucky, getting to the main hospital in Hazebrouch, guaranteed the best treatment with time to make a complete recovery, not just within his body, but within his dazed mind as well.

Doctors, nurses and orderlies worked very long hours, especially at the front in the field dressing stations. No one could ever have predicted the amount of slaughter that went on during a battle, so much so, that field dressing stations were completely overwhelmed with the casualties that came in during the carnage. The soldiers that were not expected to live were just left outside. The wounded that could walk were generally left outside too until at last there was space for them, by which time their wounds had often become seriously infected through the various germs that were in their clothing, on the ground, everywhere! Doctors frequently worked a straight forty-eight hours, sometimes falling asleep over a patient, much to the detriment of that sorry soul. The filth and squalor were everywhere to be seen, and if you got a serious wound, you prayed to be sent either to a civilian hospital or a long way back behind the lines. Soldiers prayed to their gods for the Blighty one. This was a wound that was not too serious, but would get them out of the battle and back to England, either for recuperation, or out of the army altogether. Losing an arm or a leg often seemed an acceptable alternative to fighting in the battle, where death was probably the only other option. Frequently doctors and nurses became callous towards their charges, as there were so many. Who would miss a few here and there if they didn't quite do their best? But on the whole, the medical teams were wonderful, good, well-meaning members of the human race that believed emphatically in the code of ethics they had sworn to, the Hippocratic Oath.

The battle for Loos, which was known as the battle for Artois and Champagne was an almost complete disaster. The foe knew from the Allied build-up, months before the attack that something was afoot, and prepared accordingly. The German Artillery had better guns and more ammunition. The Infantry were numerous and well prepared. The counter-attacks when they came, were brutal and decisive, which meant that gains that had initially been made by Allied soldiers, were either lost, back to the start or cost very dearly for the little ground that had been won. The village of Loos was no exception: the German infantry swarmed in, pushing the armies there almost back to square one. A great deal of hand-to-hand fighting went on, causing terrible casualties, wounds that would never heal, both in body and mind. The cost in human life was enormous. Out of living hell came nothing, just more pitiless misery for the fighting man. During the battle, which officially started on the 25th September and was finally called off on the 8th October 1915, more than forty three thousand Allied men had become casualties, whereas there was only twenty thousand German dead and wounded. This was such a catastrophe that it forced the resignation of the Commander of the British forces General Sir John French. General Haig took his place.

It was perhaps a fortunate day, when on the 5th October orders came from HQ, that the remaining London Northern Rifle Brigade should fall back to the rear for a well earned rest. The surviving remnants of the 21st Division replaced the evacuated men and held the ground well, until finally being forced to retreat back to the original lines on the 7th and 8th of October. The battle had been a mistake from the start. Haig understood the potential danger of a killing field in which the German army was in a better position to win the day. If only General French had said "No" to Joffre, many men might have been spared, at least until the next battle was planned!

Even Generals were not spared in the battle. One Major-General Capper, who became so frustrated at seeing his men dithering, not really trying hard enough to advance to their deaths, rushed onto the field of conflict to urge the men forward, and was almost immediately cut down with machine gun fire: he was dead before he hit the ground. Many other high-ranking officers also died trying to rally their men.

One of the saddest stories to come from the Battle of Loos is that of John Kipling, twenty year old son of Rudyard Kipling. He had been encouraged to join the army, and at first had been turned down on medical grounds as he was considered too slight and weak. But with the connections that his father had, he was given the chance to join the Irish Guards as a Lieutenant. This was his first battle, and only his first hour into it, when he was hit in the head by a bullet from the enemy, and died shortly after. Rudyard, who had always been a great patriot, believing emphatically in the right of the British cause, was devastated; he spent the rest of his life trying to find his son's body, but never did. Rudyard became so bitter that he wrote a great deal of anti-war papers, blaming the officer class and the government, for the death of a generation of youth.

At last the decimated ranks of the London Northern Rifles Brigade were safe behind the lines. They had been taken back to Hazebrouch, with a view to sending them once again up to attack, after a few days' rest and recuperation. But on the 8th October the attack was officially called off, which meant that the Brigade had an extended leave of rest.

It was Sergeant Kelly who first made inroads as to where Enrico might be, and on enquiring at the HQ, was told that he was in the civilian hospital right there in town. There were several members of his section of the Battalion that had found their way to hospitals all around the area, and he felt it his personal duty to track them down, to find out how they were, and when and if they would be coming back to the home of the Battalion. There were also several other deaths from Enrico's section. Barry Knight had just vanished when a shell exploded not more than two feet away from him; the only thing that anyone found afterwards was his left boot, without a foot in it. John Hutton had his arm blown off, at least nearly off; it hung there on his shoulder by the merest of threads of sinew; he screamed a great deal, while trying to fix it back on with his other arm. By the time he was found by medics he had died from blood loss. He was buried in the shell hole where he fell, after another shell landed nearby, throwing enough earth to completely engulf him, with his dangling arm tucked into his trouser belt. Corporal Harrington had been hit by a ricocheting bullet, just behind his left ear; it was not serious, except that it had left him with the worst tinnitus he had ever known. The buzzing in his head was so loud it became hard for him to concentrate on anything that was being said. He had his head bandaged, was given his rifle back and was told, "Go shoot The Hun!... *I said! Go shoot The Hun!* Are you deaf, man?" at this, the annoyed doctor moved away to treat the next patient.

Sergeant Kelly thought it was time to see how Corporal Caruso was doing in the nearby hospital. "Corporal Harrington, Ted, what say we amble over to the local infirmary and get that slacker Caruso out, maybe for a drink?"

"Eh... Drinks, good idea!" answered Harrington as he cupped his hand over his ear in an effort to lower the pitch of the buzzing.

It was not hard to find Enrico, wandering around the ward, dressed in a now clean army uniform, with one arm plastered and bandaged in a crooked position, and the other arm just picking up a bed pan that was slopping with urine and excreta from a bedridden soldier.

"Corporal Caruso!" bellowed Kelly. Enrico started with a jerk, making some of the urine slop back onto the soldier who had just given it.

"Oh, Corp! Mind what you're doing!"

But Enrico's mind was now struck firmly with the prospect of seeing two familiar faces.

"Sergeant Kelly, Corporal Harrington, am I glad to see you! I haven't found out anything since being here. You can fill me in with the latest news."

"I am not filling you with anything while you are carrying that! Get rid of it, and the three of us are off to the local estaminet for a jug or two of beer."

Enrico had never seen this side of Kelly before. 'The man is human after all,' he thought. Having cleaned the bed pan, he felt free to join his peer group for that well earned drink.

The beer was warm, but who cared? The bread was stale, but who cared? The eggs that had been promised *were* hard boiled, and ever so slightly addled, but who cared? The only thought that came to Enrico's mind was how nice it was to be on the outside again, free from well-meaning doctors, bossy nurses, and henpecked orderlies. It seemed to Enrico as if he was no longer a recruit but now a veteran, and an accepted member of the NCOs.

"Tell me, Sergeant Kelly," said Enrico, as he spilt yet more of his beer, trying to drink and talk at the same time, "how is Matti?"

"Dumbridge is doing fine. He's had a lot of scares in the last couple of weeks, and I shall certainly mention in my report how he dug tirelessly in the rubble to get to you, being the only one who really believed you would still be alive. In fact, I expect Colonel McBride will make him either a Lance Corporal or a full Corporal, for he has earned that right."

They told Enrico all about the battle, and what a disaster it had become. Kelly said that it was time for them to go, but asked in passing "how long before you get the plaster off, and come back to us?"

To which Enrico replied: "Not sure, Sergeant, but it can't be soon enough for me!"

Time passed quickly, now that Enrico had rediscovered his friends. Matti had visited him on several occasions, and on one of those occasions, when taking off his great coat, proudly produced two stripes on his tunic. Corporal Harrington had become Sergeant Harrington, and Sergeant Kelly had become Regimental Sergeant Major (RSM) Kelly. The ranks of LNRB were filling once again with new recruits being sent from London.

Raw recruits, new faces, young soldiers who stood in awe of the veterans around them. On the 15th October the Battalion, once again left the haven of Hazebrouch, back to man the old trench system in Wipers, and along with them, went a thinner, and possibly more careful Enrico Caruso, with his arm now out of the plaster, but still crooked in a sling, doing light duties, mainly within the Battalion's new headquarters, just a few hundred yards in an underground bunker, east of the Lille gate. The sight that greeted all the old group when they reached Ypres was of an even greater devastation than they remembered: there was hardly a roof to be seen anywhere, and in most areas, a tall man standing could see every-where. Enrico turned to Matti:

"This is soon to be the biggest building site anywhere in Europe!" A nod of agreement came back.

How quickly things went back to their normal agenda! Two days in front line trenches, two days in the reserve trenches, usually doing extreme hard labour, carrying yet more mortar bombs, more barbed wire, more ammunition, A frames for the new trench systems always being built, and the interminable duckboard; along with that would be the never-ending kit inspections, and general fatigues, and maybe if you were lucky two days in Poperinge with a certain amount of freedom to do as one wanted, but often as not, the rest days would be cancelled to do yet more hard labour and more front line trench duties. Periscopes were constantly being looked through, checking for any new enemy movement.

Any place that could be used to spy out the enemy's territory was used: there was even a tree trunk that stood splintered twelve feet above the forward trench near Hellfire Corner. This had been carefully measured and drawn, and a hollow iron replica was made, and brought to the spot through the trenches, and on one dark, moonless night, the old stump was taken and replaced by the metal lookout. This was manned twenty-four hours a day by lookouts that had a panoramic view over enemy terrain. Sadly for one Second Lieutenant who was doing his tour of duty, when a German bullet actually hit the replica tree, instead of there being a thud as would be expected, there was an echoing clannng, which alerted the Hun to the delusion. The next ten minutes were spent by the Germans turning the whole thing into a colander, much to the chagrin of the Lieutenant inside.

But the English Tommy was a resilient soul; though he expected hardships, moments of humour abounded everywhere, and the adaptable troops learnt very quickly to make the best of everything. It was just before Christmas of 1915 when a German shell crashed into the ramparts, a few yards away from the Menin Gate, exposing a hidden doorway into the ramparts themselves. Soldiers quick to seize upon a chance to find secret treasures stumbled into this concealed cellar to find a civilian printing press, with huge amounts of ink and paper. With the help of willing colleagues from the Sherwood Foresters they began the weekly issue of 'The Wipers Times'. This became a prized and treasured read to all on the salient, and somehow managed to get distributed even out to the exposed positions in no-man's-land. This paper comprised poetry, stories, titbits of things you needed to know, and gossip, but everything was presented in a light-hearted, humorous fashion. A typical poem with no title, and no known author was much appreciated:

> *If I were king! Ah! Bill, if I were king,*
> *I wouldn't touch an 'A' frame or a thing,*
> *I'd watch the sergeant split his blooming thumb*
> *And, when he wasn't looking, drink his rum,*
> *I'd make the corpr'l rations to me bring,*
> *If I were king! Ah! Bill, if I were king.*

Another poem ran thus:

*What matter, though the wily Hun*
*With bomb, and gas and many a gun*
*In futile fury, lashes out,*
*Don't wonder what it's all about -'stick it'*

*When soaked in mud, half dead with cold,*
*You curse that you are a soldier bold;*
*Don't heave your 'A' frame through the night*
*And, though it's wanted, travel light -'stick it'.*

The puns and jokes which were often in riddle form were in many ways the best tonic that came to the soldiers.

Christmas Day presented itself, cold, wet and gloomy. Not the truce of 1914; the powers that be made sure that mortars and guns kept firing over the entire festive season. Men were told: should any German present himself with a view to an armistice, "shoot him!" There was to be no fraternisation with the possibility of extreme grave consequences to any soldier caught disobeying this order.

Matti and Enrico had finally been given two days' leave in Poperinge, and were staying in Talbot house. There had been a beautiful carol concert, attended by one and all, with Tubby Clayton leading the almost celestial choir while playing the out of tune harmonium. This had done two things to the chums: for the first time, in both their short lives they had sat through a long service, and sung out as loud as they could to every carol, with Matti getting bolder with each chorus that went, and Enrico singing his normal flat, out of tune mono sound. But they loved it. The second feeling was that it brought back tremendous homesickness, and for Enrico, this was for sure the first time he experienced these feelings since leaving his father to go to Collingbrook mine.

"Matti, I've been thinking about my father lately. Although I said we should never contact our families, if it's alright with you, I'll write a letter home to see how he is and telling him the news."

This was readily agreed, as Matti too, wished to make contact with his beloved parents. That night, they both spent an hour writing very carefully about their exploits, but not admitting to any of the events that had brought them to this state. In a very relaxed mood, the lads fell into a deep dreamless sleep, and did not wake until after eight in the morning. This had been a rest much needed. Boxing Day arrived with a great, windy chill in the air; though there had been no snow, a thick frost had developed overnight, making all the ground hard enough, even for loaded lorries to pass over, and not get bogged down. The problem now of course, was that the solid rubber tyres slipped badly on the frozen earth. The duo had decided that this being their last day of comparative freedom, they would take a tour of the estaminets, and see if they could find the prettiest Eugénie look-alike. As they turned off the main square at Poperinge and were making their way to one of their favourite watering holes, they were both brought to a sudden stop by a car that was parked outside it. This car had already collected a group of admiring people; it was the Rolls-Royce that belonged to John Norton Griffiths, also known as 'Empire Jack'.

"Maybe this is our chance, Enrico!" said Matti. "It's like providence. This could be the occasion we've been waiting for!"

"Well, it won't do any harm to go in, have a drink, and if we get an opportunity, talk to him."

The place was steaming from the sweaty bodies, drunken rowdiness, and smoke from the ubiquitous 'Woodbine' and 'Navy Cut' cigarettes. There, in a corner table, surrounded by other officers, sat Major John Norton Griffiths, who was holding court, relating a dirty joke to the bemused crowd gathering around. Matti and Enrico closed in, just in time to hear the long drawn-out story:

"Beau Geste, having distinguished himself in the French Foreign legion was given an easier assignment. It was to a fort that was being held right on the edge of the Sahara desert. The Colonel-in-Chief stood and welcomed Beau, saying "well, Lieutenant, you will enjoy this posting; we have one of Paris' finest chefs; we have the best food that money could buy; we have a cellar of the finest vintages that France could supply, we have sport facilities that are unequalled anywhere, and there are no enemy Bédouins within two hundred miles. This is the safest and best posting that any legionnaire could get, but, mon ami, there is but one problem: there are no women at all within the fort. If the needs become desperate, then see Sergeant Chapuis, and he will tell you what exactly you must do." For several months, Beau Geste dined on the pâté de foie gras, caviar, and the best food and wine that France could supply. He enjoyed numerous sporting events, and had become extremely fit, but eventually, his other needs became urgently apparent, so he decided to seek Sergeant Chapuis "*Cough-cough*-er… Sergeant, the Colonel informed me some time ago that you were the man to see, should I be in need of female company."

"Yes, Sir, that is right. If you go into that shed over there, you will see the camel that'll do the trick."

So Beau Geste strolled, more than a little embarrassed, into the shed to find this female camel, with a ladder next to it. So he put the ladder to the rear end of the camel, and on dropping his trousers, climbed the ladder and proceeded to satisfy his lust. When he was finished he went outside again, and confronted Sergeant Chapuis "*Cough-cough*-well, Sergeant, that was not quite what I had in mind, but it certainly did the trick."

"Well, that's as maybe, Sir, but generally my officers use the camel to take them into town!"

To this the whole of the estaminet erupted with laughter. The pals had their beers, and waited quietly at a table close by for their chance to approach Empire Jack. After what seemed an age, Major Griffiths was left silently drinking his Chablis, and musing about his family left back in London, wondering when he would see his lovely wife Gwladys again.

Enrico nudged Matti, and they arose to approach his table. They stood there at attention, not daring to utter a sound. Major Griffiths was still in a dream, looking straight through them, sipping at his wine, but eventually he became aware of the two young NCOs, standing erect, blocking the view of his dream.

"Well, what do you both want?" he almost barked at them.

Enrico took the lead, as usual:

"Sorry to disturb you, Sir, but I am Corporal Caruso, and this is Corporal Dumbridge, and we were wondering if you still needed miners."

"We always need miners, Corporal. Are you miners?"

"Yes, Sir. We both worked in Collingbrook mine, and we were both face workers. There's nothing about mining that we don't know, Sir."

"Ah, Lord Collingbrook! I have not seen that old miser for many a long year!" he said, and then looked at their insignia, "so you are both with the LNRB? Why do you want to join the mining division?"

"Sir, we've been told that we can earn six bob a day."

"Only the front line clay kickers earn that."

"That's us, Sir, front line clay kickers," said Matti, not having a clue what a clay kicker was.

"Right, lads. I could use more men. Write your names and serial numbers on this piece of paper, and I will get you transferred, just as soon as I can."

Both the lads saluted Major Griffiths, but he was already deep in thought, inspecting the contents of his half filled glass.

The next day there was a tremendous barrage, and it seemed to the lads that it was the Germans firing into Wipers, and on the day that they must report back, too! 'It never rains but it pours,' thought Enrico, 'Why couldn't we have a quiet time until we are transferred?' Sure enough, the enemy was giving a general blast of the big guns all over the place. Not just the front line trenches, but also on the Menin Road, which was very unfortunate as at that time, unknown to the Germans, there was a column of troops working their way out towards the trenches at Sanctuary Wood.

The Pioneer Corps had long ago raised a curtain along the Menin Road to hide who or whatever went along it, as it was the main route for most trench systems, and it could clearly be seen from almost all the German lines. The curtain gave a little cover from view, but just by chance the shells started to enfilade, catching all the troops and their horses before they could get to cover. There was a terrible slaughter, and very little that could be done to help. Men and animals lay everywhere: death had yet again struck with unlucky or lucky consequences, depending on which side you happened to be on. Shells fell on all fronts from the enemy guns. So the British trench mortars opened up with their own bombardment. One mortar bomb landed directly inside a Hun dugout, killing all inside and making the roof fall in on itself. This dugout had been used by German Officers, and had always been quite safe from fire, but someone forgot to close the door as the bombs rained down, and it took only one direct hit to knock the whole shelter completely out. The rats dined well that night! Some of the enemy shells were now even starting to land on the road to Poperinge; this was going to be a tough hike back to camp. They were supposed to be back at HQ by twelve that morning, but running the gauntlet of shells made them careful, so it was nearly four in the afternoon when they both scrambled through the dugout doors.

"Where the hell have you two been? I could put you both on a charge for this. We thought of sending out search parties for you. What happened?" came the distinctly frosty challenge from Adjutant Major Tyler-Latham, as he signed some paperwork and generally shuffled the papers about. He glared at them with squinting eyes, and an almost curled upper lip.

"Sir, the shelling was serious all the way back; we had to duck and dive on several occasions," said Enrico, as he stood to attention looking directly ahead, not catching the Adjutant's eyes.

"You should have come back last night. There is no excuse!"

"We are very sorry, Sir, it will not happen again."

"It's lucky for you two that I have a special job for you both, or it might have meant a court martial!"

"Yes, Sir!" The pals looked at each other in a worried fashion. 'Not over no-man's-land, not again!' thought Matti and Enrico together.

"The Colonel wants you to get some prisoners; take as many men as you might need. We need to know what is shaking their tails now. Are they planning an offensive, now, or in the near future? And this time let it be proper soldiers, try and bring back a live Officer, not the cook! And another thing, on the way back, I want you to capture the machine gunner on the far left of our section; if you come and look on this map you can see just where I mean. He has been a huge worry these last few days, inflicting several casualties. We have tried shelling him with mortars and bigger ordinance, but to no avail: it is a concrete bunker, and there might well be quite a few in there, but I want to finish it off, once and for all. Do I make myself clear? The whole bunker has to go. I don't care how you do it, but I would prefer it to be quick! We will supply you with high explosives, so if you get the chance, blow it all sky high. Now you know what we want, go get ready, pick your men and report for a final briefing to RSM Kelly. Now get the hell out of here before I change my mind and send you two back for punishment!"

The two chums left the dugout in a much shaken state. "They must either hate the living daylights out of us, or they are completely mad! Either way, I don't like this operation at all!" said Matti, with Enrico nodding in agreement, but thinking furiously about how this task was to be done.

"Nice to see you are both back in the land of the living; what happened to you? We wondered if you had gone AWOL, and I would have to get the firing squad all excited about having to boom, boom you both," said Kelly with a smile on his face, and making the gesture of a pointed rifle. "Anyway, I'm glad to see you both."

"Thanks, good to be still alive. The road here was getting more than a little pasting from our friends from up the hill there," said Enrico, pointing in the general direction of the German army. "Please tell me this madness is just a sorry joke?" pleaded Enrico, with Matti looking on very dejectedly.

"No such luck, it seems important that they get information, and it is also true that the bunker in question is doing a lot of harm to us; it needs to be got rid of. My gut feeling is that you take only two with you, but that is up to your own judgement. Don't go to their lines, go direct to the bunker. With some luck there might be just what you need in there. Maybe there will be several people, get all the buggers. Bring back any information that you can, any papers, anything. Then why not leave your own calling card there. Wire the entire place with booby traps, you might be lucky and catch a few of them." RSM Kelly blew his nose on a disgustingly filthy hanky, making both the lads looking on feel quite nauseous. 'Funny, I can look at dead bodies, guts hanging out, skulls and bones lying everywhere, but somebody blows their nose and I want to throw up!' thought Enrico.

"Alright, we will do it," said Enrico, not that he had a choice. "I'll need the four of us to carry back packs full of high explosives and fuses. I'll need for each of us to be given pistols instead of our rifles; they are far too clumsy to carry with packs as well. I want rope to tie prisoners, and plenty of food, decent food, not tinned apples or beef hash rubbish. Can you help us with what I want?"

"I guess so; give me an hour, you will have the lot. What about a sack of Mills bombs as well, just in case, and good Sheffield steel?" There was a nod of agreement from both the pals. "Pick who you want and get back here for seven o'clock tonight. It will be pitch dark, as there is no moon, and anyway, look at those dark rain clouds coming over. Spend the time you have, working out your route and who to take, and how things are to be done! Well, don't let me hold you up...Scram!" then in passing, "when you all get back, the drinks are on me, promise."

"Why, thank you, RSM Kelly," said Enrico with a half bow and a wink of his eye. "We will hold you to that. Must be a first?"

Enrico found a brew being made by a soldier he had never seen before. 'New recruit, hundreds of them, I don't know anybody anymore,' he thought, as he sat on the fire step drinking the strong hot tea. Condensed milk was offered and readily accepted, "at least it will sweeten this awful concoction," he commented to Matti. "So, how are we going to take this bunker?" he said to nobody in particular. "I guess we should see if Jimmy Riddle will come with us, and maybe Whitey Boy, and maybe the little Jew? What do you think Matti?"

"Well, I think they are a good choice, we need three to help carry the load. How are we going to find this bunker? Do you know where it is?"

"Not a clue, but we will do our best, and if we cannot find it, well that's just bad luck. Find Harrington and see if he is using the three Musketeers; if not they are ours, whether they want to be or not."

The shelling had now gone back to its normal steady thump, thump. Concentrating more on the British front line trenches, after the firework display that had caught everyone so much by surprise, this was a strange twist. It was certainly not playing the game to break the norm. A gentleman could easily tell that the Hun had never learnt to play cricket. Since the beginning of trench war, a pattern had formed, showing a certain humanity between foes: in one sector of the trench system, there was a tacit agreement that a well would be shared and while in use, no soldier was fired upon by either side; in the case of the well, the British used it from twelve at night to twelve in the morning, and then in the afternoon, the Germans had access to it. In the case of shelling, it had become the norm that no big guns, mortars, machine guns or rifles, would be fired between the hours of seven to eight thirty in the morning, thus giving each soldier a time to wash, shave and eat breakfast. After all, we would not want anyone to be shot while still having sleep in their eyes and an empty stomach, or yesterday's beard still growing! When it is your time to die, you must be presentable, at least to your maker.

Enrico and Matti scurried around collecting the three friends who where going to accompany them on this little jaunt. There was not much to tell, except what the objectives were. The plan was: find the bunker, kill the occupants, except maybe one to bring back, booby trap it for the future tenants, and then get the hell back to friendly lines. Enrico thought it might take as long as three days to manage this task; after all, it must be at least half a mile to where he thought the bunker might be.

"Get some rest, sleep until we go over the top tonight. It might be the last sleep for some time!" Enrico sat and thought about everything, 'the letter home, it should be there by now. Will I get an answer, how long will it take to come? I really hope the Police haven't read it, they may well be after me. What can they do while I am fighting in the army? They can hardly send some police over to arrest me, can they?' These and many other thoughts swam past him, until fatigue overcame every other consideration and he fell asleep.

*Rat, tat, tat, tat!* Machine-gun fire awoke them all; it was quite nearby. Enrico yawned, stretched his arms, got to his feet, scratched his crotch, and decided it was now time to get everyone ready for the off. "It must have been an extremely quiet day. I seem to have slept through everything. How are you, Matti?"

"I'm fine. It has been quiet with the guns. I really don't know what is in the Germans' minds, what was all the shelling for? Do you think they had a General inspecting their trenches, and so they had to put on a show? By the way, you snored loud enough to wake anyone, that I promise you." They both grinned at the thought of Enrico's snoring outdoing the foe's guns.

"Is everybody ready for this excursion?" he said, looking towards the other three lads who had volunteered to a man, without even knowing it! Enrico looked at his watch, three thirty-four, and it was already getting dark. 'What am I doing here? I should be at home still with Dad, helping to finish the remains of Christmas food. All I have eaten this bloody year was some cold chicken at Talbot House, and that seems like years ago now,' he thought to himself. He realised that he must get out of this mood, as he knew that the other four would depend on his strength above all else.

"Right, lads, let's get to Spider for the final briefing and our packs. We can grab a bite to eat, have a drink, maybe even a little rum: that would be nice." That thought made him smack his lips together. "Then it's off we go; where we land, nobody knows?" 'What a poet I am!' he marvelled, and then smiled broadly which made everyone catch the mood.

Kelly was in his dugout, eating some bread while reading some paperwork. He had grown fond of Enrico and Matti, though he could not show it outwardly. So, as he smiled at their appearance at the dugout door, he barked, "Where have you all been, there was work to do!"

"We are ready for going over the top. Have you got the map for me, pinpointing exactly where we are going?" Enrico asked, knowing darn well that of course he had the map.

"There are five of you; I understood it was just going to be four? What changed your mind?"

"I thought that maybe we could spread the load easier with five," to this Kelly nodded in agreement, "and I really think this could take maybe two or even three days, so we must take more food and water."

All was agreed. More food and water appeared. Five packs of explosives were handed around, pistols holstered, ammunition stowed.

"Sir, any chance that the men could have a wee drop of the hard stuff, before we go?"

"I didn't hear that, Corporal, and anyway, there is only that bottle of Scotch on the table there, and I wouldn't want it finished while I go for a piddle!" At this, Kelly rose and left the dugout. The five of them made good use of their time while he was out. Feeling slightly light-headed, and indubitably warmer, the five made peace with their Gods, asked the CO if there were any last orders, and on his reply, made their way to the jumping off point. Kelly reminded them of the password for their return, wished them all God's speed, then added… "Don't bleedin' well come back unless you've done the deed. I'll be expecting a big bang… Don't let me down!"

It was now six o'clock at night. It was cold and extremely dark, as there was no moon and a great deal of clouds that threatened heavy rain at any time. As it was, the ground was sodden, but starting to harden, which made they way very hard work, picking up clods of heavy mud on their boots. They crawled under their own wire, which extended out nearly forty feet, and was getting broader by the week. They could sometimes crouch when walking, but on the whole it was down on all fours; this was safer even at this distance from the enemy's lines. They followed one another at approximately six foot behind from the one in front. No one spoke; there was absolutely nothing to say. No one smoked, that would have brought fire down on them in seconds. So bad was the terrain that they were freezing cold and soaking wet even before getting through their own wire.

'This is going to be a hard, tough assignment, that's for sure,' thought Matti, as he followed in Enrico's footsteps. All five of them were frightened; it was safer to be frightened, it kept them on their mettle, but they shook more from cold, than from fear. They had only covered forty or fifty feet from the wire, when a star shell went up from the German lines, lighting up the entire battlefield more brightly than daylight. The group froze where they crouched, but it gave Enrico a quick chance to spy out the route that they needed to take. Remembering the map that was in his pocket, he knew that he had to make a detour more to the left and slightly up that small ridge, to where the stump of the old oak tree stood in a sad splintered heap. But, to them it was first a point of reference, and secondly a place to take stock of where they were, and of what to do next. There was a brief crack of gun fire, but not in their area, much to the relief of all of them. So far, so good. *Slash!* 'Shit, what was that?' wondered Enrico, turning on his heels. 'Oh, for Christ's sakes!' Matti had slipped into a half-filled crater, a shell hole half-filled with water and dead bodies that were now bobbing up and down, looking like apples in a barrel. Matti had an expression of extreme terror written deep into his face, but not one word came from his mouth, just silent screaming. He was already being pulled deeper into the mire with every effort he made to escape from the mess. The four others crowded around the rim holding out their hands, as if to pull him out, if he could only take one of those hands. Enrico quickly remembered the rope around his pack. Lying down beside the nearest edge to Matti, he threw a length for Matti to catch. "Tie it around your waist if you can," he whispered across, hoping that only Matti was able to hear his words. Matti struggled to get the rope around himself; he was slipping deeper and deeper, with the goo now up to his chest. It seemed as if hours were passing and that Germany was looking on laughingly, just waiting for the order to open fire. 'We are all dead unless we get him out within a minute or two!' Enrico was getting desperate, as Matti seemed unable to get that rope, which was his life or death, around himself. 'What is the matter with you, arsehole, get that fucking rope around or I'll bloody well leave you to drown.' Of course he had no intention of leaving his lifelong friend to drown, but he was seriously getting worried. "Matti," he whispered, "Get your pack off, thread the rope through the pack straps and around your waist, another minute and you will be done for. *Come on, move! Move, move!*"

Matti was frantic, and now pushing the dead remains under his feet, for some sort of leverage. His teeth were starting to chatter. It became so loud, that it sounded like a Spanish Flamenco Castanet player warming up, except poor Matti was quickly beginning to freeze. It finally took the efforts of the little Jew, almost wading into the slurry and holding onto Whitey Boy, to get a grip on Matti's pack, get that out of the hole, then reach back again, grabbing Matti around the scruff of the neck, pulling for all his worth, as something surely had to give. Something did give. There was a slop, slop, slurping sound as Matti was dragged back onto terra firma. His boots were full of water, gore and mud. He stunk to high heaven. It had shaken him so much, that he started to sob almost uncontrollably. But he was safe, at least from drowning. 'How are we going to dry him off?' thought Enrico. The whispering was just loud enough to be heard by them all: "Let's get ourselves over to the oak; maybe we can dry off a bit, and rest. I think we all need it." It took another two and a half hours of crawling and stumbling, before they finally reached their objective, at least for now. Matti was almost completely out of it when they stopped. Shivering, whimpering like a lost puppy dog, he had never in his short life, been in such a sorry state. They quickly found some shelter. Some past warrior had dug a fair sized hole almost completely under the trunk of the oak. It was wet, but not full of water. At least it was cover. "Let's have some food, give us some energy, and I think we have earned it already."

" 'As anyone thought to 'ave brought a towel with them?" asked the little Jew.

"Yes, I have," replied Whitey Boy.

"Christ! You are a genius! It would never have occurred to me," was Enrico's honest retort. "Let's get Matti dry and comfortable. And Maurice, well done for saving the little idiot here! It might have been easier if he wasn't so fat." But his attempts at humour were falling on deaf ears. Another star shell shot up from the enemy lines. They were now under cover from any viewing foe, so it gave Enrico a chance to see just how bad Matti was. 'Not good, he is shivering badly; I must get him warm and dry, or he might as well return to our own lines; he'll be no good to us or himself.' After these thoughts, he asked him directly, "Matti, do you want to return to our lines?"

"Of course not, just get me dry and warm, I'm bloody freezing!"

They all took turns in rubbing Matti down. Getting his blood circulating seemed like the right thing to do, and if nothing else, it cheered him up. After some food, which always did the trick with Matti, and the continuous rubbing, he came back to life.

"Not so much food, it's got to last: we might be out here a day or two. And don't drink all the water either. I'm beginning to wish you had decided to go back," said Enrico, feigning annoyance.

"It is late; I think it might be a good idea to stay the night here. Two of you will take first watch for two hours, and then be relieved by another two, and so on. Whitey, you and Maurice, you take the first turn. Whitey, over there! Maurice, can you see that brickwork, it's about twenty yards to our right, see it? Get behind that. Fritz may well have patrols out, so no sleeping on watch, or I will personally shoot you. If you hear anything, creep back and we all will deal with whatever it is. Watch out for the rats. They are big, and they bite. No surprises, don't yell out for any reason. I don't think they realise that we are here, yet. Let's keep it that way. Right, got everything you need? Oh, one last thing, if there is trouble, try and use your knives, keep it quiet! Right! Go, back in two hours. Riddle and me are the reliefs. Matti, you sleep, don't snore, just get warm and better."

Again the guns started to boom in the distance. A couple of wiz bangs thundered over. A German machine gun rattled off a belt. 'I bet that's our boy,' thought Enrico and Matti, as they nestled up close together to conserve body heat.

The temperature dropped below zero that night. They just lay there shivering, watching the ice crystals forming on the ground around them. The clouds had parted, making the threat of rain pass; this in turn left the way clear for cold to appear like the grim reaper. The pools of water froze over, leaving them even more dangerous; if you fell into them now, without a lot of help you would most certainly drown, or die quickly of hypothermia. Matti had fallen asleep with his back up against Enrico's, but it wasn't long before he was shivering so badly that it kept Enrico awake. He lay there worrying about Matti: he could freeze to death if something wasn't done and soon.

"Matti, how do you feel?" he whispered. There was no reply. 'What shall I do? This is now becoming a very worrying situation. I don't want

Matti to go west!' "Matti, Matti, are you awake?" still no reply. Even Enrico was feeling the cold, and had lost all feeling in his feet. He turned to Riddle, who was not asleep either. "Jimmy, are you awake? I'm very worried about Matti, I think he is going into a coma. I cannot rouse him at all. Can you come here and help me with him?" Even though they were all wearing winter clothing, including thick sheepskin outer garments, they were all really cold. Matti was far worse; with the falling into the shell hole he was soaked through to his skin. Though they had all made valiant efforts to raise his temperature, they could not dry his clothing. Like the small lakes and ponds around them, he was starting to freeze up. Ice crystals were now forming inside his clothing, and also on his skin. He was now in such a state of hypothermia that unless things were done quickly, he would be dead within an hour or two at the most.

"Jimmy, let's wake him, whatever it takes, then you take him back. Can you retrace our steps?"

"Yes, of course I shall be happy to help old Matti." Again, rubbing his feet and back vigorously, it took another five minutes of hard treatment from both the lads to get any life back into Matti. But for a brief spell he became his old self again.

"What's up?" he said looking directly into Enrico's eyes. It was a look of complete trust, and acceptance of what his dear friend had in mind for him.

"Listen Matti, you are in a serious way. You must not fall asleep. Jimmy is going to take you back to our lines. You are seriously freezing. The rest of us will carry out the task ordered. No arguments, go!" There was of course no argument and he was *compos mentis* enough to realise that he too must do his bit by staying alive, and that meant no sleep. He groaned under his breath when the two tried to stand him up. Every fibre of his body was really cold. 'It is going to be hard to get these muscles working again,' he thought to himself, as Enrico and Jimmy tried to get him to his feet. At that moment a rifle fired a shot; it echoed through the night.

If they had been back in Blighty, they would have been forgiven for thinking a poacher was on the prowl, but here in no-man's-land, their instinctive reflex was to duck, even though it was obvious that the lone shot was not in their direction.

It was quickly agreed that their packs would be left while they made a hasty exit for the friendly British lines. This meant that three men would be carrying the loads of five. Enrico quietly made his way to Whitey Boy, whispering an explanation in his ear, and upon his nod of agreement, helped him with his load. Enrico now realised that the closer they got to their objective tonight, the better, and anyway, Matti showed him that it was too cold to fall asleep. Now carrying the two extra loads plus ammunition and bombs, they started off to explain the present encumbrance to Maurice, the little Jew.

They had been crouching very low, and had only gone about a hundred feet, when another bright star shell illuminated everything before them. They could see Maurice, with his head pressed close to the rubble that he had taken refuge in. He was watching towards the German lines, but more to the point, they clearly saw the shapes of three German snipers in full camouflage, and as the enemy had been observing the trajectory of the star shell, they were lucky not to be noticed. The Germans were probably less than a hundred yards from Maurice and they themselves were only fifty yards away. Getting to aid Maurice was going to be a close thing. The little Jew had also clearly seen the three potential adversaries, and judging by the direction in which they were heading, they were going to pass within a few feet of him. So he prepared himself for the worst. Enrico and Whitey Boy were now on all fours, creeping as fast as they could, but straining and panting under the heavy load that they were carrying. 'If I take the pack off, I will probably be too late, if I keep it on, the shits might hear me. Can't be helped, keep it on,' thought Enrico, as he made another surge forward. The light now went, and when darkness comes after such bright lights, it takes a few seconds for the eyes to accustom themselves to the pitch black. There was broken glass, rubble from ruined buildings, bits of barbed wire, steel fragments, and many squelchy things that Enrico or Whitey Boy preferred not to identify. Their hands and knees were taking a battering from all the debris of war.

They were now no more than twenty feet from Maurice, and Maurice was aware of their presence. As they looked at the little Jew they could just make out that the first finger on his right hand was pressed up to his lips, in a gesture of 'quiet!' Enrico indicated that he knew of the three Germans heading their way; he withdrew his knife and made sure that Maurice understood when he drew it across his own throat. Maurice nodded with his finger still over his lips, but his left hand drawing forth his own dagger. The three Germans were good, but not really good enough; because of the camouflaging, they were hard to see, but they were not hard to hear. Had you not known it was the enemy, it would have seemed obvious to you that some rather large rats were scurrying along after a meal, but it was in fact the gentle rustling of their camouflage clothing that betrayed them. The Germans were dressed in layers and layers of strips of brown, grey and black cloth; it hung from the top of their heads, completely covering them, and in day time they could creep surreptitiously amongst the detritus and blend into almost any background. In general they were a formidable force to be dealt with, but with the noise of their own rustling, they were completely unaware of the rather clumsy and noisy efforts that Enrico and Whitey Boy had made while trying to get into position for the ambush. Enrico again showed his knife to Maurice, and indicated that he should take the first man, that Whitey was to take the second, and he would take the third. There was hardly a moment to spare, just time to yet again feel the roughness of the broken ground against his knees and hands; then, a rush forward.

The three of them went steel in hand for their quarry. Sadly for Enrico, before he reached his man, he stumbled with the load he was carrying, crashing into the soldier, and both of them went sprawling into the ground, the soldier giving out a loud yell of surprise. Whitey Boy, as quick as a flash, thrust his knife in to where he thought the surprised sniper's throat was. There was a gurgling sound coming from underneath all the cloth, and the soldier with his gun slumped to his knees, with his eyes bulging, and his life juices now spreading over the cold ground. Maurice had done much the same to his, sinking his blade deep into muscle, veins and spinal cord. He pulled the knife from side to side, which almost severed the head from its torso; blood gushed and could quickly be seen through all the layers of cloth, even in the dark, but the figure of this soldier with his arms and legs thrashing about fast reminded Maurice of a headless chicken.

All this time, Enrico was struggling to hold his soldier down; in the stumble he had dropped his weapon, and was thrashing with arms and legs towards anything that resembled a human being amongst all these strips of cloth. The German was screaming at the top of his voice, and all Enrico could think of doing was to say: "*Shush, shush!*" as he thrashed out with his arms and legs once more. But this sniper knew that Enrico's intentions were not entirely friendly, and it had not taken a genius to realise that his life was not worth a carrot, and that, unless he got out of there quickly, he too, would end up yet just another statistic. Somehow he got to his feet, avoiding Enrico's attempts to keep him down; he had dropped his sniper rifle, but this did not matter. All he could think of was to run back the way he had come. His brain was exploding with panic, and he was still yelling as he started his run. All this had happened from start to finish in less than ten seconds, and before Enrico could raise himself off the ground, the little Jew had drawn the pin on a Mills bomb, and thrown it just beyond the fleeing enemy. It exploded, knocking the luckless Hun completely off his feet, with a massive gaping hole in his stomach, and his entrails spewing onto the cold ground, along with his blood. At the precise moment the sniper hit the ground, several star shells and various flares went up from the enemy lines. But the Germans could only see two fleeing figures of

British soldiers, falling down in the light, very close to the Allied barbed wire. Machine guns opened up, trench mortars blasted, and all Enrico, Whitey Boy and Maurice the Jew could think about was that it was not them being fired at.

"Maurice, help me up. Bloody load's made me top heavy!" Maurice complied, raising Enrico back into the erect position. Shells were landing everywhere, but not, fortunately, in their sector. They could talk quite openly, as the noise of the shelling was deafening anyway. Enrico pulled Maurice's head to him and shouted into his left ear: "Grab your pack, take some of the Mills and some of the ammunition from me; I'm too heavy! We've got to get out of here! Poor Matti nearly froze to death; it's no longer a good idea to try to sleep. I think it's better if we press on and get closer to our goal."

Now a few pounds lighter Enrico felt a little more comfortable, toting the load that he had. He kicked both the dead Germans to see if there was any reaction, but they had both gone to Valhalla. The three of them, stumbling as they progressed forward in their crouching mode, started on the trek towards the enemy wire. They checked the third German soldier for signs of life, but as the flashes of shell fire briefly gave a little light, they could tell that he too, had gone to his maker. Their fear, now, as they lurched forward, was of bumping into any more snipers or patrols. The kerfuffle that had stirred the Germans from their temporary slumber now had got them into a state of agitated restlessness. Their frontline troops were nervously searching the horizon for what may be a British assault. The trio had faltered around many half filled frozen shell holes, most with decomposing corpses of men and horses, and every step that they took was disturbing the thousands of rats that were taking refuge against the noise of the shelling. They came across a well used path, and they quickly realised it was a track used regularly by the Jerries which would lead to their own wire.

'This might be a good way to go; it's pretty clear of debris, and is very much akin to a sunken road. When we get near the wire, we can break off to the left, and make our way once again around the shell holes,' thought Enrico. This was going to be a much quicker route, and they were able to step out at a lively pace. Two minutes later, they had already come to the outer limits of the German heavy barbed wire. The first sight of that wire sickened all three of them, as there, for all to see, were approximately a hundred dead British, strung out like so much washing. These were the dead of a previous battle, and on closer inspection, the dead were just skeletons dressed in rotting khaki. The little Jew, on first seeing these tragic silhouettes pulled up fast, holding back the other two.

"Aaah! For goodness sake! We 'ave 'ad many a truce. Why, oh, why 'aven't they buried them?" said Maurice to the other two.

"This could work to our advantage," said Enrico, as the other two looked at him in horror. "If we follow close to this line of wire, on our left, should we need to lay prone, we might be taken for some of these… with luck!"

The three of them carefully crawled out of the sunken track, and edged their way along the craters, making sure that they were out of sight of any alert enemy.

They slithered from crater to crater, making as little noise as possible. All three of them were suffering from the battering that the hard land had given them; fatigue was fast overtaking, and Enrico was worried that they might make mistakes. Every fibre of their body ached from exertion, and though their extremities were numb with cold, they were sweating profusely from the extreme tension that was being forced upon them. Whitey Boy was the first to realise how serious their condition had become, and as they snailed their way across one large frozen shell hole, he yanked at Enrico's trouser leg to get his attention.

"This is crazy, Enrico. We must rest. It's time to find somewhere dry and safe, where we can hide and sleep."

Enrico thought about this for a second, and then nodded in

agreement, as he saw the state that the other two were in, and realised that he too, was just about done for. There were two more shell holes to traverse, when they came across a very deep one that had a dead horse on the rim, thus giving shelter from prying foe. It was deep and wide, and the idea was that they should dig out a hole under where the horse lay, then crawling into this hole, they could be out of sight and comparatively safe. They worked with a will, and very quickly made the hole big enough for the three of them and their loads.

"We should all eat, eating gives energy, and we certainly need that! I don't know where we are, but I would hazard a guess that we are only a few hundred yards from the bunker, and if we rest until tonight, we can take it without too many problems."

None of the trio seriously believed this was the end of their troubles, but it was reassuring to hear a positive word or two.

All three took food, and then it was decided that they would all sleep, close to one another to conserve heat. The one element that was on the positive side was that as the earth and water had frozen solid with the cold, this meant there was now no smell from decomposing flesh. 'I wonder what's happened to Matti. Please God, make them safe.' This was Enrico's last thought, as he slipped into oblivion from utter fatigue.

'I 'ope Enrico's all right. I knew it was time for us to stop. We are making mistakes, but I am too bloody tired to care!' were the last thoughts of Maurice Bechstein, as he too, succumbed to his state of exhaustion.

Matti reeled and staggered. He knew he must keep his thoughts focused on staying awake. 'Think positive man, you want to get home, see mum and dad. Fall asleep and you never will see anybody else again!' he thought, as he put one foot in front of the other pushing every muscle to new heights of agony. It had taken a long time to get close to the comparative safety of the Allied wire, but they now had no packs to carry. 'It should be easier, keep on putting one foot in front of the other, stop thinking of sleep… How is Enrico doing? How will the old fart manage without me…? Stay awake or you will be letting your friend down as well as your family. They all need you!… I am so cold, I just want to sleep. No, no, no, think of that lovely Belgian girl you screwed, what's her name? There is a whole world of girls out there waiting for you to lay them… Keep up with Jimmy, keep him in sight, and don't fall over!' These thoughts rushing through Matti's brain kept him going. Jimmy Riddle led the way, and pushed Matti into keeping up with him. He would not let Matti fall over or lag behind; he understood that if he fell asleep it would be his end. So with one eye on the terrain in front and one eye behind, he forced the way forward. 'It's not so far to our lines now, just get under the wire, alert the sentry to who we are, and get Matti to hospital.' Time passed slowly in Jimmy's thoughts, but eventually he became aware of the wire in the darkness. 'Before trying to get underneath, I must alert the sentries, what's the bloody password again? "Dragonetti", who by golly was "Dragonetti?"' thought Jimmy. Just as they reached the perimeter of their own barbed wire, there was an explosion. 'Sounded like a Mills bomb,' thought Jimmy. Then without a moment to think, star shells and flares zoomed skyward, lighting everything around brighter than day. "Matti, get down! They will see us!" Too late, machine gun fire rattled, starting to sweep around their area. Then a whiz-bang burst overhead. Shells began to rain in. Crash, bang, earth was thrown everywhere, some covering them. All sorts of debris showered them. Broken masonry, already shattered from many previous bombardments, got a further pasting from the shells, making it fly up into the air and thunder down thumping into the earth, smashing and breaking everything around.

The wire was taking a severe pounding too. Pieces were whizzing in all directions, acting like bullets, as they were broken off the main roll. What was worse, the wire had become rusty, and carried germs that once in the body were going to infect the wound with all sorts of terrible diseases. Matti and Jimmy just lay where they fell, head pushed as far into the ground as possible. They expected to die, or the very least be maimed, by any of the missiles that were flying around. 'Why was I so stupid in joining the bloody crazy army?' was Jimmy's thought, as yet another shell threw mounds of earth, bricks, glass, rats and human remains at him. Matti had crawled by his side, and they huddled there, tight as sardines in a can. 'If I am to die, let it be with a friend,' was their common thought. The firing changed direction, moving more to their left. Jimmy didn't waste any time. "Sentries, can you hear me? This is Jimmy Riddle and Matti Dumbridge coming through the wire. The pass word is "Dragonetti". Did you hear me?" They didn't wait for any answer, but started crawling as quickly as their terrified bodies would allow. 'Christ, some of the wire has come down further onto us, it is going to take time pushing through this lot!' thought Jimmy. 'Must keep an eye on Matti...' "Matti," he whispered, "Keep up with me, if you get into trouble just call me quietly!"

"Will do," came the very reassured reply. The intensity of the shelling was abating, which made the two young men give a huge sigh of relief. So they pushed on through the wire and closer to their own lines. *Crack, crack, zing!*, went a few bullets whizzing up just in front of Jimmy. He stopped in abject terror. 'Christ, these are coming from our own lines: bad enough being killed by the Hun, but to be shot by one of your own!' "Stop firing!" he shouted, now worrying that the Germans might hear him and resume firing shells. "This is Martin Riddle and Matti Dunbridge here, stop firing!"

"What's the password?"

"Oh shit, you have made me forget!"

"Dragonetti!" cried Matti, to save the day.

"Come through, friend and be recognised!"

"Thank God for that!" cried out Jimmy, now extremely close to disgracing himself as the terror of the last half hour had almost become too much for him. They were not there yet, still a good forty feet of barbed wire to crawl under. The shelling had almost stopped now, and anyway it was dropping far to their left, which did not offer a great deal of danger from that direction. Inch by inch, they clawed their way closer to safety. Exhaustion, mental and physical was upon them both. Matti's one thought was how he wanted to sleep. They were in pain, not just Matti but Jimmy too. He ached from every muscle, every sinew, each and every fibre of his being. All he wanted was a hot mug of tea and a long sleep. 'Sleep, yes, that's the order of the day! Sleep for at least twenty-four hours. Then a long holiday, maybe Blackpool or Scarborough, then back to the family and out of this madness forever,' thought Jimmy as he reached the parapet of the home trench.

"For God's sake, man, help us both down!" shouted Jimmy, as he noticed a bemused soldier just standing there, watching him as he struggled to get himself and Matti down onto the duckboards. "Quick, get a doctor or medic, this man's in a bad way!" The sentry ran off leaving another soldier to give aid to Matti, who was just about all in. "You're bleeding," the soldier said as blood was pouring from Matti's arm. "What? Where, bleeding, me?" He then looked at his arm and noticed that blood was indeed seeping from it, then he realised that there was serious pain coming from the right arm. "Oh, shit," he said "I must have been hit; I didn't feel a thing until now." Matti looked towards Jimmy and said, "Jimmy, you are bleeding too. Tell Enrico…" He then promptly fell to the floor in a dead faint. Jimmy moved as if to catch him, but was not quick enough. Then he too, realised that there was pain coming from his left arm, and saw the thin line of blood trickling down his sleeve onto his hand. Warm, life giving blood, and there it was, wasting all over his hand. He felt dizzy, looked at the soldier, who hadn't a clue what was going on. Jimmy swayed, tried to keep himself upright, but lost the bet with himself. There he was, next to his friend, prone; for a moment all he could see was stars, or was it the angels coming to fetch them both? He too, was out for the count.

Sergeant Harrington came running with two stretcher bearers. He took one look at his two young charges, ordered with a sharp snarl,

"Get them into a dressing station right away." This was done at a rate that would have made all medics proud, had any of them attained that sort of speed. Harrington then went off to find his friend Kelly. 'What the hell has happened to them, are the others dead?'

Enrico, Stanley and Maurice were tucked into a hole just big enough to give them cover from above. It did not stop the rats from finding them, neither the lice from irritating them. They lay there, hardly snug as a bug in a rug, but the bugs were!

Enrico had fallen asleep, but woke within an hour, tired and scratching. He didn't want to wake the other two, so just lay there getting colder and colder.

'What is that noise? Is it a rat? I can hear sounds, they sound like footsteps,' thought Enrico. He quickly realised exactly what was happening, and put both his hands over the mouths of his colleagues, bringing them immediately awake, and also aware that something was amiss. The sounds were as if something was scratching along the perimeter of the shell hole, and the three of them instinctively stiffened.

"Pssst! Ich gleibe ich habe etwas gehört!"

"Ich habe nichts gehört."

"Was war das?"

"Es hat sich wie schneichen angehört!"

"Du bist verruckt! Das waren Raten!"

Enrico heard the voices; not understanding anything that was being said, carefully, he withdrew two Mills bombs and his service revolver, and prepared himself for any action. Not daring to breathe, he laid the weapons by his side; again the scratching sound… and he just made out in the darkness the figures of five German soldiers, creeping around the rim of the crater. Surely, they could see him, lying in the makeshift hole, but he did not move.

"Ja, es mussen Raten gewesen sein."

"Schau, in das Loch, da. Kanst du etwas sehen?"

"Nur Leichen. Komm, mir ist kalt, gehen wir zürück zur Front; hier ist nichts."

Gradually, the figures crept to another bunker, and Enrico, Whitey Boy and the little Jew gave huge sighs of relief. When he knew it was safe to speak, Enrico said to the other two:

"I forgot to post a sentry; just as well, as it turned out, a sentry would have been seen. Here in our hole, we got away with it. I suggest we try and sleep some more," but scratched furiously at the itching under his arms.

"What do we do if we need a dump or a pee?" enquired the little Jew.

"Either hold on to it, or creep out and do it quietly on the other side of the crater, as far away from me as possible!" There was a little giggle coming from the other two. Enrico could not sleep, and was being bothered by the incessant itching and the extreme cold. 'Please, daybreak, come quickly, and let it be sunny!' Daybreak did come, along with the rain, at first just a drizzle, but soon developing into a downpour.

Whitey Boy and the Jew were at the back of their little cave that they had dug the night before, but Enrico was towards the front, and as the drizzle turned into a torrent, it was blowing in, soaking him. 'The misery, how long is this going to carry on? We have to stay all day here until dark, and I'm bloody freezing and soaking.' Enrico also noticed now that the water was starting to rise, and he thought it might be a good idea, before it was full daybreak, to go to the opposite rim, and dig a small gutter to the next crater which was less than two feet away from this one. As this crater was lower than the German parapet, he should be able to do it without being seen.

He crawled out of his hole, barely able to move his arms and legs from the cold and wet. Keeping as low as possible, he crept around the sloping wall of the crater, with every now and again, his left arm or foot slipping into the filth that was rising fast. At first he could claw at some of the earth; cutting into it with his hands was easy where it was wet, but where it was dry, he had to break through it, as quietly and quickly as possible. He began by using his knife, but this was really too small to make the sort of impression that he needed; then he realised he had the perfect implement on his head: his helmet. Scraping at the earth, he managed to eventually break through, and then it was comparatively easy to dig downwards, so that the gutter would be below their cave entrance. The next further shell hole was slightly downhill, and as the water rose in this one to the gutter, it would soon cascade into the next shell hole, thus giving them a further dry period which hopefully would remain, even if the rain carried on until night came again, when they must continue their assault. Now covered from head to foot in filthy, slimy, brown gooey mud, he crept back to the hole whence he had come. 'Now I know how cavemen felt,' but truth be known, he had been aware of how cavemen felt since first having to sleep in a trench.

The rain was incessant; it did not ease up for a minute, and as the day wore on, the lower shell hole began to fill, thus making the water creep up towards their shelter.

"Enrico, maybe we should take turns in bailing this water out of the 'ole; if we just push it over the side with our 'elmets, and not throw it, we might not be seen," said Maurice.

"Good point!" said Enrico. "You can be first. I am freezing and soaking, and I've probably got double pneumonia to boot!" So there was this figure of Maurice Bechstein, lying in the crater, almost at water level, carefully scooping water, and throwing it over the edge, not realising that for every helmetful that went over, half a helmet came back! It was really a losing battle. An hour went by before Maurice pleaded to be relieved, and Stanley White took his place, making an equally futile gesture. All three of them were cold, muddy and wet through. It was suggested that to eat might be a good idea. The day wore on, and now water had started to come into their little hideaway, but they knew that in less than an hour, it

214

would be dark, and they could continue. Out of sheer fatigue and cold, they had reached a state of apathy, no longer caring about the water, so long as they did not drown. Maurice withdrew a beautiful gold fob watch from his tunic, and squinting at it, hardly able to tell the time, eventually made out that it was three fifty-two. With the heavy rain clouds, it was already as dark as night. They crawled to the rim of the crater, barely daring to peer over, but as they could see nothing, it was hardly likely they could be seen in return.

"We'll give it another fifteen minutes, and then we make our way in that direction," Enrico declared pointing to the left of the German wire.

"To be honest, I'm glad to get out of that hole; at least on the move, we have a chance of keeping warm!"

The guns had been firing in a spasmodic fashion all day, but all were hitting behind the lines, and not into no-man's-land. A solitary flare went up, lighting briefly the way they had to go; this would be a slithering crawl, as they were now in the open and dared not stand, in case more flares or star shells went aloft. For every ten yards forward, they would be forced to do another few yards either to the left or right, or in some cases backtracking when shell holes full of water barred their way completely. But none of this worried Enrico, whose main fear was that the packs of explosives they were carrying and dragging, might well end up useless if waterlogged. Every now and again, they would have to move the remains of rotting human or animal flesh, as these abominations barred their way; the feel of this rotting flesh and bone against their own person was night-marish, something they would never ever forget, but the cold had at least taken away the stench of corruption. It was just before midnight; eight hours had passed since they had left their shell hole hideaway, and they had only travelled a mere two hundred yards; those two hundred yards had taken the effort of a marathon runner, but finally they had reached their goal! There, just a mere five yards away, they could make out the outline of the concrete bunker, and *there* was the door that would lead into it. As they edged their way closer, they noticed that the steel door was ever so slightly ajar; it looked as if a high explosive shell from the British lines had jammed it on its hinge, so that it could now no longer close properly. 'What good fortune! Luck is with us so far!' thought Enrico. They were now six feet away from the door, and they could just make out the light of a candle or two through the gap. Peering intently through that gap, they could distinguish the figures of three German soldiers, manning a machine gun.

Enrico nudged Maurice; touching his wrist, he whispered into his ear: "See if you can tell the time from the light."

"It's three minutes to midnight."

"Then we will wait here, because I bet you a pound to a penny that they will change the guard at twelve. Fritz is so predictable!"

Sure enough, a couple of minutes later, a trap door opened within the bunker, and up came an officer and two other men. They talked for two or three minutes very quietly, and the three first gunners retreated down the hole into the ground. The officer lit a cigarette, and looking though the slit in the bunker, he blew smoke rings casually in the direction of the British lines. Enrico whispered to the other two that they were to use their knives and kill the two Privates, and he would take the officer, and for that, he withdrew a heavy wooden and lead-tipped cosh, which he had secreted on his person since leaving the British trenches.

"We have to be extremely quiet, not a sound must be heard; we'll creep up to the door. Maurice you take the left, Whitey you take the right." They now stood by the side of the door. As the bunker itself was almost entirely under ground, there was little fear of being seen from the German lines, unless the light of the candles illuminated them too much as they rushed in. They stood there, the filthiest vagabonds the British army had ever had the misfortune to produce. Enrico put three fingers in the air, they steadied themselves, coshes and knives raised; then two fingers were shown, they took a sharp intake of breath; one finger, their eyes were ablaze, and their muscles taut. The finger went down, the door was pulled, and they were in! Two knives wheeled down fast, and a cosh landed squarely on the nose and jaw of a completely startled German officer. He slumped to the ground, senseless. The feeling of pain was to come later. The two other Germans both gave gurgling sounds, eyes almost popping from their heads, arms raised in a wasted gesture of defence, and their life juices gushing out, hitting the cold concrete floor. Steam came from their throats, for all the world looking like ectoplasm emanating. The three stood there, shaking from head to foot; Enrico quickly said:

"Maurice, bring in all the packs of explosives!" which they had left outside to do their assault, and then turning to Whitey Boy, he added "Stanley, guard that trap door, get your pistol and a couple of Mills bombs ready." He took the rope and started to bind the arms of the German officer.

"Stanley, open it up, and let's see what's down there!"

Stanley obliged, and there, below, was a tunnel which led back to the German lines, and was obviously going out to the British lines.

"Stanley, go down there very carefully, take a complete pack of dynamite, and set up a trap with a couple of Mills bombs; with the dynamite this should be enough to bring down the walls and roof for quite a way. We will place the rest around the entrance to the trap door so that the blast should set off the explosives up here."

Whitey Boy crept down the ladder, and looked sharply in both directions. He could hear the gentle tap-tapping as men were obviously working on the tunnel under the British lines. He set four grenades into the walls, took the pins out of all four but held the caps together with string that once trodden on, would release the grenades so that they blew. The bag of dynamite was left by the grenades, and exposed so that the force of the Mills bombs would erupt directly into the pack of explosives. There were dim lights from two forty watt light bulbs, both within ten yards of where he stood. When the bomb was set, he quickly went and broke the bulbs, making it impossible for any German soldier to see what

217

was in store for them, unless they carried a torch, and as electricity was installed, it seemed unlikely that anybody would feel the need to carry a light as well. He went back up the ladder, and they set more Mills bombs, hanging from string over the hole, so that when the explosion occurred, they too, would be set off. The other four packs were exposed to the open hole, and Mills placed in careful positions again ready to erupt. They found masses of German ammunition, and this too, was piled upon the packs of explosives. It was now time to leave. The German officer was still out cold, and as Enrico looked at him, he realised he might have ruined his Teutonic good looks, as he had obviously broken his nose and his jaw, and some of his teeth were lying on his tunic along with the blood that was dribbling from his nose and mouth.

"Right, we will have to drag him, and we are going to go in the most direct way that we can. So boys, there's no time to lose!"

The whole action from entering until leaving the bunker had taken a little under five minutes. They opened the door, and dragged the soldier out, and started on their way to the British lines. 'Thank God for the rain! It's so dark that nobody will see us!' then turning to Whitey Boy he made a passing comment: "Did you shut the door? I would not want a draught to get in!" he said, smiling to himself, unseen by anybody else. They scrambled, slid and flopped their way from the German bunker. It was easier now for them, their only burden being the almost lifeless Hun, and though they could between the three of them almost carry him, they had to be careful where they trod, fearing to fall into shell holes that were now completely full of water, and surely be their 'Waterloo!' if they fell in. Enrico urged them forward all the time; even though he was shivering from cold and soaked to the skin, inside he was boiling from the effort. A good forty minutes had passed when they crouched down behind the roots of an upturned tree. All three of them were panting hard, and Maurice, who had been carrying the feet of the German most of the way, dropped them, and bent down almost touching his toes, trying desperately hard to get his breath back. Vigorously rubbing his side in an effort to relieve the stitch that had formed, he began to say: "I'd have thought by now that the trap would have been spr…" but his words were interrupted as a roar developed which within two seconds expanded into a thunderclap of noise. The whole ground on which they stood shook, and in many areas, subsided; even the tree trunk in which roots they sheltered shuddered violently, and part of it slipped from view.

"Christ! We've started an earthquake!" said Enrico, then quickly realised that taking the direct route had taken them more or less in the direction of the tunnel; there was a huge shell hole with a circumference of approximately a hundred feet, which was completely full of water before the explosion, and now was emptying as if a giant plug had been withdrawn from the bottom. More ammunition was exploding, and pieces of concrete and steel were crashing down everywhere, as the bunker just ceased to exist.

"That could not have possibly been just our explosion!" and in fact it was not. What everybody on the British lines would never know was that this tunnel led directly under the British forward trenches, and was systematically being filled with German high explosives. So that, given time, they would have set this whole mine off, maybe killing hundreds of front line troops in one fell swoop. What had happened was that a cart loaded with at least one ton of high explosive was being pulled by six German soldiers and a further two pushing. They tripped the wire that set the Mills bombs that exploded the pack that set off the cart full of high explosive, then exploding the four further bags which had been placed around the trap. This blew the bunker to smithereens, and created a minor earthquake all the way through the tunnel. The poor Germans at the face were either suffocated by falling chalk, or drowned by the onrush of all the water that had gathered above. Very quickly flares went up from the German side, and then star shells began illuminating no-man's-land even through the heavy rain, so that everything was a haze and had a ghostly appearance. Many seconds had passed before all the explosions finished, and where a German machine gun bunker had been, an orange ghostly glow could now be seen.

"Bloody hell! Did we do all that?" said Whitey Boy, looking at Enrico.

"I cannot believe our five packs could have made such a mess!" replied Enrico, with edgy nervous laughter. He stood there, shaking from head to foot, and not just from the cold. German mortars started their expected bombardment, but as the Hun did not know where they were, or indeed if anybody was there, they were being sent over with the expectation of luck more than judgement. Now there was a steady boom coming from far behind the British lines, as the big guns were sending their blockbusters over in the general direction of the Hun line. The rain did not stop for a second, and they had been lucky to have rested behind the roots of this old broken oak tree which had been upended by the blasting of thousands of shells, months ago. It was already dead, but it gave protection even in its death.

"I don't know where we are, but if we keep going in this direction we must reach the lines, sooner or later, and I feel we should keep going in case Jerry sends out patrols."

Because of the precipitation, the visibility was less than ten feet, just enough to see the ground in front, but not be seen from behind, even when illuminated by star shells or flares. They went forward, two carrying the arms and shoulders of the unconscious officer, and Enrico carrying his legs and leading the way. For every step they took, they were sinking into the mud, almost up to their knees; the eruption seemed to have liquefied the ground, and there was very little solid to stand on. They struggled on for another three hours, and had probably only managed five hundred yards when exhaustion completely overtook all three of them. The real problem of the German officer was beginning to manifest itself:

"Aa-h!" The sound of this groan startled the three chums, as the German soldier began to come back to life. An instinctive right foot jerked from Enrico's grasp, then jerked back, kicking Enrico in the small of the back, sending him sprawling into a shell hole containing yet more rotting corpses. The pain of the heavy boot was nowhere near as intense as the pain of yet once again being covered in human decomposing organs and excreta. His only thoughts were: 'every bloody time it's me that gets copped for the human muck!' The two other boys dropped their German and rushed to help their friend, until they saw what he was covered in, and as quickly as their arms had shot out to help him, they shot back in, not wishing to know anything about it! Another deep groan came from the German, giving them both the excuse to leave Enrico and go back to him.

"You shitty arseholes! Can't you help me out of here?" but he was already pulling himself up over the rim of the hole, trying to brush off as much of the decomposition as possible. He glared furiously in the direction of the other two, but was unable to see their broad grins, just as they were unable to see his anger. He picked up the feet, and again they moved on, following the general flow of the water. Another hour went by, and none of them could feel any of their own limbs; the pain of fatigue was over-whelming them.

"Enrico, I've really had it! We must rest, and you'd better look at this Kraut. I don't want to be carrying a dead body!"

"All right, we'll stop as soon as we can find a spot where there is a little cover." Another twenty paces later which must have taken half an hour, and they came across the perfect place. It was a small section of a wall, sticking up no more than three feet, but it had a concrete floor which was big enough for them to put their ground sheet down, placing another one upon the top of the wall, thus making a bivouac away from the elements. This time Enrico remembered to post a sentry. Turning to the little Jew, he said:

"Maurice, how many Mills bombs do we have left?"

"Three," was the reply, "but we've got our service revolvers."

"I want you to stay on watch for an hour, just in case of enemy patrols. Then, wake me and I'll do an hour, and then I'll wake Whitey Boy.

He can get the rest, as he seems to be the most done in."

He looked at the officer and realised that his eyes were open; blood was still oozing from his mouth, but he seemed to be more *compos mentis*.

"Do you speak any English?"

"Nein." He followed this with a whimper, as he realised that by trying to speak it only aggravated his broken jaw. Enrico put his hands to the side of his head, indicating he should go to sleep, but before he crawled in beside the German, he once again tested the knots that bound his hands behind his back.

Enrico awoke when a hand was placed over his mouth and was startled by the silence. The heavy guns had ceased firing, the mortars and machine guns had halted, but worst of all, the rain had stopped; and as drops dripped in puddles, the noise seemed to be like the rattle of a snare drum. He speedily got to his knees, and heeded the invitation to be silent from Maurice. He murmured in his ear: "What's the matter?" and Maurice, pointing towards the German lines mumbled the words: "I'm sure there's a patrol out there, and I think they're getting closer to us!"

Enrico crouched and silently woke Stanley: "You're right; I think I can hear people out there." They knelt behind the low wall, service revolvers ready, and a Mills bomb each.

"What are we going to do?" asked Whitey Boy in a shaky, worried voice.

"We'll let them go past us. We haven't got enough ammunition to realistically provoke a fight, so keep still and be quiet."

There came the sound of a clunk of metal against metal, and the three pals stiffened instinctively in preparation for what might turn out to be a fight.

"*Shhh!*" gestured Maurice, as they heard the distinct sounds of the patrol closing in on them.

"Achtung! Achtung!"

To Enrico's horror, this alarm came from their prisoner, who they had entirely forgotten about. Too late to stop him, so more out of retribution, Maurice lashed out with his boot, landing a heavy blow in the officer's groin. The only sound that came was the inrush of air from the winded officer.

*Crack, crack.* The sound of rifle fire came in their general direction, but they did not return the shots, as they still could not see anybody. They could now hear the tramp of heavy running feet, and they did not have to wait long for the inevitable. Enrico pulled the pin on his grenade when he finally saw the emergence of the German patrol. He caught them right in the middle, and the resulting explosion took the leg off one German, and disembowelled another. Now they had targets to fire at, and as the Germans came on, they in turn could see the wall that the British were cowering behind, so the onslaught began.

They fired their pistols into the onrushing patrol; there had been ten, at the start, and already three were dead, and two seriously wounded. A stick grenade was thrown, and it landed just in front of the wall. The concussion of the exploding bomb hurt their ears, and the shock wave nearly knocked them over. Again Maurice fired at a surging German; another stick grenade winged its way through the air, but Stanley had seen the German throw it, and watched its flight, as if in slow motion. Like the great W.G.Grace, he swung his hand like a cricket bat, pushing the grenade further into the distance, where it exploded almost harmlessly, only managing to kill a panicking rat that was looking for somewhere to hide while the commotion went on. Still in slow motion, Stanley then raised his pistol, took aim at the grenade thrower, and pulled the trigger. He knew he hit him, but the soldier did not fall, but came on again in a determined fashion, with his rifle and bayonet affixed to it. Again Whitey Boy shot, again he hit the soldier, and still he came on.

The last shot that Stanley White fired lifted the scalp, brains and helmet completely off the head of the German infantry man, but he too, had won the day. As he fell forward, his bayonet cut right through the breast and ribs of Stanley, entering his heart, and killing him instantly. The last German tried to throw his stick grenade, but a lucky shot from Maurice had sent the bullet through his throwing arm, making him drop the grenade at his own feet. For a second, he looked in a totally bewildered state, but before he had any coherent thoughts, he was lifted off so completely that his feet were still stuck firmly in the mud. He landed at least six feet away, still alive, but dying fast. Silence again befell the area. No guns or mortars had opened up on this melee; this had been personal.

"Quick, let's get out there, and finish them, otherwise the screams and cries might bring another patrol." Both the lads drew their knives, and went off to do their deadly business. They went quickly from body to body, and they found only three that had not quite died. One was in agony, with blood gushing from where his leg had been, and there was a look of almost relief on his face when Enrico thrust the cold steel through the space between his ribs into his heart. The man shuddered once, his whole body in a huge jerk, and then lay still. The other two, they dispatched in a similar vein, but they were already unconscious, in their last moments of death throes. It was at this juncture that Enrico remembered his pal Whitey Boy. 'Where the hell is he?' They ran back to the protection of the wall to find the dead German, still with his hand on the rifle whose bayonet pierced Stanley's heart, both soldiers having sunk to their knees, on either side of the wall, as if in prayer to one another.

"Oh, Stanley!" said Maurice, as he inspected his friend, hoping what he knew to be true, would not be.

"He's dead!". Tears welled into his eyes, and Enrico too, was overcome with grief for a brief second, until he noticed that there was now no German officer. Startled back to reality, he grabbed Maurice's arm and said: "The fucking Kraut has done a runner!"

"He can't go far, he's tied!" and looking around, he could see the legs of the German officer, thrashing about wildly, as in his efforts to escape, he had tripped and fallen headlong into a puddle of water; but as his hands were tied behind his back, he was starting to drown. Enrico looked at Maurice, and he said: "I know what you're thinking, but if we don't get him back, this will have all been for nothing."

So they pulled the German out of the water; he coughed and spluttered, and along with blood he was throwing up mud from his mouth.

"It will be light soon," said Enrico. "Let's try and make it to the lines, or at least get close enough to make ourselves safer from any more patrols."

As they were now dragging the German in an upright position, they would make a faster time. Dawn was starting to break, and though they could see the start of the British wire, they knew that they would not make it, as everything was still so boggy that every step was an ordeal. They came to a shell hole that stretched approximately eight feet from side to side, but the good news for them was that in the earthquake it had completely emptied of water, and just above the mud at the bottom was a huge piece of walling, that though still wet, would keep the three of them from getting stuck in the mud. They could stay there and hopefully dry themselves with the rays of the winter sun. They lay there, covered with the remaining ground sheet, now completely beyond caring whether there were snipers ready to finish them, or if a passing shell took a fancy to settle in their midst, or whether the rains came again and drowned them. They were at the end of their physical tether; cold and in pain, they sank into a dreamless sleep.

Enrico was the first to awaken, with the unconscious groaning of the German officer next to him. He stretched, yawned, and looked at his friend, Maurice, who was lying there, mouth wide open, not making any noise, but dribbling profusely. Enrico knew it was already late, so he woke Maurice up.

"Look at your watch, Maurice. Tell me what the time is."
"Nearly two thirty."
"Have you any food left in your rucksack?"
"I've got one tin of bully beef, which I'll gladly share with you."
"Oh, gee! Thanks, just what I've always wanted!" retorted Enrico in

his most affected sarcastic mode. But he consumed it eagerly. The German, whom they now saw clearly for the first time was quite obviously in a bad way. Broken nose, broken jaw, bruised and battered, he was falling in and out of consciousness, and like his two adversaries, was covered from head to foot in mud. Enrico turned to Maurice, and said:

"Christ! I hope he makes it! I would hate this all to have been a complete waste of time."

But until it got dark, there was nothing they could do. They lay there, on their broken walling, looking up at the sky, waiting for the already setting sun to chase further west and bring the onset of night. They watched, idly, as two planes were locked in mortal combat overhead, and neither said a word, hardly even managing to blink, when one of the planes burst into a ball of flames, spilling the pilot, who cartwheeled to the ground, also in flames. They did not know whether the RFC or the Hun had won the day, and quite honestly they did not care. What's one more body in all this carnage?

Night came quickly, and they dragged themselves, and their prisoner for one last effort. 'Shit or bust!' thought Enrico. 'Nothing's going to stop us now!' They reached the wire in two hours, again exhausted from virtually dragging their prey and slopping through mud. They flopped by the side of the first batch of barbs. Enrico thought it would be a good idea to test the water, as he was not sure how deep the wire would be. So not shouting too loud, but hopefully loud enough, he said:

"Sentries, two British coming in, with one German prisoner!"

No reply. It was time to crawl through at least ten feet, and then try again. Repeat this sentence to find still a deafening silence. Crawl another ten feet; this time he changed his wording:

"Hellooo! Anybody home? Two British, one German prisoner coming in! We need medical assistance. Anybody there?"

"Why don't you shout louder? They can't quite hear you in Berlin!"

Enrico looked at the little Jew who was looking back at him with a huge grin on his face. Then he shouted out:

"I ain't forgotten. You promised to take us all out for a drink of the 'ard stuff, and I for one, is gonna 'old you to that!"

"Before you get that drink, tell me the password, you horrible little soldier!"

"Dragonetti!" bellowed both of the lads, and then followed it with: "Who the hell was Dragonetti, anyway?"

Five minutes later, RSM Kelly was busy organising three stretchers to take them to the dressing station, but he had a huge smile of satisfaction on his face, very happy to see that Enrico Caruso, the worst singer in the whole battalion was alive and safe to sing another day!

# VII

Enrico, Maurice and Lieutenant Kruger were rapidly taken to the field dressing station just inside the ruins of Ypres, deep within the battlement of the medieval wall close to the Menin Gate. This particular dressing station was more like a hospital, and could keep patients there until entirely recovered from their ailments or wounds. The view was more than a little disappointing, as they only looked onto thick concrete walls since they were actually more than thirty feet underground. Enrico and Maurice recovered fast from very mild frostbite and sheer exhaustion.

Kruger was a little the worse for wear. His nose was indeed broken, as was his jaw. He had lost his four front upper teeth; with that, and his mouth being wired up to help the setting of the bone, he was in a very sorry state. He would not be talking for a few days yet. His groin was swollen from the heavy boot that had made contact with it. It must have been agony to walk with the pain of testicles bruised and enlarged. But, time would heal them too. He lay there in the makeshift hospital bed, his legs wide apart, airing his wedding tackle, his mouth wired and swollen. He was now no longer the Fraulein's dream of Teutonic manhood. But he need not have worried, as there was a very effeminate male nurse that thought he was divine, and just could not take his eyes off looking at those huge swollen love doughnuts. Enrico hated any hospital, but this dressing station was particularly gloomy, damp and depressing. Maurice and he just wanted to get out of there again, into sunlight, even if it was raining shells. The doctors and orderlies were pleasant enough, but they just could not get used to lying in bed, watching their lives go by, even if it was just for a few days. Enrico lay there, having very unpleasant dreams about the last few days. All he could see in the sleeping hours were the dead, especially the friends that he had lost. In his dreams, Whitey Boy, stuck on the end of a bayonet, haunted him; he could hear him crying out for help, and he was always too slow to stop the puncturing of his heart by the enemy; now each night this recurring vision appeared in the colour red, which he interpreted as being his fault that the blood had been spilt. Only in the waking hours could he lay there, quietly recovering his strength, and more or less managing to keep these nightmares at bay.

On his second day in the dressing station, he got a visit from RSM Kelly and Sergeant Harrington.

"Well, Caruso, how the hell do you feel now?"

"Fine, Sir," he lied, not daring to say anything about his bad nightmares.

"You did a magnificent job out there. We were all completely taken by surprise at the extent of the explosion at the bunker. When Matti and Riddle got back to our lines, we assumed that you were all dead. Then bang, and here you are! I am very glad to see you again." Genuine warmth came from Spider Kelly; to Enrico this was entirely out of character, but he wasn't going to knock it.

"I want you to make out a report for the Battalion, but I think there will be a medal or two in there for you both. Everyone's talking about the night of the big bang. So let me in on what really happened out there, I want to be the first to know the truth. After that you can say what you like," he quipped to both the lads.

"I will be glad to tell you all, but first, how's Matti and how can I contact him?"

"Dumbridge is suffering from a not too serious form of trench foot, or frostbite. He's in hospital in Poperinge along with Riddle. They both got wounded coming through the wire, probably shell fragments. I haven't heard their complete story yet, and I haven't had time to get out there to visit them.

But I plan to, in the next day or two."

"But he will be alright, won't he?" asked Enrico with a certain urgency in his voice that prompted the quick reply.

"Yes, he'll be out and back in the Battalion before you know it."

"So come on, what happened out there?" enquired Sergeant Harrington, sitting on the side of Enrico's bed with an expectant look in his eyes. "No more prevaricating, tell all." And with that last prompt, he did just as he was told; he told them the complete story with Maurice Bechstein listening in and agreeing when he felt the need to. Lieutenant Kruger listened and heard, taking in all the information that he could. After all, there could be a war crime here, and he might use what he was hearing against the British perpetrators, when the Kaiser's army had successfully won the war! He could of course speak perfect English, though he was having difficulty understanding Maurice Bechstein when he spoke, 'sounds like a very strange dialect, must be a north Englander with that way of speaking,' thought the Lieutenant as he strained to hear.

New Year came, and went. Things in war had gone really badly for the Allies in 1915, not a great vintage; maybe 1916 would be better; there had been no reason at all to celebrate the coming of another year. Enrico was now restless to see his old friend once more. Anyway, the bad dreams were going and sleep was becoming easier; he noticed that his right hand shook a lot, which even made him spill his drinks at times. 'This will pass,' he thought, and he was desperate to leave this dark damp cave in the ground which passed for a hospital. Lieutenant Kruger had been taken away a few days before, so that he could be questioned. He was just jumpy and edgy: having nothing to do did not suit Enrico any more.

"Doctor, please can I be discharged? I feel a fraud: there is nothing wrong with me. I need to get back to my men in the Battalion. So, what about it, Sir?"

"I have been told to keep you here until tomorrow, you have an important visitor coming very soon; after that you can get up, then and only then, can you think about the war again." The doctor was a kindly old man, who had seen too much death and terrible injuries, so much so that, like some of his colleagues, he tended to keep men in the wards longer than was really necessary; at least in that way, he could keep his charges alive maybe a day or two more. It was a noble but futile gesture, as the top brass had other ideas; they obviously worked for the Grim Reaper. Between the Kaiser and the Allied Generals, death was enjoying a new renaissance.

The next day came slowly, but the boredom of sitting around, knowing that he was back to his old self, health-wise, was almost too much for Enrico to bear. They played drafts and silly card games, but soon sleep was the only way to pass the time quickly. Both the boys were woken in the early afternoon, when the doctor and some orderlies, came in to see them.

"Smarten up, lads, you have important visitors coming, and they will be here in a couple of minutes. Just sit on the side of your beds, you are sick after all," said the doctor to both of them. Enrico brushed his hair, noticing that many locks were coming out, and that it had lost its dark black lustre, being now a rather lifeless, matt black. Sitting beside their beds they only had to wait a minute. Into the ward came the figures of General Ashton with Colonel McBride and Major Bennett; following closely were Regimental Sergeant Major Kelly, sporting a broad grin, and Sergeant Harrington, whose hair was now fast going white, which shook the lads, as they had never noticed how old Harrington was starting to look.

"'*Tenshun!*" said Enrico, with only the little Jew to obey his command.

"Relax, men," said General Ashton, "this is a pleasant informal meeting; these are the sort of gatherings that I like." He came around between both beds, and to the great surprise of both Enrico and

Maurice, offered his hand to shake. 'What a firm grip,' was the startled thought of Enrico.

"It has come to my notice that you both managed something that the artillery could never seem to manage. You blew up that machine gun bunker; in fact you obviously managed to blow the tunnel that the enemy were digging under our lines, probably saving hundreds of lives in the process. And you managed to bring a German Lieutenant back to our lines for interrogation." Now smiling broadly at both the pals, he added, "It is my distinct pleasure to award you both the Military Medal, for outstanding courage in the face of great personal danger. You are indeed a credit to your Battalion and your Officers and NCOs. Well done, men, you have earned this praise; enjoy the accolades, for it will be back to work just as soon as you know it!" Then addressing himself to Colonel McBride, he said, "Well done, Colonel, I wish more Battalions had men like yours, we could win this dammed war quicker." Then turning on his heels, he marched out of the ward without any more thoughts given to the proud feelings he left behind him. Kelly shook both the friends' hands and said, "Well, what about that drink?"

As for Matti, he had been taken directly to Poperinge, after making it back to the British lines. He was in a very serious condition, with frostbite in his legs, plus wounds to his arms, most of them coming from Allied rusty barbed wire that had been blown into him from the exploding shells, when Riddle and he were trying to make it back to the home front lines.

He had been delirious for several days, from the shock of his wounds and the fatigue of the whole experience.

Martin Riddle had fared better, again with wounds to his arms from shielding his face and head, when shells started popping all around them both. He even had a deep graze from a bullet from the home lines, but that fortunately was not serious. Within three days he was back in the Battalion, but not loving every minute of it! He yearned for home. Just to see his father and mother, he would give anything. 'Why, oh why, did I allow myself to be talked into this awful bloody army? I should be in the office helping with legal problems! I'm no soldier!' were his thoughts. He seemed to be slipping more and more into himself, not really wanting to know any of his former chums in the section. He would not talk about the raid to anyone; even though he had helped Matti back to the British trenches, he would not even acknowledge him, refusing to hear anything about him while he was still in hospital. He could not sleep at night, tossing and turning incessantly to the extent of disturbing people around him. He had been very popular before the raid, but as he shunned others, they started to shun him. The more of a recluse he became, the harder it was for anyone around him to feel any sympathy or pity. When he was given a task to do, it was done in the slowest way possible, and he was starting to become insubordinate to Officers and NCOs around him. It was only a matter of a few days before he was on a charge for some minor offence, but when given two days of kitchen duties without pay, he lost his temper and started to swear at the Officer, thus then making it a more serious offence.

It was only RSM Kelly's intervention, which saved him from a more serious charge being administered upon him.

Enrico and Maurice joined Kelly and Harrington for that promised drink. They travelled to Poperinge for the treat, and treat it was, as 'Spider' Kelly was not known for his generous gestures, so they had two things to celebrate: free drinks and freedom from that awful claustrophobic cell in the battlements of Ypres that was called hospital. Not that Enrico fretted about the treatment, just the place itself. He had come to the conclusion that he no longer appreciated being underground for any length of time; but before drinks, a visit to see his good friend Matti.

"It *is* good to see you, Matti; I didn't know if you were alive after we saw the bombardment that you were getting which was meant for us. How are you feeling?"

"Well, better now that you are here. I wondered if you went west too. I have been told about the medal and all. Well done, I am sure you deserved it. So why the four of you, no, don't tell me… 'Spider' Kelly is honouring his debt?" This caused a titter out of them all, except Kelly who feigned a hurt expression on his rugged exterior of a face.

"I am renowned for my generosity, maybe when you are out of here you can see it for yourself, not that I will buy you a drink now! You can just suffer and watch the others enjoying themselves. That'll teach you to be more polite." Again a snigger came from all.

"Matti, how is your leg? You really had me worried, I was sure you were going to die in that hole. You had gone into a coma, and I thought I wouldn't be able to get you out of it."

"The leg hurts like hell, and it has gone from being blackish in colour to bright red, which the doctor says is good news, though anything that hurts that much is never good news. But I expect to be out of here before too long. Maybe we can get some leave?" he said in a very pointed hopeful way, that didn't go unnoticed by Kelly or Harrington.

"We must go, a thirst you would not believe is upon us all," was the last casual remark that Enrico made to his friend, before leaving him again.

"Get well soon, we need you back. You won't know any of the section any more, all new faces, and so young and inexperienced." This comment by Sergeant Harrington, made them all think of how easy it had been, to lose those who had become good friends, moving on to new people, as if you were just changing a daily paper.

Two more weeks went by; the weather had turned extremely cold and snow was in the air. Matti was due back to the Battalion that day, and Enrico had news for him.

"Welcome back to the family, not that you will know too many people now. The Hun has been doing well with their snipers and we have lost a steady stream of good men, and the new boys just don't seem to last too long. But I have some news, good or bad I don't know yet. We have our seven day passes, with tickets home to Blighty, if we want to go. When we get back we have a temporary transfer to the mining division, as per request." Enrico jested as he said these words, making out to be overly delighted.

"Surely, that's good news, isn't it?"

"To tell the truth, Matti, I am not at all sure that going back underground is going to be a good thing, I feel extremely nervous about it. But the good news is, it's just temporary, we will be back in the Battalion for the summer. So, I guess I can stand it if you can?" He paused, and then quietly added:

"I have some bad news too. Jimmy Riddle has gone AWOL, and I seriously think he has gone mad. But if the MPs catch him, I suspect it will be the dawn chorus, and that would be awful. And another thing, Sergeant Harrington is being sent back to Finsbury to become a training Sergeant for new recruits. His nerves are shot to pieces, and he's losing all his hair which has gone completely white. He looks terrible. Nice chap too, I really got to like him."

"So, where are we going on leave?" said Matti completely ignoring the bad bits of news. 'This has to be a good news day only,' he thought to himself. "Let's go home!"

"Home! What's that? I have forgotten all about home. I never got a reply to my letter. Home... maybe we could at that." Enrico went into a thoughtful mode; hand on chin he wondered, 'Can we get away with it? It would be great to see the old man again.' "Yes, I agree; let's go home. Bugger the police, it's been long enough for us to be low priority, we can get in and out without anyone ever noticing."

"How much money do we have?" enquired Matti.

"More than enough to have a really good time."

Home had been a place other people go to, not Matti or Enrico. The nearest either of them had been to home, was the meeting of Matti's brother Alan; since that encounter, nothing, no letters, no news.

Blighty just didn't exist for them, and now it shone like the Star of David, guiding them to their Jerusalem. The thought of home was now making them both so excited that tears welled up in their eyes. 'Must stop acting like a sissy boy, men don't cry,' thought Enrico, as he wiped away a couple of tears.

The passes came through the next day, and it was time to leave. The Wipers guns were unusually quiet, though the occasional boom could be heard; who had fired or where to seemed completely irrelevant; this was a day to savour, not to be spoilt by any loud reports.

Enrico and Matti were spruced to the nines, they looked good, and they felt great. This was now their time. The train was crowded with the wounded, but they managed to find space. Being a hospital train, it got priority on the line and sped through the French countryside to the port of Calais. In fact the train journey had still managed to take three and a half hours from point to point, but it seemed to be quick. They were by the dockside showing their passes to the Military Police, even before twelve noon, and they could board a ferry within the hour. That ferry would land in Newhaven or Brighton within four hours, so with luck they could be on a train to Liverpool in the late evening, maybe catching the Northern Mail train. But hope springs eternal.

They caught their ferry as hoped, but halfway out into the Channel a U-boat was spotted and chased by a Frigate escort ship; the ferry had to be given another port to go to, and this meant more time. The Frigate never caught the U-boat, though many depth charges were dropped, and a lot of fish were executed in the place of German submariners. But no U-boat was landed as a prize trophy. One had to suspect that the Captain and crew of the U-boat were also going home for leave and really didn't want any fuss. For a U-boat, coming through the Channel was asking for trouble, and one would seriously wonder why the underwater ship would dare take the risk? The laying of the mines was done in a deliberate fashion to catch the unwary U-boat Captain;

they lay at every depth, just waiting patiently. Submarine nets had been placed in many of the channels; these too were almost impossible to break through, once a submarine had got itself caught.

Fishing boats were on the look-out, ready and eager to catch the biggest fish of all, and they carried guns and mines to make sure that if a submarine surfaced, it would be finished off there and then. Then of course, there were the roving Frigates. These extremely well armed and very manoeuvrable ships could chase anything that moved under or on the surface of the sea, if they chose to. Very few submarines then made their way through the English Channel, opting instead to go right around the British coast line, to enter German waters coming around the Norwegian coast; much longer, but infinitely safer. So why would one or two make that almost suicidal attempt of the quick route? Usually, because they were running out of fuel or had seriously injured crew on board. Maybe that was the reason that Enrico and Matti's ferry was diverted for safety reasons to Portsmouth. And because of the extra journeying, they never landed until three in the morning of the next day: day two of a seven day pass. Time was already running down, and it made them both very depressed at the thought. It was cold and wet when they stepped off the ferry onto good old English sod. Enrico nearly bent down to kiss it, but noticed just in time that a dog had been there just before him. 'What is it about things that smell bad and me?' he thought.

The train to London would not leave until five thirty, and there was nowhere to even get a hot cup of tea. All they could both do was walk up and down the station playing the waiting game. The train was late, which was now no surprise to anyone. When it finally appeared, having broken a wheel bearing, it had to be replaced and of course that took time too. But at least now, the station buffet was open and they could get some meagre breakfast, with hot, strong tea. Ten thirty came and went. Enrico was pulling his hair out with frustration, whilst Matti stayed much more pragmatic, with an air of "what must be must be." This made Enrico even more uptight. The train was finally boarded at twelve twenty-three of their second day. They arrived in St. Pancras station at just after three fifteen. Then they made their way to Euston station to catch the next train to Liverpool, but were told that the only train they could get would be the five fourteen, arriving in Liverpool at ten thirty-three in the evening. "Where's our luck? We will not be home until midnight, and then we will have to leave again in a couple of days. What's the point of this nonsense?" complained Enrico, but he was secretly very excited about the chance of seeing his father once again. This journey proved to be no problem, with the train running on time. And they arrived in Liverpool at ten twenty-nine, a result at last!

They got a taxi to Tranmere, as that at least would be quick. Matti's home came first, and Enrico just had time to see the tender loving care that was bestowed on his friend. They agreed to meet later the next day at Matti's address, and then the taxi drove off to the Lokowski household. Enrico knew immediately when the taxi drew up to the address that something was wrong. The house looked empty. He emerged from the taxicab, asking the driver to wait, knocked on the door, but that hollow echo that comes from an empty building came back to haunt him. 'Where the heck is the old bugger? It's so late I cannot knock up any of the neighbours; anyway, I don't want anyone to know I'm still alive and around. There may well be a profit in someone informing the police that I'm here, back in Tranmere.'

"Driver, do you mind taking me back to Liverpool? It seems my father is out, and I know a priest that is a good friend of his; maybe they are playing cards or something?"

"No trouble, gov'nor! You're paying, I'm driving. Just tell me which church and guide me if I don't happen to know the way."

It was well after one thirty in the morning when Enrico paid the cabby off and walked into the porch of the Manse. His heart was in his mouth, 'Would Father Lyon know where father is, would he still talk to me

238

knowing of my terrible secret; what has happened while I've been away?' He knocked on the door, then knocked again even louder; he kept knocking until after a couple of minutes, lights appeared, coming down the stairs and to the front door. There stood his young saviour, now getting much older, Father Lyon. "Yes, my son, who are you and what do you want at this unearthly hour?"

"Father, it's me, Enrico Lokowski!"

"Lokowski…Enrico, mon Dieu, is it really you? Where have you been, though I can see you are in the army? So you don't know about your father?"

"I have come home to see him, and the house seems to be empty. I'm sorry to trouble you, but I could not think of anyone else to ask for information. Where is dad?"

"Enrico, come on in, it's cold and wet. I have a story to tell you and you are not going to like it!"

Enrico knew what was going to be said, but still he obediently walked into the priest's parlour. "Sit down, Enrico, would you like a drink?"

"No thanks, Father, I'm so tired that a drink will just send me straight to sleep. Say what you have to say to me."

"Right, then. Your father died a week ago, I buried him yesterday. He had a good funeral, all his neighbours came. They had all grown to respect and like him very much; it was nice to see all those faces, but the one he would have wanted most of all was not there for him. Why did you not write to him, you could have told him about joining up, he would have understood. Did you have some sort of falling out with him? He was talking about opening a shop in Darwen, so as to be near you. He was making good money and had saved a lot. I have the money in a bank; it will be transferred to your account if you have one? So what happened?" The priest had withdrawn a new bottle of Scotch whisky from the Welsh dresser, and started to pour himself a large glassful.

"Father, I did write to him, and he must have got it. But I guess he has never told you about the trouble I was in; the Police must have given him a hard time looking for me?"

"I have never heard anything about Police looking for you. The times he has been here, we drank and talked. He thought you had run away from the mine and gone to Scotland. He was always expecting a letter, and it never came. Maybe the letter will be at the house now? I have heard of no such letter, I can assure you. Maybe it is time that you gave me your confession? I will be happy to hear it now, should you wish to?"

"Sorry, Father, but with all that I have seen and experienced I really don't want any confessions right now."

"Your choice, my son. Would you like to have a bed for the night? You will not find a hotel at this time. Then tomorrow I will tell you all about what happened to him."

"Thank you, Father; I'm not sure that I will sleep, but I'm really not taking anything in now." Enrico was shown to the spare room. The priest left him to his own devices, allowing him time to grieve alone. Enrico sunk onto the bed. At first, all he could think about was that it had been hardly worth coming home, and then he started to think about his father. 'Father, what have I done to you?' He burst into a crumbling heap and sobbed. After some minutes, he fell into a trance-like sleep, with nightmares of dying soldiers; his father was there in Wipers with him, asking him 'What are you doing here? Why aren't you back home with me?' Always death in the dreams, always death! Enrico awoke exhausted after the dawn had broken. A sunny cold day, but nothing but gloom in his mind; there had been no rest in that sleep, only confusion and suffering. Washing didn't break the feeling of complete and utter exhaustion, and when he went down the stairs to join Father Lyon in breakfast, the good father looked at him in a very worried fashion. "Did you sleep at all, Enrico?"

"Not really, Father. I dreamt awful dreams that all included my own father."

"Have some breakfast with me, food can be a great restorer," he added with no real great conviction.

"So Father, tell me, how did he die?"

"Well, my son, your father never got over the death of your mother, and after he became friends with me, we used to spend many a night chewing the fat over a bottle of whisky or two. He enjoyed the drink; it seemed to me it had become a habit that he could not break. It was alright when he was here; I kept him to a reasonable amount, but on his own at home he would seriously overindulge himself. Others were not aware that he had developed a drink problem. He never got drunk and he never disgraced himself. But it took its toll on his organs: two weeks ago he was rushed into the infirmary with obvious signs of liver and kidney failure. He lasted a few days, went into a coma from which he never recovered. Don't blame yourself though. Of course he was heartbroken at not seeing you again, but it was the loss of your mother that was the origin of his drinking. I will take you to see his grave. I am the main executor for his estate, and of course it will all belong to you, but I am sure you can trust me to arrange and pay for a fine headstone for him?"

"Of course, Father. When you're ready I would like to see his last resting place, then I shall leave you in peace, and I will go seek out my friend Matti Dumbridge."

"Please don't feel you have to leave; why not stay here with me for the days you are on leave?"

"Thank you Father, but no. I will find Matti and maybe we can do something together, if he wants to, or I shall stay with his folks, then it's back to France for us. Besides, you are a very busy man, and I wouldn't want to be any sort of burden. I have got used to being self-reliant; it is not a problem for me any more. Anyway, I'm alone, and it's time to stand up and be that man my father would have been proud of."

"He was always proud of you, Enrico. His sorrow was that he couldn't provide for you the way he wanted to. You must do as you wish, but please remember there is always a bed here for you while I am priest of this parish. Now let's go and see your father's grave."

The grave was unmarked, just a mound of earth, tucked nicely close to a huge yew tree. "Father would like this position," Enrico imparted to the priest. "You have done him proud, and I'm very grateful to you. You were his best and only friend. At least he could talk to you; we all need someone to talk to. I too am lucky enough to have Matti; he may not be Albert Einstein, but he cares about me as I do him. We will see one another through these awful troubles with Germany, and then maybe there will be a chance for us to make something of our lives?"

"I hope so, my son, I truly hope so. One thing is for sure, nothing will ever be the same again. Things must get better after all this death. Do you think it will all end this year?"

"Father, some say it might go on for years. I think there will be a big push either by the Hun or ourselves, but one way or another, it has to be resolved, and we have to break the lines; there cannot be an endless supply of soldiers, sooner or later all the youth of the world will have died from either machine gun fire or shelling. But of course, I hope it will be our side that wins the war, but sometimes I just wonder if it matters."

"Surely you don't believe the Kaiser's army should win!"

"No, Father, I don't want Fritz to succeed, but I don't want this stupid waste of life to continue. It's so easy to watch someone dying that surely, Father, it must be better to watch them live?"

Enrico called a taxi and gave Matti's address; he sat in the back, looking out at the grey, filthy buildings, thinking of his father, and how he had come to let him down so badly. Tears welled in his eyes once again, but now he could not really tell what he was crying for; was it the loss of his father, the death of Youth, or just for that hollow, empty feeling within his body and mind? He paid off the taxi, and proceeded to knock on Matti's door. A little old lady appeared whom he now recognized as Mrs Dumbridge. Just over a year had passed, but the Dumbridge parents had aged a century.

"Come in, Enrico. Matti has been waiting for you. We knew about your father, and were very sorry to hear, but it was not our role to tell you last night."

When going into the parlour, he saw, sitting close to the coal fire, Matti's father. To Enrico's eyes, he was a wizened, skinny old man who had been beaten by life's labours, and he sat there, huddled, deep in thought, with his hands wrapped around a mug of tea. He did not even look up, or acknowledge Enrico's presence.

"Enrico, Ma told me about your dad, I'm so sorry! What say we both go and have a drink down at the local? By the time we get there, it should be open."

"Good idea. I don't know how I feel, but I do feel like a drink."

"Landlord, two pints of your best bitter, please!"

"Coming up right away, Sir!"

As Enrico and Matti gulped their first pint down, Matti put his hand on Enrico's arm, squeezing it slightly in a comforting gesture. Enrico smiled at his friend. 'I may have lost my mother and father, but with my pal Matti, I'll never be alone.'

"So, what's it like being at home with your mum and dad?"

"It's funny, really. Since we left to go to Darwen, and now to the army, I suppose, like my brothers before me, I have become independent. To tell the truth, Enrico, I'm bored. One night at home, and I did not know what to talk about. But one thing I did discover, the police don't seem to have made a connection to us in Tranmere. I suspect that we have been protected by some of the witnesses from the pub that awful night."

"Yes, even Father Lyon had not heard of any visits from the local Constabulary, so maybe, their line of inquiry will have gone cold, at least where you and me are concerned. But we should always stay vigilant, and expect the worst. We should be optimistically pessimistic."

243

"What??"

"Hope for the best, but expect the worst."

They both laughed and ordered another two pints.

"Matti, what do you want to do with the rest of your time here? We really have to leave, at the latest the day after tomorrow."

"To tell the truth, I think we should leave first thing in the morning. Speaking entirely for myself, this is not my world anymore. I don't recognise anything, it all seems too long ago; even my own mother and father seem like complete strangers. What do they know about our living conditions? My mother could only ask if I'm keeping myself clean, and am warm enough at night. They don't know how to kill a man quietly with a knife, or how to blow the top of a man's head off with a rifle. They can never imagine the filth and squalor and degradation that we have to endure every minute of every day, living with the rats and dead bodies. How can they ever imagine that?"

Enrico looked at Matti with a new found awe; he had never heard him be so eloquent before. He did not even know that Matti had hidden depths that were now starting to surface.

The lads leaned back with their third pint each, Enrico putting his feet onto another chair and surveying the public bar they were in. An old picture of Queen Victoria, fading badly under years of tobacco smoke, hung on the wall opposite to where they sat. The floor was covered in sawdust to receive any spilt drinks, or the vomit that often comes from too much drink. The bar itself was solid oak, but stained from a thousand sloshed drinks; there were three pumps for the three beers offered, and pewter tankards festooned the underside of the ceiling above the bar, each one probably able to tell a rather depressing story. The landlord was a huge man, weighing at least twenty stone, but being at least six foot two, carried it very well, and with the broken nose and deep scar above his right eye, he looked more like an all-in wrestler than a jovial, welcoming publican.

"How will you tell your mother and father that you are going back early?"

"I guess I will do what I always do, lie!"

This was not a happy homecoming; both lads felt as grey and grimy as the buildings around them. It had once again become cold, and it looked as if snow might well appear over the horizon. The beer was not doing its job, and a fourth pint only induced a more acute sense of melancholy.

"Well, Matti, drinking has not solved our problems. I suggest we go back, have a nice sleep, and leave early in the morning."

"Agreed, but don't waste your money on a hotel; if you don't mind the floor, you can share my room."

"The floor, heaven! Anything's better than sleeping on a cold, wet fire step!"

But somehow, strangely, that cold, wet fire step now seemed more like home than Tranmere ever would again.

The lads left the house before first light. Matti had written a short letter, explaining that they had been called back to the Battalion early, but was aware that his mother would never believe this and see through the fabrication immediately. They caught the first available train back to London with no problems whatsoever, and then went to Charing Cross station to get the next train to Dover. At Dover station there was an omnibus just leaving to go to the dock, and having shown their passes they were quickly ushered onto the steam ferry.

"It's bloody amazing how much easier it is to go to war, than to get back from it!" Matti laughed in agreement.

The ferry went to Boulogne, but they still arrived there with plenty of time to find a hotel room for the night, with a view to reaching Wipers the next day.

"Enrico, what say you and me find a really good restaurant, and have ourselves a decent bottle of red wine and some frogs legs?"

"One out of two sounds good, *but you can stuff the frogs legs!*"

It was tough finding accommodation, as Boulogne was crowded with troops from all corners of the Empire; Indian soldiers, some in turbans, many leading horses, looking more suited for a battle at the Kyber Pass than a melee on the Western front; Canadians with the odd American recruit thrown in for good measure, looking very much more casual, wandering around the town without a care in the world. There was a Battalion from little Newfoundland with its staunch pro-British tendencies gathering in Boulogne, waiting to go up to the front. That small enclave of the British Empire had managed to raise an entire Battalion of ten thousand men, all now in France, believing they were there to protect their mother country, England. The different colours of the uniforms were nearly outdone by the different colours of soldiers' skin; Boulogne had become a truly multiracial collecting point.

But the pals did find a place to put their heads, albeit a church hall belonging to the local Catholic church. They shared the room with fifty other men, so it was not going to be a quiet night. It was not easy to find a restaurant that had tables to spare, but eventually they did; just a little way away from the harbour was a small intimate bistro, that was filled with French men and women, but who nevertheless welcomed the two lads into their bosom. Enrico could speak no French, and the French certainly were not going to speak any English! So when the waitress said:

"Et pour vous, Monsieur?" they looked at one another, and Enrico smiled at the young lady, and with his hands indicated that he wanted two enormous piles of food, and gave the eating motion.

"Ah! Vous voulez de grosses portions! Je vais vous apporter un bon gros steak frites. Que désirez-vous boire?" she went on, indicating with her right hand a drinking motion.

To which Enrico, still grinning, nodding energetically, showing two fingers indicated the number of bottles required.

"Bon, alors deux carafes de vin rouge!"

The little bistro had come to a dead stop, with everybody's interest firmly planted on these two English soldiers, but as soon as the waitress had taken the order and walked away, the place went back to its normal hubbub of noise and chitchat. The smell of Gauloises, wine, and fried food had an intoxicating effect on the two men, as the hunger pains made their stomachs rumble and the various aromas made their mouths salivate. The food came in abundance, much to the delight of the entourage that had again silenced themselves and watched with wonderment as the two Tommies tucked into their food with such a relish as to make them all think they had become devotees of the French national pastime. The food was delicious, the steaks thick and juicy, with a sauce made from the juices of the meat, a few pats of fresh butter mixed with some fine red wine. The frites were thin and beautifully crispy, and came by the bucketful, closely followed by a crunchy green salad. Two carafes of red wine went nowhere, and soon two more were ordered. With the second round of wine came a selection of French cheese, which at first both the lads turned their nose at, but soon found themselves tucking in with a will. Faced with such enjoyment and enthusiasm for the food, the waitress took it upon herself to bring them a delicious tarte aux pommes 'on the house', which they promptly demolished. The waitress raised her own glass of wine, called for silence, and said: "Messieurs-dames, buvons à la santé de nos alliés. S'ils se battent aussi bien qu'ils mangent, nous ne pouvons pas perdre la guerre!" This caused a huge cheer from the now genial gathering, and they all added with raised glasses: "Vive la Grande Bretagne!" thus making the Entente Cordiale even more cordial! Enrico and Matti, completely bemused, and understanding very little, when seeing the glasses raised, and hearing the cheer for Britain, stood, raised their own glasses, and said: "Vive la France!", and then they asked for two more carafes to be brought, the contents of which they promptly distributed amongst the friendly populace. Enrico turned towards Matti, put his left hand on his shoulder, and with a drunken lurch slurred: "I can't remember when I *lasht* had *shush* a good time!" To which Matti replied: "Yerrr drunk!" but however hard he tried could not raise himself from the chair.

Enrico looked down on his friend, who had now lost any feeling in his legs from the waist downwards, and added: "and you think I'm *s-drunk!* I think we should get *sh-ome co*-coffee..."

The waitress and regulars were completely beguiled by this alien duo, and made sure that when their time came to leave this establishment, they would leave in a safe and sober state, so coffee was employed in great quantities to successfully do the job. This had been a wonderful night; they had never experienced such friendliness before, and the barriers of language had been overcome by just good will and friendship. Though the waitress tried to keep the cost of the meal to a minimum, the lads lavished a lot more money upon her in gratitude for such a fine evening. As the two left the bistro, they were made to shake the hand of everybody there, and were warmly wished "Bonne Chance" by one and all. Their way back to the hall was made all the easier with the memory of the cheering from all the customers witnessing the kisses the waitress gave them on both cheeks.

The journey back to Belgium was almost uneventful, except for the reminder of war as the big guns blazed from Ypres. They had got within three miles of Poperinge, when the train was halted through more work being done to the line, so they decided to walk to the town and stay one night in Talbot House. It was a cold, windy day, and though there were no clouds, the sun gave no heat, as the Siberian cold winds won the day. After two hours of walking, they made it into Talbot House, and were astonished to find SRM Kelly, sitting there, smoking and having a strong cup of tea.

"Lads, what are you doing back so early?" asked 'Spider' Kelly.

"To tell the truth, this is more home to us than home was," said Enrico, without mentioning the demise of his father.

"I know what you mean, nobody really understands what we go through here, and when you try to explain what it's like, you get that look of disbelief on people's faces. When this bloody war is over, it's going to be damn hard to readjust." There was a long pause from Kelly, and then he added in a softer tone: "Boys, I've got bad news for you. Martin Riddle was caught casually walking the gangplank of a ferry, trying to get back to England, and there was a court martial yesterday here in Poperinge. I personally pleaded that he had always been a good soldier, and was just suffering from a complete mental and physical breakdown, but none of those bastards would listen; and even the fact that Riddle did not know where he was, and could hardly answer any question coherently, they just put it down to dumb insolence. He's going to be shot tomorrow morning as a deserter."

*"Fuck! FUCK!"* said Enrico, bringing his fist hard down on the table, startling all that were close to hand.

"Are you going to be there, Spider?"

"Yes, I am!"

"Can I come too?" followed by: "Me too!" said Matti.

"I'm glad you said that; he's a good boy that Riddle. He needs us around him for his last moments."

Just before dawn, the next morning, the three of them presented themselves to the Captain in charge of the firing squad.

RSM Kelly asked the Captain if they could be in attendance for Private Riddle, and be the ones to lead him to the post, just before the Padre said the final blessing. This was agreed; when they opened the cell door, all they saw was a completely broken young man, who not only did not know them, but really did not know himself, or what was about to befall him.

"Martin," said Kelly, in a soft, friendly gentle tone that once again startled the two lads who had never realised until recently just how much Spider cared for his men. They felt the warmth of his voice, as if directed at them too.

"Matti and Enrico are here with me, and we are going to walk you out in the courtyard, we are going to say a prayer together, and everything will be over very quickly; there is nothing to worry at all about, you are with friends."

Private Riddle looked up at the three of them, with a half smile on his face; he had not really understood anything, but he was relaxed and at ease with himself. Matti took one arm, and Enrico the other, and the four of them walked very slowly the twenty or so paces to the post. Martin was still smiling when they tied his hands behind the post, and still smiled when the priest gave his blessing, but recognition dawned, as the firing squad was quickly marched and lined up. Then he said, almost screaming: "Matti, Enrico, what are they doing? Why am I here? What is happening?" Horror entered the faces of Enrico, Matti and Kelly, as suddenly they had to contend with a *compos mentis* Martin Riddle who now realised his fate was sealed. The Captain of the firing squad came over, and while Private Riddle was frantically trying to break free of his bonds, read out the charge: "You have been found guilty of desertion, and have been sentenced to death by firing squad. Have you anything to say?" but a look of sheer terror was in Martin's eyes, and the Captain did not wait for any words to come from his mouth; he quickly placed the hood over his head. Private Riddle was screaming: "NO, no, you can't, this is a mistake. I'm no deserter!" but the Captain had already moved away, had called the squad to take aim, and just as Martin was saying: "I never deser..." the order to fire came.

A loud report echoed around the small courtyard, and Martin Riddle slumped to his knees with blood gushing from his torso. The Captain returned to the prisoner; lifting the hood, he could see that Private Riddle was very much alive. "Oh, Christ!" said the Captain, as he withdrew his service revolver, cocked the trigger, and put it towards Riddle's temple. At the same moment Riddle looked up at him, and he tried to speak, but froth and blood gurgled from his mouth, and the Captain pulled the trigger. The bullet finished the job that the firing squad had started, but it blew blood, brains and scalp everywhere, some even hit Kelly, who reeled, almost sick to the stomach at the spectacle that he had just witnessed. The firing squad were marched out, the witnesses were marched away, and the Padre gave the sign of the cross over the limp remains of Private Riddle.

Enrico, Matti and Kelly, now white as sheets, removed themselves from that place.

"Spider, Martin's father will be devastated when he gets the letter, telling him his son was a deserter. Would you please write to them, and tell them the truth?" requested Enrico.

"Of course, I will do that, but I will ask them to be discreet; at least until this damn war is over, otherwise the indiscretion could cost me my job."

Matti and Enrico shook hands with Kelly, and as both of them were in very sombre mood after this experience, they said their farewells, and decided to make their way back to the Battalion, and then onto the new phase in their life.

And all the time the guns barked out their message of welcome…

# VIII

Coming back to the Battalion now seemed to be the holiday that the duo had thought they needed. Why, they were even glad to see the miserable face of Major Tyler-Latham, the Colonel's Adjutant. Though that thought didn't last very long, as when they appeared in the entrance of HQ dugout, he scowled at them in the most unfriendly way. "Where the hell have you two been?"

"On leave, Sir; we had passes, and are not actually due back until tomorrow," answered Enrico in a not too friendly way.

"Well, forget your leave, you are back now and I expect you both to get to work right away. Go and see Sergeant Cakebread immediately; tell him I said you were to start work now." At the mention of Cakebread both the lads stiffened, trying hard not to laugh at the name. 'Jesus, if I had that as a name I would change it by deed poll before joining the army. And what the hell has rattled this arsehole's cage?' thought Matti, still with half a smile on his face.

"And you can take that look off your faces right now!"

"Yes, Sir, sorry, Sir. We will find Sergeant Cakebread right now and do as we are told," said Enrico, putting a real emphasis on the name of Cakebread, with tears now starting to form in his eyes, and holding his breath as much as he could, so as not to laugh out loud. 'Laugh and we are dead. This piece of dog's do is dying to charge us with dumb insolence.' They both stood to attention, saluted the Officer, and left as quickly as possible. "Where the hell is the Cakehole?" asked Enrico, to the riotous laughter of Matti, now feeling the relief of being able to let his feelings flow out. "Let's ask someone, or we will be charged with disobeying an order from a superior Officer, and that would never do, would it?" chided Matti, still chuckling. "That shit should take a German bullet if there was any justice in this world," said Enrico, as they walked into the trench system. '*Home sweet home*,' was the common thought.

"Private, come here!" shouted Matti to the first soldier he came across. "Who is Sergeant Cakebread, and where might we find him?"

"Corporal, he is our chief cook. You will find him back near the Battalion HQ. How come you don't know him?"

"When did he arrive here?"

"A few weeks ago, I should guess."

They found Sergeant Cakebread baking some pies for the Officers. He was a huge fat man, who would have been more suited for working in a fancy restaurant than catering in the army with the harsh conditions that he had to toil under. He was sweating profusely as the duo approached. His trembling wheel of fat which covered his body, turned a second or two after he had swivelled, making the very uncoordinated man look like a clown in the circus.

"Yes, Corporals, what do you want?"

"Well, we are supposed to be on leave, but Major Tyler-Latham insisted that we come to you for some work, but as we are being transferred tomorrow to the mining division, you can get stuffed about any work and leave us to our own devices. Just thought you ought to know, that all." Enrico looked at Matti who had spouted this abuse at the Sergeant, looked back at the Sergeant and waited for the explosion. Nothing happened.

"Oh, all right then, what do I say if he comes around here looking for you two?"

"Tell him that Matti Dumbridge says hello and wishes him a pleasant day." This one just made Enrico double up with laughter.

"Well, what about a quick drink with me before you both disappear for the day?"

"Why, Sergeant, you are a real gent after all. What about it, Enrico, fancy a snifter?"

"I never say no to a gentleman, you know that, Matti," he jibed, and then added, "what's your tickle, Sarge?"

"Good army rum, of course. You didn't think I would go out and buy some, did you, now?"

"Well, Sarge, as we don't know you, and have no real intention of seeing you again after today, I think it would be extremely impolite of us to refuse. Don't you agree, Matti?"

"I so heartily do, old friend. Get those glasses out, Sarge, and let us at it."

Smiling with a grin as broad as his fat stomach, he produced three glasses, and then poured generous portions of rum into each one. "Cheers!" was said by all three, then down in one. Another round appeared as if from nowhere, down in one again. 'My goodness!' thought Enrico, 'it's going to be a boozy day, that's for sure.' After a few more rums were poured, another bottle was produced from another secret hiding place. "Well, lads what about some serious stuff, then?" Enrico was already feeling terribly groggy, and Matti was looking extremely cross eyed.

"We've only been having a couple, but I can hardly see," were Matti's drawling words.

"Speak for yourself," interjected Enrico, who had taken no notice of what Matti had been saying.

"Call yourself soldiers? Come on, this is going to be fun." Sergeant Cakebread was enjoying this: his favourite pastime, with two cheeky young whipper-snappers to put in their place, teaching them a salient lesson in manners

"Come on, lads; you've a lot of making up to do!" Picking up his glass full almost to the brim with a dark treacle-like rum, he made sure that the lads clinked glasses with him, and downed the contents almost in one go.  Filling the glasses again, he insisted on yet another "Cheers!"  By now, with only half an hour gone since their arrival at the cookhouse, the trio had consumed almost three whole bottles.  Enrico could no longer see his hand in front of him, and anyway, who needs hands?  Matti was sitting on a box, swaying from side to side, convinced that he was on a ship in a very rough sea.  Sergeant Cakebread never got drunk, and was enjoying himself.

Another glassful of rum each and Matti, now believing that the ship he was on was sinking, had gone completely green, and was looking ready to give it all back with interest, but instead fell to the floor, completely unconscious.  Enrico, seeing his friend with his face in the dirt, his arms by his side, and his bottom sticking up in the air, pointed at him, burst out laughing, then promptly joined him in that prone position, he too, being completely numb to the world.  Cakebread was laughing almost hysterically, but thought it prudent to get them, the glasses and the bottles out of sight.  He dragged them both behind some stacked boxes of bully beef and some sacks of potatoes where they could lay unseen until they recovered.  He then gluttonously gulped down the rest of his rum, and went back to his pies, as if nothing had ever happened.  Lunch, as well as the evening meal came and went, and it was eight forty-five in the evening when some kitchen orderlies, hearing a moaning sound coming from behind the stores, informed Sergeant Cakebread of the existence of two drunken louts sleeping it off.

"I want four of you to carry the two lads out here.  Get some strong coffee brewing, and an empty bucket.  I've a feeling they're going to need it!"

The two lads were plonked unceremoniously on two makeshift chairs; neither really knew which day of the year it was, they did not even know if they were alive or dead.  If they were dead, they had made the Grand Trip to Hades; if they were alive they still had made the Grand Trip to Hades!  'I think I'm going to be sick!' was all that came to Matti's mind, and as if with telepathic powers, Enrico thought 'I am going to be sick' in response.  Quickly grabbing the empty bucket, he did his best to fill it; Matti, who was becoming more aware of his surroundings, on seeing his friend heaving, snatched the pail from Enrico, and promptly deposited a load there himself. Enrico, now trying to come to terms with the fact that he was *not* dead, squinted through bleary eyes to see five sets of eyes staring back at him; one of those sets was attached to a large, swollen, ruddy face that sported a huge grin and rotten teeth.

"Sergeant, how come you're not as bad as we are?" asked Enrico. Five sets of eyes burst out laughing, but only one gave a very profound sentence back in reply.

"Son, you could never outdrink me! I've been practising all my life. You two are amateurs, you happened to tangle with a professional. Now, are you two suffering from headaches?" The answer came with two sets of nods, quickly followed by two sets of groans, as it was definitely a mistake to move their heads.

"I have the perfect answer for you; it might make you leak at both ends, but it will do the trick. Orderlies, two of you stay here, and watch the 'prisoners'," which provoked huge laughter from the four orderlies, "and you two come with me, and help me prepare the medicine. Charles, bring me the coffee, Louis, bring me vinegar, mustard, pepper, lemon and some rum."

There, was Sergeant Cakebread, his huge bulk wobbling up to the table, as he mixed equal portions of rum and coffee, then added a generous tablespoon of pepper; half a glass of vinegar was blended in, then another generous spoonful of mustard powder. All this was stirred vigorously, with the piece de resistance of a soupçon of lemon.

"What do you think, Charles? Is this up to our usual high standards?"

Private Charles Hacker leant forward to smell the concoction, and nearly fell to the ground in disgust.

"Sergeant, you are a true master. I do believe this creation is the best ever!" They poured two glasses and took them back for Enrico and Matti to indulge themselves with.

"Look, lads, you won't like this, but trust me, it will do the job. You feel bad now, you'll feel terrible in a minute, but after that, you'll be able to handle again what the world throws at you. Right, boys, hold their noses, Corporals, open your mouths now!"

With that, the two glasses of so-called medicine were emptied down both Enrico's and Matti's throats. There was a moment or two, as the duo gasped for breath. Mount Vesuvius was starting to erupt again, only this time, the lads had to hold on to their trousers as well.

"Charles, quick, take them to the latrines! Louis, follow up with the bucket, it may yet be necessary."

Twenty seconds later, Enrico and Matti were sitting side by side with their bowels continuously emptying. It was just as well that neither of the lads had ever taken up smoking: had they struck a match to light a cigarette, they would have finished the job the Germans were trying to do since the start of the war! After five minutes of eruption from both ends, it was true the headache was passing, and they started to feel of sound mind once again.

The boys stood to attention in reverential respect for Sergeant Cakebread.

"Sergeant, you are one of a kind. You put up with our bombastic ways, and taught us a lesson, one we probably will forget tomorrow, but today you are our hero!" With that, the boys extended their hands to be duly shaken by this worthy opponent; again beaming from ear to ear, the Sergeant slapped them both on the back, and said: "Boys, it's been entirely my pleasure!" to which everybody laughed.

"There's some pie left. Fancy some?" but the very mention of food had sent Matti and Enrico scurrying back to the toilet.

"Corporal Dumbridge and Corporal Caruso, today you are being transferred temporarily to the mining division. You will make your way back to Zillebeke; there, at the ruins of the old church, you will be picked up by a lorry, and taken to Lankhof. Then you will report to Major Norton-Griffiths. You will have to leave now, as the lorry will be waiting for you as from ten o'clock; so you have time to pack your belongings, and be on your way. I wish you good luck, and look forward to seeing you back here with the Battalion in the not too distant future."

"Thank you, Sir."

Both the lads standing erect saluted Colonel McBride, turned on their heels and marched out of the dugout. They could not go without saying goodbye to 'Spider' Kelly, who had now become a strong stalwart of the duo.

"I'm not sure that you two men have done the right thing by volunteering for the mining division, unless it's for the extra money; it may be dangerous here, in the trenches, but I've heard of seriously nasty incidents taking place in the tunnels. So, lads, stay alive, and stay healthy!" With that, he shook hands, and turned on his heels and left: none of them were good at emotional goodbyes.

The two lads quickly assembled their few belongings; grabbing two thick slices of bread covered in 'Ticklers' apple jam from the cookhouse, they set off through the remaining trench system till they reached the track that led to Zillebeke. This now had to be done carefully, as even though they were several miles from the German trenches, this whole area was overlooked, thus exposing it to shell or sniper fire. One went along this track as quickly as possible, listening intently for the familiar whine of a German shell.

The German artillery must have been having its pumpernickel and sausage, as they were completely ignored, and grateful to be so. They made it to the ruined church with a lot of time to spare, and so looked for a watering hole to top themselves up: yesterday's escapade had left them very hungry and dehydrated. Much to their amazement, local villagers were still living in many of the ruined buildings, and there, in the middle of this devastation, was an estaminet that sported no doors, nor windows, as they had been blasted by shell fire. But it was still able to muster up two fine plates of ham, egg and chips.

At ten o'clock, they went back to the ruined church to find a covered lorry waiting for them. As they climbed into the back, they were greeted by the sight of seven other mining recruits who had come from various Battalions within the neighbourhood. The lorry pulled away, trying to get some speed, as the only road took them past the infamous Shrapnel Corner; there they turned left to get to Lankhof. Though it was only a mile and a half away, it took them the best part of forty minutes to arrive, as the road was so pitted with shell holes and debris; but they got to Lankhof just before twelve, and were told to line up and wait. They waited in line, at ease but not allowed to move from the spot. They remained there until six fifteen, when a chocolate-and-black Rolls Royce turned up, just as if it had come from a day trip outing to the seaside. How the German artillery had not blown this obvious show of British Officialdom to Kingdom come, was a mystery to one and all. There stood this symbol of all things great that come under the banner of Great Britain, with its Officers strutting around, in full view of the Hun and his artillery, yet nobody ever fired at it. Were they missing their best opportunity, or was there a master plan, something much more sinister waiting for that chocolate-and-black Rolls Royce and its occupants?

Out stepped the imposing figure of Major Sir John Norton-Griffiths, also known as "Empire Jack". Talking to other Officers, he at first ignored the soldiers still in line and feeling extremely weary. Then a good five minutes and several jokes and laughter later, he turned sharp on his heels in the direction of the new intake of recruits.

"Men, sorry to have kept you waiting. We are a happy crew here, and I expect you all to enjoy working in this Division. You will be working on a six day schedule, twelve hours on and twelve hours off. In your free time, you can do more or less as you want as long as you don't leave this area. You will get three days in Poperinge after two weeks of work. The nine of you will be working under the supervision of Sergeant Clamour." Looking around he wondered if that blasted Sergeant was around when needed. 'If he is drunk again, I will have him sent direct to front line troops, which will teach him a lesson!' "Has anyone seen Sergeant Clamour?" No answer came back. "Right, I will find him and introduce him to you all. Stow your kit in one of the dugouts, just over there. Get some chow, and then take it easy. You are to start work at six in the morning, and you will all be working in shaft number M4. Remember that, number four. Also remember that everything you do here is top secret, and there is to be no talking to strangers, or you will be for the high jump. Your stupid talk could and would cost lives, let alone the wasted time on the work. Corporal Dumbridge, ah, there you are, dismiss the men." Empire Jack turned and walked away, as if looking for the missing Sergeant.

"Right, men, attention... Dismiss." Matti looked at Enrico. "What the hell have we come to?"

"Don't ask me, Matti, I was already wondering the same thing. Let's get our kit sorted and find food, I for one, am in need."

The night was cold and wet. Sleep came, but very fitfully. At five o'clock in the morning reveille was 'sounded' by a kick at the end of your legs by a marauding Sergeant, but just for good measure, he was known to tip your bunk should you have one, and yourself onto the wet floor. 'Welcome to the mining division!' thought Matti as he scrambled into his working clothes. After shaving and washing and doing the usual toiletries, they got a quick mug of hot tea and some bread, usually with "Ticklers" apple jam on top. 'Always "Ticklers", is there nothing else in this man's army?' thought Enrico, as he squirmed at the thought of yet more of the same. The truth is that there had been a huge surplus of apples over the last few years, and making jam for the army seemed the patriotic thing to do, so there was now a mountain of apple jam for the fighting boys.

They congregated at the edge of M4 shaft, waiting for signs of Sergeant Clamour. When he finally appeared, he looked very much the worse for wear, and smelling of whisky, which made his bad breath smell even nastier than before. He stood by the entrance, coughed that hacking chesty cough that only comes from smoking more than forty cigarettes a day, spat out the residue, then spoke. "Men, you will be going down this shaft which is eighty feet deep; it is hot and wet down there, and we must always be on guard against gas. Gas is the main killer, which is why we always take these caged birds with us. If they keel over, get the hell out as quickly as possible. Understood?"

"Yes, Sergeant," came the mumbled response from the entire squad of men assembled.

"When we are down there, your jobs will be divided into diggers and collectors. Two will clay kick, two will gather in the spoil, four will pull it back to here for immediate careful heaping around the camp area. But the spoil must be disguised to fool the enemy aeroplanes that might be watching, kidding them into thinking that all is normal: they must not know about these mining operations. Understood?"

"Yes, Sergeant," this time the response was more positive.

"The last one of you will work with the Officer within the tunnel; his job is to listen for enemy countermining operations. And believe me, these go on all the time. Watch yourself. If the enemy break through to our tunnel, we do not surrender; we kill them or die trying to. Understood?" This time he didn't wait for a response but continued, now in full flow. "You all carry knives and clubs and you all have been given service revolvers. Use the knives, not the guns. If you miss with the pistol, you may end up shooting one of your own. The knife is silent, and that's how we like it. If we come into one of their tunnels, we might be in a position to do them some serious damage, by exploding their bombs under their own lines. Or we might just wait there and kill as many as we can, as they come down their tunnel. There are endless possibilities, so be on your toes at all times. Silence is the rule. If you have to speak, do so in a whisper. If you need to shit or piss, dig a small hole and just do it. Food will hopefully be brought to us at various times. Though don't hold your breath, it often sadly gets overlooked, so for future reference, it might be a good idea to take food and water down there with you. Just in case you get hungry or thirsty.

There are few lights, only every fifty feet or so, and they are only forty watt bulbs. The idea is that if the Hun breaks through into our tunnel, they won't be able to see much. The trouble is, neither do we! So, all we are waiting for now is the night shift to come up, and then we go down. Is everything understood?"

"Yes, Sergeant, but who is going to start the clay kicking?" asked Enrico.

"I have been advised that Corporal Dumbridge and Corporal Caruso are experienced miners, so those two will start. I will show you how to start the clay kicking; we are using quite a clever little device, makes your life easier, plus it is silent. *Shhhh!* Here come the night boys."

The lads did not hear a thing: as hard as they listened they could only hear the guns from Wipers. Then, just as the Sergeant predicted, out came the dirty and tired faces, carried by the equally weary legs, of ten men and an Officer. So intent was the squad in watching this motley crew emerge from the shaft entrance, that they did not witness the arrival of their Officer in charge. He was a tall lean man in his early thirties; his haggard features were made all the more prominent by the extreme tiredness that emanated from every fibre of his being. This was a man that was on the edge. 'My God, can we trust our lives to this creature?' thought Enrico, 'he looks as if he's just about to pull his hair out and run away screaming!'

"My name is Lieutenant Sykes, I am in charge, and you will do exactly as I say. First, check your equipment. All helmets can be left behind; you won't need them where we are going. Torches, strap them to your chest, or carry them in a way that you will not drop them. Your knives, are they really sharp? Always make sure that you can cut anything quickly with them. Your trench club, have it tied to your belt in a way that you can pull it off and be able to swing it instantly. Your service revolver must always have a complete chamber of bullets, but keep the safety catch on, unless you want to fire it." Here, a small weak smile appeared on his lips. "Water, always make sure your canteen is full. You might not be re-supplied as often as you may wish. Your trench shovel should be slung from your belt, always keep it handy, it could save your lives in many ways. Right then, your name?"

"Private Richard Bruce, Sir."

"Right, Private Bruce, you will stay besides me this entire shift. You will assist me in any way that I wish, but our objective is to listen out for enemy diggers, and believe me when I say they will be there, doing just the same as us. All of you keep alert!" Just as they were to descend into the tunnel, Sergeant Clamour came beside Enrico and Matti. "Stay by me, we will lead to the tunnel face. I will show you how to do this kicking process. Two hours on, two hours off, that should keep you happy!"

"Right, Sarge, with you all the way."

The tunnel was dark and wet; as the squad reached below eight feet, they came upon chalk. Every fifty feet or so, a forty watt bulb illuminated about six inches of blackness, with just enough light to see the next bulb shining like a distant star in the black night sky. The tunnel was quite straight, but every few hundred yards it would veer either to the right or left, depending on how the Surveyor wanted the line to run. It extended to approximately half a mile, and it took them a good ten minutes before they reached the face. There, were the kicking boards next to two empty man-sized metal carts; one of which the two-man team filled with spoil, and it was then dragged by the four-man team to the outside for the sur-face crew to dispose of. While the four-man crew were taking a filled cart, the two-man crew were filling the next, and so on. All the time this was going on, the kickers were whacking at the chalk, dislodging huge chunks to be taken away. Sergeant Clamour took Enrico and Matti to the two frames that were to be their seats for the next two hours. The frames looked like upturned crucifixes, leaning backwards. The kicker would rest his backside upon the seat that was the bar of the cross, leaning back against the upright section of the cross; one could then exert great pressure on the special digging spade that had a longer handle than usual, with two pedals at the sharp end to put your feet on and press down. Once going in full swing, a good kicker could get out around twenty five lumps of chalk a minute. In a shift's work, they could expect to have created a further five feet of tunnel.

Enrico and Matti went to work with a will. The clods came thick and fast; soon the first cart was filled and was being dragged uphill towards the entrance. Sergeant Clamour would busy himself with whatever was needed to be done, wherever. Two hours went by; Enrico and Matti were relieved by two of the cart pullers, the two loaders then transferred to pulling, and Matti and Enrico became loaders. Then two hours after that, change again. All the rotating helped take away that feeling of fatigue and futility. Four more hours passed before Enrico and Matti took their turn again at kicking.

But the Officer was pleased with this day's progress. He had spent the day with Private Bruce and a long thin steel rod, with a circular flat end to act as an ear piece. This he would insert into the ground, walls or ceiling at various places along the tunnel and listen. His was the most terrifying part of the whole operation: he was listening for the Hun, who was probably doing exactly the same thing as him. Every now and again, he would signal for complete silence. Then with furrowed brow he would stand, kneel or even lie upon the bottom of the tunnel in the greatest state of concentration. He was straining every sinew in an attempt to catch the odd thump or rattle, clang or even sounds of voices, which would indicate trouble ahead. This first day, it never happened. The canary sang as it reached air again, the Officer smiled and looked relieved, as did Sergeant Clamour, who had quite obviously been drinking some alcohol down in the tunnel: he looked bleary-eyed when they went down, he looked far worse when they entered the trenches again. He had trouble actually standing without swaying. It was perfectly obvious that Lieutenant Sykes was aware of the illicit drinking that went on, on the part of the Sergeant, but turned a blind eye, as long as it didn't get in the way of work. Anyway, the Lieutenant too was in such an imminent state of near breakdown, one would hazard a guess that he too could and should be reported to a higher authority, but this was never going to happen. Men for mining were in short supply; better the Devil you know, than the Devil you don't know, was probably the order of the day. Their first day was such a long day of labour, without many breaks for rest that the men could hardly drag themselves out into the fresher air. A quick wash and brush up, followed by a big repast, as much as could be crammed on a plate, seconds if you wanted more. A hot cup of tea, maybe a cigarette or two, then bed. Get as much sleep as possible, until the body got used to such hard continuous work.

This is what the routine became, each day hard toil, desperate nervous tension, breaks of heart-stopping terror, when lights went out or the Lieutenant thought he heard something. The further and closer they dug to the German lines, the more nerves became frayed. Small incidents often turned into major catastrophes, nearly wrecking everything they thought they might be achieving. A full cart turned over, spilling all the contents, making very little noise, but to the men working, this was an earthquake, which could probably be heard in London. But no Germans broke through; no Hun exploded a bomb to collapse the tunnel while they were working in it. Actually, they had been extremely lucky, with no major incidents at all. Then two weeks were up; hard work over, freedom for seventy two hours. Money to spend, baths to be had. Clean clothes, heaven! Get rid of the lice, even if it is for only some hours, heaven! Good food to eat, wine and beer to drink, heaven! Meet other people, maybe a woman or two, heaven! Most of all, the chance to get away from mines and mining!

Just before they left on the lorry for Poperinge, they were warned yet again, "No idle talk…Spies are everywhere, watch your drink, but most of all watch your tongue!"

"Where shall we stay, Matti, my old mucker?" Enrico enquired, knowing what the answer would be.

"Let's stay in Talbot House: it's cheap, clean and friendly."

"Your wish is my command, oh hairy one," teased Enrico.

Seventy-two hours is a wisp of time, and it is over, hardly before your mind and body have started to appreciate the rest. But along with the food, which was more plentiful and more interesting than bully beef and bread and jam, they enjoyed a blissful bath, and a welcome de-licing of their clothing. 'So there is a God in heaven, after all,' thought Matti, as he dressed in his clean underwear, with nothing biting or irritating him. 'Bliss, *pure bliss!*'

All too quickly it was back to work, only now they were on the night shift, and that was far worse than day time work. Night brings terrors induced by imagination; ghosts of the dead might not appear, but they are there just the same, maybe merely in one's mind, but that can create the worst demons of all. The squad was at the face with Matti and Enrico kicking at the chalk; things were more than quiet, which made everybody jumpy and on edge. Lieutenant Sykes was in a terribly shaky mood, hearing all the demons that he could conjure within himself. He was calling for quiet every few minutes, which meant very little work was getting done. "*Shhhh.* I really hear something now. It sounds like running feet, and they're just on the other side of this wall," he said, pointing to the right side of the tunnel from the entrance. "*Shhhh.* It's getting louder. I want four of you to dig a small hole in this area, and see if we can reach them before they reach us."

"Matti, get your shovel and dig right here with me. We will see if there is anything there, or are we all just badly shaken tonight?" whispered Enrico, almost right into Matti's ear.

"Quietly, lads, I don't want the Hun to know we're on to them. Can you hear anything, Dumbridge?"

"Yes, Sir, I think I can. It does sound like running, but there must be dozens of them, to make so much noise."

Matti and Enrico dug very carefully at the offending wall just about two feet above the floor. All of a sudden: *Whoooosh!* Water came gushing in.

"Christ, men, we have hit a river. Get out of here quickly!" shouted

Enrico. Nobody needed telling twice, and the race was on. The water gushed so fast that before anybody had gone fifty feet it was up to their knees. Then the lights fused. Darkness fell like a heavy lead weight on all of them. They could only make their way scrambling over each other and all the debris that was being swept along with the huge tide of water. The smell was the first thing that struck Enrico, as the water rose beyond his knees to his waist. The stench was of more putrefaction, as well as rusty iron. 'Strange, I cannot remember such smells around water before,' thought Enrico, who, though scared, was in command of what he was doing and what had to be done. "Matti, all of you, stay close and keep moving. The water is really cold, but just keep moving!" Enrico had now taken complete control.

They all struggled forward, but as the water got higher their movements got slower. It was up to their chest and still rising. The noise had become much louder, as the hole broken through was widening under the pressure from the gushing torrent. There were still two hundred yards to cover before reaching the entrance, but at least the ground was rising, making movement that bit easier. Every step took them higher and closer to the tunnel's way out. Enrico now able to stand upright again, stopped to find out who was with him. He shone his torch. The first by him was Lieutenant Sykes, his eyes almost on stalks, bulging in terror. He was babbling something completely incoherent; as he rushed past, his only thought was of getting out. Then Matti stood beside Enrico, shivering badly, but surprisingly calm. "What's to do?" he said looking at Enrico through the light of the torch. "Make sure that everyone is safe by counting them through." More water pressure pushed at them, so they both moved higher up the tunnel. One by one, the squad moved past, making their way to safety. "Nine, there is one person missing, Matti. Did you see who it might be?"

"No, I thought everyone was safe. The canary has had it though!" They looked at one another, and then gave out a nervous laugh. "Let's get out of here, nothing to be done. If anyone is left in there they have gone west."

All the squad made their way finally to the surface, to find ten soldiers in various forms of attire, some even in their pyjamas waiting at the entrance. As each man appeared, a large tot of rum was presented to bring life back to the wet, freezing bodies. The first out was the half-crazed Lieutenant Sykes, who was totally beside himself, gabbling nonsense, as if speaking in tongues, but he was coherent enough to take the mug of rum being offered and down it almost in one gulp. Gradually, other men appeared, all shaken, all cold and all ready for that rum ration. Finally, Matti and Enrico came up, trembling from the fatigue and icy waters that had flooded the mine. Dust was gushing out of the entrance: as the water rose, it was forcing the oxygen and carbon monoxide with such strength that huge clouds of dust were being forced out along with the gases. Enrico, once more took charge: "Who's missing?" as he looked around, counting off. A voice came: "Sergeant Clamour, he's not here."

"Right," said Enrico.

"One of you, Privates," pointing to one of the soldiers who was fully clothed, and watching the proceedings, "come with me, bring a torch, and we will go down to the water line, and see if he's there." They went into the tunnel entrance, and descended no more than eighty feet, when they came across the water. Shining their torches along the surface, they could see nothing, except one or two floating packing cases.

"Oh, shit! I'm afraid Sergeant Clamour has paid the price for too much rum; he's a goner."

They made their way back to the trench system to inform the others; even as they got there, a team of other soldiers, of which Enrico knew none, were assembling sections of pipe together, and bringing forth a motorised pump which would be lowered into the water to see if the tunnel could be salvaged.

The next morning at exactly nine o'clock an entourage of vehicles headed by that familiar chocolate-and-black Rolls-Royce made its way into the camp. Yet again, no enemy artillery fire, making 'Empire Jack' look as if he had a charmed life! The salvage crews had set up their pump with several hundred yards of piping leading further down through the trenches to the lower levels, where the water could be pumped away without fear of it coming back. Major Norton-Griffiths called for a meeting to discuss whether M4 could be saved. At this meeting Corporals Dumbridge and Caruso were asked to attend. Major Norton-Griffiths turned to Enrico and asked for an immediate explanation of what had occurred. Standing to attention, Enrico retold the story as he knew it, then glanced at Matti to see whether he wanted to add anything that may have been left out, but Enrico's explanation was enough to satisfy 'Empire Jack', who turned to him and said: "Relax, Caruso, this is an informal meeting, not a board of inquiry; nobody is on trial, here; in fact, Corporal, I have some good news for you. With the demise of Sergeant Clamour, I'm making you up to a full Sergeant, as of right now. So, congratulations, Sergeant Caruso! You obviously handled this incident extremely professionally, with a cool head."

Norton-Griffiths then turned to his Chief Engineer, and asked two obvious questions.

"Firstly, do you think it was a river that flooded the tunnel? And secondly, can it be saved?" The Engineer, one Captain Roberts, looked back at Sir John, and answered his question, as truthfully as was possible with the data known.

"Sir, I have no doubt in my mind that it was not a river, but just a large cistern of water that had collected over years, being unable to permeate through the chalk. As to the second question, we will know for sure within a day or two, but I rather feel that it could be saved, albeit that the excess of water now within M4 will make it a dangerous place to be, after the water has been emptied out."

"But you feel we could save it?"

"Yes, Sir. I will know for sure soon, but I think probably."

"Right!" said Major Sir John Norton-Griffiths, turning back towards Matti and Enrico. "Until we know for certain whether we can continue in M4, I will transfer all the men working on M4 to a new site, which will be M5, and you'll start a new tunnel at that given location. I want you to liaise with Captain Turner here, who is our Chief Surveyor."

Turner beckoned to Enrico and Matti, and the three of them went outside into the cold, fresh air. Captain Turner undid a new packet of Senior Service cigarettes, withdrew one, put it in his mouth, then as a second thought, offered the open packet around; but the duo declined, being non smokers. Drawing heavily on the cigarette, then exhaling a lungful of grey smoke, Turner turned to the boys, saying: "Follow me to the car; I'm going to get the driver to take us on a little drive." They reached the car, and set off in the direction of Shrapnel Corner. Then making their way down the Kemmel Road, they reached a heavily shelled track, which led to a deserted hamlet called Vierstraat; they crossed a small beck, and just on the other side, under the cover of some ruined buildings, they parked the car. Turner got out, followed by the two lads. Producing a map which he laid on the ground, he showed them exactly where they were.

"We will start an entrance, just about where we are now. This track that we are on is completely shielded away from civilians and not easily overlooked by the Germans. All the spoil will be bagged, and used as trench reinforcement. We are going to dig through in a south-easterly direction to a heavily fortified wood, which is called Kroonaardhoek. There we will put in a lateral gallery, extending the length of the wood, and off the lateral gallery, we will put in six explosive chambers. We will turn that wood with one fell blow into a matchstick factory. For within that wood, there are five or six machine gun bunkers, and our spotter planes have noticed bigger concrete bunkers being built, which could be used for the housing of large Howitzers."

"Sir, when is this going to start?" enquired Enrico.

"Why, Sergeant, us being here has made it start! Tomorrow the digging will proceed, and while you are digging the mineshaft, I'm bringing in other Sappers to dig general trenches for accommodation, storage, gun emplacements, and anything else that will fool enemy aircraft into thinking this is just an extension of the existing trench system. Again we don't want them to know the truth, so secrecy is the order of the day. You will be working entirely under my command, and anything you need to know, you will ask me direct."

"Sir, may I ask one question? What has happened to Lieutenant Sykes?"

"Lieutenant Sykes has been relieved of all duties. I'm sorry to say that as we speak, he's being sent home to England. The pressure, sadly, was all too much for him. He has had a complete physical and mental breakdown."

'Christ! He gets sent back to England. If that happened to one of us, it would either be at best, extra work and punishment, or a line-up at the dawn chorus!' thought Matti.

That night, under the secrecy of darkness, twenty lorry loads of men set off for Kroonaardhoek. The next morning, just before dawn, breakfast of bread and jam, along with some sizzling bacon which had been stolen by the Quartermaster was served to all. Bacon! a rare treat and one that was savoured by all. Work started immediately with a wide new trench being dug, and the spoil being thrown up facing the enemy for protection. These had to be very secure trenches, as they were to contain all the things necessary for the tunnelling, so brand new extra wide A frames were to be used. Enrico himself, with the guidance of Captain Turner, selected the exact spot where the shaft was going to be sunk, and they started to excavate a six foot by six foot square hole. They had only gone down two feet when the sandy soil started to give up a grisly secret: Enrico pushed his spade into the ground, and was aware of a hissing sound. He also heard his spade knock against something metallic.

"Matti, I think I've hit a gas shell! Can you hear the hissing?" Matti came across hardly daring to breathe in case it was true that either chlorine or mustard gas was seeping from the spade's cut into the ground.

"It sounds more like water bubbling than gas. Push your spade forward slightly, and let me look into the opening."

It was true, a certain residue of water was bubbling up from where his spade had impacted.

"Carefully bring up that spadeful of spoil." This was duly done.

"Oh my God! You've just chopped off a man's head, and that bubbling is the decomposing gas, permeating up through the mud and water. Look, there's his helmet, and what's left of his head."

Matti bent down and pulled the helmet from the ground. The smell was terrible, and the helmet contained clumps of matted, black hair, bone, and bits of rotting flesh and brains. Holding this with two fingers, as far away from his nose as possible, he opened a sack and dropped the remains in.

"Enrico, old boy, you've found yourself a Frenchie."

"The smell is awful! And we'll have to dig the rest of him out, but his life will not have been in vain, as he's now going to be part of the parapet."

The remains of the poor Frenchman were duly dug up and deposited into four other sacks; his gun, along with a pair of binoculars, and a trench compass were going to make good trophies. The man himself would soon impact down, and set in his sacks as hard as concrete, but it was not long before one Frenchman turned into five more, and it was a grisly day, placing all these human remains into sacks. At the end of the day, when a new team replaced them to carry on the work throughout the night, Matti and Enrico looked for a place to wash themselves thoroughly. Remembering the beck, just about a hundred yards behind their new lines, they went with a view to have a wash. But no matter how hard they tried, they could not rid themselves of the smell of French decaying flesh. Indeed it was to take several days before that particular aroma passed. The next morning, Enrico and Matti returned to do their shift in the hole, which now already went down twelve feet. They made sure that all four sides were shored up thoroughly, and a pulley system was now in place for bringing up the sacks of spoil. The hole was now deep enough for four men to work at one time, two digging and two filling sacks. All was going well.

"Two more days of this, Matti, and we'll be able to go horizontal towards our goal." They were now digging into solid chalk; going down into chalk was harder than going horizontally through it.

The trench system had been finished; the mineshaft too had been completed, and they had dug horizontally for fifty yards, when Easter greeted them. It was amazing how in all that devastation, where hardly a square yard of land had not been blown to Kingdom come on at least several occasions, the grass still grew, along with the bluebells and daisies, and dandelions. It was as if overnight, their world had been carpeted with greens and yellows. Along with the longer days, the men's spirits also became reborn. Man could destroy practically everything, but the war was always won by nature. Though still quite cold at night, when the sun shone, you would often find men bathing in the beck. It made them clean, but it did not kill the lice.

On Easter Sunday, there was a surprise visit: on a motorcycle and sidecar, there was this larger than life figure of the Padre, Phillip 'Tubby' Clayton. He went into the trench system, and asked for an area to be made ready for an Easter service, in which men could take Communion. Anybody who was not on duty willingly attended, and had the Germans seen more than a hundred soldiers having a service just behind a ruined farmhouse, they could have had a field day with the artillery. But like on many other occasions, the opportunity was either ignored, or was just unseen in the first place. In this instance, no one will ever know why the artillery did not fire, but there had been many other cases when the Germans could have opened fire on obvious religious ceremonies going on, and did not, out of reverence for the Almighty. It seemed incongruous that in such slaughter, with so much human suffering, moments of kindness could, and did occur.

One can visualise this picture of 'Tubby' Clayton, with his portable table as a makeshift altar, his bottles of cheap red wine as the blood of Christ, and his long French loaves representing the body of Christ. Next to that, was his motorcycle sidecar in which was precariously perched a portable three octave harmonium. He asked the standing, sitting and kneeling men to remove their helmets out of respect for this special day. They sang three hymns, had several prayers, aimed mainly at the wounded and dead of all the armies, then Communion was started. Men lined at the table, as the bread was broken into small pieces, and handed out with the words: "This bread represents my Body. Eat it in remembrance of me." Then the wine was placed into a chalice, out of which every man took a sip, with the words: "This wine represents my Blood. Drink it in remembrance of me." There was not a soldier there, young or old, who was not moved, almost to the point of tears by this special ceremony performed by this true humanitarian. At the end of the ceremony, they all sang the hymn 'Rock of Ages' then dispersed back to their various tasks. There was still a little wine left in the chalice, which it was mandatory for the Padre to finish. Having done this chore, Phillip 'Tubby' Clayton presented himself to Captain Turner, inquiring if there were any graves that needed blessing, or any injured men that he would like him to minister to.

"Bless you, Padre, but we have not been shelled or attacked in any way. The only injuries have been through accidents, and those men were sent back to better equipped dressing stations. I wish to thank you for that wonderful service." Shaking the Padre's hand vigorously, the Captain showed 'Tubby' Clayton to the door of his dugout, and said: "Many thanks, Padre."

"And God be with you, my son."

The beginning of May 1916 came. The tunnel was progressing well, and there had been very few serious accidents. 'Empire Jack' came on several occasions to see for himself how progress was going on M5. On one of his visits he requested an update from Captain Turner, and was told, "Things are going well, in a way too well. Nothing serious has gone awry, but I cannot help feeling we are in for big trouble in the not too distant future."

"And what of that Sergeant Caruso, is he pulling his weight, is he of use to you?"

"Yes, he's a fine example to his men. In fact I sometimes have to tell him to delegate more actual work on to his men. I visit the tunnel and find him still digging along with everyone else. He should be doing more supervising, and oversee the work, but he will insist on doing things his way. But I am very happy to have him. He does understand what we are trying to do, and it does get done; why, Sir, the interest in Sergeant Caruso anyway?"

"Well, Captain, we are going to lose him and Corporal Dumbridge within a week or two: they have been requested by their old Colonel to rejoin the London Northern Rifle Brigade. It seems there is going to be a big push in the next few months, and they need their experienced NCOs back as they are short of men."

"That will be a big shame: I could see Caruso going the whole way with the mining division; maybe he could be in line for a Junior Officer's post?"

"I rather think that is unlikely, it seems NCOs are considered more use than Junior Officers." Both Norton-Griffiths and Turner laughed at the very thought of that.

"Any other news for me, Sir?"

"M4 is now reopening, but I believe your suspicions are right about it being dangerous. I fear for the squad that takes that one on again."

The very next day was when the incident occurred.

Enrico and Matti had taken their squad down into the mine at the usual eight in the morning, after the previous shift had shown itself at the entrance, and things were going well, mainly because of Enrico's hard work in the organisation of the working of the tunnel. He had proved himself in many ways, to the extent that M5 was probably the safest and cleanest tunnel for the miners to be working in. In point of fact Enrico knew that when they were to explode this mine, with all the explosives packed into the six chambers, he for one would be extremely sad to leave what had become his own personal project. He had made some very good alterations to their working environment; electric light shone all throughout the tunnel, now with sixty watt bulbs; these at least shone down to the floor. He had forge-type bellows installed, working around the clock to remove foul air, pumping life-giving oxygen to the face kickers.

There had been several deaths from asphyxiation, before they had installed the bellows. The system was not perfect, often breaking down, but it was infinitely better than what had gone before. He had introduced guards to work with the listening Officer; these were armed soldiers, rather on the same lines as the marines had been in Nelson's time, there to guard the ship and its crew, or in this case to be on guard within the tunnel in case the enemy did break through, thus not relying entirely on the miners to defend the tunnel. These guards carried pistols, and more important Mills bombs, and a plentiful supply of them. Each miner still carried his own weapons, which included knives, clubs, small deadly shovels, which were often sharpened, to the point that they could be used for the cutting of wood. There was also the obligatory service revolver, with a full chamber and an ammunition pouch loaded and waiting.

Enrico saluted the Officer, Lieutenant James Fisher, as he approached, checking his personal gear as he walked. "Morning, Sergeant," he said with a warm smile on his face. He was a very young man who had just left University, with a first in philosophy, hardly a suitable degree for warfare. "Good morning, Sir," came the answer from Enrico. Matti stood next to his friend, as he always did, and always would, yawning heavily, and showing that he could hardly keep his eyes open.

"No sleep, Corporal?" was the smiling enquiry.

"No, Sir, the bloody guns got to me last night; they don't usually, but there seemed to be something more urgent about them, even if they did not fire off any more rounds than normal."

"Corporal, you are dreaming. Last night, the night before, tonight, they are all the same. We have the Hun on the run, I am sure of it."

They all lowered themselves down into the tunnel from the shaft entrance, the Lieutenant so sprightly that he almost danced his way down the tunnel. They had only gone fifty yards or so when the first shell burst over their trench system. "What the heck, I had almost forgotten how a bursting shell sounds. I hope it didn't do for anyone?" said Enrico to no one in particular. Then another one fell, and another. Then it rained continuously with heavy metal. The explosions could be felt more than heard. It made the tunnel shake and shudder as big shells would hit over head. "We're safer down here, than up top, that's for sure!" remarked Matti, getting slightly closer to his pal than usual. 'It has been a while since we felt a bombardment. I didn't like it before, I don't like it now,' thought Matti. The walls started to shake as each shell was blasting more craters within existing craters. The pressure of air expanding, as gasses were released through the shuddering walls and roof, made the squad stop walking and wonder what was coming next. It was only a minute before their question was answered. Water jets squirted from cracks that appeared in the walls, not so serious as to cause a flood, but serious enough that if a jet of water hit, it hurt like heck, and it was sometimes strong enough to knock one of the men off their feet. This in turn caused more pressure to build up, which quickly produced headaches and bad tinnitus in the ears. The shelling was as rapid and ferocious as Enrico or Matti had ever experienced. "They must be taking one hell of a pounding in the trenches. Do you think this is the prelude to an attack?" This question was asked by Enrico to Lieutenant Fisher, who answered with, "your guess is as good as mine!"

A huge shell landed extremely close and the electric lighting went out. "Light the candles," called out Matti.

"Is that wise, what about the gas escaping?" asked the Lieutenant.

"Sir, we have to see where we are going, it's pitch black in here, and if there is gas, then it's more likely that it will just put the candles out, not be ignited by it."

"Well, if you say so." The Lieutenant was a charming young man, but without any real confidence in his own judgement. The trouble was that, with Fisher relying on the knowledge of an even younger but more experienced person such as Enrico, it gave absolutely no confidence in the officer on the part of his charges. This was no time to be worrying about who was running this tunnel; Enrico took complete control. "Sir, I want you to take two or three men and start listening: this is just the sort of excuse that the Hun needs, to start an attack within the tunnel."

"Right, Sergeant, yes, you are right. You three grab some rods and follow me, keep your candles alight so we know exactly where we are."

"The rest of you, spread out right up to the face, and let's be prepared for whatever might happen. Keep your guns holstered but be ready. Nobody fire a gun if you can use your knife. If anything happens, keep a tag on who is around you; we don't want any nasty accidents now, do we?"

They all moved further into the tunnel. The lighting now consisted of just a few candles that were carried by the men themselves. You really couldn't see more that the hand in front of your face. But then, that meant neither would the attacking force. Nerves were on full strain, everyone trying to hear from the possible attackers, but only able to hear the roar of their own breathing sounding like an express train passing through a black smoky tunnel. Enrico tried not to breathe at all, as he too could only hear himself. His chest was heaving from the lack of clean oxygen, 'but as long as we're quiet and stay conscious, we can get through this nightmare,' thought Enrico.

Lieutenant Fisher whispered that he wanted absolute silence, as he thought he could hear something... *Booooom!* A huge explosion came thundering up the tunnel from near the entrance. It now seemed obvious that they had entirely missed the fact that the Germans had known where they were all along. Private Pierce came running up the tunnel towards Enrico. "What has happened?" asked Enrico.

"They have blown in our tunnel from their own, which must run parallel to us. All this time and we never knew."

"Keep your calm men; this is no time to lose your nerve. Are any of the enemy in our section of tunnel?"

"I don't think so, it's probably too soon, but they will come, that I am sure of," Private Pierce was almost crying with tension as he said those words.

"Anyone missing?"

"Yes, Sergeant, I'm sure Lieutenant Fisher has been hit by debris and buried. The force was such that he's for sure dead. It has brought our roof down, and I would think for quite a way. That means we are trapped in here!" He was now almost hysterical with the thought of being buried alive. Unseen tears were flowing freely now. All Private Pierce could think about was 'I will never see Carol again, she will never know how I died!'

"Right, listen, men, we are trapped, and while the shelling bombardment goes on, we can do nothing to save ourselves, and nobody is going to be able to rescue us, not until the shelling stops. The only real thing to do is to break through to the German tunnel: that will give us more air, then blow them up as close to their trenches as possible. So, quietly start digging right about here. That should bring us about halfway across no-man's-land; it's either fight or die, and I for one am not about to die. Start digging but don't let them hear us. With luck, they might think we all copped it in their explosion."

They all started to burrow into the wall beside what they assumed to be the German tunnel; it must have been several yards away, as they made quite a large hole without hearing any sounds from the enemy on the other side. 'Christ, I hope we have got this right? We could be miles out, their tunnel might be above or below us, how can we tell?'

"*Shhhh*. Let me listen, maybe I can hear feet walking or running. It might give us the direction of their tunnel?" Enrico listened very intently, and he was quite sure he could hear feet moving up and down not so far away. "Right," he said in a very low voice, "I'm sure we are close by. Careful now, and be ready to rush in and do what must be done. No guns, just knives. Don't forget!"

They dug again; this time they could distinctly hear voices and movement, and it was just a few inches away. Matti and Enrico picked carefully at the chalk, and then quite suddenly there was a small hole into the adjoining tunnel. Enrico could see several of the enemy scurrying around carrying more explosives.

"This is our chance men, they obviously are not aware of our existence, and there is TNT waiting to be used again. Let's oblige them, by using it on them, on my command. Now gather close and put out the candles."

Enrico pulled the lumps carefully all the way to the floor of their tunnel which happened to be at least two feet above the German one. Within a minute there was just a paper-thin veneer of chalk that could be pushed down when they wanted to. Enrico watched and waited until he thought there was nobody close by on the other side, and then one push and they were in. The remaining eight of them rushed into the German tunnel, looking every which way for the enemy. All was quiet. Enrico could hear that there were some soldiers up at their face, laying more explosives. 'The bastards are going to lay a huge mine right under our lines. We must stop that and turn it onto them.'

"Men," he whispered, "we must creep up and finish them off;

keep behind me, don't use the guns," he emphasised again. Creeping back towards the British trenches, they had to walk at a crawl nearly two hundred yards. A German soldier was walking back, not really looking and walked right into Matti who lunged at him, pushing his knife deep into the soldier's chest. A surprised gurgle came from the dying lips, and he crumpled to a heap on the tunnel floor. 'One down, how many to go?' wondered Matti.

They moved on again, watching and listening for any movement. They could hear whispering in German but it was still some yards off. Enrico could see candlelight dead ahead. One, two, three… six, maybe more soldiers, but at least six lights.

"Let's rush them from here, watch out for the explosives. *Now!*"

They all ran down the tunnel with little sound being made; in fact it was further than it seemed, candlelight can give a wrong impression of distance. The nearest German peered back on hearing the running feet, but thought it was going to be some of his own kind. The surprise that he got when he saw at the last moment the outline of a British uniform made him far too slow to react. Cold steel struck him clean in the jugular vein, and he fell to the floor in his death throes, blood flooding out, as life slipped away. A scream came as Germans realised that their surprise had come back on them. Knives flashed and were wielded to and fro, many shrieks sounded before all went silent. There had been seven of them, and they were just putting in the fuses within the vast amounts of explosive that was packed neatly up against the tunnel face, which now must be under the British front line trenches.

"Just bloody made it! Right, Matti, disarm this pile. Men, start picking up these boxes, with care. It's back up the tunnel for them. Watch out for more Germans, their screams will almost certainly have been heard. Follow behind me."

There they were, eight British Tommies, carrying the German explosives up the German tunnel, to put under the German front line trench. Like a line of worker ants they scurried up that tunnel, toting that load of future excitement, or at least some of it. Enrico led his motley crew, Matti close behind, then the rest of the squad following behind him: a line of brave, but foolish young soldiers, playing at their deadly games.

Sure enough, not far from where the two tunnels connected, a crouching sniper let go with a crack of fire. A bullet shot passed Enrico, but hit a friend of Matti's, Private John Snoop. He dropped like a stone, almost cold before he hit the floor. As he fell, so too did the explosives. "Shit...watch the TNT, it'll send us all to hell if it goes off!" Enrico, now full of fury, pulled his revolver from his holster and charged forward, completely taking the sniper by surprise; he, in turn tried to reload, but in his extreme terror no longer knew how to. Shots rang out, all from Enrico. The sniper even tried to put his hands up in surrender, but there was not going to be any prisoners. The very next bullet went through the terrified German's chest, taking out most of his left lung and several ribs. He fell to the floor, bleeding profusely, also dead. Enrico knew that they must be quick and get some of this explosive set off, or the element of surprise would have passed. "Come on, men, get that fucking stuff up there, we are not there yet." Still they moved forward. More shots rang out, hitting the walls all around. 'There must be several Germans up there now,' he thought. "Give me a couple of Mills, quickly!" He was passed what he wanted, told everyone to get on the floor, and then threw the first bomb where he thought the Hun might be. *Bang!*...lots of smoke and coughing. He threw the other. *Bang!*... silence. They moved forward yet again. The sound soon came of more German soldiers heading their way. Enrico had already reloaded his pistol, asked for more bombs and was ready for anything. He didn't have to wait long: more shots came, this time more rapidly. *Crack, bang, bang, zing, smack!* Bullets were flying everywhere. Two more of Enrico's squad fell wounded. "Down, all of you!"

*282*

Matti and he started firing from a prone position; there was little cover but nobody could see them, so everyone was firing blindly. Enrico threw yet another Mills grenade in the direction of the firing... *Boom!* Followed by a huge smoke ring that came back along the tunnel and engulfed them all; then another bomb and another. 'Why don't they throw stick grenades back?' thought Enrico, 'Of course, they know about the explosives, they're frightened of setting off the whole thing.' Realisation that they held the upper hand was pure delight, and it had given him the glimmer of an idea. "Follow up behind me, and pass me a bomb each time I throw one." Enrico with three other men, crawling up behind him, crept forward a few yards, then threw a bomb as far as he could... *Boom!* Crawl another five yards... *Boom!* another five yards... *Boom!* He now came upon the first dead; pushing them aside, he threw another bomb... *Boom!* then another. This he kept doing for nearly a hundred yards. He had killed and wounded many of the enemy with this creeping bomb-throwing movement. It had worked: he kept the Germans from coming forward, always keeping them in retreat. "Matti, another grenade!"

"You've had the last!"

"Right then, let's fire the rest of our pistols at them." But they had no need to. They came to a bend in the tunnel, one that kept them safe from bullets. 'This will do nicely!' thought Enrico. "Bring up the explosives; this will be our Alamo Fort: we will blow this whole tunnel in on itself, just like they did to us."

Gradually the boxes were brought forward to the point where Enrico wanted them stacked; as soon as one was laid, the carrier would scurry off to the face to fetch more, but it only took an hour before they had enough to do the damage that they wanted to inflict, and still they managed to prevent the Germans from attacking. Enrico put in the fuses, making sure that he primed them properly. More gun fire could be heard and bullets were zinging into the wall opposite, doing no damage but letting them know that they were not forgotten. Then, horror of horrors, a stick grenade came hurtling down, and crashing against the wall opposite. Without thinking, Enrico rushed across, picking it up and throwing it straight back. Not a moment too soon… *Boom!*… followed by some light screams, then silence. Again he cocked his pistol and fired into the darkness. No sounds came back. "Get that bloody fuse lit. Let's get out of here!"

As he spoke, he could make out the obvious hissing sound of a lit fuse. 'Shit, let me get past this lot, it will go up any second now!' All the men had rushed away, picking up the wounded, and had crammed through the hole back into their own tunnel. Hardly safe, but it felt like home. Two seconds after they had all got through, Enrico followed, panting wildly.

*Crash!* A huge explosion occurred, winding them all yet again. After the explosion came the smoke, choking, black, lung-searing smoke. All of them were coughing badly; ears were ringing, eyes watering. At least they thought they were safe. After a long while, the smoke cleared by settling everywhere, but mostly on the men, making them look to the entire world like ghosts in the candlelight. Nervous laughter ensued, and a great deal of trembling, nerves being shot to pieces, even if the flesh wasn't.

"Right, men. Let's assess the situation. You," pointing to Private Pierce, "go down our tunnel and see if anything can be done, and you two, go down the German tunnel, and start collecting in the rest of the boxes of explosives. Before we leave here, we're going to make sure that their tunnel will never be used again. Matti, you stay with me, let's see what that bang did… How are the wounded, anybody taken the trouble yet to see if anything can be done for them?" No answer came. "Right, let me look at them." He bent down to peer at the first man he came to. "He's dead!" Then, moving on to the other, he said, "Can you manage here for a while, how bad is it? The trouble is we will have to try and find some first aid equipment; I don't want to leave you in this dark, but we will have to for a while. Are you going to be all right on your own?" "Sergeant, do what you must do. Nobody ever did anything for me in the past, why start now?" Enrico squinted in the direction the voice came from, and said "Listen, you little dick, we will all try very hard to get you out of this tomb, I will try and get everybody out, but you are not going to die: you have been shot in the shoulder, and it looks more like a serious graze than anything else. Stop feeling sorry for yourself and act like a man! I will leave you now, don't move, but most of all, don't make a noise. We will all see you soon."

Enrico followed Matti to the cave-in they had caused in the German tunnel. Smoke was still emanating from the rubble, and they wondered how far the fall went. They didn't have to wonder for long, as digging sounds could be distinctly heard coming from the other side. "Hear that, Matti? They're coming for us. Let's get the rest of the explosives up here and bring the rest of the roof down!"

They all laboured, bringing up the cases of high explosives; there were ten more, and it took the best part of forty minutes to fetch them all. "Me and Matti will stay here until you have stacked it all. Two boxes on top of each other, then a gap of six feet, and so on. That should be enough to make quite a bang. Matti, I think they're almost through at the top there; if you listen closely they sound about a foot away. What d'you think? Have we got long? Get up there with your pistol, and any head that pokes through will be sent to Hades."

"Right," whispered Matti, "you can see the rubble shaking, put out the candles, and quiet!"

A few moments went by, when they heard the sound of moving chalk debris, and then another, before a chink of candlelight could just be seen. Enrico and Matti raised their weapons, waiting for the moment that a head appeared. They could quite distinctly hear German speaking voices coming from the direction of the hole. Then a face emerged. With a start, Enrico opened fire – *crack, crack,* straight into the face. He knew he had made contact as he felt warm blood running down his own face, and it was not his. There was a frantic sound of pulling, as the now dead enemy soldier was pulled back to the opposite side from them. "Quick, block the hole before they start throwing stick grenades through!" The two of them were frantically shovelling rubbish in the general direction of the hole, when *boom!* A grenade had exploded within the space of the hole; the shock threw Enrico and Matti down onto the floor, but a rumbling sound told them that more of the ceiling had collapsed within the hole, making them safe for the minute.

"Are those fuses set yet?" Enrico screamed at the others. One of his team was struggling, trying hard to get the fuse primed and ready for lighting, but was fumbling badly. "Matti, do it for him!" There was just enough light from the candle to see if everything was in order. Enrico listened once more. "*Shhhhh!* Quiet!" He could hear the sound of more digging, and this time it sounded more earnest than before. "There must be a dozen of them behind this lot. We might catch them all if we're lucky. Get out of this tunnel all of you, take that arsehole in our own, and get as far away as possible. I shall stay and light the fuse, but hurry. Go right now." The frantic waving of his arms seemed to do the trick; they all scurried away in the direction of home.

Enrico waited: the nearer the Boche got, the better the chances of catching the lot of them. 'The fuse should be around a minute, that should be enough time for me to get back, way into our own tunnel out of the concussion range of this detonation. Blimey, the air is thinning badly: the candles are giving off very little light, only a red glow. Is that them coming through? They must be close now! Yes, I can see some movement as the chalk shakes. I'll light the fuse now.' He proceeded to light the fuse, but to his horror, it just fizzled and went out. 'Shit, the oxygen is weak, the bloody fuse doesn't want to light.' He tried again. This time it fizzed, and started to burn down. But Enrico didn't trust it, and he was not wrong, as it fizzled out once more. 'I will have to explode the TNT with my pistol, how good a shot am I?'

He moved back into the tunnel, but knew he could not go far. 'Christ, can I hold my hand straight? I feel so nervy! When should I start firing?' He moved back another twenty paces. 'The blast will kill me for sure here. But if I go any further back it will only be a lucky shot that makes it.' He could now hear the obvious sounds of digging, and he knew it was time to do the deed. He moved a further ten paces back, took out his gun. *Crack, crack, crack!* Nothing, except the digging sound now stopped, and then started again. *Crack, crack, crack!* Nothing! 'Must I get closer? No way! I shall just keep emptying my revolver in the general direction and hope upon hope that it strikes something explosive. *Crack, crack, crack!* Now he could hear the sound of the diggers, much louder, scratching at the chalk, and he knew that they were through. *Crack, crack, crack!* Again nothing, except a small moan from the tunnel face where the enemy had penetrated. 'Maybe I hit one of them?'

Indeed he had, and the very irate German didn't think much of a bullet in his shoulder: why, he wasn't playing the game! In fact he thought two could play that game, so he lobbed in a stick grenade for good measure. *Boom!* went the stick grenade. *Booooom!* went the explosives, being set off by the unsuspecting Hun, with his gesture of annoyance. Enrico was lifted into the air: his feet had left the ground. He knew he was dead. But he could think and feel. 'So this is what it's like to fly? My goodness, feel that heat! Something has just gone past me, I wonder what it was. I think the ceiling is coming down. God, please forgive me for all the killing I have done. Forgive me for all my past sins. Forgive me for leaving Matti, whom I pledged never to leave. Please forgiv…' *Thump!*

He hit the ground again, only approximately ten feet away from where he had started to soar, a microsecond ago. He could hear the ceiling was cracking and falling. 'So, I'm not dead after all. Thank you, Lord!' as he picked himself up and ran in the direction of where he thought the opening to their tunnel was. He fell straight through and onto their tunnel floor. 'Not safe yet, must get further down!' As he thought, more ceiling was collapsing; this could be distinctly felt even in this tunnel, which was shaking badly. So was Enrico, whose every fibre shook, more out of excitement than fear, though there was plenty of that too. 'I must find the others; I don't even know how many of us there are? God, that candle we left for Stanley is low, no, it's not: it's because of the lack of oxygen. I had better get to our cave-in and give a hand.' The candle was indeed burning very badly, and now Enrico became aware of just how poor the oxygen was within the tunnel; his chest started to hurt from the exertion of the trials that had befallen them all, his breathing was becoming short. There was a smell that he did not recognise, 'what is that smell? Oh, no, it smells just like gas. That cannot be possible: the fall-in would have completely stopped any further digging from the Hun, what is it?' He soon found himself at the cave-in. There, was Matti and the three others clawing away at the shale of debris, trying hard to make an impression, and get themselves out of this hell hole. The wounded man was lying quite still, not far from where they were working. Enrico decided to approach him for help. "Hello, Stanley, how are you feeling?"

"I'm feeling like shit, Sergeant, but I will live, at least I hope so."

"You at least sound better, and your attitude is a marked improvement. I have a job for you, if you think you're up to it?"

"Anything that can take my mind off the pain in my shoulder! What d'you want me to do?"

"I want you to get your revolver out and guard the rest of us, just in case the bloody Germans do get back in. Is that all right, do you feel capable?"

"Sure, let me at the buggers!"

"Now I can help with the digging. Matti, quiet a moment; are the guns still shelling our positions?"

Silence befell the tunnel. The guns were still blazing away. "Well, that does it, it's up to us to get out of here, and we'd better hurry, the air is running out; keep to just one candle. I know there's little light but the more candles we burn the quicker the oxygen will get used up. Better we're breathing it than the candles."

Just one candle was left alight, giving no real light, but they all knew what they had to do. "Dig for freedom!" That had been a poster displayed all over Britain, to get the populace to grow more food for themselves, thus taking the pressure off the shipping, as the ships were being sunk by the U-boats at a terrible rate. It seemed as if the hierarchy thought it best that ships should be sunk carrying armaments for the army, than food for the people. But now the saying had a completely different meaning, one that was much more profound to the six surviving souls down M5.

"Matti, how are you? How's your breathing?"

"Anything you can do, I can do as well. You keep breathing this foul smelly stuff we call air, and I will too."

"You can smell it too, then?"

"Enrico, I thought you had farted," which caused a ripple of laughter from the beavering squad. "The smell is methane, isn't it?" said Matti.

"Bloody hell, of course you're right. Methane, that's it. It must be seeping through with all the bombardment. As if we didn't have enough problems, now gas as well!"

They worked harder than ever, realising that every breath they took would use up the precious supply of oxygen. The candle grew dimmer as the time went by. The spoil of chalk was getting much bigger, as they worked their way through the ceiling fall-in. It then occurred to Enrico that maybe they were going the wrong way. "What if we cannot get through this heap? Maybe we should be thinking of an alternative route?" This was not a casual remark from Enrico, who had now stopped work for a minute; he was serious, as if he had a plan.

"What d'you mean, this is surely the only way out?" said Matti puzzled by the stop, and wondering if his friend was suffering from gas fumes.

"Maybe we should go upwards through the ceiling to daylight?"

"Enrico, how do we do that? Stand on one another's shoulders to dig? Come on, get digging, we cannot have much time left," scolded Matti.

"No, stop Matti, just give me a minute. Didn't we have some more explosives around here? There's a box of Mills bombs somewhere. I'm sure they haven't been used up. Find them, dig a small hole in the roof, plant a bomb, Bob's your uncle, and so on… until we make air."

"And where are these elusive bombs to be found? I don't know of any."

It was then that the voice of Private Stanley Spooner called out. "Is it this box I'm lying besides?"

They moved cautiously over to where Stanley was lying; sure enough, there was a full box of twenty Mills bombs.

"Oh, you little darling!" said Enrico to Stanley.

They took the bombs, and then decided it might be a better plan to explode a hole into the roof a little further down the tunnel, thus also giving a chance to the others to keep digging their way through, just in case it didn't work. They moved twenty paces away from where the bombs had been found, dug a small hole, just big enough to squeeze a grenade into, pulled the pin and ran back. *Boom!* A chunk of roof fell to the floor, but it only went into less than a foot of ceiling. Another hole was dug, and the procedure was done again; *Boom!* Another six inches deeper; and again, and again, and again.

Before long, the air was now almost completely used up; the diggers had more or less given up, and were starting to accept that death was their next option. Enrico and Matti had to scramble over heaps of chalk which had been brought down in the grenade explosions, and each time Enrico was lifted by Matti to dig the next little hole. *Boom!* This time, along with the big chunk of chalk came several hundred gallons of water. But there was now quite a cavern up in the ceiling, making it very hard to reach in order to dig yet another hole for another grenade. "Give me a hand here, fellows, this old sod is heavy and I need some help to lift him to the ceiling." Help came from two of the others. They lifted Enrico up towards the new ceiling, and he dug a bigger hole. 'Better to explode the last three grenades together, might do the trick?' He pulled the pins one by one, jumped down and moved everyone out of range of the explosion. *Boom! Boom! Boom!* A huge piece of roofing chalk came down, bringing yet more water. And more and more water.

"Oh, I hope this isn't another cistern of water, I don't want us to drown down here. Keep close to me, Matti," said Enrico. Then the water stopped and they all realised the guns sounded much louder. They had broken through! Clean air gushed into that gaseous hole in the ground. The squad breathed deeply yet again. But the guns were causing a great deal of damage, and the fear of a shell coming through was a real one. "Better we get further up the tunnel ourselves. Having gone to all the trouble to get air again, it would be a crying shame to get killed by enemy guns."

They moved back into the darkness yet again. "Matti, light some candles, at least we should be able to see something." The water had risen to four inches all over the tunnel floor, not enough to drown anyone, but certainly enough to make them cold, wet and irritable. In the dim light of the candles they could survey the extent of the new hole to freedom. It was crater size, almost completely round, extending a good six feet from side to side. It must have been ten to fifteen feet from the new hole up to the ground above. If it hadn't been for the weight of the water, their grenades would never have been enough to get through topside. Enrico and Matti both realised just how lucky they were, yet again! Clean cold air was reviving them all, and the squad quickly gathered their thoughts, moving back further towards the German trenches again. As they progressed forward, Enrico trod in something: it was the body of a dead soldier that had come down with all the spoil from above. The smell was immediate, making him heave slightly and not for the first time. "Oh, not again! Matti, I have trodden in someone, and whoever it was is all over my boots and legs. Please help me wash him off!" There was the sound of marching feet, but no word from Matti. 'You are not getting me there!' thought Matti, as he moved away as quietly and quickly as possible.

Soon they were in a safer part of the tunnel right beside where the German tunnel had fallen in. "Can you hear anything?" said Enrico, as he called for silence.

"No, not you too! There is no way that the Germans could dig that much spoil away, not this side of Christmas anyway. You sounded just like Lieutenant Fisher then! We are safe from the Hun here, surely? Aren't we?"

"Yes," answered Enrico, "I would think so, but better to be safe than sorry. We will all keep quiet and wait until the shelling stops. It cannot last forever." But as quickly as he said it, he knew darn well it could. They would have to get food and water if they were to survive any length of time down there. Maybe they could escape through the new hole? But again, that was not a great idea, as they were smack in the middle of no-man's-land. No, when the shelling eased or stopped, they must dig their own way out. But Enrico's thoughts were on a high really: after all, hadn't he suggested their new air hole? They would have suffocated by now. But the shelling was excessive, huge mortars and howitzers making their presence felt.

"I wonder how they are faring back topside in the trenches," Enrico remarked to Matti, knowing that he wouldn't have a clue either.

"Who knows?" came the predictable answer.

Hours went by, day turned into night, though it was always night down there in the tunnel. The shelling seemed to get worse, instead of easing off. Matti and Enrico had now started to fret on their predicament, all the time dwelling on how they could get out. "How much food and water do we have? I want us to pool everything, so we can share it out if we are going to be stuck down here for a long time." Then he added: "I left my own food and water bottle near the German face, when I was picking up a case of explosives, for someone to carry. It's still there. So what do we have?"

Matti was the first to come forward with his water bottle. "Half empty!" said Enrico. "No, half full!" One by one they produced their meagre rations, which in total added up to roughly half a loaf of bread and four canteens of water.

"This will last us just a day or two at the most. We will give it another few hours, then we go back to digging." There was just the first hint of desperation in his voice, but enough to make Matti look up and start wondering. The air was cleaner, but there was still that musty smell of methane which was clinging to the floor, like icing sugar on a birthday cake, white, thick and sickly to the taste. Besides, there was also that disgusting smell of putrid, stagnant water. These smells were becoming more and more obvious to the surviving six. The hours went by, slowly, and each man took his turn in listening duty. It was while Private Stanley Spooner was on duty that the shelling eased dramatically. He woke the others.

"Sergeant, the shelling, it's changed."

"Yes, you're right. I think they've gone back with their range," as the shells seemed to be falling much further away. "Matti, maybe it's time that we moved forward again, and started digging."

They had been digging for not more than three hours, and the morning light was beginning to creep into their new air hole. Just as Enrico looked up the new opening, there, above the rim of the new crater, three faces appeared. They saw him at the same moment. Just in time, he dived for cover, as a stick grenade was thrown down, but on this occasion, it exploded on the wrong side of the fallen debris, making a huge echoing bang, and a pressure wave that nearly knocked the four Tommies off their feet.

"Jesus Christ! Are you all right, Enrico?"

"*Sssshhh!*" came the terse reply. Matti and Private Pierce were crammed into the small space that they were digging to break through; Enrico was still lying prone behind some fallen rubble. It was Private Charles Foote and Private Stanley Spooner who caught the full blast of the next two grenades that were thrown into the hole at the right angle. Spooner died instantly, as his head left the rest of his body, and Charles Foote was seriously wounded with fragments of grenade embedded in his stomach; but it was not the grenade that killed him, it was falling into just four inches of water in an unconscious state, making him drown. Enrico knew that this was not the end, and his fears were confirmed when a hissing noise was heard. He could distinctly and immediately smell gas! 'They're trying to gas us out! I'd better make my way closer to the others!' Crouching next to Matti, and trembling badly from fear, he said: "Matti, they're gassing us!" but Matti had already worked that one out for himself.

"Enrico, stop flapping! There is a way out of this. Pierce, you listen too. This is chlorine gas, and I remember them telling us in training how to neutralise chlorine gas. All we have to do is take out our hanky, and piss into it; there is a chemical in our pee that can counteract the effect of chlorine." At this point, Private Pierce interjected with: "Yes, I remember that, it's the ammonia in your pee that does it."

Matti was demonstrating with a huge flow of urine, which he had been meaning to part with for hours. Pierce did the same, but much as he tried, Enrico could get none to come out. Now almost in a panic, he grabbed Matti, saying: "I can't fucking pee!"

"Oh, for Goodness sake, Enrico! Give me your sodding handkerchief!" It seemed Matti had an endless supply. Their eyes stung from the heavy concentration of gas, but at least they could breathe and stay alive. Another three stick grenades were dropped in from above, exploding harmlessly, and helping to clear the gas. A flare was dropped in, giving an eerie light and casting huge shadows. The head of a German soldier came into view, as he was lowered from a rope. He looked around in the light, and saw the gruesome, bloody remains of the two dead Tommies; he assumed that all were dead. While they were crouching, wondering what was going to be the next move, they could hear the distant rattle of a machine gun, followed by: "*Ahhhhh!*" At the same moment, the torso of the startled, dangling German came crashing down onto the heaped fragments below. For a second he lay there, stunned, but that second was long enough for Enrico to shout: "Get the bastard!" and rushing forward, withdrawing his sharpened shovel as he went, he lammed into the dazed foe, hacking everywhere with his tool.

One second later, Matti and Pierce were doing the same. The German really never had a chance, as the three of them nearly chopped him to pieces. Not one sound came from him; as they kept hacking away, blood, bone and guts lay everywhere. His head being nearly cut off, had completely caved in, as blow after blow had cut through all the bone. His chest was mangled, with bits of rib, clothing and vital organs minced into one odious mess. His right leg twitched, even as Enrico was still hacking at it, cutting right through the bone in many places.

"Stop, stop, stop! I think we finished him!" The three of them backed off, and allowed the sun to cast its rays of hope onto this pile of gore. Enrico remembered that there must be other soldiers up there, and they thought it prudent to get out of the area of exploding grenades immediately. But no grenades came; the British machine gun had seen to that, catching the three enemy topside, with its burst of deadly fire. After half an hour, they thought it was time to go back, and start work on the face again, as the chlorine gas had now dispersed, and it was obvious that no fire was going to come at them from above. They dug like crazed men, knowing that it would just be a matter of time before another enemy patrol would come this way. After what seemed many hours, they could hear the distinct noises of digging coming from the other direction, and it was only another thirty minutes to wait until the grinning face of a British miner stared at them.

When they finally got up from the shaft, they were able to witness for themselves the devastation that the shelling had done to their trenches. Though the shaft had not been hit, the whole of the trench system had been badly mangled, and many Tommies had been blown back to their maker, without a chance of ever retaliating back at their tormentors. Several officers had died under the bombardment, plus several NCOs. Though there had been no attack from the Germans, the bombardment had been brought about as a diversion, so they could destroy the tunnel and the tunnelling divisions, but the bombardment itself had stopped when a dozen British aircraft had found the German artillery, and bombed and strafed it into silence.

That night, drinking a copious amount of rum, while giving their report to Captain Turner, they were informed that no only had they done a great job on killing many Germans and destroying the enemy's own tunnel, but they had also done some further damage with the explosion to part of the German front line trench. He then added quite casually, as if in passing: "Of course, I'm going to be sorry to see you go!" A startled Enrico and Matti looked at Turner, and with a puzzled frown Enrico asked: "Go, go where?"

"Why, you've been seconded back to your old unit. Didn't you know?"

"No, I had no idea; seconded back to the old unit? When is this supposed to happen?"

"Well, Sergeant, I'll get you two organising the reclamation of M5, then it's on your bikes!"

"That could take a couple of weeks."

"Well, then, you'd better get to it!"

The next seven days were spent frantically clearing all the waste, removing the fallen comrades and surging forward at the tunnel face, knowing that every time a claykicker removed a chunk of chalk, they were getting closer to the Hun, who knew they were coming.

On their last night with the mining division, Captain Turner had invited Enrico and Matti to dine with him, and crack a bottle of whisky. He had grown to admire these two young men enormously, and this was very unusual, as an officer fraternising with NCOs was frowned upon by the hierarchy.

"I'm going to miss you two. When you first came, I thought you would be a total waste of space, but you've certainly proved that wrong! You have both been hard working, diligent and professional in everything you have done."

"Thank you, Sir. And speaking for both Matti and myself, I don't relish getting into any more scrapes like the one we've just got out of, but I must admit the whole experience has been a very exciting one, and it's one I'll be able to tell my grand children about with a certain amount of pride. And yes, Sir, we will miss you too." Matti was nodding in agreement, and just for a moment, their eyes misted at the thought of the friends that had been hard to win, and easy to lose. Their drinks were finished and final farewells said, with a shaking of hands and two smart salutes. Enrico and Matti went for the last time to their billets, and the last time to sleep in the company of the mining division. Just before falling asleep, they once again became aware of the guns booming over Wipers…

# IX

Life back in the London Northern Rifle Brigade, which in June 1916 meant Ypres, or Wipers to the more enlightened, was then anything but calm. The losses that had befallen them while doing trench duties had been devastating. So many killed and wounded that the original numbers had been decimated, and the ranks were being filled at such a rate with raw recruits that nobody knew anyone else. It became hard to befriend someone, as you didn't want to see a friend get killed, and new boys were being killed at such an alarming rate, that it seemed better not to get too close to anyone. The Germans always had the trenches within their gun sights, so knowing this, the enemy artillery could fire almost at will, wherever and whenever they liked. If they thought a new detachment of troops was entering the system, they just opened up with a few dozen rounds of howitzers or mortars and they were sure of some success.

But the Allies had a master plan, a plan that would drive the Hun out of Belgium and France, right back to Berlin. There was going to be a new front, one that would be devastated by British and French artillery delivering a bombardment that was going to last for twenty-four hours a day, for seven days. There were going to be no Germans left alive in their trenches, the barbed wire that always stopped an advance was going to be obliterated with all that shelling. The attacking troops could and should walk across no-man's-land at an amble, smoking their pipes and cigarettes; why, it was going to be such a shelling, that they would be in the German trenches in time for a bacon and eggs breakfast! But all of these plans would be for nothing if spies got wind of anything that might be afoot. The

*298*

Germans didn't need spies: it was perfectly obvious from the preparations gathering momentum within the Allies trenches that an offensive was going to be forthcoming, and it didn't take any genius in Germany to work out where it was going to take place; this made it the worst kept secret so far within the Great War; a tragedy of Biblical proportions was about to unfold itself.

The Battalions were reforming. With the continual loss of the youth of Britain and its Commonwealth, numbers could no longer be sustained at their previous level, so it seemed the obvious solution for the top brass was to bring the Battalions into mixed Corps, sweeping aside hundreds of years of regimental history. This was to give Kitchener's Pals Brigades a chance to be slaughtered en masse, along with all the others whose lives were fruitlessly wasted. And this oncoming battle was due to be exposed, for all of Britain to 'marvel' at: the battle of the Somme.

The French were suffering tremendous loss of life at Verdun, and the Germans knew that Verdun was the life blood of France; destroy Verdun, you destroy France. France needed a respite, something to take the pressure off. A joint action with the British was necessary; at least that is what was being told by General Joseph Joffre. On meeting General Foch, he insisted that the latter make a detailed study of the possibilities of a combined British and French assault within the Somme region.

"If this is not done soon, and an all out assault is not forthcoming, France will cease to exist, the flower of its manhood being killed or wounded. Make that offensive and the pressure on Verdun will ease." The French were to attack on the thirty-five mile stretch from the River Somme, all the way to Lasigny. The British were to attack north from the River Somme to Arras. General Joffre wanted to start this major battle as soon as possible, and when talking to General Sir Douglas Haig, just after the 19th December 1915, after Haig had officially become Commander-in-Chief of the BEF, he became extremely upset when being told by Haig that there was no chance of a battle being fought before August or even

September 1916. But under tremendous pressure from his French counterpart, the new Commander-in-Chief agreed to a compromise date of the 1st July 1916. 'Thus the seed was sown, the die cast, Berlin here we come.'

Since the end of 1914, when the BEF were being decimated by the Hun with his machine guns, Lord Kitchener had appealed to the nation and the entire British Empire saying that men were desperately needed. Every little village, town and city started to recruit men, with the slogan 'join together, fight together.' Thus were born the Pals Brigades.

These Brigades were formed from every walk of life, men straight from Colleges and Universities; not just the students, but the professors as well, joined up en masse. You would get a Brigade made up of just City men, bankers, stockbrokers, men of great wealth and importance, men that theoretically ran the finance of the entire country. Firemen, musicians, farmers, builders, miners, in fact every profession one can think of, they all came together with a single will to defeat the Hun, send Fritz back to Germany with a flea in his ear; all well meaning, all completely unknowing of the true extent of the squalor that awaited them. What they were told, and what was the real truth about death, were really two entirely different things: not quite the glory that they had been duped into believing, but a painful and often ignominious end to life, a complete waste of the manhood of the world. Over the entire Empire, several million men enlisted to do their duty for King and Country, in many instances, to fight for a country they had never seen, or were never going to. Indians, Pakistanis, Ceylonese, Australians, New Zealanders, Canadians, Afrikaners, New Foundlanders, Nepalese, Chinese from Hong Kong, the whole of the British Empire.

To the people of Britain, including Ireland, the war had now become completely global, the very first World War. And all these men were ready, willing and eager to meet the Hun in action, as if they knew what 20th Century action was.

It was against this background that Enrico and Matti rejoined the

Battalion in Ypres.

"Sergeant Caruso, Corporal Dumbridge, welcome home! I've heard very good reports of your conduct within the mining division, and the way things have been going here, I'm glad to have two capable NCOs back in the fold," said Colonel McBride to the duo, standing to attention in clean uniforms and highly polished boots, looking for all the world like professional soldiers.

"Thank you, Sir. It's true, we had a few scrapes down in the tunnel, and I think I speak for both of us when I say it's good to be back."

"Sergeant, we are going to need you with all your skills to re-train our raw recruits, as we are heading away to be reformed along with the Kent & East Sussex. As far as I know, we are both going to be used in a support capacity in a huge offensive that will be happening very soon, exactly where and when, I am not at liberty to say. Our trench system here will be taken over by another Battalion, and I understand, a Portuguese Division will be in support here, too. We have seven days in which to withdraw, along with all our equipment, and allow the relief Battalion to take our place. It is your job to support RSM Kelly, as now you are the senior Sergeant left within the Battalion."

Upon hearing this, both Enrico and Matti started, as they had not realised just how serious the casualties had been.

"So, men, go have some food, stow your equipment, find RSM Kelly as time is very much against us."

The seven days went quickly, and though the guns still blazed from both sides, the casualties had been comparatively light, and the switch-over day had come with no serious hitches. The London Northern Rifle Brigade was for the first time in its history to be reformed, albeit temporarily, along with the Kent & East Sussex Rifles to make a new Division. They were to form at the little hamlet of Daours, which is eight miles east of Amiens, just nestling on the north side of the river Somme. The Battalion boarded trains at midnight, a few miles south of Poperinge, arriving in Amiens just after two in the morning; there had been no hiccups and no casualties. It took two hours to unload the various trains of their soldiers and equipment, and another hour to get assembled, ready to march to Daours. So that when they finally trudged into the sleepy little oasis of peace and tranquillity that was soon to become the most horrendous battle yet known to man, they were all ready for a good long rest.

"RSM Kelly, men will have plenty of time for sleep, but first, we must dig them in," said Colonel McBride. This was duly done, and once the field kitchen had been set up, breakfast of a sort was administered.

"Men, you can have the rest of the morning to recover, but this afternoon we start training, and it will be training in earnest. No slackers will be tolerated, so if you think you're ill, or going to be ill, see the MO now!"

Enrico and Matti both worked with a will to dig initial slip trenches which would soon become yet more major trench systems. By nine am, the trenches already started to appear, and all along could be seen many sleeping soldiers, or soldiers at rest, writing letters or postcards, smoking cigarettes or just reading the latest issue of the 'Wipers Times', but generally the men were well fed, relaxed, and quite contented. It reminded one of sheep that were in a field, fattening up on their last meal, just outside the doors of the abattoir.

"Matti, fancy a stroll down to the river? It would be nice, as it's such a sunny warm day, to maybe have a wash, and put one's feet in. What do you say?"

"Sounds good to me! Let's go!"

They strolled the remaining quarter of a mile, till they came to the bank of the river Somme, and there, was a beautiful, large weeping willow, which had grown directly out of the river bank, and with its trunk, branches and foliage was hanging entirely over the river. If it was not for the noise of the guns in the distance, this could have been an idyllic setting for a young lover's tryst, or a family outing picnic. Enrico took his shoes and putties and socks off, rolled his trousers up to his knees, walked down the bank, and sat on the trunk of the tree which leant out into the river. Matti had joined him, and the two were sitting down side by side and about to put their feet in the water, when the war came back to hit them both.

"Oh, my God! Is that what I think it is?" Both of them pulled their feet up quickly, away from the water, because there, just under the surface, was the swollen body of a German soldier. As they looked at this misshapen corpse, they could see the arms of another corpse, wrapped around him. Getting a stick which lay nearby, Enrico prodded the body to move it and see what was underneath. There, to his horror, was the sight of a bloated French soldier, looking as if it had died in a lover's leap with his German comrade, but on closer inspection, it could be clearly seen that each had stabbed one another with their bayonets, and thus locked together, had fallen into the river, to spend the rest of eternity in one another's arms. Having disturbed the corpses, which now started to float again down river, Enrico and Matti were brought back to reality by the smell of rotting flesh.

The first day of training was very light, with just drill and kit inspections, but on the thirteenth of June, the men were woken at four thirty in the morning, and told that they were going on a full-kitted route march. They had to carry their entire kit, along with several large pieces of stone, so that their total carrying weight would be about eighty pounds. The march went all the way around Amiens and back, which was approximately a twenty mile trek. That night, exhausted men, far too tired, even to eat, fell into their makeshift bunks, and most were asleep before the Sergeant had time to come and tuck them in; the next morning, another four thirty wake up call. Again with nearly eighty pound weights, they had a tedious, long, and hard obstacle course to contend with, which again exhausted them. Dinner was served immediately they got back to camp, and ravenous appetites were sated with copious quantities of something that reminded them of a type of Irish stew which had dozens of hard boiled eggs thrown in for good measure. Though the meat tasted a little gamey, it was only later that they discovered that they had eaten one of their own artillery pulling horses, which the day before, on grazing merrily in the field, had yawned lazily, looking towards the sun, and just keeled over, being probably the only horse in the history of World War One to have died of old age!

Yet again the men slept soundly. The next day, bayonet practice; more drilling, more throwing of Mills bombs, more kit inspections, and so on, and so on...

There had been many lectures by senior staff officers, especially aimed at junior officers and NCOs concerning the forthcoming battle, and what was expected of each Division. At the end of each address, the men would be just as confused, regarding what their particular role was going to be, as before each lecture. All they knew was that in reality, the London Northern Rifles and the Kent & East Sussex Rifles were left as Reserve Divisions, to be used however the commanding General thought was best, maybe even not at all. They knew now the basic battle plan, but being reserve troops, their own role was always left as a blank. They had been told of the huge artillery emplacements along the whole of the fourteen mile front, with three million shells at their disposal. Like General Haig said: "Not even a lice will live through this bombardment!" They learnt of the seventeen huge tunnels that had been built, and were at this time being stacked with high explosives. They knew that the mines were to be exploded at seven twenty-eight a.m., the shelling would then stop, and at seven thirty, the attack would start. Not far from their encampments, the cavalry were preparing themselves, knowing that it was their task, once a hole had been punched through the German lines, to exploit that hole by sweeping out into open country. General Sir Douglas Haig believed emphatically that it would in the end be the cavalry that won any battle, but then General Haig too, had been brought up with nineteenth Century cavalry campaigns under his belt. So each day went by, with all the familiar toil and training, until that morning of the twenty-fourth, when everybody was awoken by the monstrous sound of the opening bombardment. Guns of every calibre were laying their seeds in the harvest of battle. The actual earth shook, even though they were fifteen miles from the front, and in the pre-dawn, the whole of the East was alight with the colours of death.

"How could anybody be alive, after this?" said Matti, as he leant across, stealing a quick drink of water from Enrico's canteen.

"Well, surely, old bean, that's the idea. We kill them all!"

Ears began to ring with the horrendous roaring, and the concussive reverberation from the continuous explosions, but yet again, human endurance started to show its determination to withstand all sorts of discomforts as they got used to the guns. Hours went into days, and the bombardment never ceased, even for a second. Guns would become so hot that barrels had to be hosed down with water to stop them from cracking; in some cases, the really big calibre guns were losing so much metal from within the barrel that they had to be withdrawn from service, for fear that they would blow up, killing the crew. There were three major problems that were going to cost the British dear: firstly, the Generals had not taken into account how deeply the enemy had been allowed to dig themselves in; often the German dugouts were twenty or thirty feet deep, making them impervious to all but the largest calibre shells. Secondly, the German wire was not being cut, as the bombardment had meant it to be, because of the simple fact that most of the shells were shrapnel shells, rather than the high explosives needed to break the wire. And, last, and probably most important, was that, possibly up to a third of the entire stock of shells, turned out to be duds, and would often explode when the attacking troops ran into them.

On the 29th June 1916, the joint troops of the Corps, Divisions and Brigades moved up to their various jumping off trench systems: men from all four corners of the globe, each man having to carry the equivalent of eighty pounds weight extra, as well as his rifle and ammunition. He would be carrying A-frames for the new trenches that the attackers were going to occupy, duck boards for the floors of the said trenches, barbed wire, stores of all sorts, plus the normal guns, ammunition, and bombs. Just as well the artillery was sending in nearly three million shells, otherwise the enemy would catch the Tommies with their trousers down. The Kent & East Sussex and the London Northern were no exception to this rule. Even though they were going up to the reserve trench, they too had to tote huge loads of stores and war implements. So many men cramming into all the systems of trenches, waiting for the whistles to blow and to climb out of their own holes to find new ones in German held lines! Waiting for two days, and two nights in such conditions was hell in itself, and on top of that the German artillery was also firing back into Allied trenches, with heavy mortars, howitzers and like the British, guns of all calibres. Their deadly deeds were executed with efficacy, causing many casualties long before the men were due to see the enemy. The shrapnel shells were creating havoc, and the stretcher bearers were getting plenty of practice in before the main event. Casualty clearing stations were getting a taster of what was to come, and they were already not coping well with the injured now!

In the reserve trench, Matti as was his wont, stood next to his friend Enrico, tired and sore from the carrying of stores; conscious of the fact that a good meal would not have gone amiss, he looked at pal Enrico and said: "You will stay close to me if we do have to go over the top, won't you, Enrico?"

"Yes, of course I will. Don't I always stay next to you? Why, I can hardly go for a dump before I'm aware of you passing me a sheet of the "Daily Sketch," and offering to help wipe my arse as well! We are always together."

"It's such a beautiful day, warm and sunny, what in heaven's name are we all doing here? We should be on the beach at Blackpool, getting a tan, and having a few beers."

"*Shhhh!* Matti, can you hear that song thrush? With all the crashing and banging, the birds are still singing. It gives hope to a better existence, that's what it does. Look, I hadn't noticed before, but look at all the yellow wild flowers, what are they?"

"Buttercups, you idiot!"

"Well, I don't care what they are, it gives me hope when I still see colour in all this desolation."

The sun shone down on the crouching troops, sun that gives life, but also shows up extremely shiny objects, and glistening objects make good targets for the artillery. So along with the sun comes the rain of death in the form of a steel scythe, one that harvests all the ripe soldiers.

There were pools of water in shell holes, still left over from a wet, cold winter. These were the homes of many dead swollen corpses from bygone battles, and as the water shrank, it then exposed these rotting clumps of human flesh and bone. As each body started to show itself, the flies would come and lay the eggs which quickly turned into maggots, then bluebottles. When a shell landed near a shell hole containing these remains, millions of bluebottles would take to the air for a few seconds, but in such great quantities that they swarmed like a cloud of dust, so thick one could not always see through them. With the bluebottles came diseases and this caused great anxiety to the Generals; they wanted the fighting soldiers to be able to do their duty, before going down with Typhoid or worse.

Still the shelling went on. 'How could anything be alive after this?' thought Enrico.

Then came the evening of the 30th of June; the shelling had intensified with a view to using up the remainder of the three million shells. The very ground shook, even to the extent that British front line trenches were in danger of collapse. Some of the parapets of these trenches had started to fall in under the terrible shaking that everything within several miles was subjected to. One good thing that had come from this bombardment was that the rats had abandoned the sinking ship. For that entire week, not a single rat had been seen within the Allied lines. 'Let the Hun have the lot!' was the general view upon this piece of good luck. It was a black night and everyone was becoming very tense. MPs had moved up into the front lines trenches, and every fighting soldier knew why they were there! Any malingering would be dealt with quickly, taking no prisoners for court martial. A bullet to the brain was going to be the order of the day. No cowards would be tolerated, anyone who came back, unless with orders from Officers or on a stretcher, wounded, would be dealt with, summarily. The rum ration was brought out, ready for distribution to each man; a hefty slug would be administered like a dose of medicine, and this was used as a quick nerve tonic. The rum would be handed out thirty minutes before the whistle was blown, and the attack was on.

Weary men stood waiting with full packs, rifles slung over their shoulders, waiting for that moment when either it would become a stroll in the park, or a nightmare only imagined within bad dreams. Many planes had spotted for the front line soldiers, some even getting shot down by friendly shells as they took huge chances to see the enemy front line trenches, and what was occurring during all the shelling. The prognosis had not been good. Many pilots had reported that the wire was still very much in place, having sustained little damage from the shells. This was ignored by the Generals, who put it down to bad eyesight on the part of the pilots: looking through all that smoke and choking cordite, they had obviously got it wrong. Then scouts were sent out into no-man's-land to see what was happening. They too, came back with the grim news that the wire in most places was untouched, and where it had been blown up, it had curled into tighter rolls, thus creating an even harder obstacle for the attackers to overcome. Again, the Generals put this down to just not going to the right places. They were going to have their battle no matter what! Seven o'clock in the morning came, along with beautiful sunlight, a wonderful day. 'Good omen,' thought Lieutenant General Congreve, the commander of the reserve troops. But still his arm twitched badly, and his voice was extremely shaky from nerves. The minutes were now ticking down to zero hour. Soldiers were becoming tense, ready for the fray that was to come, pepping themselves up with the rum ration. Tensing all nerves and fibres, waiting for that moment when they would have to climb the ladder and walk into what? Men thought of home once more. Would they ever see their wives, mothers, sweethearts, family, or even country again?

Seven twenty-eight minutes past midnight on the morning of the 1st July 1916. Seventeen huge mines exploded. The biggest was to become known as "Lochnagar Crater" and was filled with eighteen tons of high explosive; the spoil from this explosion was thrown many hundreds of feet into the air. It was so devastating that even some British front line troops were buried alive when the waste came back to earth. Two minutes later, at seven thirty exactly, silence! The artillery had expended its huge stockpiled shells. Whistles on a fourteen mile front started to blow, and up surged the attacking Tommies from their trenches. Each was carrying their eighty pounds of extra equipment. So heavily laden were they, that to run or jump about was impossible. Almost ninety percent of the attacking force had never been in action before, since they were all recruited within the last twelve to sixteen months; all willing, but all raw and untested.

Captains and Lieutenants were the first from their trenches, standing on the top of the parapet, urging all the men to quickly climb the ladders. No more than ten seconds had passed before the initial *rat-tat-tat-tat* of machine gun was heard. At first, it was a long way away, but soon other machine guns were heard, and in less than two minutes, all the German trenches were manned with soldiers, firing their rifles and machine guns. Where had they come from? Why weren't they all dead? It was shortly to become very clear that, far from being dead, although they had suffered very badly from the continuous shelling, in most cases, it was more from a mental point of view than a physical one. What the British and French had failed to find out was that the defenders had dug themselves deep dugouts, and though being bombarded continuously, only suffered serious casualties from direct hits from the biggest shells. They had been deprived of fresh food and water for a week, but they were alive, and now they were mad. They wanted revenge for the deprivation that had been inflicted on them, and the Tommies were going to pay dearly.

Enrico and Matti were looking through periscopes from the reserve trenches, and were horrified at the sights that confronted them: soldiers were not even making it to their own wire, as German machine guns swept the line of moving men. So their fate had been decided: this was *not* a picnic in the park, but a nightmare of bad dreams. Men were falling over themselves, falling over comrades, falling over the barbed wire. In many cases, the attackers could not even see the enemy trenches, they were that far away, but still the German rifles and their machine guns took their toll. Line after line of Allied troops crept forward, many having learnt by now to dump their loads, or even use them as shields, as they quickly made their way into shell holes. The bravery of the soldiers was never in doubt, as through all this rainstorm of bullets, they still struggled to go forward. Many got into the middle of no-man's-land, only to have the German artillery open up, creating a further wall of death. The artillery had had months to work out every square yard of land, so their shells could fall precisely where they wanted them to. Still more troops entered the front line trench systems, yet more climbed the ladders, some were even being killed as their heads went above the parapets, and others dodged from dead body to dead body, using their comrades as human shields. Surely the corpses would not mind!

Some of the first wave had even managed to get close enough to the German wire to use their own guns; many defending soldiers, realising they were on a Sunday turkey shoot, had thrown caution to the wind, and were actually standing on their own parapets, so that they could get clearer shots at the attacking Tommies: those foolish Huns were swiftly dealt with, but how did you cross the wire? Only in a few instances had any wire been cleared by shelling, and where it had, the Germans had quickly mounted several machine guns, so as to catch the funnelling advancing troops in a deadly crossfire. So many soldiers had rushed headlong towards the Boche wire, and had fallen victim to a wounding bullet and got themselves impaled on the barbed wire to die in abject misery over minutes, hours, or even days of agony! The screaming from the wounded could be heard even above the screaming of the shells overhead.

The battle was costing the Youth of Britain dearly; in the very first hour, it was estimated that forty-eight thousand casualties were sustained, and over the whole day, more than sixty thousand had fallen victim to enemy rifle and machine gun fire, shelling, stick grenades, mortars, and in some cases were burnt alive from the German flame throwers. This indeed was proving to be a slaughter of Biblical proportions.

All this was observed from the reserve trenches, and seeing all this death and mayhem had made the soldiers very reticent about the possibility of also being pushed forward to fill the yawning gaps.

"Oh, dear God!" sobbed Matti with tears of compassion streaming down his face. "I hope I never see anything like it again in my whole life!" Enrico too, had tears rolling down his cheeks; his mouth was agape, and though the sight of this massacre made him almost sick to the stomach, he was as if hypnotised, unable to withdraw his eyes from the ghastly spectacle that he was witnessing. All the men that could watch were watching, and it affected the morale extremely badly.

"How could the Generals have got this so wrong?" asked Enrico to nobody in particular. They all felt the urge to comfort out of pity their wounded and dying brethren, but their mandate would never allow them to leave their trenches without special permission. The sight that was there to behold was one of piles of men, writhing and wriggling, like a fisherman's box of worms. Some of the wounded were crawling in agony to try to make it back to their own lines, only to receive yet more bullets, or shell fragments finishing them. German snipers were taking careful aim to shoot anything that moved at all, and machine gunners were systematically sweeping the living, wounded or dead with more and more raging bullets. This was proving to be the greatest death toll ever on any given day.

The stretcher bearers were taking tremendous chances, often being killed themselves in the effort to save a wounded soldier, and in the first hour of the battle, the hospitals and medical clearing stations were completely overwhelmed with the influx of the wounded: men were laid side by side, and an orderly would go up and ascertain whether the luckless soldier could be saved or not. And if the verdict was 'not,' he would be left there to pass away without any assistance being administered. The priests and padres were working overtime, and the sappers could not dig the graves quickly enough; generally the bodies were left to their own devices.

Yet, in all this death and destruction, the attack had not been a complete failure everywhere: there had been some gains, some enemy trenches had been taken, some villages in the rear had been overrun by attacking Allies; in fact the news that was getting back to the General Headquarters had become very confused; Generals Haig, Rawlinson and Gough had been getting contradictory reports on how the battle was faring. Haig was under the impression that they were on the threshold of a huge historical victory, Gough was even talking about bringing the cavalry into play to exploit the obvious breakthrough that was occurring, and this was the signal that was getting back to the many newspaper reporters who were not allowed to be close to the fighting, but nevertheless were eagerly waiting for reports that they could wire back to their various editors. The real truth of the battle would be a long time in coming...

By nightfall, there had been very few realistic gains, but between La Boiselle and Fricourt, there had been penetrations of up to half a mile into enemy territory, with even the capture of the village of Mametz. Further south, there had been some success, and one Corps had managed to complete all its objectives, from Pommiers redoubt east of Mametz, to Dublin redoubt north of Maricourt.

The mood in the reserve trenches had not altered from the first gloom that had appeared after the witnessing of the undeniable slaughter befalling the frontline attacking troops. Both the Kent & East Sussex and London Northern Rifle Brigades had sat back, trying mentally to prepare themselves for the call-up that they feared was inevitable, but instead of being ordered forward, the men were told to stand down and organise guard duty rotas. Field kitchens were hastily assembled, and a hot, mushy but nourishing, glutinous stew was produced for the men. It smelt awful, and tasted worse, but soldiers had learnt that when food was in the offing, it should never be refused. While they ate, the slaughter in the field continued, but some of the wounded were now managing to get back, and many German soldiers, whose bloodlust had been high, had become sated; many turned a blind eye so that the British wounded could get back to the safety of their own trenches. Thus with the Germans' surprising com-passion, many hundreds of seriously wounded British soldiers were able to make their own way, or be rescued by the heroic efforts of stretcher bearers and be taken to the swamped advanced dressing stations, at least giving them a chance of further life.

The attacks continued, the hours blended into days, and on the 14th of July, now having committed more than four hundred thousand men to the attack, the sheer weight of numbers had turned the tide, more in favour of the Allies than of the defenders.

General Rawlinson had decided that the battle should concentrate on three objectives: the taking of Bazentin-le-Petit and Delville Woods and beyond those two targets was the dark and oppressive goal of High Wood.

The attack was made, after just a five minute dawn bombardment, along Caterpillar Valley. At exactly three twenty-five in the morning, twenty thousand more attacking Tommies moved to gain control of these three woods. The sudden bombardment and then the attack had been a huge surprise to the defending Hun, and within minutes, a five mile stretch of the German second line was overrun. Shortly after that, on the left, the first objective, Bazentin-le-Petit Wood was taken. Then the attack started on Delville Wood. It took a further six days, and many thousands of British and South African troops' lives before Delville Wood was taken, but the main goal, the austere High Wood, was going to be much harder. The attack on High Wood had started with the seventh Division, on the same day as the attack on Delville Wood.

At first, the gains had been quite good, in fact good enough for two squadrons of cavalry to be made ready for that famous breakthrough that was supposed to come. The trouble was that it was only the Dragoons and Deccan Horse who were in the attack: the rest of the cavalry Divisions had gathered in the town of Albert, and knew nothing of the role they were supposed to be playing. So in the initial attack, when the Germans had recovered from seeing these horsemen with sabres and lances, galloping across the cornfields into the sights of their machine guns, the slaughter started. Every horse was killed, and many of the riders too. Only a few managed to crawl out of the cornfields with their tails very much between their legs. At first the seventh Division made some progress into the wood, but was soon driven back by the defenders. Then the serious battle for High Wood developed. The British artillery was given orders to zero in on what was fast becoming an infamous place, and planes were deployed for the spotting of the artillery. The problem with using cannons in an unknown area was that they often fired shells on their own men, thus adding to the huge casualty list that was developing.

It was decided by Lieutenant General Congreve to use the Rifle Divisions as support troops in the attack at High Wood, and on the first of September, the soldiers of the London Northern and the Kent & East Sussex Rifle Brigades, along with their own artillery, and their officers and NCOs, were marched through the infamous Caterpillar Valley, and into the relative safety of the new trench systems at Bazentin-le-Petit Wood.

"Colonel McBride, I want you to devise a plan that includes taking your Division of Riflemen up the sunken road, capturing the German Switch Line and breaking through into the northern part of High Wood. You can use your own twenty-five- and thirty-pounder artillery to shell the German sector of the wood. Once you have captured the Switch Line, send a runner back to inform the artillery, and then a further attack will be mounted from the seventh Division lines on the south side of the wood. If you look on the map, here," said Brigadier Cutler, pointing to the chart on the table within the ruined house that was now the Headquarters on the edge of Bazentin-le-Petit, "you can see distinctly that the wood is roughly one half mile long, running east to west, by a quarter of a mile wide. The artillery has already made massive inroads in destroying enemy bunkers and trench systems, but we have not been able to successfully drive the enemy from the wood. Before we can go any further, *this* we must do! Once you have taken the German sector of trench, any withdrawal on the part of the Germans can be dealt with by your Lewis gunners and riflemen. Can you come back tomorrow, and give me a detailed account of how you intend to do this?"

Colonel McBride saluted the Brigadier, rolled his map, looked at his own officers who had been listening and watching, and beckoned them out and back to their own dugout. Once there, he turned to his senior officers and asked for their ideas on how they were to take the Switch Line. Captain Northern was the first to come up with an idea.

"Sir, if we get the artillery to open up just before dawn on the enemy positions, and then to stop, start again, stop, start again at irregular intervals, this will, hopefully, confuse Fritz into thinking that each time it ceases, attack is about to happen, but then after a minute or two, starting up the bombardment again will completely throw them.

Under the guise of these mock attacks, the Battalion can creep forward, using the cover of the sunken road, plus the corn, which in many places is still waist high in the fields around. I think that we can, and should, attack at two positions in the Switch Line; having taken those, we can leave a small section of men to protect the rear of the main body, as it moves forward along the line, taking and killing the Germans as we go. If we are really quick, we might well be successful, and as long as runners keep in touch with the artillery, we can use it to make a creeping barrage along the trench system, just ahead of us, thus all the time keeping German heads down, until it is too late."

"Sir," the hand of RSM Kelly went up, "may I further suggest that you get the use of the Seventh Division Artillery, or at least some of them. They can shell the north side of the wood, hopefully creating yet more havoc and confusion. Then using two sections to take the two positions within the Switch Line trench, we can hold back the entire Battalion as reserves for the aftermath gains."

"These are all good ideas," said Colonel McBride, rubbing his hands together as if trying to dry them, with great enthusiasm. "We have the basis for a plan here already. I like it!" That whole night was spent writing up all the details, and making accurate drawings, to show to the Brigadier the very next morning.

The Battalion had once again dug in and made itself as comfortable as possible. Food was served, and morale started to buck up somewhat after the tragic events of the last few weeks.

"Maybe we're now going to be able to contribute to this 'ere battle?" remarked Maurice Bechstein, while trying to eat, drink and smoke a cigarette at the same time.

"Well, I for one, will be happy to get things moving; watching all that was going on and feeling so helpless has been a source of nightmares for me," said Enrico, to the general assembly of men who happened to be sitting, standing and sleeping around him.

"What d'you think we'll be doing, Sarge?" enquired Peter Simpson, a new recruit who had joined the ranks after training just a few weeks ago.

"No idea, we seem to have been brought up here for something, though. Maybe it's to do with that wood there?" he added pointing in the direction of High Wood. Laying back on the fire step, he slowly allowed his eyes to close, 'maybe I can snatch a couple of hours' sleep. For sure I need it.' Enrico was snoring before he had finished the thought.

Two in the morning of the 2nd September; a hand shook Sergeant

Caruso to wake him. It was RSM Kelly. "Enrico, wake up! I need your help. Are you awake?"

"What's the problem?"

"Come for a little walk with me, I want to show you something and get an opinion from you."

Enrico yawned, stretched his arms, and shook himself as the night had turned a little cooler; he scratched the itching that was coming from his crutch, and got up to follow his friend Kelly.

"What's the problem, Spider?" asked Enrico again.

The guns were firing spasmodically in all the sectors, and every now and again, a huge explosion would even go off in the High Wood area. But on the whole, things had quietened considerably over the last few days.

"We have to try and take that wood in the next couple of days. It has already been the death of thousands of soldiers from both sides. I want your feelings on the whole thing?"

"What, that wood there? Thousands you say? What on earth happened?"

"It has already been named as one of the biggest killing fields of this battle, and you saw what happened on the first day!"

"Bloody hell! What's the plan?"

Kelly gave him a rough outline of the plan that had been devised, explaining that if it was approved, the attack would be in two or three days, when enough shells and bullets were brought forward for their use.

"D'you have a complete layout of their gun emplacements? Do we know where their machine gun nests are?" asked Enrico with a worried frown on his brow.

"We have an idea, but I thought, why don't me and you go take a look?"

"When?"

"No time like the present! Anyway there's a very weak moon tonight, that should help us."

"To be honest I'd sooner sleep, but as I'm now awake, I say let's do it. Oh, let's get Matti too!"

"Right, go get him."

The three of them moved furtively through the undergrowth until they got to the sunken road; they could only move along it for one hundred yards before they came upon a very jittery machine gun post, with two Lewis machine guns pointing in the direction of the German Switch Line.

"Alright, alright, stand easy, there's no need for formalities here. Keep your eyes peeled for enemy movement, and anyone who falls asleep is for the high jump. Back to your posts!"

That last remark from 'Spider' Kelly about the high jump had them wide awake again. "We're going out on a little reconnoitre, our password to you is 'Goldfish,' don't forget it, understood? We should only be gone an hour at tops, so no wild shooting!"

There were machine gun pickets all across the divide between the British and the Germans, so finding out how far it was exactly to the enemy emplacements was vital for the artillery and the attacking soldiers. The trio crept along the sunken road, passing the dead of both sides. Suddenly a flare from the enemy went soaring into the sky, but they were well used to such tactics and had thrown themselves to the ground long before anyone could have seen them. But that flare probably meant that the Hun knew something was going on just inside no-man's-land. Care was the byword of the day, as they crouched down just behind the brow of the rise on the road, trying hard to see what could be seen. A match was struck not more than fifty feet away. This made all three hearts stop, then beat at twice the normal rate. Kelly beckoned the other two to his side, and then very carefully whispered into both their ears… "I think we have to creep a little further through the corn field here, what d'you think?"

Matti looked at Enrico, more a pleading look than anything else. 'A person could get himself killed here, let's go back, please, Enrico. Come on, hear my plea!' thought Matti, but moved along with the other two without saying a word when Enrico agreed with 'Spider'. With hardly a sound they pushed into the corn, inch by inch they edged forward, trying desperately hard not to move a single stem for fear it would be heard.

Another flare went up, again the trio froze. No shooting; at least that was a good point. Then carefully they came upon something they would have preferred to have missed: there in front of them, stinking to high heaven were the first dead horse and rider of the Dragoons that had so heroically rushed forward, in the vain hope of creating that elusive breakthrough the Generals so easily demanded and hoped for.

The creatures were already alive with maggots, and the smell made the three of them come to a halt and put their hands over their mouths and noses. Passing the first pair of horse and rider, then a second, then a third, they quickly realised that the entire field which lay before them was in fact the sorry remains of the Dragoons and Deccans lying everywhere. This also created a further problem as the corn had been beaten down and had not risen back up again. 'This is it; we can't seriously go any further without being seen,' thought 'Spider'. He took out his binoculars and started to examine the vista ahead. He could now clearly make out the German wire. 'Not very deep, maybe less than six feet, that shouldn't be too much of a problem, could even jump it on a good day.' He turned to Enrico and said… "I think we've seen all we can, time to retreat back and report. How many gun emplacements have you counted?"

"Well, they have some field Howitzers just on the edge of the copse over to the left. That should be blasted first. Then we have at least four or even five machine guns facing out, in fact there may well be many more. Look, you can see the holes that some of them are hiding in." He was pointing all over the place, trying hard to discern shapes in the dark. Matti too, had not wasted his time, and was busy pointing out possible sights for machine guns in the direction of High Wood. "For sure, this is going to be no picnic, taking this wood after all!" said Matti to the others.

They got back to their own trenches roughly an hour later, and then started feverishly to write down all that they had observed: time was very much of an essence. What was needed most of all was good cooperation between all the forces involved. It was time to show the finds to Colonel McBride; men's lives were at stake, and the plans must be well formulated and approved by all concerned. McBride was impressed, but a little annoyed that RSM Kelly had taken two of the best NCOs on a mission into who-knows-what, without permission, but secretly he wished he had been there too.

So, the final plan which was presented to GHQ was as follows:

A LOCAL BOMBARDMENT WAS TO TAKE PLACE ON THE ALLOTTED TIME; THIS WOULD COMPRISE OF THE ARTILLERY OF BOTH BRIGADES OF THE RIFLES, WHICH INCLUDED TWENTY-FIVE- AND THIRTY-POUNDER GUNS, TWENTY-FOUR IN TOTAL AND ANOTHER FIFTY HEAVIER GUNS OF THE 7TH DIVISION, WHICH ALSO INCLUDED TRENCH MORTARS. THIS BOMBARDMENT WAS TO BE ON A STOP-START ROTA FOR AN AGREED GIVEN TIME; A HUNDRED SOLDIERS OF THE LONDON NORTHERN RIFLE BRIGADE WOULD CREEP UP THE SUNKEN ROAD TO ATTACK THE ENEMY SWITCH LINE TRENCH; HAVING TAKEN THE TWO SECTIONS OF TRENCH AGREED UPON, ANOTHER FIVE HUNDRED MEN WOULD DO THE SAME TO STRENGTHEN THE GAINS. A CREEPING BARRAGE WOULD THEN BE PUT IN PLACE TO GRADUALLY ALLOW THE ATTACKERS TO MOVE FORWARD TO THE NORTH END OF HIGH WOOD; ONCE A FOOTHOLD WAS ESTABLISHED, THE MAIN BODY OF THE 7TH DIVISION WOULD ATTACK FROM THE SOUTHERN END OF THE WOOD, AND THEN SWEEP THROUGH TO MEET UP WITH THE RIFLE BRIGADES. TIMING THROUGH THE USE OF RUNNERS WAS GOING TO BE VERY IMPORTANT, BUT WITH GOOD FORTUNE AND THE RIGHT DETERMINATION, ALL COULD WORK.

'Simple and to the point.' That was the general thought of GHQ, and thus the plan was accepted. All equipment was to be gathered and made ready for the attack to happen a week from the presentation of the plan. Colonel McBride was satisfied with the entire concept, and insisted on heading the main attack himself. This was not considered a good idea by the hierarchy, but nevertheless they gave in to his demands.

McBride had never been a brave man, and had risen to the rank of Colonel through sheer hard work. Most of his professional life had been spent sitting behind a desk in an office, pushing papers around, and signing scraps of written word, often not knowing or caring what had been written, or understanding it when it had been read. But he was a good officer, one who cared deeply for the men he commanded, so this was his moment to prove that their lives were not to be wasted needlessly, as he wouldn't waste his own.

The week was spent feverishly shepherding the shells, trench mortars, and general machine gun and rifle ammunition. All the men were expected to do a fourteen hour shift of carrying. By the third day, soldiers were almost ready to collapse through lack of sleep and sheer exhaustion, but as the ammunition was stockpiled, the labouring hours were relaxed.

On the fifth day, all the NCOs and junior officers were given their final tasks; some would be front line troops, while the rest would be used in reserve yet again, either to back up in case of failure, or hopefully, to exploit any serious breakthrough. On the sixth day, the troops themselves were told of the plans and their role in it. The artillery dug in, and now, after many plane observers had given better information on enemy artillery emplacements and machine gun nests, the gunners thought they had zeroed in on most of the salient points to attack.

The front wave troops were going to consist of Colonel McBride, Captain Northern, Lieutenant Hughes, RSM Kelly, Sergeant Caruso and Corporal Dumbridge, along with one hundred riflemen divided equally from Kent & East Sussex and The London Northern Rifle Brigades. At three in the morning of the 9th of September, all the men were assembled within the sunken road, and the bombardment started at three ten precisely. It lasted for thirty minutes, which gave the troops a chance to reach beyond the sunken road, and into the corn field. Machine gun pickets had dug several nests throughout the last seven days, and had lain hidden, just out of sight of the enemy, and though the foe knew that things were afoot, because when patrols were sent out to investigate, they never returned, they did not know exactly what the activity meant.

Now these machine guns were going to be used efficiently. During the first bombardment, the accuracy of the guns had been good, and they had managed to knock out three of the five field guns by the copse, and several machine gun posts. At three forty a.m., when the bombardment ceased, many front line German troops, believing that the attack was imminent, rushed forward to fill the gaps left by the dead and dying machine gunners, but themselves now got caught in the deadly enfilade of the attacking machine gunners. At three forty-seven, the bombardment started again, and only went on until three fifty-nine. Once again the Germans surged forward to reman the vacated positions, and once again, they were caught by this incessant rate of fire from the British machine guns. Four-fifteen: a new bombardment began; this one lasted until 4.50 a.m., but this time the Germans were wary, and crept low towards their own gun emplacements. At five o'clock, the last bombardment got under way, and this one went on until six a.m. By this time, the Germans were completely confused, and as the guns went silent, the leash was let loose, and a hundred men plus officers and NCOs surged the last two hundred yards to gain a foothold in the Hun trench system.

The confusion had spread to the British lines too, and as the men headed straight for the unbroken wire, at their head, waiving his swagger stick frantically, could be seen the erect, well groomed, bespectacled fifty-three year old Colonel McBride. They reached the wire, more or less at the same time as the defending soldiers started to regain their composure, and though they had no time to bring up any more machine guns, they made good use of the rifles and pistols. One of the first men to be hit was Colonel McBride; he was shot straight through the chest, and was dead before he could have ever felt a thing, his limp body falling directly across a section of the German wire, bringing it down, and making a bridge for some of the attackers to cross. A whole batch of Mills bombs was thrown into the German trench, killing many of the defenders, and this was happening just as the first wave of attackers were jumping down into the Switch Line with their bayonets fixed, slashing and thrashing as they went. At this stage, no prisoners would be taken, and though it was frowned upon, it was generally agreed that the enemy wounded would be despatched forthwith. The two sections of the trench attacked were taken with no more than five dead and thirteen wounded men. The section of the trench between was quickly overrun, and then the process of mopping up and moving along the trench began.

. At this point a pre-selected runner was sent forth to give the news that the Switch Line was now occupied, and that the other five hundred men should promptly be brought forward. It was then that the artillery of the Rifle Brigades would open up, with their trench line coordinates fixed, so the creeping barrage could start, away to the right of the trench, following the trench system through to the northern section of High Wood. The fifty guns of the Seventh Division had been busy from the very first bombardment at three-ten a.m., with a continuous random barrage of the northern sector of High Wood.

"Sergeant Caruso, take your men as quickly as you can to the starting point of the creeping barrage. I want you to mop up anything that remains alive, and where there are deep dugouts, don't bother to take them, but blow them up, and bury the buggers."

German dead lay everywhere, and it became the gruesome job of some of the pioneer troops to lift their remains onto the northern section of the trench, so as to use the bodies for more shelter, should there come some further attacks. The stretcher bearers had speedily done their job in removing the wounded, and RSM Kelly ordered the removal of the body of Colonel McBride, 'silly old sod, why couldn't he have stayed behind his desk and left the fighting to the real soldiers?' thought Kelly, shaking his head, as if in disgust at the waste of this officer whom he had never really admired, but had respected for the fact that the job he did was done with military efficiency.

As this attack was going on, a much more straightforward frontal attack was started by the troops of the seventh Division, the idea being that they would rush and fill in the southern sector of the wood, while the Rifle Brigades pinned down the northern sector; all was starting to work well: as the seventh Division moved into the southern sector, they were surprised at first by how little resistance they encountered. They pushed in deeper, and were disconcerted to be stopped in their tracks by the appearance of not more than a dozen German snipers, who had positioned themselves high up in some of the trees. The soldiers had to fire at any dense foliage to see whether there was an enemy there, but this often gave away their position, and another sniper then did his deadly deed.

More and more of the Seventh were moving into the wood, when the German artillery decided it was time for them to come into play, and now a serious bombardment started. The British artillery, with the use of spotters from the air, had to maximise the range of some of their heavy Howitzers with a view to try and knock out the enemy artillery. So an artillery duel earnestly began to develop.

Enrico and Matti were pushing forward, and at every turn in the trench, took several Mills bombs and lobbed them round the corner, but generally did not catch live defenders, as most had been dealt with by the creeping barrage using shrapnel shells. They had come across two deep dugouts; not waiting to find whether there were humans in them, they had just tossed down parcels of TNT, which brought the roof and walls down. Had there been anybody inside, they would have either died from the blast, or been crushed and suffocated by the ensuing fall of debris. All of this action had taken place from 6.02 a.m., and had reached the boundary of the wood at 8.15 a.m., with the ending of the creeping barrage. Enrico looked at his friend Matti, who was black with gunpowder smuts, dirt and the spluttering of blood from the remains of the dead foe.

"My God! You're a scruffy bugger! You're a British soldier. Can't you smarten yourself up?" said the grinning Enrico. "Hold the line here, Matti, I'm going to go and get the mass of our troops to come up to the line and start pushing within the main trench systems to take the wood. I think you and me have done our bit for the day."

"It would seem that the Hun has done a big runner; most of those that are dead were killed by the barrage, not by anything we've done. So be quick, the few of us that are here, I will keep here, but if there's a counter attack, remember we're in a vulnerable position."

Enrico, crouching down, ran back along the zig-zagging trench until he reached the main body of the Rifle Brigades, who were now filling the whole of the trench system with potential firepower. Enrico was confronted by Captain Schultz, who did not know Enrico, and had wondered where he had come from. Captain Schultz was a professional soldier, and very loyal to the Kent & East Sussex Rifle Brigade. His background was that he had been born in Deal, Kent, had gone through the English educational system, and had got a degree in Chemistry at Canterbury University. But his major problem was one of parentage: his father and mother were both very Bavarian in their demeanour, and as soon as the war looked likely, they had returned to their native Bavaria, leaving a very confused Hans Schultz to his own devices. He had become a hard taskmaster, carrying the burden of a German name, and his men, wary of him, had long learnt to jump when he barked an order.

"Who are you? Where have you come from?"

"I'm Sergeant Caruso, of the London Northern, and I was in the advance party to take this trench, Captain."

"Don't you know to stand to attention and salute an officer when you see one?" Schultz barked, with veins sticking out in his throat.

"Sorry, Sir! No disrespect meant, but we are in the height of battle."

"That's no excuse for insubordination, but what have you come back for?"

"Sir, we need help. I want men to start taking the wood ahead of our position, and keep up the attack before the enemy have a chance to regroup."

"You want what? Who the hell do you think you are? Are you the Brigade's tactician? I think not! I will come and assess the situation, and will make the decisions, and until then, go back to your post, or I will have you arrested as a potential deserter!"

"Yes, Sir, I will go back, but can I take some men with me?"

"No, Sergeant, not until I have assessed the situation. Now, go!"

With this, Captain Schultz turned on his heels and headed in the opposite direction. Enrico felt it might have been a good idea to have shot the stupid cretin there and then, but nevertheless, turned around and made his way back towards Matti and the frontline.

Five minutes later, as he told Matti what had gone on, they realised they were in a serious situation, since there were only nine of them holding the front, and they would immediately be overrun, if there was a counterattack from the Germans. Fortunately, they were in a slightly higher section of the trench, which gave them a commanding panorama of all the sectors, once standing on the fire step. Enrico realised it was now foolish to go any further, and positioned two men with a box of Mills bombs to hold their place in the line, in case of any incursions along the trench by the enemy from the wood side. The rest of them, he spread out along just fifty yards of trenches, knowing that if there was any rush at all, they were all finished anyway. As he looked towards High Wood, the British shelling could be seen to be doing its job: of the many acres of trees that had furnished the wood, about two thirds had been hewed by the incessant shelling, but this was a mixed blessing: though it killed snipers who had taken refuge in the tree tops, it also gave the defenders valuable areas of sanctuary beneath the tangle of trunks, branches and upturned root systems - easy places to defend, hard places to attack.

'How many Germans are there in there?' wondered Enrico. 'And how the hell are we going to winkle them out?'

One hour and fifteen minutes had gone by, when Enrico became aware of flames coming up the jagged trench system from the wood. This meant that the Germans were using a flame thrower to move back along the trench. Enrico called to Matti, who came and saw the problem advancing towards them.

"Matti, when that flame reaches just this corner of the trench," he said, pointing to the section not more than thirty yards away, "I want you and the other two to throw some Mills bombs in there to get them. But we'll have to be accurate, as once they start popping, the Hun will know roughly where we are."

"No problem, Enrico; if we lob six or seven grenades that should do it." Just as he finished talking, a German shrapnel shell burst a little further to their right, seriously wounding two of their mates. Enrico knew that the German artillery must be lining up to make their own creeping barrage, but first things first: they had to deal with the flame thrower. Enrico crouched low, his chin in the dirt, watching the ball of red and black creep ever closer, whilst Matti came back with the two Mills bombs throwers with their box of tricks.

"Any second now! Wait for it... Just let them get a little closer... Right, go for it!"

The three of them started to throw their bombs, at first too far, but that was better than being too short, as now the flame thrower soldiers knew they too were in for trouble. But as Enrico was in a better position to see, he grabbed a handful of bombs, began pulling the pins, and lobbed them in the general direction. Much to his horror, a stick grenade came spinning through the air, and landed by his side. Without even having time to think, he picked it up, and threw it away from their position. It exploded harmlessly. Again they kept throwing their bombs, and they knew they had scored a hit when there was an almighty *Woooshhh!* A huge ball of flame and choking black smoke soared a good fifty feet into the air. Instead of the six grenades, it had taken almost the entire box, and what Enrico and Matti were never to know, was that none of their grenades had done the job. For, as the flame thrower operator had been inching forward, followed closely by several storm-troopers who wielded the stick grenades, one of those troopers had stumbled just as he was about to throw one, had lost control of the grenade, and it had exploded, killing them all. At the same time, it detonated the flame thrower's fuel oil and nitrogen.

"Phew! That was a close one!" said Enrico to his friend, visibly trembling.

"There's no question about it, Enrico, we *are* immortals! We might get wounded, but nothing is going to kill us two."

"I have the self same feeling; it's true: no matter what we do, when we should be dead, we get away with it!"

"Where the hell are these reinforcements?" asked Matti, his voice taking on a more despairing tone.

"I really don't know, but I do think we have been forgotten by the stupid captain who said he was going to come and assess the situation. Maybe we should retreat a little bit ourselves, because for sure we won't have been forgotten by the Germans."

Shells were starting to burst over the captured trench, now making a withdrawal dangerous as well.

"Oh, shit! We got ourselves penned in, here!"

Where Enrico and Matti were standing, they could clearly see that the German guns had found the range, and were enjoying a small renaissance.

"Matti, check how much ammunition and supplies there are around, because I think we are stuck here for a long time!"

Matti did as he was bid, and returned a couple of minutes later, with the less than satisfactory news that there was only seven Mills bombs, and about fifty rounds of 303 left, hardly enough for repelling the inevitable onslaught. Half an hour passed, and the shelling, though intensive, had not come their way, which indicated to the lads that the German artillery did not want to shell their own troops. It was obvious that this section of the trench was going to be retaken.

"Enrico, what are we to do?" pleaded Matti.

"Well, there isn't a great deal we can do! We can put up a fight with what we have; the trouble is, with that idea, the Hun won't wait for us to run out, and then ask us if we'd like to quit, they'll come in, all guns blazing, which will mean our end. We can wait here, and live in hope that nobody comes, but the reality is, they will! Or we can chance a retreat through the barrage, with the hope of rejoining the main body of troops."

He had no sooner said that, that a stick grenade bounced about ten feet to their right, and exploded, doing yet more damage to the two wounded Tommies lying on the decking.

"Well, that makes up our minds for us!" said Enrico. "We have to press forward, I think, and do what damage we can, and gain any of the enemy guns and ammunition which we can put to our own use." But for once, Enrico felt no real confidence in this plan. He decided there and then, there should be a democratic vote, something entirely alien to normal army life! He called the other five to crowd around.

"This is not an order, but I really don't feel we can stay here; if there is anybody who is prepared to volunteer, and get reinforcements to come along the trench system, that would be good, but I'm not going to order anybody to do that. Corporal Dumbridge and myself are going to press forward, as retreating or staying here seem to have the same intensity of danger, but I am freeing each man to do his own bidding. We might be lucky, and come across some German guns and ammunition. Although it's not a good plan, it's the only plan I have! Who's coming with me?"

As if in a single voice, the five remaining soldiers agreed to follow their Sergeant Caruso.

"Good! Maybe we can do a little damage. Matti, check the two wounded, make sure they've got some water, and are as comfortable as possible."

Matti got within three yards of the two prone riflemen, then turned and came back.

"Enrico, there's no need to look too closely, they're both dead."

"Right, men, there's seven of us, and a few thousand of them, which puts the odds in our favour! Let's go and do some damage!"

Matti and Enrico headed the thin line of troops, as they snaked their way forward, around each bend in the trench system. As they rounded the second bend, they came across the completely charred remains of the smoking flame thrower operator, and behind him, the remnants of three storm-troopers.

"See if there's any guns or grenades that we can use. Check them carefully, and I will go up to the next corner. Give me a Mills, Matti."

Enrico walked to the next corner cautiously, grenade in his right hand, ready to be thrown, if necessary, but no-one was there. A minute later, his friends came up behind him.

"Just two stick grenades," said Matti.

"Right," declared Enrico, "to the next corner then."

As they turned, there, across the top of the trench, lay a huge beech tree, which had been brought down in the bombardment. Enrico and Matti used the cover of this tree to check if there was anything of a threat above them. They could see that there was a machine gun nest manned by three soldiers; fortunately for them the gun was facing in the opposite direction, not more than fifteen feet away; the three soldiers manning it were all so intent on looking the way they thought an attack would come, they were oblivious to anything that might appear from behind.

Enrico withdrew his service revolver, and indicated to Matti that he should use his bayonet, and they crept forward. They had got to within six feet of the pit that held the three men, when the breaking of a twig by Enrico startled one of the Germans into looking around. He was looking directly into the face of Matti, and had frozen solid, but so too had Matti. The stalemate was broken when Enrico pulled the trigger, and the bullet went through the side of the German soldier's throat. With this, the other two Germans turned and raised their hands in a gesture of submission, but Enrico could not think about taking prisoners. One was shot directly in the face, virtually taking his head off his shoulders, and the other one screamed in horror, as the realisation hit him that his death was imminent. The next shot went through his chest, but he did not die, and thrashed about on the floor, and this brought Matti back to reality: he threw himself on top of the writhing Boche and despatched him quickly with a bayonet swipe through his heart. Both Matti and Enrico were shaking with nerves and adrenalin; they knew they had got their first prize: they had captured their first Maxim machine gun!

Enrico was about to turn and fetch the others, when he heard a crack, a scream and then a lot more firing. He knew without seeing, that the rest of his men were being fired upon from within the trench itself. Inching back to the parapet, to see what was occurring, he could hear the muffled voices of German troops, as they came running along the trench. Taking a Mills bomb, he waited until the majority of the troops were directly below him and then dropped it in their midst. The explosion was tremendous, and at least one German was thrown almost completely out of the trench. He had killed three, and seriously wounded another three, but there were at least a dozen more coming up behind. Fortunately for Enrico, the Germans thought that the bomb had been thrown by the escaping Tommies. Several stick grenades were tossed through the air, and again he heard another scream, which meant that the German aim was really quite good. Enrico peered once again cautiously over the parapet to see the Germans surging forward anew, and this time, he dropped his last two remaining grenades in the middle of them all. The explosions were so loud that they almost burst his own eardrums, and the detonation gave the opposite trench wall a serious shudder, letting loose a small landslide of earth.

Enrico could not see how many he had killed or wounded, but

believing that caution was the better part of valour, he turned tail, and got back into the machine gun dugout, next to his friend Matti. The duo quickly put the three German bodies over the side, and turned the machine gun around to face the German trench. They could both hear a lot of shouting and they primed their newly liberated weapon, ready for use. There were now obviously several dozen Germans just a few feet away, and they knew that it was just a matter of time before the enemy remembered the machine gun nest. Enrico frantically searched the small dugout that housed the machine gun, in the hope of finding yet more grenades; unfortunately there were none. It was up to them and their Maxim…

After a few minutes, which seemed to stretch like hours, the noise abated, as the Germans had obviously cleared their wounded and dead away. A voice shouted something entirely incoherent, but patently German and plainly a query aimed in their direction. Two or three seconds later, a steel helmeted storm-trooper's head, with thick rimmed glasses and a button moustache, popped over the edge of the parapet, only to pop out of sight again. The lads kept their nerve, and the head popped up again, followed by a second and a third. The enemy obviously knew that the nest had been taken, but they were unable to see any British still there, so the three of them had been ordered to retake the position. They heaved themselves onto the top of the parapet with the help of the fallen beech tree. They were creeping forward when Enrico decided to open up. *Rat-tat-tat-tat*, barked the Maxim, and the three storm troopers slumped forward, and though still twitching, they were quite dead. Matti leapt from the shell hole, went to the bodies, and frisked all of them. He found six grenades, a Luger pistol, with around twenty rounds of ammunition, plus three sharp bayonets: they were adding to their arsenal. Armed with the grenades, they both crept to the parapet, and did not have to wait long, before the sound of running feet could be heard again.

A dozen or more storm-troopers surged around the corner, giving a very good aim of fire for the two. The Germans saw them, and were so bunched up they were unable to do anything. When Enrico started to fire his revolver into the group, the confusion that it caused created mayhem. Matti started to toss the stick grenades, and used four before Enrico stopped him throwing a fifth.

"Matti, stop! Take it easy! I'm quite sure they're all dead! And if they're not, it's going to be real hard for the medics to find the right bits to fit here or there!"

"Enrico, may I suggest we take our prize, and retreat a little further into the wood? They know we're here, now, and for sure there's going to be no quarter given! It's shit or bust time now!"

"Matti, not only are you a great philosopher, but you are a fucking poet to boot! Let's grab all the water and food that we can, and we'll creep a little further into the wood."

They discovered upon the dead Germans three canteens of water, a half bottle of schnapps, two loaves of black bread, and a highly 'scented' garlic German sausage, which had obviously been nibbled at one end by the rats. Thrusting these trophies in an empty German satchel which was lying around, they picked up all the ammunition they could carry, and taking the machine gun, edged their way into the dark tangle of broken trees.

The shelling from both the British and the Germans stepped up at least three gears, and all of the bombing was in the wooded areas. Enrico and Matti were lucky to crawl into the remains of an upturned oak tree, getting their gun and equipment plus themselves hidden underground with the help of the old tree that now lay shattered by the bombardment from both sides. What had those wonderful trees done to deserve this ignominious end? It was just yet more great loss of life, albeit not human.

When Enrico left Captain Schultz and returned to the wood end of the trench, he was promptly forgotten by the Captain; even though he had said he would come to that sector and assess the situation, he never did.

Instead, he had taken his troops and without considering the plan of action, they had attacked the enemy to the left of the trenches. This had a disastrous effect on the men, as they bottlenecked within the trench, and soon became the whipping boys for the Hun. Men were falling all over one another in their efforts to reach the enemy, but the enemy had fought and ran, thus giving them the old adage of "he who fights and runs away, lives to fight another day".

The German soldiers simply fired a volley, then backed into a further section of the trench, awaited the storm of British and did the same again. This drew the attackers into the mistaken belief that they were putting the Germans to flight. The truth was that they just got deeper into German held territory, where the defenders could seriously reattack and create havoc. And there, at the head of these attacking British was Captain Schultz. Another volley of fire brought down half a dozen British soldiers, also creating confusion as the soldiers behind, in their eagerness to reach the Hun, fell over their fallen comrades. Then the unthinkable happened! The artillery of the Germans knew exactly where to fire their rounds of shells, thus causing even more trouble. The first to catch a shrapnel shell and be dispatched was the annoying Captain Schultz. Several red hot balls of lead passed through his shoulders and face, killing him within a couple of minutes. This brought the advance to a rapid conclusion, and the enemy were ready to deal with this falter in the charge. The turn was immediate and deadly, as the shells fell onto the British: those still advancing fell into the troops trying to flee the shelling. Then the enemy troops made their attack dominant, causing as much death and destruction as possible before the British could reform once again. Within the space of ten minutes several hundred British troops lay dead or dying. While the German artillery had found the British, their British counterparts were once again searching for the German guns, to try and put them out of action all together.

The one area that the British had become masters of was the air.

The planes were used to good effect, spotting for the British artillery. It was less than an hour before they signalled exactly where the enemy big guns could be found, and then the duel was started up again between the heavy calibre weapons. Fortunately, the British won that duel, and after just a few dozen rounds of shells, the Germans pulled the movable guns away, to relocate.

That space was enough for the troops in the Switch Line trench to reform, and prepare for whatever was to follow. The shelling did not stop there; once the artillery had reformed, they got their sights set again, and this time concentrated on the trench that was occupied by the Rifle Brigades. The respite had been almost enough for the now defending troops to dig in deeper and prepare themselves for the onslaught to come. But the damage had been done: instead of the rout that was expected, and the capture of High Wood, the British soldiers were now very much on the defensive, having lost several hundred men to the accuracy of the German ordnance. In the middle section of the trench, 'Spider' Kelly had carefully placed his troops in defensive positions, awaiting the inevitable attack from storm-troopers. More troops were coming along the sunken road, and were trying to make their way to reinforce the Switch Line trench. The reserves were bringing more ammunition, food and water, and it was sustenance that was soon to become most desperately sought after.

Stretcher bearers were extremely busy, trying to rescue the wounded, and evacuate them, way back to aid stations. There were numerous wounded, and the Germans were firing indiscriminately, so it was not long before even the stretcher bearers became targets. It was late afternoon, the sun was only just above the western horizon, and Kelly had managed to strengthen the line. The day had been so hectic, that he had not had time to think about his old friends; they must take their chances, along with all fighting men, but he had given thought to what was happening within High Wood, which was the reason why the attack had been put into practice in the first place: to take High Wood from the Switch Line trench, occupy the northern section of the wood, neutralise the eastern and western machine gun redoubts, and meet with the 7th Division, having successfully taken the whole wood. Good plan, easy on paper, not so easy in practice!

RSM Kelly became aware that the shelling from the German artillery had eased considerably, and this seemed to him like the prelude to the attack. They were not going to come along the existing Switch Line trench, that would not make any sense at all; there would be a charge from a secondary trench lying further back to the north. Machine guns were positioned and primed ready for use, riflemen standing on the fire step in preparation for that charge that hopefully would not come, but deep down was acknowledged by everybody. 'This has all been too easy, they have allowed us to take this trench, and now I'm beginning to feel like a fish caught in a net, and the net is about to be pulled on board,' thought Kelly, as he ran up and down the trench, steadying men's nerves, giving words of encouragement, and generally making sure that all the soldiers were ready.

"Pass the word: fix bayonets, and prepare Mills bombs. If they get into the trench, drop your rifle, and use clubs and knives, and hopefully we won't have accidents amongst ourselves."

All of a sudden, silence fell on the trenches. Kelly looked up: the sun was now casting long shadows, making the entire landscape into an eerie, spectral, dreamlike picture. As he looked into the sky, he noticed the skylarks whirling in the thermals, catching the myriads of insects that were caught in warm updraughts.

For a moment, he forgot the war, and he was back home, out walking in his beloved Laindon Hills. He could visualise the river Thames, lazily meandering its way around Canvey Island and out into the estuary, ebbing into the sea…

*Bang, rat-tat-tat-tat, boom!* Back to reality! There, in the distance, were the charging storm-troopers who had been waiting in reserve, just for this moment. Several riflemen fired indiscriminately, hoping for some success, but the distance was unrealistic.

"Hold your fire! Wait until they're a hundred yards, then let hell break loose. If they make it to the wire, use the Mills, if they break into the trenches, do as I've said before."

There must have been a good few thousand German shock troops, running wildly towards the trench. Fortunately for the British, the Switch Line trench was on the brow of the hill, so for once, the British had the high ground, and Fritz had to run uphill. The artillery had been alerted, and now opened up onto the onrushing hordes. At first the shells were falling short, but up there, just above the skylarks, was the trusty Sopwith Strutter, guiding the artillery to where the shells should go. But this horde of Boche was not going to be stopped by shelling alone, and in no time, they could be plainly heard, shouting and screaming, as they got within just two hundred yards of the wire.

"Fire! Let the bastards have it!"

All along he line, the rattle and crack of machine guns and rifle fire could be heard. The Germans fell everywhere, and soon the dead and dying lay like a wall of human flesh, but this still did not stop them. German snipers, now finding good positions, started to systematically take out the British, and as it was just the British heads and arms that were sticking out, it was an unpleasant sight to see your comrade firing next to you one minute, then in a split second, his head bursting like a ripe melon. The German troops were now running from shell hole to shell hole, but all the time surging forward. The British machine guns were scything death, just as the grim reaper had taught them, but nothing could stop them coming on, as there were many more attackers than defenders. The Boche made it to the wire, and began to lob stick grenades at the same time the Tommies were throwing their Mills bombs, and everywhere the screaming of the dying was very quickly drowned by the inferno of the battle.

Some soldiers had crawled through parts of the wire, and been killed by the British, others had tried to leap over it, but had been caught by the deadly enfilade of lead that had been let loose. But the dead had their uses, because as a German fell across the wire, either dead or wounded, he created a bridge for his comrades to pass over. Just five minutes more, and the first wave were at the parapets, trying to jump in, guns and bayonets flashing in the fading light. Again the continuous volleying of the British Tommies was creating havoc in the Kaiser's men, but some of the first wave had managed to get into the trench, and now hand to hand fighting was taking place all along the line. The machine guns were doing a fine job: as the second wave of Germans approached, they were being cut down faster than they could be replaced, so the second wave was initially stopped and the Boche either went to ground, or did an about-face and retraced their steps. The British were faring well in the trenches, and as Kelly had advised, they had dropped their cumbersome rifles, and taken to using their maces and daggers. Though many British had been put out of action, they had caused all the attacking Hun who had made it into the trench, to be despatched.

Now a new threat was developing: a section of the Germans were coming up the trench from the left, while many of their comrades were rushing on the parapet itself, firing into the dense mass of Tommies, killing and wounding many. It took a long while before the threat was understood, and several officers tried to organise a batch of men into making a counterattack to stop the assault; using many Mills bombs and carefully positioned machine guns they started very gradually to repel the charge of the enemy. Night had now fallen, and the main attack had faltered; all the Germans within the trench were dead and just the occasional crack of a sniper's rifle could be heard; even the shelling had now ceased.

Battle does a funny thing to soldiers: as the adrenalin rushes through their bodies, they become terribly thirsty and hungry, and men would give their right arm for a bar of chocolate, or something sweet. So it soon became obvious to Kelly that in a very short time, they would have run out of food and water, and though there was a steady stream of men coming up the sunken road with yet more supplies, the German artillery knew every nook and cranny. As soon as they suspected that men were there, shells would be sent over. 'If they were going to be stuck in this trench for too long, resupplying them was going to be a major problem' thought Kelly. The German dead were taken from the trench and thrown over the parapet. One could hear the groaning and the whimpering of the wounded and dying German soldiers, and it rattled the very soul of those who were within earshot. There was going to be no sleep that night.

Enrico and Matti knew that they must cover themselves with as much debris as possible to stop being seen by any German patrols; more imminent was the fear of being blown to kingdom come by the incessant indiscriminate shelling which was falling all over the wood, and coming from both sides.

"Keep your head down, Matti, and try not to make any noise. Keep an eye out for any passing Germans; we might be lucky and not be seen, but if we are, we must finish them before they do for us."

Matti was shaking almost uncontrollably, not so much from the fear of being killed, as they both believed that was now quite impossible, they were destined to survive this little trouble between the Kaiser and the King!, but because he knew that he could be wounded, and wounds tend to hurt, and he really didn't fancy any more pain. The same went for Enrico: pain is very overrated in the pleasure department, and he wanted more pleasure from life before he wanted the pain of it.

"The noise of the shells is awfully loud; I can hardly hear myself think," said Matti, almost having to shout the words into Enrico's ear. So much for keeping quiet! With the noise of the shells exploding, who was going to hear anything else?

"Give me some of the water, please," asked Matti. He was passed the flask, shook it and said, "I think we will have to ration what supplies we have, or we'll soon be in trouble, unless we break out of here."

"Matti, think about what you're saying! How the hell can we break out of here? We're surrounded by the enemy, shells are falling all around us, and we have enough ammo to last about one or two attacks, at the most. Please be sensible!"

Then he added, as if it was perfectly obvious to one and all. "We have to make a stand here, at least until we either run out of ammunition, or there is a break in the shelling which gives us a chance to slip away. All we have to do is stay put. If any German patrols come around and find us, we fight, other than that, we keep our heads down. But let's get that Maxim fixed up and ready to fire, just in case."

As if to emphasise their problem, a thirteen pounder shell landed smack on their tree trunk, not more than ten feet away from the root system they had dug themselves into. It shook them to their marrow, and they dug in even deeper, making sure that there was a great deal of wooden cover around them both. Unless there was a direct hit, they should be safe where they were. The shelling went on and on, hardly letting up for a moment. They became extremely hot under the tree roots, which made the active lice itch more than usual, the scratching making both of them thirsty then hungry. Time passed slowly, but it did pass. At four thirty in the morning, the shelling slowed to just an occasional burst. Without realising it, both the lads had fallen into a deep sleep.

Thirst woke Matti up first, and then his movements awoke Enrico. They decided to eat some of the black bread and sausage. The sausage was more than eighty percent fat and gristle, with a very chewy consistency; it was the garlic that gave it the little taste that it had. The bread was made from rye, but had a percentage of sawdust mixed within.

"If this is the best they get, we picked the right army to be in," remarked Enrico, swallowing the food with great difficulty.

"The blockade of the German ports must be working well; this is really just garbage compared to what we get."

"Ticklers apple jam and bully beef!" Both said this more or less at the same time, which made them laugh just a little.

"Quiet!" whispered Matti, "they might be round about. They could have heard us laughing!"

"D'you realise that the shelling has stopped?" asked Enrico, holding his arm as if to ratify that statement.

"Christ, no! We were both asleep. We get used to everything, even when it's not there!"

"Quiet! I hear something."

Sure enough, in the silence, a definite creeping sound could be heard: the occasional crack as a small branch was broken, the swish of leaves and wood being trodden on.

"There is a patrol just across the way. Is the machine gun primed and ready to fire?" murmured Enrico.

"You know it is!" whispered back Matti. "What are we to do?"

"Wait and see how close they come to us, how many they are and if they see or hear us; that will be the decider as to whether whoever is out there lives or dies!"

"And whether we do, too!" said Matti, with a worried frown on his face and a slight crack in his voice. Just across the tree trunks, not more than twelve feet away from their hole, they could just make out the legs of several leather-booted Hun troops. All of a sudden a hissing sound came, which sounded like rain, then water was splashing on the branches that covered their hideaway. 'Jesus, the bugger is peeing on us!' thought Matti. The urine was just starting to penetrate through the foliage and onto the lads, and this made them both very aggrieved. 'Being peed upon is bad enough, but *German* pee! What did I do to deserve this insult in my young life?' thought Matti with a reluctant smile, as he realised the irony of the situation. 'So close to us, but unable to see us, or even know that we're around at all, that is a serious bit of good luck for us. They must have found their dead colleagues, and they must have noticed that the Maxim has gone; so why so casual?' thought Enrico, hardly daring to breathe in case it was heard.

The peeing stopped, some half whispered words were spoken, then movement again. This time the feet moved onto the fallen trunk above their heads. There were at least two of them, but were there more? Enrico looked at Matti, and then very carefully removed his knife from its scabbard; Matti followed suit. 'No point in thinking we can deal with them with the gun, far too cumbersome to use down here, it will have to be knives.' This went through Enrico's head, and without saying a word, Matti had understood. Movements seemed a little further off, and then another twig broke close to home again. The two lads froze once more. They were both very scared, and thought that they were in trouble yet again. 'How many of them? They seem to be all around us!' Matti was frantically trying to count the number of footsteps he could hear.

*Bang!* A shell went off, not more than fifty feet away; there was a scream, which meant one of the enemies had been caught by the explosion. There was frantic scurrying across broken trees and branches; not much pretence of not being around now, as the German soldiers were trying to retrace their steps before more of them were blown up by the incoming shells.

All of a sudden a foot crashed through the roof of their lair, and unhappily the offending foot landed on the machine gun. Its owner knew immediately that something was not right there, as he moved his foot back and forth across the gun. A hand appeared and started to feel around. The pals knew what to do. Grabbing the hand quickly, they pulled him down and into their little hole. The surprised German didn't have time to say a word. A startled look of bewilderment and fear was showing on his face, but nothing was said; he couldn't talk even if he had tried: Enrico had cleanly cut right through the trooper's vocal cords, in fact he had nearly cut right through his neck. The poor Hun didn't shudder or fight, but simply fell limply to the floor of the two lads' hole, spurting hot blood all over them. There was a small gurgle, coming from the void that had once been his larynx; his eyes still had that startled expression, and somehow the life still shone in those eyes, even though it had left the body. This worried Enrico terribly, as he felt sure that the luckless soldier was looking directly at him. The duo pulled him in completely and repaired the big gaping hole that he had made. Shells were still falling around, so that the noise they made in the restoration of their hideaway was drowned by the inferno around them.

"If he's missed," said Enrico, "they will think that he bought it through a shell, at least I hope so."

The German's blood was still oozing all over the floor, and now with the three of them, and the machine gun, it was getting a little crowded. Matti sniffed, and then sniffed again. "Have you dropped one, Enrico?"

"Not me, mate, but now you mention it, I can smell something too." Enrico bent over the lifeless corpse of the dead enemy, and realised that the poor man had defecated in his death throes. "Oh Christ! We'll have to drag him outside, and dump him somewhere. I can't live with this stink!"

"Let's check the body first, for food or water, and anything we can use." He had a canteen with less than a cupful of water remaining in it, but no food, except for some American chewing gum.

"Where the hell did he get this from?" enquired Matti.

"Ain't got a clue!"

They decided that they would, once again, break out of their den, and drag the body out into the open, but far enough away, so that when it was discovered, it would be assumed that a shell fragment had torn his head off. It was a dangerous enterprise to undertake, as the British shells could not discriminate between friend or foe. But there was no time like the present! Matti got up, grabbed the legs, and started to pull. A shell burst twenty five feet away to his right, and fragments of red hot metal showered around him, but none luckily caused him any harm. They got the German to no more than ten feet from the entrance, and they decided to throw him up onto another fallen tree. This they managed, and rushed back to their secret refuge.

For the first time, the lads were aware autumn was coming; there was a slight mist in the air, and with the cordite from the explosions, it only added to the heavy atmosphere permeating High Wood. Enrico could also hear in the distance the clatter of machine guns, and wondered to himself how the rest of the Battalion were faring. Matti was thinking about steak and kidney pudding, with mashed potatoes, to be followed by steamed suet pudding drowned in oodles of custard. As they sat in the back of their lair, Enrico frowned with worry, and Matti drooled with hunger.

The day went on, with shells bursting everywhere; another big one had hit their tree, making the back wall subside a little, and the whole tree came down another six inches, creating an even better place of safety for them. Once more the shelling eased, and the lads were aware of a new threat to their being: there was a smell of chlorine in the air. Enrico nudged Matti who was nearly asleep, and he warned: "Put your gas mask on, our boys are sending over chlorine!"

They both fumbled into their pouches and got their masks out, and Enrico helped Matti put his on first. "Don't forget, if it starts coming through the filter, just remove it and pee on it." Enrico donned his mask to the sound of incoming shells, and instead of explosions, the sound was more of a plop. Enrico had been right: the British were shelling this sector of High Wood with chlorine gas. All the lads could do, was to sit there, huddled, and wait for the gas to clear.

Many hours went by, and the distinct sound of gun fire could be heard all around. Maybe an attack was in progress; Enrico checked the Maxim yet again, and made a little spy hole to see if there was any movement outside.

It was now late afternoon and the sun was beginning to set. The gas had finally disappeared, and neither of the lads was any worse for wear from that experience. Enrico noticed that a shell must have landed close by where the dead German had been, as he hung down over the tree, with what was left of his head dangling, and the first thing that Enrico noticed was the Hun's eyes staring directly at him. He drew his breath sharply, and then fell back into their hole, white as a sheet.

"What's up?" whispered Matti, "you look as if you've seen a ghost!"

"I think I have! That bloody German is just hanging around! Stick your head out and have a look!"

Matti jumped back, too.

"Bloody hell! The bugger is staring right at us!"

They drank the last of the water to calm their nerves, and ate the remaining food, but this did not quench their thirst, nor sate their hunger. They both knew that unless they got provisions, and soon, they were in for a miserable time.

The shelling had once again died down, and the machine gun fire was also intermittent. Enrico thought it could be a good time to venture out to answer a call of nature. It was now dark, and he could not see the German, but went to the left, away from him, anyway. Mist was swirling, and even though there were not many trees still standing, the rustle of leaves made a very eerie sound in the darkness and the mist. The call of nature took but a second, and he scurried back to his hole; Matti had also decided to answer the same call. Enrico suggested he might like to turn right instead of left, and in the darkness, Matti dropped his trousers, squatted and relieved himself. He turned to find some leaves to wipe himself with, only to be confronted with the bloody remains of the upturned face of the dangling German, not more than six inches away from his own. He let out a scream, that surely could be heard back in Ypres, and tried to stand up and run, but as his trousers were still down to his ankles, he stumbled and fell badly, cracking his head on a broken branch. This too, made him emit a small cry of fear. Enrico, on hearing the first scream, emerged from the dugout, just in time to see Matti's head crack on the branch, and without any thought for his own fears, helped drag the bleeding, whimpering form of his friend back into the lair. The mist was everywhere, swirling. The sound of the sighing wind brought the reality of a million dead souls passing through High Wood, as if on an eternal journey. Matti was in a terrible state, and Enrico helped him put his trousers back on.

"He was watching me, Enrico! I tell you, he was watching me!"

"Calm down, Matti! Put a hanky on the gash on your head. He can't see us, he's dead, but it is a ghostly night, and I think you and me are going nowhere."

It was a long night, and the mist started to lift as the dawn broke in the east, and the spirits of the dead left in search of new places to haunt. With the dawn, came yet more shelling, and more machine gun fire, some now quite close, but for Enrico and Matti, the night had, indeed, been one of great horror, as in their mind spirits and ghouls had fluttered and flown everywhere. They had not slept, and were now thirsty, hungry and exhausted. Gradually the shelling moved away from the sector they were trapped in, and they did not have to wait too long before the familiar cracking and snapping sounds of twigs could be heard: the enemy were coming back. On hearing the sound, Enrico nudged Matti until he was sure he was fully *compos mentis*. They only had to wait two minutes before numerous German troops came into view. They were creeping as quietly as they could, for fear that the British might be coming from the other side of the wood, and they were coming out with snipers to ambush any attackers. Enrico could see three private soldiers and a Sergeant, examining the body of the hanging German, and they were obviously in deep conversation as to how he had died. Then one of the privates pointed to the ground, to the pile of excrement which was so obviously human; again there was murmuring, but Enrico knew that their luck was probably running out, when the four of them started to look very cautiously about. Enrico nudged the muzzle of the machine gun in their direction, and there must have been some sort of metallic sound from this action which gave their position away.

*"Achtung! Achtung!"* screamed out the Sergeant, but that was the last word he would ever utter, or his comrades would ever hear. The noise of the splattering Maxim seemed deafeningly loud, but it had done its duty by the two lads, as all four Germans lay dead or dying on the ground. Enrico grabbed the muzzle again and pulled to the other direction, and was in time to catch another couple of Germans who had been standing almost by the side of where the two lads hid. They were brought down when a hail of machine gun bullets tore through their legs, and in the same burst ripped through vital organs, killing them instantly. There was confusion everywhere, not least of all, under the roots of that fallen tree.

"Well, Enrico, they know we're here now! It's shit or bust again!"

At that, two stick grenades landed just at the entrance to their hole, and the ensuing explosions wounded both Enrico and Matti, as they were peppered with grenade fragments in their legs. Their wounds were not life threatening, but the pain that they had so dreaded had come a'visiting. Both the lads lay there, groaning, more from shock and blood loss than anything else; when Enrico became aware of tremendous machine gun clattering, rifle fire and grenades exploding, he elbowed his friend, and said: "Sounds like the cavalry attacking the Indians to me! Surely that rifle fire sounds like our Lee-Enfield 303s!"

The Germans did not know what had hit them; the British attack had not come from the south side of the wood, but from the Switch Line trench in the east, which meant that the combined Rifle Brigades had made an important inroad into the north side of the wood, taking the eastern machine gun redoubts and the very trench systems that now surrounded Enrico and Matti. Germans were running wildly everywhere, but were being cut down by the onrushing Tommies. One German officer even tried to crawl into the den that held Matti and Enrico, but on seeing them, plus the Maxim machine gun, he gave out a tremendous yell of surprise, and backed off, only to be bayoneted by a charging Tommy. Within a few

347

minutes it was all over, though distant machine gun and rifle fire could still be heard.  Matti, in great discomfort and distress, looked on his friend, and thought that the latter was dead as there was no movement from him, and he lay in an awkward position as the dead often do.  He looked towards the daylight, and there he could see the outline of what was obviously a soldier in khaki, wearing putties.

"Help!"  He made a feeble attempt; no movement from the soldier…

"Help me, please!" a little louder this time, using all his strength.

"Who's down there?"

"Corporal Dumbridge and Sergeant Caruso, who if you don't get help quickly, will be 'late of the London Rifle Brigade!'" Blackness then descended.

Consciousness came back to Matti, as he realised he was being jolted along within a rigid-tyre ambulance.  He looked around to see that the ambulance was full of wounded, but to his great joy, on the next stretcher, was his soulmate, Enrico Caruso Lokowski.  Though Enrico was still unconscious, Matti knew he was alive, as the army never wasted resources on the dead.  A smile of ecstatic pleasure beamed from Matti's face; then he felt the pain in his legs, and promptly became unconscious again.

# X

Matti was the first to emerge from his deep unconsciousness; woolly-brained and woozy, he could not work out where he was, or even what he was doing here, but the pain in his legs soon reminded him that he was recovering from severe deep wounds inflicted by a couple of German stick grenades. A low growling moan came from his throat and it brought a female nurse to his side.

"How are you feeling? Can you hear me?" said a voice. Through the pain Matti fell in love: 'what a beautiful woman, she looks just like an angel, and she is talking to me!' were the first coherent or at least nearly coherent thoughts that went through Matti's mind since…when?

"How long have I been here?" then quickly as his mind started to clear; "I'm alright, I guess, though both my legs hurt like hell! Is Sergeant Caruso around here anywhere?"

"He is in the next bed, but still in a deep exhausted sleep. But he will live, as will you. As to your question, you have been here for nearly a week now, most of the time in a state of stupor, and often rambling away, sometimes about a policeman and mining! But nothing that one could really understand. I have been next to you on and off all the time."

"Nurse, please, where am I?"

"You are in Calais, and now that you are recovering, I expect the doctors will send you back to England for rehabilitation. I do not expect you to be rejoining your Battalion for some time yet, if ever again; now what about something to eat and drink?"

The magic words! Food and drink… Now Matti started to realise that hunger was in there somewhere, and was going to make its presence felt; that's what stomachs are for, aren't they?

"My goodness am I thirsty! Food, yes, please, but only by the bucketful if you don't mind."

The nurse smiled and gave a delicious little laugh at his whimsical remark; this brightened up the colourless face, which lay there in the bed looking at her, with nothing but love and longing.

"Before you organise that, nurse, please tell me your name."

Another little laugh came, then a broader smile, which now turned the ashen face of Matti into a bright red beaming sunset.

"Now, Corporal, you know I am not supposed to fraternise with the patients, shame on you. But off the record it is Nurse Dawn Williams, and before you tell me, I know your name is Matthew Dumbridge. I know a great deal about you! So what about that food and drink?" Then she was gliding off, before Matti could react. 'Oh, what a wonderful woman! Please, God, let me get to know her before I'm taken from this life!'

On this thought Matti turned to look towards Enrico. His friend lay in the bed next to him; he looked very pale and there was a tent to stop the sheets and blankets from touching his legs. He didn't look at all well; this went through Matti's brain, as his head started to spin, and he thought he was going to be sick. He lay looking at the peeling plaster on the ceiling, and glimpses of the last weeks started to leak back into his memory. 'What had happened out there in High Wood?' then he thought of that German corpse hanging upside down, with those eyes looking directly into his, then blackness.

He awoke when Nurse Williams sat by the side of his bed, trying to get him to sip some hot drink. 'Tea, that's what it is.' He coughed, and spluttered some of the hot liquid all over the bed.

"Never mind about that. Is the tea nice to drink? Would you like it sweeter? More milk maybe? You just ask for whatever you want." Another huge grin came from Dawn's lips, showing a wonderful set of white teeth, which to Matti sparkled in the dim hospital light. The moment was quickly broken, when Matti's stomach gave up the ghost and a huge rumble burst from below. His face now went crimson. "Sorry about that, I guess I'm a little bit hungry after all!"

Food was quickly administered, and the pangs of hunger abated. One problem is alleviated; another one takes its place: the pain in his legs began to worsen, and Nurse Williams could see from the expression of discomfort on Matti's face that he was having difficulties.

"Is it your legs? Do they hurt badly? I can get you some mild painkillers, but nothing too strong. We want you to know that you have been in the wars," she said, with that smile beaming again, "anyway, the pain is the leg mending, no serious infection, you are fine. I'll get you that aspirin."

"Nurse, please keep me informed about my friend Enrico; I guess I rambled on about him too, in my delirium?"

"Yes, you did, and that is why he is in the next bed; the doctor thought that it might be important to both of you."

Three days went by before there were any real signs of life from Enrico, but on that third day, Matti heard several moans coming from his friend, so he then called the nurse. "Nurse Williams! Can you look at Enrico? He has been making some very strange noises just now. Maybe he's coming around?"

Dawn went to Enrico's bed, smiled as was her wont and looked back at Matti, then listened close to Enrico for a change in breathing or pulse. "I think he is now coming round; I shall get the doctor to look at him, but yes, I do think he is coming back to life."

"Wonderful, and so are you, Dawn!"

"Now, Matthew, that's enough of that sort of talk," but her smile said other things to Matti.

The doctor came and scrutinised closely the still sleeping Enrico. He was a kindly old Major, who was much more suited to looking after his sick patients than worrying about army procedure. He never knew when to acknowledge a salute or got extremely uncomfortable when NCOs and Privates jumped to attention around him. Doctor Bartlett he was, Doctor Bartlett he wanted to be called. That is why at sixty-two years of age he was still a Major, and had not climbed that army ladder to anything higher in command. All Bartlett's patients were either son or a first name, with never a reference to rank or such. Subsequently anybody who worked with him, or who was treated by him, had nothing but the highest respect, or even love for him. Bartlett looked over Enrico, checked his pulse, listened to his breathing, and lifted the sheets to see how his legs and feet were doing. Then he gently slapped Enrico around the face several times. It only took three gentle pats before a groan came, then a squeaky voice said, "Yes, who's there?" Enrico was back alright, albeit hardly knowing where he was or who was around him.

"Mr. Caruso, my boy, welcome back; you have been asleep for nearly ten days, time to start getting back to normal. Can you hear me? Can you see me? Have you any pain?"

Enrico only needed a few seconds to collect his thoughts.

"All three questions are yes to. How is my old mate Matti? Is he close by?"

"He is fine, and there he is, in the next bed. What about something to eat and drink? You must be starving!"

"Well, if I wasn't before, I am, now that you mention it. But please no Ticklers or Bully Beef; any chance of something different? I don't mind what, just something different."

"Nurse Williams, you have another patient here that needs your attention, too. Some hot broth and maybe a couple of slices of good thick white bread and butter will help build the inner man again." The doctor winked at Dawn, who smiled, then went off to do his bidding.

"Enrico! How the bloody hell are you?" said Matti with tears of joy in his eyes and a break in his voice.

"Well," croaked Enrico, "I've known better days, but I guess we are still immortal!"

"We *are*, though for a moment back there, I had my doubts."

"Matti, my legs hurt very badly, did you get it the same way?"

"Same damn legs as you and you'll be happy to know that mine hurt like hell too." A small burst of laughter was followed by both the lads wincing, as the pain in the legs was aggravated by the sudden movements that laughter brought.

The next day being a Sunday, Matti was made to get into a wheelchair and attend a church parade. It was the first time that he had been able to rise from the hospital bed and the feeling of air passing by him as he was wheeled down into the little hospital chapel was exhilarating and gave him his first real buzz at being alive again. His heart was filled to overflowing as Nurse Dawn Williams was his escort. The service took place, unheeded, as his mind was on a completely different plane.

"Dawn, is it possible to have a little stroll around the grounds of the hospital before going back to the ward?"

"I don't see why not. It is not cold, the sun is nearly shining, and if you keep that blanket around you, I will be happy to show you the fish pond that is in the middle of the garden; it is quite unusual, with some really huge carp in it, and so tame that they will take feed from your hand," then she added with that normal twinkle in her eyes, "anyway the air will do you good, that I am sure of."

"Dawn, you are a peach, and I love peaches."

"Stop that, you…I will go bright red if you keep that up." And sure enough she did.

To Matti, this was the greatest day in his short life, and he was now hopelessly in love with his Florence Nightingale. She wheeled him through the darkish oppressive corridors, until they reached an opening into the hospital's little oasis. The hospital building was more than five hundred years old, once being a Monastery for the Benedictine Monks. It had been vacated during the French Revolution, and subsequently, it had become a school for the children of the town until 1914, when it was taken over by the BEF, as their first line of hospitals, before evacuation of the wounded back to England.

The courtyard was no more than one hundred feet square, and right in the middle was this quite large, for the space available, fish pond. It had been there in the yard since the building conception, having been put in as a Thursday pond. That, to the uninitiated, is a pond built for housing fish that could be caught on a Thursday to be eaten on the non-meat day of Friday, according to Catholic customs. The garden itself was really colourful with many variations of flowers still blooming in the warm autumn sun.

"Oh this is so beautiful! I have never in my life seen anything like this, Dawn."

"Matthew, where have you spent all your life? This is lovely, but England is full of such places." She as always smiled at Matti, then her smile turned to a frown as she realised that tears were streaming down Matti's cheeks. "What is the matter? This is for joy not tears."

"Dawn, for the first time in my life I'm really happy. I just don't want this moment ever to end."

She smiled again, then gave a nervous giggle, and placed her hand on his left shoulder. His heart jumped a beat, and he brought his hand very nervously up to take hers in it. She didn't refuse, so he stroked her fingers with his. She was smiling and was looking directly into his face.

"I ought to tell you, Matthew," she started...

"Please, Dawn, everyone calls me Matti, can you, too?"

"Of course I can, Matti. As I was starting to say, before being rudely interrupted," another smile and chuckle, "I am here in France because I wanted to help you boys who are doing so much for the cause. I was engaged to a wonderful boy from Hastings in Sussex; I loved him very much and we were to be married next July, but he was killed at Mons in 1914. There has been no one else in my life, and that is what I thought I wanted. I am twenty-two years old; you are… how old?"

"Dawn, I am twenty!" he lied, but thought it prudent to do so. Dawn smiled again, but he knew it was a remote, wistful smile, one that was meant for someone in Mons.

"Dawn, I know there's a special bond between us. I don't want to rush into anything with you or anyone else. But this war has taught me one thing, life is too short, and one must live it as fully as possible, and to the best way one can!" He coughed, scratched his armpit more in instinct than actual itching. "I really do think I'm in love with you. I cannot promise anything, I have nothing yet to give, but I would be honoured if you would consider me as a real close friend and give me that chance to find out if there is anything that can develop between us; what do you say?"

Dawn didn't say anything; she just bent down and kissed him with the tenderest of kisses on his forehead.

"Come on, you, what about those carp?"

"Dawn, give me that chance, please. Will you?"

"Yes, Matti, we will see what we will see."

Before he knew it, the day was over, this day that should never end. He was back in bed, next to his closest friend, one that he loved above all else, until now!

"Enrico, are you awake?"

"Well I'm now, thanks to you. What seems to be the problem?"

"I am in love…and before you say anything, I really am in love. I have fallen in love with Nurse Dawn Williams, and what is more, I think she feels much the same for me."

"Well, that's a turn up for the books! Well, I guess it is because she saw you before I was *compos mentis*; otherwise it would be me saying this to you. Matti, don't you realise that every soldier sees his Nurse as a special person, and love is often felt between healer and patient? There is a bond that develops between the two of you, but that happens with all soldiers, so what makes you think you're any different from the thousands that have said the self same thing to Miss Williams before, over the last few months? She must have heard the love lines hundreds of times, and each soldier meant it just as you think you do." Enrico was saying what he thought; his words were not meant to hurt or wound, but just the truth as he saw it.

"I hear what you say, and don't think I have not thought about that, and what is more you may well be right, but Enrico, you must understand, I have to find this out for myself."

"Matti, I do understand, and you know me well enough to realise that I would wish you nothing but happiness. Who knows? You have as much chance as anybody. Be an optimistic pessimist which means hope for the best, but expect the worst."

"Enrico, we have both grown older and wiser since joining the army, and speaking entirely for myself, my experience with women has been a complete non-starter, so of course I am pessimistic about Dawn and my future."

"*Dawn* - is it?"

"But we all want some happiness from this life, and our futures, yours and mine, have looked very bleak up to now."

As he said these words, Matti's voice lowered, and he looked around the ward to see if any of the other twenty-eight patients, or medical staff had been listening to his conversation. He then added in a softer tone: "I know that our future could end with a noose around our neck on the gallows, or it could end through a bullet, or being blown to kingdom come, but you and me, we have changed; neither of us are the innocent, green little boys that ran away to the army. I for one feel like a man, and that man wants a future. I think that if I survive this war, I will have changed so much from the bottle-wielding miner of a couple of years ago into a responsible adult who could give something back to society, and contribute to help make a better world."

Enrico looked on, listening carefully, with his jaw almost hanging down to his knees. He smirked loudly, and then added:

"Matti, what a load of old bollocks! You sentimental old bastard! I've never heard so much claptrap in all my life, but I love you dearly," he said, wiping his drooling mouth on his sleeve. "But if you believe what you have spouted, I'm always prepared to give you the benefit of the doubt, and I wish you nothing but health and happiness, you dozy bugger, you! Tell me, does she know how old you are?"

Matti, who was looking intently at his pal, now turned away sharply, and reddened brightly…cough, cough, "er… sadly, she threw me by asking that very question, and I lied. I told her I was twenty, and she is twenty-two."

"God, man, she's an old woman!" This broke the conversation which had become too serious, and both the lads burst out laughing. Enrico put out his hand to his friend, who took it willingly. As they shook hands, Enrico loudly smacked his lips as if to send him a kiss:

"That's because you're the finest person I know, and no matter whatever you say or do, I want you to know I'm your best friend, and I'm there for you."

Both the lads beamed broadly.

Later that evening, after Doctor Bartlett and his medical staff had done the rounds Dawn came into the ward to see how her patients were doing before settling them down for the night. She first went to Enrico's bed, but Enrico was in no mood for the niceties of life, as he was feeling distinctly uncomfortable from the pain in his legs, and when Nurse Williams asked him if he wanted anything, he shook his head, and turned it away to hide the fact that tears were welling in his eyes. She tucked him up, and smartened his bed, and then turned her attention to Matti.

"Hello, Matti. How are you feeling?"

"Much better, Dawn. The pain in my legs has eased considerably," then he added with a wink: "it's the pain in my heart that should be worrying you!"

Dawn gave one of her beaming smiles, flashing her beautiful white teeth. She whispered to him: "Well, we can't have you lying here with a broken heart, so I'd better come back tomorrow morning, and with the Doctor's permission, get you on to the parallel bars, so you can get those legs up and working again!"

Matti said in a very quiet voice, loud enough so that only Dawn could hear: "Dawn, give me your hand a moment!" She passed her hand rather surreptitiously; he took it gratefully, carefully brought it up to his lips and gently kissed the top, then tenderly kissed each finger. Then as a final act of defiance, he turned her hand over, and deeply kissed her palm. A little gasp of surprise came from Nurse Williams, and she looked at Matti, with a new gentleness.

The next day the ward was roused early, to the clatter of orderlies, wheeling trolleys of bedpans and washing bowls. Matti awoke to all the joys of living; he knew he was getting better; his wounds were healing fast, and though his physical scars would show for ever, he was progressing at a rate of knots that would have made a captain on the Blue Star line envious of his speed of progress. Matti turned to Enrico and his joy quickly evaporated when he realised that his friend had fared badly during the night, and that it was obvious that Sergeant Lokowski was experiencing a recurrence of the fever that had wracked him after the battle of Loos. Matti immediately felt anger, that orderlies had not picked up on this fact and started to treat him during the night.

"Doctor, Nurse, come quickly! It's Sergeant Caruso! He's bad!"

Two orderlies appeared as if by magic; one felt his pulse, the other placed a thermometer in his mouth, and felt his forehead for signs of high fever. A little while later a junior doctor joined the group, and confirmed that indeed, Enrico was suffering from high fever, obviously caused by the wounds in his legs, and the stress and strains of the past weeks in battle. It was suggested by the doctor that he should be taken to another ward, but Matti interjected very quickly by saying: "Doctor, leave him here; if he goes into the dying ward, he won't come out alive. If necessary I will give my life for Sergeant Caruso, so I'm buggered if I will let you take him away from me!"

Matti said this in such a threatening manner, and so loudly that everybody in the ward heard him. But the arrival of Doctor Bartlett immediately defused the situation which was becoming somewhat tense: "No, son, we won't take your friend away from you. He has nothing that you can catch, so I think it's important that when his fever breaks, the first people he sees are the friends around him, so that's how it's going to be."

"Thank you, Doctor!" said Matti, much relieved.

Two nurses came, placed some screens around the bed, took the sheets and blankets off, and removed the soaking pyjamas from Enrico's sweaty body. They then proceeded to fan him and sponge him down with clean water. Enrico's legs were very red and inflamed, and the doctors and nurses were worried that gangrene might set in. Their fears abated, as after many hours of patient nursing his fever broke, leaving him exhausted but awake.

"You had us worried there, you old bugger," said Matti to his half *compos mentis* friend.

"I'll do anything for a decent night's sleep, and I must have slept for hours, but I still feel exhausted. What happened?"

"You went into a coma, and had a terrible fever; the nurses worked on you for hours, but eventually got your temperature down."

"Well, I don't feel great now, and I'm a little cold and wet, and I could sure use a drink, and maybe something to eat. *And ooh! Do I need a bottle!*"

The days went by, in a productive manner; both the lads were now recovering quickly, and both were managing to walk with the aid of crutches. Enrico's progression had been slower at first, but with the enthusiasm of his friend, along with the encouragement of the doctors, and not to forget Nurse Williams, his first faltering steps had been taken without any major mishaps.  He was quite obviously going to recover completely.

Matti had been spending all the time he could with his precious Dawn; on many occasions, she had wheeled him around Calais, and they had had the chance to get to know one another.  He learnt that Dawn had been born and bred in Bexhill in Sussex; she had come from a large family like Matti; she was the youngest of five daughters.  She had left school at the tender age of fifteen to study nursing.  Her fiancé, one Raymond Pritchard, had been her mentor at college, before becoming her lover, and when the call came in 1914 for doctors to enlist, he had been one of the first to go.  He had met his end bravely at Mons: when trying to rescue several young wounded soldiers, he had been caught by a stick grenade and had joined the ranks of the deceased.  Dawn had been devastated and heartbroken, but had decided that if her beloved Raymond could give his life so willingly, the very least she could do, was to offer up her own.  Unfortunately for Dawn, though she was readily accepted as a nurse within the army ranks, no army nursing staff of the female gender was allowed within front line areas.

On a Friday morning, Dawn appeared with her wheelchair, ready once more to take Matti on a stroll around the town.  They were making their way to the docks to watch the trains being loaded with their human cargo directly from the ships: more troops being wheeled off for the slaughter.  Then what might have been the self same trains returned what could have been the same troops, but by now battered and seriously wounded, taken to the ships for transportation back to Blighty.

Dawn was standing by the side of the wheelchair, and they were on the shorefront, watching the ships coming and going; it was a cool day, with very high unbroken clouds in the sky; then as if from nowhere, a pulsating throbbing, sounding almost like a ship's generator echoing across the sea, but out of sight from land, was heard.  Instead of that expected ship, the grey clouds parted briefly to allow a glimpse of the most terrifying spectre that they had ever seen: coming into view was a Zeppelin.  It was several miles north of them; this great lumbering black monster put the fear of

God into all who saw it. As it passed through the clouds, it created minor electrical storms, which, apart from looking ghostly, could have had a devastating effect upon the gases used within that monster. All the ships started to sound their horns, defence guns aimed skyward, and a great panic ensued. Guns blazed in all directions, but the giant was too far off to be hit, and after a few minutes it had again risen into the protection of the clouds, and gone onward with its mission to bomb London.

"Matti, I've never seen anything like that!"

"Neither have I, Dawn. They are skyships but are called Zeppelins. I heard of one recently being shot down in north London, and as the thing started to plummet to earth, some of the crew had to jump in the hope of lightening the ship so it could save the few that remained; that one did not make it, and crashed not far from Tottenham. It was said in the papers that people came from everywhere, and bribed the soldiers guarding it to get remains as souvenirs."

"Those poor sacrificed men! What a terrible death!"

"Dawn, my dear, any way you die is terrible! And at times I have as much pity for the Hun, as I do for our own troops."

Matti stiffly got out of the wheelchair, moved to the back to where Dawn was standing, put his hand on her shoulder, and gently drew her towards him. Once again she smiled that tender smile, and those lips just begged to be kissed. Her eyes met his, and for the first time, a real understanding took place between the two of them, and he kissed her full on the lips. For Matti, this had been the first time he had kissed a girl with serious passion, and as she pressed against him, she too, became aware that he was very much alive. His hand ran down her back, but she stiffened as he reached the small of her back.

"Matti, this is too quick for me! You must give me time. I know you are sincere in what you say, and I know you realise that I too, care for you, but you must understand that I am confused, and not quite ready to give myself to you!"

Matti understood, and though more than a little disappointed, he went back to sit in the wheelchair, and allowed himself to be pushed around again.

The next morning, Doctor Bartlett was late reaching Enrico and Matti, but when he did arrive, he approached their beds with a broad grin, and some very cheery words.

"Good news for you two! You have made such good progress that you are both going back to Blighty tomorrow! You are going to a hospital in a small rural town, some miles from the centre of London. The town is called...er..., what is it?" turning to the junior doctor,

"Beckenham, Sir."

"Ah, that's it, Beckenham! This hospital is a converted school, called Balgowan. Now, you lucky boys, the good news for you two is that it's within easy reach of sixteen railway stations, and you can get just about anywhere from there. The countryside is just up the road, and you are not that far from London. You're going to have a ball; enjoy it while you can, because your Battalion will soon be calling on your services again."

Then in a flurry, he turned on his heels, and Doctor Bartlett and his entourage swept out of the ward. Enrico's eyes had lit up with the prospect of Blighty and a change, but Matti was downcast at the thought of leaving behind the woman he was so much in love with. He looked around to see if Dawn was within the ward; she was not!

"I'm going to find Dawn," said Matti in a low upset tone to Enrico, "I will see what can be done about this!"

"Good luck," was the reply from his pal. Dawn was not in the hospital, so Matti looked around the outside of the building, hoping upon hope that he would catch a glimpse of his lady. There was rain in the air, and the temperature had dropped by several degrees, showing clear signs of the oncoming winter. Grey days make grey people. Matti waited outside the main door, getting more and more depressed at the thought of the inevitable. The old adage sprang to mind, making him feel even worse…'out of sight, out of mind.' Then, just as Matti was starting to get wet, as the rain permeated gently through his clothes and was making his dry skin now clammy with damp, Nurse Dawn Williams strolled around the corner and into his line of vision.

"Dawn, my sweet! I've been waiting for you. Did you know I was going to be sent back to Blighty tomorrow?"

"Yes, Matti, I did. But I couldn't tell you, I am sorry."

"But Dawn, I love you, and I don't want to leave you. What can be done?"

"Nothing, my dear man. If there is a real love between us, then the passage of time will make it grow stronger. Anyway, I do get leave every now and again. And we could always write to one another. Darling Matti, have you never heard the saying… absence makes the heart grow fonder?" Her smile once again lit up his life, even the wet cold rain meant nothing to him now. In front of the hospital and casually passing people, he kissed her full on the lips, and she kissed him back.

"Will I see you before we are shipped out?" enquired Matti in an excited voice, full of expectancy.

"I finish work at seven tonight. Why don't I take you back to my room and cook you a meal?"

"You can do that?" he asked now, with the blood rushing through his veins.

"No, but I will… for you."

It was agreed that nothing would be said during the day, but at seven that night Matti would be waiting outside the hospital building, crutches and all. Dawn would order a taxicab and they would be together that night. He kissed her one more time, after which they both entered the building but went different ways. The day dragged very slowly for Matti, who could only think about meeting Dawn, and the moment when he would be alone with her, going back to her room.

Enrico had performed the exercises that the doctors had prescribed for every day, for the purpose of strengthening his muscles and ligaments; he had walked up and down the ward with the aid of his crutches, and generally tidied after himself. He now waited for this day to end and the next to start. A new beginning, and back in England! What was this going to hold for them? He, like Matti, felt a certain fear of returning. Though the last time they went on leave, there had been no mention of police or murder, they both had that sinking feeling that as soon as their feet touched terra firma in Blighty, there would be the police waiting at the dock with a warrant for both their arrests. He could still feel that noose tightening around his neck, and the thought brought him out in a sweat.

As for Matti he spent most of the day standing at the ward's entrance, hoping that Dawn would just happen to stroll by. Occasionally he did spy her, running from ward to ward, carrying out her duties, not having any time to notice him. This made him feel very depressed; in the end he gave up trying, went back to his bed and attempted to read the book "Moby Dick". Having read twenty pages, he gave up when he realised that he could not remember one word of what had been written.

Lunch came, and so did a visitor: RSM Kelly stood in the doorway of the ward, beaming from ear to ear. "Well, there you both are! I thought you were dead, at least I hoped you were; I'm getting tired of all these hospital visits, it's a strain on my nerves."

"Well, hello to you too!" answered Enrico, recovering from the shock of seeing his friend Kelly standing there. "How the hell are you anyway?"

"I'm fine; you're the two that are laid up with some phoney complaint or other," laughed Kelly, as he reached the bed and shook Enrico's hand really warmly, and then turned to Matti, who was still standing in the middle of the ward, now with his jaw hanging in wonder.

"How the heck do you keep finding us?" asked Matti, as he too, shook Kelly's hand.

"No point in being an RSM if you can't pull strings and find your friends now, is there?" then added almost at once, "anyway, there are so many that bought it from our Battalion that those that are wounded I like to come and see. I hear on the grapevine that you two fellows did rather well in that wood. Are you going to give me the lowdown on what went on?"

"Actually, speaking for myself," said Enrico, "I was shit scared that we had ended up in Hell's Wood, I don't know about High Wood! But I'm happy to spend a while telling you how brave we both were."

"No bullshit, I had already heard that you had performed rather well...yet again. Bucking for more medals?" Kelly laughed. "The way you two are going, there won't be enough war left for the rest of us."

The three of them sat around the bed and the story of High Wood unfolded before their eyes once again. There they sat for two hours talking about all their problems concerning that accursed wood. Kelly too, had had awful experiences in the trenches. The Germans had attacked and been driven back only to attack again. Eventually after seriously hard fighting, with many casualties, the Hun had started to win the day. The Battalion could not get supplies up to the front quickly enough, and Fritz had plenty of time to prepare before the battle had even started. So many good men fell; after several days of attack and counterattack, the Germans had forced the British back to their original lines at Bazentin-le-Petit. Kelly was fuming about the lack of good leadership, which led to the excessive loss of life within the Battalions. Then just as things were reaching fever pitch, he stopped his tirade in mid-flow, and suggested that the three of them go out for a drink. Matti quickly held his arms up in an apology, saying…"I have a date, sorry fellows, but I've had a better offer."

"I shall take his place though, if I'm good enough?" smiled Enrico, expressing himself as if he was a girl. Kelly laughed, tickled him under the chin, winked and said…"You'll do lovely, my dear!" Off they both went, leaving Matti even more nervous than before. All good things come to he who waits, and eventually seven o'clock came around, which found Matti standing outside the hospital in the pre-arranged zone. He didn't have to wait long: two minutes later, out through the doors came the ever smiling

Dawn, and she walked straight into Matti's arms. They kissed hard and passionately. After coming up for air, they hailed a taxi, and went the two miles to the room that had been allotted to Nurse Dawn Williams by the hospital administration, after her arrival in France.

It was a cold room, approximately sixteen feet by twenty feet, with only a bed, table and two chairs. Wooden floors that had almost worn clean, with a threadbare carpet that once had a pattern upon it. There was a sink next to the window; it was a very deep sink, which could have served for many uses, had the room been used by a man. The window had a clean, but totally worn curtain hanging, though how it could be drawn either open or shut beggared belief. The bed was an old iron frame bed, with a thin mattress and half a dozen blankets that again were clean, but once more had seen better days. Though Matti scrutinised everything very closely, he was too polite to say what he really thought of her accommodation.

Instead, he smiled lovingly, squeezed Dawn's hand approvingly, drew her close to him, and once again kissed her squarely on her ever smiling lips. They both reddened as they thought of the moments to come.

"Let me make some food," said Dawn, as she gently pulled away from Matti's arms. "I only have some meat and salads, I hope that is alright?"

"Of course it is; do I look the sort of person that needs to eat much?" with a cough, at which they both laughed.

Matti helped lay the table with two plates, one of which had a rather large crack through it. Knives and forks were polished and placed around the plates, glasses filled with wine, a nice red from Cahors. This was a wine that had once been favoured by the Kings of England, and would keep for many years; it needed careful preparation, but Dawn knew her wines, and when it was drunk they both appreciated it very much. The meal consisted of ox tongue, slithers of finely cut veal steaks, ham off the bone cooked in honey, and several more precious meats, that even in peacetime would have been hard to get…"How on earth did you manage to get these wonderful cuts of meat?" enquired Matti.

"It's not what you know here, but who you know. I have made a friend of the local farmer, after helping his wife give birth to their fourth child, a little girl. She was having a very bad time, and I came along and gave assistance. He was so grateful he promised me meat whenever I needed it. I have never used it until now. So Matti my dear, eat and enjoy."

They ate and drank; an old gramophone was even produced from under the bed, and an old recording of Beethoven's violin Concerto was played. Matti had never heard such music before, and was really moved by the beautiful melodies and tunes. Even though the sounds coming from the horn were very scratchy, and the record jumped through excessive wear and tear, none of these things mattered. This was a magical evening, one that would be held in his memory for ever.

"Dawn, we have talked a lot, and you know my feelings towards you, I love you. I would like to think that there is going to be a future for us," and he held up his hand to indicate that there was more to that sentence before she could interject with her own thoughts. "But before I can promise anything to you, we have the little matter of the war to consider, and you already have lost one fiancé; I don't want you to lose two. Enrico and myself have come through many serious scrapes, actions that might have killed other men; we believe, and I'm serious in this, that we are immortal, but we still don't take any chances, and we still get wounded and feel pain, but neither of us really have any doubts that we'll come through this war together. But before you scoff at what has just been said, I too realise that it's a stupid, unreal opinion; it's one that gets us through these terrible battles that we've had to be a part of. I have done things that beggar belief. I think you know me well enough to know that I'm a gentle person by nature; in fact, I was the one that was always bullied at school, and it was Enrico that used to protect me, but I've killed and wounded enemy soldiers, and Dawn, I tell you now, it's never easy to kill, but I've done it in the name of King and Country and the so-called freedom that we are fighting for, but, my darling, I'm not proud of what I've done. So in this long, roundabout way, I'm really trying to say that after this is over, I yearn for a peaceful existence, along with all the trappings of normality. My own home, wife and children; the home I will supply, the wife I hope will be you, and together, we will produce the children… That's probably the longest speech I've ever made, so what d'you think?"

Dawn, once again, smiled brightly, and those teeth almost glistened in the gas light as she answered: "Matti, dear, I agree, the war comes first; let's get that over with, and then I too, will be prepared to think about the future. This romance has been too quick," she said, reaching across to hold his hand, "but the bond between us is there, and like you, I feel a great comfort when we are together. I had not thought about finding anybody else, but one thing I have learnt, is how incredibly resilient us humans are. In my mind, you are taking up the space in the void that was left by the death of Raymond. We will write, as often as you like, and we can see one another when we have leave. I don't know how much longer the war will last, but the time parted will give us strength, and we will have had time to explore our real feelings towards one another, but, my darling, there is something I must tell you, and for some men, this could be a serious problem to overcome."

"What on earth is it?"

"Well, Matti, you should know I'm not a virgin."

Matti's hand squeezed Dawn's ever so slightly harder, and as her eyes had been downcast when making her confession, she now looked up to meet his eyes, and saw that there was true compassion radiating from them, along with a gentle smile that wrote the word love on his face.

"Dawn, I care nothing of the past, we all have pasts; yours is perfectly understandable: you were engaged to somebody, but I have done things which will haunt me for the rest of my life. All I know is that I love you, that I want you… right now!"

Matti stood from the table; still holding Dawn's hand, he gently beckoned her to rise and led her to the bed. They sat on the edge of the bed, and he kissed her. Gradually his hand slipped, and lightly touched her right breast. Her breathing became faster, but she did not resist his touch. He found the buttons on her white blouse, and started to undo them. He slipped his hand inside to be closer to her breast, but she still wore a slip and a lawn chemise, into which, no matter how hard he fumbled, he could find no entry point. This broke the moment between them, and Dawn stood up, looked directly into Matti's eyes and said: "Why don't we take our clothes off, and get into the bed?"

"Shall I turn the gas down low?" But before she could answer, he had already done so. Matti was not used to undressing in front of women; in fact he didn't much like undressing in front of men either; indeed to say he was more than a little shy about his body was putting it mildly. Very quickly, he was down to his underpants, which remained on. His clothes were piled in an untidy heap, upon the threadbare carpet. With one leap, he sprang into bed. Dawn took her time, and Matti watched on with excitement. She carefully folded each garment as it was removed, and placed it over the chair. Soon she was completely naked, showing herself totally unselfconsciously to Matti. She pulled back the bedclothes so as to climb in and grinned when she saw Matti lying there in his long john underpants, with his hands covering his erect penis, as if trying to shield her from the sight of it.

"You forget, Matti dear, that I am a nurse. I have seen hundreds of completely naked men, and you too. When you were unconscious, I always knew when you were just going to urinate by the fact that you had an erect penis, and if you're not going to urinate now, I deem it a compliment that it has expanded at the sight of me! Please, darling, remove these ugly woollen underpants, and those thick woollen socks before I get in next to you!"

Matti reddened fiercely, but did just as he was bid. Dawn climbed in by the side of him, and they kissed yet again, but this time as real lovers. Matti in his eagerness tried to mount Dawn too soon, and was chastised lovingly and told exactly what to do. The night went far too quickly for Matti, and soon it was daybreak. It had been ecstasy, and he had told her that, on the three times they had made love. The sun rose on a cold and blustery day. The inside of the bedroom was damp and musty smelling; only now, when it was time to say goodbye, was Matti acutely conscious of the miserable state of the room: there was green mildew growing in the corners and the wallpaper was peeling through damp. The drabness of the room was echoing the emptiness in his heart as the moment of leaving approached, and this was exacerbated by the greyness of the weather outside.

"Matti, it's time you left. You should have been back last night. You will be in trouble when you get back, and if people put two and two together, so will I! You will have to get a taxi; if you go to the railway station you should be able to pick one up there. Would you like me to come with you?"

"No, my dear. I'll manage; it's best to say goodbye here."

He dressed quickly, cleaned his teeth with his fingers, washed his face in the cold water, and slicked his hair down with his hand. He looked at her one last time; he bent down, gently caressed her neck and cheek with his right hand, and kissed her on the forehead. Putting his hand carefully over her eyes, so that they shut, he then turned and on his crutches left the room. When he was outside the building, he looked up at the window and could see her face peering down at him. Tears welled up in his eyes… 'stop this, you sentimental fool!'

He turned and walked in the direction of the station. He had gone but fifty yards, when an army ambulance came rattling down the cobblestone road towards him. Realising that it was probably going to the hospital, he waved it down, managing to procure a lift.

"Where the hell have you been?" enquired Enrico, as Matti sat on the side of his bed. "The doctors and nurses have been in a panic, here. They thought you had done an AWOL. I had to make up some bullshit,

370

saying that you went to see a long-lost aunt!"

"Thanks, Enrico! But last night was worth any trouble that I might be in."

Doctor Bartlett and his entourage appeared at the door of the ward. He came striding over to Matti, and said in a matter-of-fact voice: "Did you have a good night, lad?"

"Yes, Doctor."

"Good! Now, one final check over for you two, and it's off you go, back to Blighty."

The sea was rough, due to the north easterly winds which were creating a large surge of water coming from the North Sea, down into the English Channel, and everybody on board the ship was affected by the swell. Most of the passengers and crew deposited their breakfast over the furniture or floors of the ferry. What should have been an easy journey yet again turned into a nightmare. Once more the weather was so inclement that the waves prevented safe entry into Dover Harbour, so the ferry headed for Sandwich and went into Pegwell Bay, then into the estuary of the river Stour, before managing to dock at the railway terminal, opposite Ramsgate.

This whole mile-long terminus had been taken over entirely by the military for the making of landing craft and small military boats, such as torpedo boats; some of which were used as raiders in enemy waters. This little empty wilderness had been turned into a hive of activity, just like the Romans nearly two thousand years before had done. There, they had built Richborough Castle which was for the Romans, the gateway to Britannia. Unlike the Romans, these soldiers were not conquerors, but wounded men who were returning to Blighty with mostly nightmarish memories to contend with, scarred in body and mind.

The ferry was unloaded, and there was a considerable wait while the trains that were due to transport them came through from Dover. Eventually Enrico and Matti, with tags around their necks stating where they were to be relocated in big black letters, as if they were children going to a picnic, boarded the special compartment that had Bromley South on each window. Two hours later, they found themselves climbing the stairs of Bromley South station towards waiting ambulances, to be taken the short journey to Beckenham, and Balgowan School Hospital.

This Edwardian rural school had been converted for the sole use of soldiers who had been wounded in the legs. The local fields and spring water were considered very beneficial to recovery. The four major rooms of the school housed fifty patients, and since its conversion to hospital, it had never been anything but full. All the surrounding fields were flat, and the paths made good, easy walking. Watching the cows ambling from the fields to the farm, in preparation for milking, was considered a fine way to spend the day by most of the wounded soldiers. The many country pubs became the entertainment in the evenings.

The town of Beckhenham was a sleepy little place, with a large parish church called St Georges; being High Church of England it always had a large attendance of middle class parishioners. These parishioners had chosen to live there because of the convenience of the sixteen railway stations that festooned the area, and in so doing created the beginnings of suburbia. The town had grand Council buildings, and next to the church were the alms houses. These delightful little cottages had been generously built for the sole purpose of the elderly poor of the parish. The town itself was almost dominated by the large Kelsey Estate, whose lodge house backed onto the river Beck. Because of the low lying area that Beckenham was in, it was often subject to flooding.

Just across the way from Balgowan Hospital, was the river Chaffinch which backed onto Clockhouse Road; this also had developed because of yet another railway station. The Chaffinch was prone to flooding too, and on such occasions, it was known for men to have canoe races up the partly made Clockhouse Road.

On reaching the hospital, the six new inmates were greeted by an army major, one Major Stollbright, and two nurses. He checked the tags, as if to make sure he had the right consignment, though the fact that each of the six had leg wounds should have been enough.

"Welcome, my brave boys! The rules here are simple. Get really well, and get out! Those of you that will be going back to the army are subject to the normal rules and regulations of army life; this means," as he bent over slightly as if to emphasize the words with his clipboard tightly pinned under his right arm, "that there will be no wandering off without authorisation, no home leave until you are completely fit and ready to make any journey that might be detrimental to your health. Visitors will be allowed, but only upon agreed dates. Now this sounds as if we are regimented, we are not; as soon as you can, you will be encouraged to leave the premises, and go for long walks. Those of you who might be discharged will be here, having treatment until we feel the time is right for you to go and face the rigours of home life again."

He paused, looking at the four seriously wounded stretcher cases, and then turned to Enrico and Matti, who were standing with the aid of their crutches: "I expect that you two will be rejoining your Battalion within the next few weeks, as your wounds are not that serious."

Then with a wave of his right arm he smiled, with his left hand he curled his broad moustache, and ended by saying: "The nurses here," pointing to the two nurses standing by him, "will show you to your beds, and as it's been a long day for all of you, arrange for hot food and drink. Are there any questions?"

Everyone being quite exhausted, there were no questions. Enrico and Matti were glad to be going to their beds, even if it meant sleeping in a ward full of broken bodies. The men all had lost one or both of their legs, and the two pals were the only ones who could walk, or even were likely to ever walk again. Some of the men also had other severe wounds, and one poor soul, had lost most of his face, and eventually would be taken on to Queen Mary's at Roehampton, Putney in South West London when a bed became available, and where his shattered face could in time be partially rebuilt. Nobody knew his name, or where he was from. He had lost his nose, eyes and jaw, so that his extended tongue lolled all over what was left of him. He could not speak, and only gave out low growls, as his body would become racked with pain. A screen was placed all around his bed so as to shield him from view, but curiosity often got the better of other patients, and they would creep by the screen to see the horror lying in the bed before them. Yet, however terrible the damage was, somehow life kept on going.

Because of the terrible injuries that were being caused by the shells, machine guns, gas and many other weapons that had never been used before, plastic surgery came into its own. People were being rebuilt by doctors who just experimented on them, because leaving them as they were was too awful to contemplate, but in many cases the injuries were untreatable, and even if the soldiers afflicted could be identified, they were often posted as missing presumed dead, so that sweethearts and kin could be spared the terrible consequences of having to deal with the impossible. Queen Mary's Roehampton Burns Hospital became famous for the treatment that it administered to these sad unfortunates, and many were to stay, almost as prisoners within the wards, for the rest of their lives.

The only word that could describe the medical staff, from doctors down to the lowest of porters, was stoic. Often the doctors would work for twenty-four hours a day, until the job was done or they fell down from sheer exhaustion. But knowledge about medicines and treatments grew in leaps and bounds. It is a sad indictment of humanity that it takes a war for science to progress forward. Only in the slaughter of human beings does the money seem to appear from government for the betterment of mankind.

Enrico turned to Matti, and in a low, depressed, dull tone he said, "This is a sad place for us to end up in. I do not like this ward; look around you, Matti, these poor souls could have been us."

"I wouldn't want to live if I was like any of these. Just shoot me quickly if this ever happens to me!"

"Oh come on, now... Enough of that sort of talk, let's get some sleep, and maybe we can explore more tomorrow?"

"Good idea. Though I'm serious about being shot if I am going to be crippled! Now I just want to write a quick letter to Dawn, then sleep."

The next morning, both the lads were feeling somewhat better, thanks to a good night's sleep. Amazing how rejuvenating sleep can be! They woke to the sound of a tea trolley being wheeled around the ward.

"Tea! I thought we would have to wash and do our ablutions before we would be given sustenance," remarked Matti, as he grabbed the cup offered and downed the contents eagerly.

"Crikey, you finished that before I even got a chance to tell if it's tea or coffee. What was it you drank anyway?" enquired Enrico.

"Good question that; for the life of me, I don't honestly know. Could have done with a bit more sugar, but it was strong, hot and wet. So whatever it was, it was good."

After they had had their breakfast, done their wash and brush up, they waited patiently for the doctor to come around and give the alright for them to do some wandering.

"Where shall we go?" Matti asked Enrico.

"Well, we can start by seeing what Beckenham has to offer. D'you realise we could down a couple of English pints?"

"My friend, I'm ahead of you there. But it might be nice to see if there's any life in this 'ere place."

"Oi, mate," came the voice from a bed next to Enrico's, "can you do me a favour?"

"What is it?"

"Can you get me some shag? I'm completely out, and it would be nice to 'ave a smoke outside in the garden before I croak it."

This was the voice of John Jackson, who had fought bravely on the Somme, but had lost both his legs when a Mills bomb had been thrown by a dying comrade, and it fell to John's feet. He had been in Balgowan Hospital for the last four weeks, and now was starting to get used to the idea of never walking again. He was from Swindon, and had worked as a train carriage fitter before joining up like so many others, for his King and Country. Now he too needed fitting out.

"No problem, pal," said Enrico, "though if we are allowed out, I don't know what time we'll be back."

The doctor came with his small team of nurses and junior doctors. He went from bed to bed, examining most of the patients, and marking their charts accordingly. When he reached Matti and Enrico, he said in a matter of fact way: "You two will be here for a little while yet. And before you ask, yes, you can go out, but take care, use your crutches, and if you get tired, stop and take it easy. You are not here for nothing: you have both had quite serious wounds to your legs. You might think you are mending well and quickly, but overdo it, and you will yet get an infection and be put back weeks or months. And no drinking, at least don't get caught." Then for the first time since arriving at the hospital, the lads saw someone smile.

Depression lifted; 'we are going out of here for a stroll... and maybe a beer or two,' thought Enrico. All of a sudden the clouds outdoors parted to show a hazy, but warmish sun. Just as soon as they were allowed, the two friends headed up towards the centre of Beckenham: two lads with two sets of crutches, both hobbling along as fast as they could without falling down upon the ground in front of themselves.

People they passed viewed them either with a sort of reverence, as heroes returning from their latest triumph, sporting wounds as trophies, or they watched them with indifference, almost with contempt as if they were taking precious resources: after all, if there hadn't been a war, there wouldn't be shortages on the home front, so in some way these wounded soldiers were to blame. There was even those who resented them just being alive, having maybe lost someone themselves; and in their mind, survivors should not be there flaunting themselves.

There were many sad people; war creates sadness, grief and anger: people could turn very nasty to one another for no reason whatsoever, just because, and that was that.

On that walk to town, they were on the receiving end of this variety of feelings, had they cared to feel or look.

Beckenham had become like every other town, village or hamlet within the British Isles: each road, sporting its black curtains, showing the world that some young man had been lost during a campaign. The Somme had become the British killing field, and with so many dead from so many pals Battalions, whole communities were grieving from the loss. Enrico and Matti did not want to be aware of any of these feelings: they were just glad to be alive themselves; after all they were immortal, and yet again that had been proven by the fact that no police had been waiting for them when they got off the boat at Sandwich or off the train at Bromley. Nothing was going to get them, nothing!

Beckenham was a sleepy little town, with several shops, which included two butchers with fresh meats, mostly rabbit and pigeons hanging for all the town's people to see; two greengrocers, full to the brim with potatoes and carrots, but precious little else. There was also a hardware store, stocking everything from farming equipment to whatever one would need for the home. Next to a very small fire station, that looked as if it had never had its doors open, let alone fought a fire, was the George Public House.

"Just what the doctor ordered. Well, not quite, but he would approve I'm sure," laughed Enrico, struggling with one of his crutches over the doorstep.

"Make mine a pint of best, please, Matti, I'll be with you just as soon as I stop falling over this bloody crutch!"

They made it into the public bar just in time to see two more soldiers from the hospital buying themselves something wet.

"Hello there," said Matti.

"Hello, Corporal, can I get you a drink?"

"Why thank you, the Sergeant and myself will have a pint of best bitter each. That is very kind of you. What are your names?"

"I'm Private Jenkins of the Scots Guards, and this is my mate Private Cousins, again of the Guards. And you are?"

"I am Matthew Dumbridge; forget the Corporal bit for now, of the London Northern Rifle Brigade. This is Enrico Caruso, Sergeant but again forget that for now too. We are together, grew up together, worked together, lived in the same digs, joined up together, were wounded together, both of us in the legs… together."

"Thanks for the drinks," said Enrico, as he acknowledged their presence. Several drinks later, when stories had been swapped, and bullshit ruled the day, Enrico looked at Matti, who was drooping, quite obviously under the influence of intoxicating liquids, and commented: "Matti, it's time we moved on. We have fought all the battles and won the war single-handed, but you and me are getting heavy, and it's only early afternoon; let's carry on with our exploring of this Old Saxon town."

"How did you know it was Saxon?" asked the barman, who had been wiping glasses and listening to just about every word that had been said.

"It stands to reason," said Enrico, "Beckenham is two syllables, Beck and Ham, both are Saxon words, Beck is a stream, Ham means village. Around the corner, according to this local map on your wall, is the river Beck or river, river," he spluttered. "Ham is the village that stood beside it…thus, Beckenham!" A loud clap came from the other three soldiers. The barman looked dumbfounded… "Is that how it came about?"

"No question about it," spouted Enrico, then turned and winked at Matti, and whispered "Bullshit rules!" They both said their farewells to the pub and the two new friends that they had made there. They walked out into a grey afternoon, with the sun hidden from view thanks to some high grey clouds, the sort that threatens rain, but never delivers.

Using their crutches to support themselves, once again they struggled; now also under the extra strain of alcohol, they turned right back onto the High Street and walked no more than one hundred yards when they came to the river. Looking right yet again, they could see the entrance to Kelsey Estate via the gate house, and then an unmade road off to the right again called Manor Road. This they followed until, on their left, within the grounds of the estate, they could see a large pond, which fed into the river.

"Let's explore over there, might be some good fishing to be done in the future," said Matti. They turned across the open field towards the pond, though more a lake than a pond, but a sign said 'Welcome to Kelsey Pond, no fishing allowed, bye-laws must be observed.' There was a small jetty going out approximately ten feet over the lake. The lads managed to get themselves onto this rather rickety structure, without losing their footing; the water would be cold, and not at all nice to get their wounds covered in water that fish do their business in. Fish… there they were hundreds of them. It was obvious that the locals came here to feed them, as they were quite tame, used to seeing the images of human beings standing above them, giving them food. People must have looked like Gods, offering manna from heaven. Some of the carp were huge, maybe weighing twenty or thirty pounds. Some were almost three feet long.

"My God, Matti, have you ever seen such monsters? They must have been here for many years. Nobody fishes these buggers out."

"Please, Enrico, don't suggest what I think you are going to suggest. If other people don't fish them then neither should we. Play the game, or we'll be in trouble."

"Don't you give it a thought, my old mucker. Let me do the planning; after all, what would it matter if this vast expanse of water lost two fish? Salted carp, lovely!" He laughed, Matti frowned.

"Yes, Matti, you don't want to give it a thought. By the way, did we pass a tobacconist?"

"Yes, there was a small one, not far from the fire station, on the curve in the High Street."

"Then I think we should get the shag, and gently make our way back to Balgowan, because, I don't know about you, mate, but I'm getting to be very hungry."

They got back in time for their evening repast; when the meal arrived, both their faces dropped: there on the plate, were the watery remains of a somewhat overboiled piece of cod, some potatoes, that had spent the last hour swimming about in boiling water, so that when one tried to pick them up, pieces would slip between the prongs of the fork, and cabbage that once would have had some goodness in, but now looked more like mushy paper, without the print on it. Matti and Enrico looked at one another in horror, but glancing around the ward they noticed that all the other patients were tucking in with a will.

"Oh, shite, Matti! Look at those poor bastards gannetting this mush down! You know what that means?"

"No, but you are going to tell me!"

"It means, dear boy that this slop must be the norm; these blighters have got used to it."

"Then, Enrico, so must we!" And so Matti tucked into the plate of what was once good food, as if it was the greatest meal he had ever partaken of.

"Christ!" said Enrico. "If I was not so hungry, you could have mine too!" Then he too, tucked in, stoically.

A week went by, somehow; the days dragged, only relieved by occasional walks in and around the area; they felt the boredom acutely, and were fretting for a proper day out, as they had now realised how close they were to the Crystal Palace, where their exploits first began. They thought it might be fun to retrace their steps to the dinosaurs, maybe even look around the exhibition within the glass structure itself; and if the doctor allowed, maybe to end the evening by going to one of the two music halls that were offering regular entertainment. The next day, again after the visit from the doctor, permission was granted for an exciting day out. By now, the strength in their legs was improving almost by the minute, and Matti had abandoned his crutches for just the use of one walking stick. On this special day out, Enrico was going to do the same.

Before they could go out, an orderly came running into the ward, and was relieved to see that both the lads were still there.

"Boy am I glad I caught you! Doctor Stollbright has informed me that you must not disappear, as a Colonel Collins and his staff are coming early this afternoon to interview you both."

Matti gave a quick glance to Enrico, and worry lines appeared on his forehead. When the orderly had disappeared he said: "Crikey, Enrico, I don't like the sound of this interview business. You don't think they're finally onto us, do you?"

"I'm sure that's not it, Matti," but still there was a worried frown on his face, too. "If anybody was onto us, it would be the police, and they would not be announcing their intentions to come. We just would have been arrested and taken into custody."

"I still don't like it, though. It's the word 'interview' that bothers me," said Matti.

"Me too, but I suggest we really smarten ourselves up. Whatever it is, we should look our best. Why, maybe we have time to get a haircut."

Doctor Stollbright agreed that they should go and smarten up; after all, they did not often get full blown Colonels coming to this little hospital. Several hours later, two young men, with new clean fatigues, and short hair, sat waiting patiently by their beds until a familiar marching sound announced the arrival of a small entourage coming down the corridor, and breezing into the ward.

"'T-tenshun!" barked Enrico, and they both stood erect, thumbs pointing down the seams of their trousers and eyes looking directly ahead of them.

"At ease, at ease, at ease! This is a friendly visit. I'm here to give you some good news. Your extraordinary courage during the fierce engagement at High Wood has come to my attention, with the fact that the two of you captured a Maxim machine gun nest, and personally killed more than a dozen German soldiers. While you were resisting the Germans, both of you were wounded quite severely in your legs, so it gives me great pleasure to inform you both that at a certain date, you will be presented at Buckingham Palace to King George V, where each of you will receive Britain's highest award, the Victoria Cross for courage above and beyond the call of duty."

Both the friend's jaws had dropped; they just looked at Colonel Collins with utter amazement. 'Can they really mean us?' wondered Matti, still standing bolt upright.

"Come now, lads, stand easy, in fact sit down and let your brain take it all in. I have read your histories very carefully, and I have to say I cannot think of a more worthy duo than you two. Of course there will be a lot of publicity, which will be good for your Battalion and the army in general. The day at the Palace will be special, that I promise. You will be shown the correct procedures on how to behave in front of the King. I only wish I was there with you both. So jolly well done, and if you want, write home and tell your parents."

"I have nobody, Sir," said Enrico, "and to be honest, I really don't feel worthy of this honour, and I hate publicity; I don't want my name or picture in the papers, if that can be arranged?"

"Take your time and think it all over, but one thing is for sure, you both have earned this honour, so I don't wish to hear anything to the contrary, understood?"

"Yes Sir, thank you, Sir," said Matti, yet still looking straight ahead. "I have parents, though I never hear from them. But I would like to write to them and tell them of this. But I do agree with Sergeant Caruso, I would prefer no publicity either; if that is alright, Sir?"

"Well, I must say! You two just astound me! Whatever you want, you will get. But once again, take your time, think it out before refusing the publicity, you might regret it."

"Yes Sir, we will think it out."

'Not a chance; we don't want any nonsense that could get us hung, now do we?' thought Enrico.

Congratulations were extended all around from the entourage, and a clapping started to come from patients who had overheard the whole procedure. Doctor Stollbright beamed delightedly at the thought of having two VCs in his hospital. He looked at Matti and Enrico, and added: "Well, lads, tomorrow, you can have that day out and really enjoy yourselves. I can only echo what Colonel Collins has already stated, and say it seems you have earned it!"

"Right, lads, I have other news to give out to other people, so we must go, but my office will be in touch when the date is confirmed."

Colonel Collins shook their hands once again, turned on his heels and they all trooped out, just as they had trooped in. Matti looked at Enrico, and those now familiar worry lines that looked like sand dunes from the Sahara desert showed themselves on his brow.

"Enrico, what are we to make of all of this, then? What should be a magnificent day could be once again our downfall."

"There's no point worrying too much, we'll have to sort it as we go along." The excitement had exhausted Enrico more than Matti, and he now complained of a slight headache. He decided to have a siesta, so Matti took the time to write all the news, firstly to Dawn, then to his mother and father. That night, the only celebration came from the overcooked Irish stew that they were presented with.

"This has to be the only chef I have ever known, who manages to overcook water!" jested Enrico. "I've seen better presented food, floating down the trench!" This last remark causing raucous laughter from all that could hear, but still they ate voraciously. After all, what else could you do with it?

The next morning, as per norm, they were woken when the tea trolley came rattling in. The only resemblance this had to tea was the colour; but they were now used to it and anything hot and wet was better than nothing. Both the lads quickly did their ablutions, and spruced themselves up to the nines. Once Doctor Stollbright had completed the rounds within the ward, the friends grabbed their walking sticks and hastily beat a retreat from the red-bricked building that housed them. The chums had to walk up to Clockhouse station, where they could pick up an omnibus which would take them to Penge. From opposite the police station at Penge, they could catch the tram that came from Anerley, and would take them up to the terminus at Crystal Palace.

The day was yet again overcast, with high grey clouds. It had that autumn warmth that one felt could go nowhere but towards winter; at least there was very little chance of any rain. When they alighted from the tram, Matti suggested that they see if the kiosk was still there, where they had had a bacon sandwich, all that time ago. It was indeed, and still the same chap running it, not that he would have recognised them, anyway. They each had a hot cup of tea, and a round of sandwiches.

"Now, this is more like a decent breakfast!" said Matti, as bacon fat dripped from his lips.

"*Mmmmm…!* Shall we see if there are any exhibitions on?"

They walked towards the entrance to see a poster, advertising a grand exhibition of 'Captured German and Turkish Artillery and Weaponry'. They paid their three copper coins, and gained entrance to the grand glass palace. The first thing they noticed was how close the air was; at least seventy-five degree Fahrenheit, and quite steamy. Palm trees were positioned everywhere, and many exotic, colourful flowers blossomed. There were several large fish ponds, with beautiful, multi-coloured Japanese carp, swimming luxuriously, like models parading in dress shops. Parakeets, some flying freely, having escaped their tethers, added to the bright, tropical feel of the structure. They walked around, taking in the surroundings; they had never experienced such luxury and grandeur. There were life-size copies of ancient Egyptian artefacts, which included a huge plaster copy of the Sphinx. There was a wonderful, huge stage, constructed in the main body of the building. Often great concerts would be performed, where only large scale productions could find accommodation. There had been orchestral settings, using four hundred plus musicians at one time, making very exciting productions.

At the far end of the huge glass structure, the end nearest to the tram terminal, they came across the exhibition of captured armoury. There were many large calibre guns, some damaged, but many completely intact. For the boys the strangest thing to see was the captured Turkish field guns that would have been suited to a war a hundred years previously. There was a nice little cafeteria, where they got a very tasty salad lunch, with something entirely new to them…Pilchards. This strange fish, in its tomato sauce, was quite unique for these two country bumpkins. Having finished viewing the interior, they decided to stroll down into the park, and look for their old sleeping place, in the Iguanodon sculpture.

There she stood, looking proud, despite the gloomy weather; it was as if she recognised them because the smile was still on her face. The lads addressed her with a deep bow, and wished her well for the future. They then followed the path around the artificial pond, and started to make their way to the Penge exit. By the time they had made it to Penge, evening was closing in on them, but they decided to check out what the programs were at the music halls. The one nearest to the police station was staging an end-of-the-pier type show, which included many Pierrots. To the lads, this looked like a disaster waiting to happen, and was definitely not up their street, so they crossed the road and turned into Croydon Road. There, was the Palace Theatre, putting on variety acts, and starting at seven thirty. They could see from the poster that at the top of the bill was a comedian called Kenneth Wyatt.

"Now, that's a bit more like it! Hopefully, we'll have a few laughs, and then at least we can go back to that bloody Balgowan place with a smile on our face!"

"Enrico, it's been a great day, though, hasn't it? I can't remember ever enjoying myself more. Well, except with Dawn, but that's something else."

There was a public house, right on the corner of Croydon Road, and there, they could maybe get a drink, and see whether the landlady could be persuaded to rustle up a sandwich, or two, knowing Matti! Well, they got the drink, but no landlady was going to do any favours to these northern reprobates, so a pint of beer was all they were getting.

Two seats in the stalls were there for the taking, and they were straining their necks to see all that went on, up there on that dais. The first few acts could only be described in polite terms as terrible; there was a woman, who whistled popular songs of the day, but like Enrico, she whistled at least a quarter tone sharp. But it did not seem to matter, as most of the audience were drinking, talking, or sound asleep. There was a man, who had trained a dog to leap through hoops, do a dance on his back legs, and even walk on just his front legs, but it was obvious that the poor creature was ageing badly, as it would sometimes fall on its face, or just keel over on its side, with its tongue hanging out, in a state of exhaustion. At least this act created some reaction from the audience, as they started to chant "Rubbish, get off!" much to the dismay of the luckless performer, and the management. The dog obviously no longer cared either way!

Then a singer, Jack Charman, who was famous for entertaining the troops with some bawdy songs, at least entertained the good people of Penge, with his final rendition of "Goodbye, Dolly Gray". They cheered, and clapped vigorously: "Good old Jack!" At least one performer had lightened the load of the management.

Finally the last act was the local comedian, Kenneth Wyatt. His first joke got people chuckling; he then went from strength to strength, and ended his eight minutes with a monologue that included the quick changing of many caps and voices. Young Kenneth Wyatt went down extremely well, and the audience called for an encore. It had been a good evening, in fact, like Matti said, it had been one of the best days of their young lives.

The next week went by just as slowly as it could. Walking around Beckenham had become quite boring, and going further afield had only tired them badly. Gradually they had sunk into a gloom of despondency. What was needed was a complete change of scene such as going back to work.

Colonel Collins' Adjutant, Major Brimshaw had been in touch through the hospital administration to say that the Palace visit would be the week before Christmas. Orders would come before in writing to explain procedure to them both. "Christmas, I'll go mad through boredom! It's time we got back to our Battalion. What say we contact the new Colonel in Chief?"

"I suppose so…" replied Matti in a listless tone.

Though both sporting a slight limp, they were now walking without the aid of sticks or crutches; it was time to be moving on: that was the order of the day, at least as far as they were concerned.

"Major Stollbright, may I have a private word with you?" enquired Enrico.

"Yes, come to my office." Enrico followed him into his room. Papers were lying all over the place, which surprised Enrico, as he had had the Major down as a right stuffed shirt, all prim and proper. "What can I do for you, Sergeant?" asked the Doctor.

"It's more what we can do for you, Sir. It's time we gave up our beds to more deserving wounded soldiers. Both Corporal Dumbridge and I feel like frauds still being here. What we both want and need is to get back to our Battalion; maybe you would be kind enough to help us?"

Stollbright shuffled around some papers, found what he was after, and then said, "You have just reminded me that I was to call you anyway. Yes, you two are on your way. This is an order from Finsbury barracks asking for you both to be sent there if you are now fit enough. I guess you both are, so I shall make some travel arrangements for you. You can leave tomorrow. How do you feel about that?"

"Fine, Sir, and thank you for all you have done. But I know I speak for Dumbridge too when I say it has been years since we felt better, we are just a little stiff and rusty. Some drill and exercise will soon put that right!"

He was lying through his teeth, and he knew that the MO knew it too, but it was true: the hospital needed its beds: there were patients coming from all over the battlefields with precious few beds to accommodate them. Stollbright dismissed Enrico by saying, "It is agreed then, Dumbridge and yourself will leave first thing tomorrow morning; maybe you will be given home leave when you get back to Barracks."

Enrico stood to attention, brought his leg sharply down, and gave a fine salute to the Major. Bringing his leg down hard hurt like hell, but he did to show that it was now quite usable.

On returning to the ward he imparted what had passed to Matti, who was happy at the prospect of leaving and getting something more substantial under his belt, and he didn't just mean the work.

"What about a good meal tonight to celebrate?" asked Matti.

"I have it all in hand, but first I must discuss it with Cookie."

"Oh no! Come on, Enrico, we can get something in a restaurant, that's what I had in mind."

"Matti, trust me. My way's going to be fun." Then off Enrico marched to see his Sergeant friend… Cookie Simonne.

Everything was quickly arranged, but Matti was not to know what was up Enrico's sleeve until much later!

Up until eight o'clock that evening Enrico had been out of the ward and Matti had been resting. Matti had eaten dinner as usual, but nobody else in the ward had touched a thing. 'I know it tastes like paperpaste, but it fills the void that a good dump leaves you with. Why am I the only taker in eating this mush? Strange that nobody even got offered anything!' thought Matti, but in his heart of hearts, he knew.

Darkness had fallen; most of the medical staff had left for the night, just a skeleton crew remained to take care of any emergencies that might occur. It was pitch black outside, with absolutely no moon: a dark night for dark deeds.

All of a sudden, in came Enrico dressed completely in black. He was carrying a set of dark overalls which he tossed at Matti.

"Here you go, Matti, put these on and cover up any bare skin."

"Oh no you don't, I thought you were up to no good earlier! Now forget it, if we are caught we could be in serious trouble."

"Then, old fruit, we must not get caught!"

"I won't come; you can take the rap on your own. I mean it, Enrico; I'm not going to catch those bloody fish with you."

"Right, that's understood: so much for friendship, and trust. You promised to keep me from getting hurt, you promised to look out for me until the day I die…you said that, and I have witnesses."

Up came a loud chorus from the rest of the ward's patients. "Yes, you promised, we all heard you!"

"What a load of crap!" laughed Matti. "Well, if we are to do it, let's go."

Outside the hospital was Cookie, waiting with a small Austin car, revving up and trying to keep the engine from stalling. "Quick, jump in! The faster we do this, the better. Anyway, everyone is starving, and I have

389

managed to save some fine potatoes and garden peas, so we can all have a feast."

They drove the mile to Manor Road, turned out the lights and checked very intently to hear and see if anyone was around. All was quiet. Matti and Enrico got out of the car and strolled silently over to the lake within Kelsey Estate; still no sound, just the rustling of the trees, in the cool night air. Enrico had brought a huge blanket that had seen better days, plus an old loaf of bread. They skulked their way across the grass and out onto the wooden pier that stood out into the lake. Enrico knew that what he had to do was first to frighten the fish away, but as they were all used to being fed by the 'Gods', they would soon overcome their anxiety, and the bread would attract them back to the feeding spot. He threw a small stone into the water; some fish moved, most stayed put. He threw another, then another. Now they moved. Holding long lengths of string and tying stones to the corners of the blanket he cast it out into where the fish usually were. It took a little while to sink, but sink it did. Then he started to drop small pieces of bread into the water. At first nothing happened, as the fish had all backed off to safer pastures. Then, after half the loaf was finished, and a good fifteen minutes had passed, the first big beast approached and start-ed to take the bait. After another ten minutes, all the fish were eating away as if nothing had altered within their little world.

"When I say the word, pull the string very carefully, lifting the stretched blanket to the surface. When I say quick, pull it all in."

"Got you!"

"Right, I think there is enough there. Start pulling gently. Right, that's getting it. Crickey, those stupid fish haven't realised yet that they are for the pot. Steady now..."

*Bang!* A loud report sounded, and something scattered across the water surface. Someone had fired a shotgun.

"Oi, you two, don't move or I will be forced to fire at you. I am the game keeper and you two are poachers. Stop right there, the police are on their way."

"Quick, get them up now!" yelled Enrico.

Matti pulled and was surprised at how heavy the blanket had become. "We have caught about a dozen, let's get out of here! That old sod is across the way and it will take him a minute or two to get around here."

They had scooped up their catch and as it all wriggled within their blanket, it felt like a ton weight. They hobbled as quickly as they could, carrying and dragging their ill-gotten gains.

*Bang!* Another shot rang out; this time, much nearer to them. "Christ, man, it would be extreme bad news to get killed here in Blighty after all we have been through," chuckled Enrico, whose bad leg was now beginning to play up again. They got to the car as Cookie was revving up.

"Get this beast out of here. The law is after us," urged Matti.

"Don't panic, we are going."

Five minutes later, and a few pounds of sweat lighter, they all emerged from the car at Balgowan Hospital shaking, more from excitement than fear.

"Well, Cookie, we have done our bit, the rest is up to you."

"Blimey, the whole car smells of fish. They have only been in there five minutes. Don't run away, someone will have to help me clean them, peel the spuds and generally help around the kitchen. There is enough work for both of you, so come on. First let's get the buggers in the kitchen and out of sight of prying eyes."

The eight large fish were killed, cleaned and dressed. Placing rather more salt than one would normally use, rubbing it well into the fish, takes away the muddy taste of carp and gives it more flavour. The potatoes were peeled, the cans of peas opened. Before an hour had passed, the only fine meal ever to come from Balgowan Hospital was presented to the inmates that could still eat something. A huge cheer went up when Matti and Enrico appeared at their ward's door, carrying two huge platters of beautifully cooked locally caught carp. Cookie had spent a couple of pounds of his own money to buy lots of bottles of stout, so that all the participants there would be able to drink to the health of all injured soldiers.

The atmosphere was like a midnight bean feast within a public school, naughty but fun to do. This was to be a fantastic tonic for all the patients, one they would probably never forget. It was well after midnight when all the chores had been completed, and Cookie went home to his wife.

"Blimey, I'll be back in a few hours; no peace for the wicked, eh?"

"Cookie, you're a star: fantastic fun. Well done! I do believe Father Christmas came early this year." Enrico shook Cookie's hand warmly, then so did Matti, who endorsed all that Enrico had just said.

"Just as well we're leaving tomorrow! I don't think it would take that gamekeeper long to work out what happened to his beloved carp, do you?" Matti smiled, and then added "I must write this all to Dawn before I forget it."

# XI

The journey from Beckenham to Finsbury was an easy one. They were special soldiers now: to be presented with the Victoria Cross was the highest honour a country could afford one of its own, so a staff car was sent to pick them up with an officer's chauffeur who seemed to be attached to the steering wheel on a permanent basis. Not once did he lower himself to stand to attention, open the doors or even acknowledge the occupants in the rear of the vehicle. This annoyed Enrico beyond reason.

"That Private is a bloody snob!" he complained to Matti. So as a Sergeant, he ordered the driver to first take them to Trafalgar Square, and when they arrived there, he ordered him to stop just below the statue of Lord Nelson. "Right, Private, out of the car. We're going to see how good your close order drill is." A squeak of a protest started from the driver's throat, but Enrico was having none of it. He marched him under the statue, made him look up. "Salute the officer," barked Sergeant Caruso. "About turn, left right, left right quick march. About face, left right, left right. Slow march. Halt!"

This went on for a good five minutes; by now a large gathering of onlookers had collected, really in amazement as to what the heck was going on. 'Is this all that is left of our army?' were the general amused thoughts. "Pretend you have a gun. Slope arms. Order arms. Right, stand at ease, ready for inspection. Sloppy lad! Show me your nails... Just as I thought, chewed and dirty. Look at that crease in your trousers, very poor! Corporal Dumbridge, take this man's name."

Matti could hardly contain himself, and spluttered out. "Name..."

"Private Jones, Corporal," came the almost tearful reply.

"Can you drive that vehicle?" barked Enrico, with his face not more than four inches away from the luckless Private.

"Yes, Sir, I mean Sergeant!"

"Then let's see you do it, and this time as you should have done."

Private Jones rushed at a pace to get to the car. He stood there to attention, and as the lads approached opened the door for them, then closed it when they got in.

"Much better, I think we can drop the firing squad after all, Corporal Dumbridge."

Matti, nearly in tears with laughter, said "Oh! I wanted to give the order to fire, you promised!"


There, coming into view, were the imposing gates of Finsbury Barracks. Private Jones drove right up to the doors to the main building, stopped the car, jumped out, opened the back door and stood to attention, with eyes front. Out of the car stepped Sergeant Enrico Caruso and Corporal Matthew Dumbridge. Enrico winked at the still shaken Jones.

"You'll do alright, boy, but just remember, that when an officer goes for a dump, his shit smells as bad as everybody else's. Which means, my boy," coming from Enrico this sounded more than a little affected, as he was at least ten years younger than the officer's chauffeur, "that officers are just flesh and blood, like everybody else, and everybody deserves respect, unless they have proven otherwise."

"Yes, Sergeant, sorry, Sergeant."

It was a curious feeling, entering the barracks once again. This time around, the building did not seem to be so big or imposing, and it certainly was going to be strange, with a new Colonel since the demise of Colonel McBride. The new Colonel, a John Barnes, was a middle-aged career soldier, who had had a public school education which had culminated in him

394

receiving a first in Ancient History at King's College, Oxford. He was a very shrewd man who did not waste human life, and this being understood, made him popular with his subordinates. There, in front of the Colonel's office, stood the two lads, looking at the nameplate on the door, and remembering this man's predecessor with more than a little affection. They knocked on the door.

In a very deep and authoritative voice came the order: "Come in!" They entered the office to see this balding, rather large, bespectacled figure, completely alien to what they were expecting, looking over the top of his glasses at them. Realisation dawned on John Barnes, and a broad smile, showing less than perfect teeth, stained brown from years of pipe smoking, illuminated his face. The two lads stood to attention, but Colonel Barnes rose to greet them, and shook their hands warmly.

"Sergeant Caruso, Corporal Dumbridge, I presume? Welcome back to your old habitat! Must seem strange after all this time to be back here!"

Still standing to attention, the lads visibly relaxed.

"Yes, Sir, it is strange to be back; a lot of water has passed under the bridge since our basic training was here," said Enrico.

"Indeed, Sergeant, you can say that! I have your files on the table in front of me right now! You two have proved to be heroes, which has brought great credit to the Battalion, but now life is going to be a bit easier for you both, as we want NCOs to be able to train the raw recruits as they come in, and believe me, that's not going to be a picnic, as they come by the tens of thousands! Now, I have been advised by a higher authority, that you both might like to have some leave, and I will be very happy to give you both a ten day pass."

Matti's eyes lit up. 'Maybe I can get back to Calais to spend a few days with Dawn!' then he added to the Colonel: "Sir, I have a sweetheart in France. Do you think it would be possible for me to go back to spend some time with her?"

"I'm sorry to say that only essential personnel are allowed on the ferries, so I have to say it's rather out of the question. What about going to visit relatives in this country?"

"I've never had so much as a word from mum and dad, so maybe I should go and visit them."

"And you, Sergeant?"

"No, Sir. I don't want any leave. I have no family, and quite honestly, I'd sooner get on with the work now."

"Well, Corporal, you have ten days home leave. Enjoy yourself. When you come back, maybe I can get you two to give a little talk in the officers' mess about your exploits in the trenches."

"Sir, I can assure you that there is nothing remarkable about what happened with Corporal Dumbridge and me. Any one of the soldiers who were with us, would have, or did perform, as we did. The truth is, Sir, that Corporal Dumbridge and I really don't want any publicity for what happened in Belgium and France. We both saw soldiers that deserved more credit than we are getting for real heroic deeds, but they were overlooked, maybe because they were killed in action. We just happened to be in the wrong place at the right time. We are not heroes, just survivors."

"I have to second that, Sir," said Matti, trying hard to emphasise the point for Enrico.

"Well, I am sure that what you say may be true, but heroes are made up of people doing courageous things which are not their norm. Whether you like it or not, you are both heroes. Accept it and be pleased. But I will relent on embarrassing you both in the officers' mess."

"Thank you, Sir; I'm glad that we have cleared that up. I would like very much to have just a couple of days off, say until Monday of next week, then I'd like to get right into whatever you have in mind for me."

"That applies to me too, Sir, if that's alright with you?" said Matti, following in his friend's footsteps once more.

"Of course. You are both dismissed until nine o'clock Monday morning. We will keep you both extremely busy after that. And thank you for your frankness. Now go get your trains, I have work to do. Take my car, but only this once, so enjoy it while you can."

"Thank you very much, Sir," said Enrico. They both stood sharply to attention and saluted their new Colonel.

On leaving Colonel Barnes, the lads decided it was time to have a beer or two before thinking of going north to Tranmere. They made their way to the Sergeants' mess, and there, large as life, drinking a beer with a whiskey chaser was Sergeant Harrington.

"My God! Look who has made it back to Blighty!" said Harrington, nearly choking on his drinks. "When did you two get back?"

"We have just arrived to meet Colonel Barnes, seems a decent sort. We are now going on leave until Monday; four days is just about enough for us two," said Enrico, who was looking at Sergeant Harrington with a rather shocked expression.

"I know, I have gained a little weight, but will soon lose that. Lost my hair too, but sadly that is gone forever. And before you say it, I am not drinking too much, just a small pick-me-up to get through the day, nothing serious," he slurred, and he knew he was fooling no one. "I heard on the grapevine that you two had performed rather well out there. Was it bad?"

"It was worse than bad. We have seen and done things no man should ever have to do. Speaking for myself," said Enrico "I'm happy to be back in Blighty. Though I somehow think we will all be back out there before this war is over."

With these last words, Harrington visibly shuddered, and the shaking of his hands was there for everyone to see.

"Can I buy you boys a drink?" he said.

"Just the one beer is fine, we must leave after that. Have you heard from 'Spider' Kelly lately?" enquired Matti, with real concern in his voice.

"No, not a word, I think he has forgotten me. Maybe he has bought one."

"Not that old sod. We saw him in Calais just before we got hospitalised in England, he was fine. He cares for all his men, he's a good man, and I like him. He's also one of the biggest bastards I know, but I'm glad he's on our side." As Enrico finished saying these words about his friend Kelly the three of them burst out into spontaneous laughter.

"Yes," agreed Harrington "I guess you're right, he is an arsehole of the first order, but the best one to know in trouble. I liked him too."

They had their drink of beer, agreed to return the favour after Monday, left the mess to look for Private Jones once more, and then got a train up to Tranmere.

They arrived at Matti's home very late, and once again Enrico had to spend the night on the floor, before going on to visit Father Lyon. The priest was happy to see him and insisted that he sleep in the manse without any arguments. Enrico spent the time wandering around Liverpool, went to the flicks to see a comic silent movie, but he knew this was never going to be his city again, and vowed that this would be his last visit there. 'A brand new start in life, that's what is needed,' thought Enrico. 'When this bloody war is over, I'm going to find that ship to America, I will take my inheritance and make that new beginning that mum and dad so wanted for us all. This time, there will be no mishaps, just a complete change.'

Matti's homecoming was tinged again with sadness. His brother John who was in the Royal Engineers had been killed in the Battle of the Somme. Matti felt great guilt for not finding him as he had been quite close by, but he told his grieving mother that he would find the grave and make sure that there were flowers on it. His father had sunk into a far deeper depression and didn't even recognise Matti when he came through the door. He was aging so fast, and had become so thin, that nobody expected him to live much longer. For Matti, this was a very sad homecoming, he couldn't even tell his mother about Dawn. 'I should have taken my chances and tried to get back to France. Seeing and being with Dawn is all I need now. I will ask her to marry me when we next see one another.'

The lads had agreed to meet early Sunday morning at the railway station, so that they could be back at the Barracks early enough not to think about the Monday morning start. The army was their life now. They were both good soldiers, and they knew it. Actually, life in the army for Enrico and Matti had been hard but fair. The bull that had been inflicted as part of their own training had stood them in good stead. Now they were going to pass this knowledge on to other recruits, with the hope that they just may make men out of boys, men to finish the job that had been started in 1914. But without doubt, the raw recruits were much younger than the volunteers they had enlisted with, just a couple of years ago. Some of these boys were just out of school or college, knowing nothing of life and yet ready to give up their existence before their lives had started. It was Matti and Enrico's job to give them a fighting chance, and it would not be easy. Once in the trenches on a fighting front, life expectancy was shortened by inexperience.

Monday came to the barracks, along with rain and cold; winter was setting in with a vengeance. The weather was starting to make one think that God was on the side of Fritz. The lads reported to Colonel Barnes dead on the stroke of nine o'clock.

"Good morning, Sergeant! Did you both have a nice week?"

"Yes, Sir," lied both the boys.

"Sometime this morning, we will be getting about a hundred new recruits. I want you both to take them through their paces, and then starting to-morrow, I want you to arrange proper training sessions. I have here," said the Colonel, as he passed two army manuals to the lads, "two training manuals. I want you to spend the time until the recruits arrive, reading through them, and making plans of action. Any questions?"

"Yes, Sir, one. How long do we have for the training?"

"Precious little time. Basic training will only be six weeks, and then they will be passed on to field training, which will include the use of new weapons, and we will be looking for drivers for the Mark IV and Mark V tanks that are being produced. Things are moving fast, we have to meet the challenge, and that is where the NCOs come in."

Enrico and Matti were dismissed; they adjourned to the Sergeants' mess where they once again found Sergeant Harrington, slumped over an empty glass, sound asleep and snoring gently.

"My God, the fellow's heading for a breakdown! Just as well he's not at the front; he would have fallen apart completely."

"Look at his face, Enrico. It's almost crimson, surely that can't be right!"

"I would not have thought so, anyway, enough of him! I think we'd better start reading."

For the next three hours, they worked together to formulate a plan of action for whipping raw recruits into fighting soldiers. They thought they would have a spot of lunch before the new batch arrived; it was Matti who noticed it first, as he looked at Sergeant Harrington. He could hear him breathing, but the breathing did not sound right, and his face and neck were completely purple.

"Oh, my God, Matti! He looks awful! I think we must get the MO immediately."

The doctor was duly summoned; with a sense of déjà-vu they watched Doctor Bennett approach as he went straight to Sergeant Harrington.

"Quick, lads! Get the orderlies to bring a stretcher. I thought this might happen, and I think Harrington has had a massive stroke."

Enrico ran to find the orderlies; they brought the stretcher, to find Major Bennett with two fingers on the side of Harrington's throat, trying to find a pulse. He stepped aside to let Harrington be lifted onto the stretcher, and taken to the infirmary. Just as the latter was taken away, Private Jones came in with a message from Colonel Barnes, to say that the recruits had arrived. Enrico and Matti smartened themselves up, and quickly used the back of their trousers to polish their footwear. Once at the entrance, they found approximately a hundred young men milling about. The veins in Enrico's throat bulged angrily, as he screamed the word: "Atten… shon!" at the top of his voice. The milling stopped, and startled youthful faces looked bewildered in the direction of the voice.

"My name is Sergeant Caruso, and this is Corporal Dumbridge. You call me Sergeant, and you jump to attention before you do so; likewise to Corporal Dumbridge. Just remember, you are in the army now; you don't think, you just obey! Remember my word is Gospel! And if you need anything, you come and ask me, so that I can say 'no'! Right, right!" he barked once again, "I want you to line up in four equal lines, and do it quickly! Now!"

The young men threw themselves eagerly into action, trying to appease the screaming Sergeant, but it seemed impossible for them to work out how many should be in each line.

"What a fucking shower! Have you ever seen anything as bad as this, Corporal Dumbridge?"

"No, Sergeant, they're bloody awful! I don't think any of them have got any fathers, because they don't know what discipline is! But we will teach them, won't we, Sergeant?"

"Yes, Corporal, we'll show the little bastards, and we'll teach them that this 'ere army is run by us NCOs, so we are the ones they've got to fear! Don't worry about the Generals; it's us you've got to worry about!"

Enrico and Matti spent the next hour, trying to get the recruits into four orderly lines, and each time that a mistake was made, the whole platoon would be made to do twenty press-ups, which was quite impossible for many of the young men. It was cold and wet, and at the end of that hour, the young men already wished they had never thought about joining up! Then Enrico relented, and led them all to the canteen. As he did so, he gave each man a number to remember. They were given several slices of bread, and a bowl of thick vegetable soup. Sergeant Caruso spoke once more to the men: "You have half an hour to eat your lunch, then we will split you into two groups; one group goes to the MO, while the other gets an estimate for a haircut. Odd numbers, MO, even, haircut. Then when that's complete, we change over. Then after that, you will get your uniform and bed, and we will show you how we expect you to keep your things tidy and clean. Then first thing tomorrow morning, at 05.30 you will be woken by reveille. Breakfast is at six, exercise and drill at 6.30."

He left them to finish their food.

Time passed quickly for the recruits. New experiences, so much to take in. For Enrico and Matti, this was also a time for discovery. Teaching boys to be men, teaching them to destroy other beings, who probably felt exactly the same as they did; this was going to be a tough project to fulfil.

The training of the recruits became a routine of exercise, drill and bull. Generally speaking, the work was long and hard, with very little time for the young men to have for themselves, the idea being that you turned the new soldiers into machines, more scared of the officers and NCOs than the enemy that they would soon have to face. Never give a recruit a chance to philosophise about the war, keep it black and white. The British, French and Belgians were the goodies, Germans and Austrians and Turks were the evil baddies. After all, every padre would tell you 'God is on our side!'

Days of training turned into weeks; they were no longer clumsy recruits who did not know their left from their right; when an order was given, they jumped to it with a will.

It was the second week of December, and the order had come through from the Palace that one Sergeant Enrico Caruso and one Corporal Matthew Dumbridge should present themselves at the Palace gates, not later than ten a.m. Friday the 18th of December 1916, whereupon each of them would be awarded the Victoria Cross for bravery above and beyond the call of duty. The citation read: — 'That while the rest of their detachment of men had either been killed, or driven back by the enemy, Sergeant Caruso and Corporal Dumbridge had, under their own volition, captured a German machine gun post and held off an attack of the enemy, killing and wounding at least fifteen Germans; holding their position, without any thought of a retreat, they stayed fighting for three days, and when relieved, after a counterattack by the London Northern Rifle Brigade, were found to be seriously wounded.'

The whole of Finsbury Barracks buzzed with the pride that the award was going to bring to the Battalion. Enrico and Matti were far less enthusiastic and still feared that any publicity could get back to Tranmere, and it would not take long for the police to put two and two together. Colonel Barnes strutted around like a male peacock during the mating season; his chest was so extended that if he breathed in, he would explode. He was so proud to be the Commander of two such young VC winners that he was for ever doing special ceremonial parades, so that any medals having been won could be displayed for all to see, and as Enrico was already a recipient of the Military Cross, he was required to stand at the head of his men. The next two days were spent rehearsing, so that the pair would know exactly how to present themselves, when introduced to King George V. Learning how to bow when backing out of the presence of their monarch proved very difficult for both Enrico and Matti, but after several failed attempts, Colonel Barnes personally showed them how to do it.

"When you bow, Sergeant, it just is at an angle of forty-five degrees, never so far that you are going to fall over, and then when you take steps backwards, you can do so with just your head slightly bowed. Never, and I emphasize never, turn your back on the King! That would be very bad form. If the King deigns to speak to you, make your answers succinct and to the point. Now, let's try that again." Soon the duo was word perfect, and could bow and scrape along with the best of them.

The big day came, and Private Jones was there with the Colonel's staff car. This time he stood to attention, and proceeded to open the back door for the two NCOs.

"Private Jones, how nice to see you! So how do we look? Are we smart enough for the King?"

A broad smile came over the chauffeur's countenance.

"Sergeant and Corporal, you both shimmer in the delight of this sunny day!" he retorted in a sarcastic manner, to which both the lads laughed heartily.

"You'll do for me, lad!" chortled Enrico.

They reached the Palace gates, almost an hour too early, and were informed by the guard that it would be a better proposition to go for a drive around Hyde Park, as it was bad to arrive too early, just as bad as it was to arrive too late: present yourself on time.

It was a beautiful sunny day, and for once London seemed clean, though this would probably have more to do with the cold. As they drove around Hyde Park, the grass was white from frost, and it was a pleasure to see young people, taking advantage of the ice on the ground, and making a slide of it. There was movement, laughter, and gaiety, and it all was a million miles away from the Ypres Salient. As they drove past the Serpentine, the water was frozen on the edges, and it was a delight for the lads to watch the ducks waddling across the ice and losing their balance before reaching open water. Presently the car reached Speaker's Corner, which immediately took the lads back to their first visit to the capital, but all too soon, they had to speed up, this time to make sure that they were there at the gates for ten o'clock. They were ushered in with several other fighting men into one of the antechambers, and there for their pleasure, were canapés and soft drinks. The first to be presented was Major Cudgeon, who had been severely wounded, but still managed to capture a section of German trench, and personally shot and killed six enemy defenders, also taking charge of enemy mortars, turning them and using them against the reserve trench. Because of his action, it was thought that a counterattack, which was just about to happen was foiled, and in the process of his heroics, the wound in his left arm turned gangrenous, and it had to be removed. Thus it was that he won the VC. The second to be presented was Second Lieutenant Parker, who before he joined the Marines, had been an eminent landscape painter; a very unlikely hero, yet while making the rush across no-man's-land, in the first wave of the battle of the Somme, he had been wounded twice, but still managed to get to his feet and beckoned to his troops to follow him. He finally fell from loss of blood, when he and twelve other men broke through the enemy wire to gain a foothold in the enemy's trench. Even when he was prone on the trench floor, he fired his service revolver, and killed two enemies who were heading a counterattack. For this gallantry, he too, received the VC.

Soon it was Matti's and Enrico's turn, and when the doors were opened for them, they marched smartly up to the line indicated, and stood to attention. Beads of sweat started to show themselves on the lad's faces. This was proving to be a lot harder than fighting the Hun in enemy territory. King George V was a slight man, and in the eyes of the duo, a more unlikely royal there never was. In Matti's eyes, the King would have been more suited as a librarian than the head of the biggest empire the world has ever known. Their citations were read out by the King's Adjutant, who then handed the medals for the King to pin on their tunics.

"Were your wounds bad?" asked the King to both the boys.

"Yes, your Majesty. We had shrapnel in our legs from stick grenades," replied Enrico, who then looked at Matti, visibly relaxing, and added: "Yes, your Majesty, and they 'urt like bloody 'ell!" To which King George V beamed gleefully, and burst into laughter. The moment was all too soon over, and as they had been prompted by Colonel Barnes, they did their perfect forty-five degree angle bow, and backed off in precision to the open door. Once back in the anteroom, their heads swelled with pride, as they enjoyed the adventure. All good things come to an end, and before they knew it, they were back at Finsbury Barracks, and this would drift into yesterday's memory, as the real world came thundering back.

Christmas came and Matti was allowed four days' leave, and this time arrangements had been made, so that he could spend two days in Calais. Seeing Dawn again had been a very special experience for him; he had declared his love, but more importantly, she had reciprocated in kind. Enrico had spent Christmas with his friends at the barracks, and though the weather had been appalling with extreme cold, sleet and snow, anything was better than the trenches where the poor devils were dying of frostbite, trenchfoot, influenza, not to forget bullets and bombs.

At the front it was a far cry from 1914, when a truce had been held; now any sounds of Christmas joy were answered by sixty pounder shells and Mills bombs. So for Enrico, drinking beer and having hot food was a bonus almost beyond words. Safety from enemy fire and the elements was something that he was starting to get used to.

All too soon, Matti was back, beaming from ear to ear. When alone with Enrico, he blurted out the news: "Enrico, I have proposed to Dawn, and she has accepted!"

"I'm a little confused about all of this. I want you to be happy, of course, but have you told her your real age? And I'm sure you haven't told her our troubles up in Darwen. After all, how could you marry a girl if we were to be arrested? She could be a widow before she knows it: we may yet end up on the gallows. The police won't forgive and forget, and the fact that we are supposed to be war heroes won't make a blind bit of difference. If they find out who we are, we are done for!"

"Oh, Christ! I came home with such high hopes, and you have brought me right down! I don't know what to do. All I know is that I love Dawn, and she loves me."

"Have you some sort of date in mind for a wedding?"

"Well, no. We're still in the army, and we're committed until this war finishes. Though to tell you the truth, Enrico, I'm seriously thinking of staying on."

"Yes, it's crossed my mind, too, and it does seem that we have found a profession we're good at. I'm very glad that you are not rushing this wedding."

At that moment Colonel Barnes came into the Sergeants' mess. "Ah, the very two I am looking for! I wanted to ask whether you two would be interested in recruiting volunteers to become tank crews."

Matti looked at Enrico, and when Enrico's eyebrows raised, he answered for both of them: "Sir, I think it is a capital idea!" and as Enrico was nodding in agreement, he continued: "Both Sergeant Caruso and myself have been talking about staying on in the army when the war is over, and as the future seems to be in this new weapon, the tank, it might be a good idea to get in at the bottom."

"Good news, good news!" exclaimed the Colonel.

It was not until the end of January 1917 that the transfer orders came through for Enrico, Matti and twenty-two other volunteers to report to Bovington Barracks in Dorset. They were going to be trained in the new art of crewing tanks. Tanks had already been used in battles and it was Winston Churchill, being the first Lord of the Admiralty, who had seen the potential of this new weapon. The Mark I prototype had been used to take the town of Fleur during the battle of the Somme, and General Haig had been quick to realise that, had he had hundreds of these lumbering beasts, the army would have broken through the lines much more easily. For the Germans the appearance of iron monsters, which seemed impervious to machine gun and rifle fire, was likened to some hellish creature from Götterdammerung, but after the initial shock the German officer class soon realised that petrol-driven machines could easily blow up, and mortars and cannon fire were used to stop them.

On Monday the 1st February, the new squad of men, under the leadership of Sergeant Caruso reported to Major Brookes for their first day of training.

"We are going to keep all of you together, and you will all have a

Second Lieutenant who will be in charge of each vehicle. We expect the training to last two months, by which time, each of you will be able to steer and shoot, and you will all understand the workings of the combustion engine, and when necessary change tracks on the tank. I don't need to tell you that each of these vehicles has cost many thousands of pounds of taxpayers' money, and we will not tolerate any slovenly behaviour. You will treat these vehicles as if your life depended on them, and in the height of battle, that is of course the absolute truth!"

At Bovington Barracks there were eight hundred new recruits, who would crew the hundred new Mark IV tanks, and the plan was that by June, there would be another two hundred of these land ships ready for use. There were two sorts of tanks available, the male and the female. The male was different by the simple fact that it sported two six pounder cannons, one on each side. The female, by contrast, had machine guns mounted on each side instead of cannons. The trouble with the cannons was that to fire them with any sort of accuracy, the vehicle needed to be standing still. The machine gun sprayed bullets everywhere anyway, and as the task of tanks was to cause as much mayhem as possible, the machine guns won the day. Better to kill the enemy than to take aim at certain targets, which the six pounder was probably not going to destroy anyway.

It took a crew of eight to successfully drive and shoot from the MK IV: two gunners, two steerers, two brakemen, an engineer for the workings of the engine, and lastly the Lieutenant whose job it was to coordinate all the workings of the huge twenty-eight ton monster. One of the major problems facing the men was that the engine that drove the tank was seriously underpowered, so much so that it was constantly breaking down. The noise from the engine was terrible: men had quite literally to stand next to the person they wished to speak to and shout in his ear. Not a lot of fun if you were under fire. The fumes from the motor would soon fill the tank and it didn't take long before men were passing out from the poisonous infill of carbon monoxide.

The top speed, on a good day with the wind behind you, was no more than three miles an hour; any rough terrain and the beast came to an absolute crawl. Going in and out of craters was an awful nightmare for the crew as the tilt of the machine would throw them and anything loose around like a cork in rough sea. There had been cases of gunners of the six pounders dropping a shell in the upheaval of being thrown from pillar to post, and in some extreme cases the shells had exploded, killing all inside the tank concerned. Another problem was the tracks, which completely enveloped and sandwiched the vehicles compartment; these tracks were prone to breaking, and when they did, it presented the crew with an awful predicament. And as sod's law always applied, these tracks would invariably break during a battle, thus making the tank a sitting target, or a vehicle to abandon, once disarmed.

But there were good points too. The fear that it put into the foe, once seen, was worth most of the troubles; it was also the only thing that could be sure of creating a way through the barbed wire. The infantry could follow close in the rear and just jump over the debris left by the lumbering monster. They could also traverse trenches, often straddling over them and machine gunning the luckless occupants while doing so. Haig knew these would be the answer to the stalemate, if ever there was going to be enough of them.

Another downside for the crew was that at first, machine gun bullets just indented the sides and front, but that dent would cause splinters of metal to shear off on the inside, often causing terrible wounds. This was quickly overcome by giving the occupants a form of chain mail to wear: the splinters would not pass through this mail. But Fritz was a wily bird, and soon learnt how to produce armour piercing bullets and shells, then the troubles for the crew grew tenfold. Once a shell hit, and passed inside, there was little chance of any of the crew surviving.

Training was a hard, severe test to all that took part. There was not one facet of the workings of the tank that any of the crew did not master.

Everyone, given time and tools, could dismantle the engine completely and rebuild it again. All learnt how to use the weapons to a standard of perfection; after all, being able to shoot could in the long run save theirs and others' lives. If any member of the crew was disabled for any reason, another member could take his place. But all of this took time, and time in war was a precious commodity. Tactics were taught to all, not just the tank commander; any member of the crew had to be able to know where they were going and what the objective of the journey was. It was not long before the Lieutenants, NCOs and other ranks became like families, all for one and one for all. Thus it was for Matti and Enrico too. Sadly for the two lads, they were to be apart, crewing in different vehicles. The hierarchy decided that only one NCO per vehicle was necessary; so for the first time, since early childhood the two friends were separated, though still in the same Battalion. In fact, Matti made sure that whoever was commanding his tank would always be close by to Enrico, never to be out of eyeshot.

The weeks turned into months, and gradually everyone knew exactly what their role would be in whatever battle they were to be placed in. They had all become tank enthusiasts, moulding themselves into fighting machines, and even believing that they could have a major role in winning the war, not just a battle. Their enthusiasm knew no bounds, and they were all eager to get back across the Channel and into the fray again, especially for Enrico and Matti, who never felt comfortable being in England, always nervous that a knock on the door would come, with a policeman standing, offering up a charge to them both. No, they wanted to get across to France as quickly as anyone else, maybe more so. And of course, the war had not stood still since they had arrived back in Blighty. Things had been going on, even without them.

On April 9th 1917 Canadian troops attacked one of the strongest German defensive positions in France, Vimy Ridge just north of the town of Arras. They had planned the attack meticulously, and by the means of digging tunnels that could be opened up just before the German trenches, they managed a spectacular surprise on the Hun. By midday of the 9th the Canadians had managed to take most of the German-held front. The only stumbling block had been Hill 145, which was still in German hands, and of course overlooked all that had been taken, which made it a major strategic point to be captured; but that too fell the next day. The enemy had suffered more than twenty thousand casualties, whereas the Canadians lost less than half of that. So things were beginning to look up for the Allies, albeit at a terrible cost in human life.

On the 7th of June the third battle of Ypres had started. General Haig was desperate for a clear-cut win, one that could show the politicians back home in London that his way of war was bringing results, something that Prime Minister Lloyd George seriously doubted, as he believed that a change of army chief might well be what was needed.

On the 7th June the opening salvo of what became known as the third battle of Ypres started with the capture of the Messines Ridge, just south of Ypres. This Ridge was taken by exploding nineteen mines, which had been dug and laid over the last two years; one of these was the tunnel that Enrico and Matti had been involved in the digging of. The mines were exploded in the morning, and within three hours the entire German position along the Messines Ridge had been taken. The explosions were feared by scientists, even back in London, as they thought it might make a tidal wave in the Channel big enough to flood London. Instead, when the mines did erupt, Paris thought that an earthquake was occurring, windows in Lille were blown in, and the rumble was felt and heard all over the south of England. But it did the trick. More than ten thousand enemy soldiers were killed or seriously maimed by the force of the blasts. The soldiers who survived were so traumatised by their experience that they just stood around and waited for the British to come and take them into captivity.

When the British did advance onto the devastated Ridge, it was with the help of a creeping barrage, something that, had it been used earlier, could have saved many Allied lives. In 1917, the artillery had grid referenced the entire front line, so that accuracy of fire could and was maintained. For the British, this was probably the first real victory in the conflict up to this time. The big problem was to come afterwards, when the victory had sunk into the minds of the politicians and the Generals. Why did General Haig and the other Generals not plan for a victory, for when it came as in Messines, they were once again completely unprepared. They should have taken the next step and driven straight on to take Passchendaele Ridge, then driving the Hun onto the coast, taking Ostende and Zeebrugge, capturing the U-boat pens, which were a huge thorn in the side of the British. But alas, as usual, the army stood their ground on what had been achieved, and never moved into another attack mode until the German army had regrouped and rearmed. General Sir Douglas Haig and all his entourage were of course not entirely at fault: when you have had so many stalemates, why would you seriously expect anything other than yet another one? When the army was ready for its next advance, it would turn into the greatest slaughter of all time.

The battle of Passchendaele Ridge started on the 21st July 1917, with a ten day bombardment with the use of three thousand guns of all calibre. The shelling was so fierce that it was later estimated that five tons of explosive shells had been hurled at every yard of the front. Day and night, without a moment's break, the shelling continued. The defenders were sent crazy with the noise and explosions. From the air, which Britain now had complete control of, there was absolutely nothing to show that a town with streets had ever been there. Then on the 31st July at 03.50 a.m., the troops started to move forward to attack the Ridge. But as in most of the battles before, the Hun had had plenty of time to regroup and dig in. To make matters worse for the attackers, the moment the whistles blew for the attack, the rain started to pour down. Being a low lying country and with a fragile drainage system destroyed by three years of shelling, Flanders began to flood.

Duckboarding was placed down for the troops to walk on, but if for any reason a man fell off one of the boards, he might well fall into a flooded shell hole, and he was just as quickly sucked under and drowned. In spite of the lines of men stretching for miles, no one was allowed to help him back onto the walkway: anyone who tried would be holding up the rest, and the offender was liable to be shot by an officer on the spot. Many men died long before they reached the attacking area.

But the Germans had not just sat back and waited to be overrun like at Messines Ridge; this time they intended to be counted and fought to the bitter end. It was not until the 10th November, that the 2nd Canadian Division finally occupied what had once been the town of Passchendaele, and the blood bath was considered to be at an end. Lt. General Sir Launcelot Kiggel, Haig's Chief of Staff visited the troops at the front after the battle was concluded. On witnessing the conditions, he was seen to burst into tears, and was heard to say "Good God! Did we really send men into this hellhole to fight?" Even General Sir Douglas Haig seemed appalled at the amount of casualties that the British had sustained over the sixteen weeks it had taken to capture the Ridge. It was estimated that thirteen British soldiers had died for every yard of soil taken. More than three hundred thousand had lost their lives, and more than two hundred and sixty thousand Germans died there too. On the 10th November, the rain stopped.

In London, the Prime Minister Lloyd George, could hardly contain himself with the rage he felt for the loss of life. But nevertheless, it was considered unwise to change the head of the army, even with these awful mounting losses. With the slaughter on the Somme and now Passchendaele, the fine youth of England and the Commonwealth was depleted; nearly a whole generation had just disappeared under the mud of Flanders Fields.

This had finally become 'The War To End All Wars.'

Passchendaele was at last another victory, though at such a cost that no further thought was given to taking the ports of the Channel, and ending the U-boat menace. But Haig needed another victory, one that should not cost lives: an attack in an area that was vulnerable, one that could possibly be easily overrun. There was such a place near the Somme, an area well defended by the newly constructed Hindenburg Line, a German line of defence thought to be impregnable. It might have appeared impregnable, but it was grossly undermanned. In fact, as the British GHQ learnt through a luckless German prisoner, it was manned by the aged remnants of Germany's army and was thus called the 'Geriatrics Posting Place'. This new battle was going to be at Cambrai.

By the end of August 1917, Enrico, Matti and the hundreds of other tank crews, were getting themselves prepared for a journey. Everyone was proficient in anything to do with male or female MK IV tanks. These weapons simply shone, not just for pride's sake, but out of that feeling that people can get for inanimate objects: they become things of great sentimental attachment, almost greater than the feeling for other people around them. So there were more than a hundred shining tanks, just as if they had been delivered from the factory that day. Each tank had been named as well as numbered, often being called after loved ones. Enrico's tank was called 'Deborah'; Matti's vehicle being named 'Dawn' would make one think that he had had something to do with the naming… On August the 28th, three trains had pulled into the nearest spur junction to Bovington; they were pulling nothing but low lying open wagons. It took two days just to load the trains, and on more than one occasion, there was nearly a serious accident when the tank would not respond to the driver's command and nearly went over the wagon onto the next line. But eventually, the train was loaded, and all the men said their farewells to the barracks and prepared themselves for the next phase. They had been trained well, so by definition knew all the pitfalls too. They understood how much things might depend on them in any future battles, and they made no excuses for their inadequate Leviathans, with their ridiculously underpowered engines. They were there to nurse these monsters through whatever problems might befall them; they would *not* be letting any infantry down for whatever reason.

It took three trains to tote the hundred MK IV tanks, three enormous lumbering workhorses, puffing black smoke from their stacks, straining hard to get that first traction with the rails, and start that complicated journey around the south of England, firstly to avoid low bridges, but also to keep the contents that they carried from public gaze. All the tanks were covered with tarpaulin, but it would take a dolt not to be aware that something special was passing by, if one happened to be near.

All the crews had to help with the loading, covering and tying down. Then the men positioned themselves around their particular vehicle, for what was going to be a very uncomfortable journey. Normally, a train journey from there to Newhaven would take less than two hours; this time it took almost eight hours, as it twisted and weaved around the south coast avoiding hazards. When they finally pulled into the dock area of Newhaven, it was early morning of the 1st September. Unloading was much quicker, taking just a couple of hours, but by the time this was completed, the entire dock area was awash with metal beasts. The waiting period was only minutes before the loading onto special cargo ships started. Now the men could relax for a while, as this loading could only be done by Dockers. Some hours later, when the first ship had been loaded, names were called for the appropriate crew members to board, along with their iron charges. Enrico was on that first shipment; as the ship steamed out into the open sea, two things hit him; one, this was the first time that he had done something without his friend Matti, and though it had only been minutes since he had waved goodbye, he already felt a cold loneliness creep over him. Two, as the ship weighed anchor, a second batch of trains was pulling into the vacated sidings, also carrying a huge load of tanks. This really surprised him, as there had been no mention of yet more armour being made or trained elsewhere in the country; he had wrongly assumed that they commanded the only tanks that there were. 'How many are there, what is this all about?' wondered Enrico, scratching his now unshaven chin. 'I need a bath and a shave.'

It took seven and a half hours of continuous zig-zagging before the first ship docked at Dunkerque. The zigzagging was carried out as normal naval wartime manoeuvres, firstly to avoid rogue U-boats that may be lurking within the Channel, and secondly, as there were distinct routes that a ship had to follow to avoid minefields. In the time that it took from Newhaven to Dunkerque, Enrico had had time to facilitate the three Ss: shit, shower, shave. And though it was a crisp, cold day, the sun shimmered on the millpond-like sea, which gave a chance for many of the soldiers to lie upon the deck and rest.

Once in Dunkerque, the tanks were discharged immediately, and were once again loaded onto trains for yet another onward journey. This time the loading was much quicker than at the barracks, but nevertheless everybody was on high alert, as there had been a Zeppelin raid the previous day. Gradually, ship after ship docked with no incidents whatsoever, and unknown to Enrico, who had long since departed with his crew and tank, there had been more than five hundred and forty armed vehicles brought to France. Now they had to be distributed to various sectors, and hidden from prying eyes. Generally each tank was camouflaged to resemble a huge pile of bricks, so that if any passing German plane should spot it, it looked innocuous.

How quickly had Enrico forgotten the general hubbub and noise of war! And now back in France, the guns could be heard once more. Enrico's thoughts dwelt upon past memories and those friends who had all gone west: Thomas 'Hill Billy' Hill, Harold 'Harry' Gimson, Robert 'Bob' Gregg, William 'Scottie' Scott, Martin 'Jimmy' Riddle, Richard Allen, Barry

Knight, John Hutton, John Smyth, Stanley 'Whitey Boy' White, and Brian Baxter. They had all been close friends, but now gone sadly the way of all flesh; and he thought 'what has become of the little Jew Maurice Bechstein, and our special friend 'Spider' Kelly?' Now that the original recruits to the London Northern Rifle Brigade had been killed, what had happened to the Brigade itself? Were the surviving troops scattered like the four winds to other units and brigades, maybe not even aware of its proud history that had unfolded, over the last couple of hundred years?

This melancholy feeling had crept over Enrico, brought upon by the simple truth that he felt alone, no longer having the close proximity of his chum, Matti.

Second Lieutenant Frank Heap, who was the Commander of 'Deborah', had become very easy with his crew, whom he now thought of as an extended family.

"Enrico!" he called, no longer Sergeant Caruso, formalities being kept to a minimum, except when brass was about. "Get the men together. I've just found out where we're off to." Enrico did his bidding, and five minutes later, they were all sitting either around or on the tank.

"Men, I know you're tired; it's been a hard few days, but I know where we're going, and with a bit of luck, we'll be there in a couple of hours."

"Where's that, Lieutenant?" said the left brakeman, Mike Smart.

"We are going to a beautiful little town, one that my folks used to take me to, on many occasions before the war. It's a medieval town called St-Pol-sur Ternoise, and we are lucky enough to be billeting Deborah and ourselves in the grounds of a fantastic old castle, called Château d'Olhain." He simply bubbled with excitement, rubbing his hands together like a little boy. Unfortunately, his enthusiasm was not contagious, and it was the right brakeman, James Poole, in a very sarcastic tone of voice who said: "I hope the women there aren't medieval too!" But no sarcasm could take away the euphoria that Frank Heap was feeling for a return visit.

Second Lieutenant Frank Heap was an extremely popular man with his crew, and generally answered to the name of Guv; like most tank men, he was not very tall, standing approximately five foot four inches, but he was very muscular for his size, and though you could never tell by his gentle features, he had won medals for boxing and Greco-Roman wrestling whilst studying structural engineering at Durham University. Just before the war, at the tender age of twenty-four, he had married his childhood sweetheart, Deborah Manning, and when Frank had joined up in early 1917 into the newly formed tank corps, Deborah had given birth to a son, whom they had named Justin. Frank loved his son and he loved his wife; he was fond of his crew, and adored his iron land ship, which he had named after his spouse. He was the eternal optimist, who could always see the good side of everything, even when there was not one, and his smile and laughter were always infectious, making the crew respond to orders with a willingness not often encountered. Andrew Potter, the engineer, who had an incredible skill for nursing that underpowered engine through all sorts of difficulties, smiled with approval. Andrew was a much older and wiser man, being in his early forties; one of his sons was also an engineer in the tank corps, though while serving they had never come across one another. Ernie Grays, the left steerer, turned to John Winston, the right steerer, and in a not overly convincing tone: "If the Guv says this is a good place, I'm sure it's going to be! As long as we can have a few beers in an estaminet, and meet the odd Mademoiselle, life will be just cherry pink!"

Peter Mitchell turned to Enrico, "Sarge, do you know about this place? Will there be a chance for gunnery practice?"

"No, I've no idea what there will be there. What you hear is the first time I've heard it too, but honestly, I ask you, have you ever been anywhere in this army where there has not been gunnery practice, drill or inspection?" To which they all half-heartedly laughed.

It was early the next morning, when the trains disgorged their Leviathans again, at St-Pol-sur Ternoise, and this time they journeyed the last couple of miles to the castle grounds under their own power. The noise of the trudging beasts disturbed all the residents of that beautiful medieval town, which had been virtually untouched by the ravages of war. The idea of keeping tanks a secret from the enemy seemed rather pointless, when all a person had to do, was open a window and watch a hundred or more vehicles pass by. Gradually tank after tank entered the vast acreage of Château d'Ohlain, and Enrico asked his friend, Frank Heap, as each tank was being lined and camouflaged: "Frank, do you mind if we keep a space next to 'Deborah' for Matti to park 'Dawn' in? It would be nice to have Matti close by, and I know he would be feeling much the same way as I do."

Lieutenant Heap smiled knowingly at Enrico, and placing his hand on Enrico's shoulder, he said: "Of course, it's fine by me, but you better go and tell the Sergeant Major over there with the clipboard, as he seems to be the one checking us in, and also positioning us. Then you better go over to the gatehouse, and wait for 'Dawn' to come through, and that could be hours."

Enrico went and saw the Sergeant Major, who was a very stiff, erect fifty year old ex-guardsman; he was more suited for paperwork than chasing around battlefields with a gun in his hand. But he readily agreed to the request, and left a space large enough for 'Dawn' to park up next to 'Deborah'. Enrico then ran as quickly as possible, taking Ernie Grays with him, past the gatehouse, and waited until the familiar outline of 'Dawn' came into view. It was nearly three hours later, and the tanks were still lumbering into the grounds, making thick, muddy ruts where gardens had once been. Even though it had not rained in several days, the huge weight of these vehicles seemed to draw up water, as if from some subterranean pool, and everything was gooey and sticky with the chocolate coloured mud of the region. Eventually, one tank came into view, belching more smoke than most. 'That would be 'Dawn'! The way he's jerking along, they must have some problem.'

As 'Dawn' came up to get past Enrico, he banged on the side door, where the machine gun protruded. The door was swung open, and out billowed a cloud of carbon monoxide, along with a black minstrel-faced Matti, coughing and spluttering as he tried to smile at his friend.

"What the Hell's happened to you?" said Enrico, as he chuckled. "This heap of rubbish seems only fit for the scrapheap!"

"Listen, mush, there's nothing wrong with this beauty, except maybe for a few problems with the engine, chassis, tracks and guns! Replace those, and we have a good tank!" said Matti, as he stuck his head out further to breathe in some real, clean oxygen.

"Enough of this idle banter! Follow me, I've wrangled a space next to 'Deborah' for you. I knew that if you were not next to me, you'd only cry yourself to sleep at night!" A noise came from within the smoky, smelly and noisy cavity of the tank. It was the voice of the right brake-man, Tom Rider.

"Come on, you two Nancy boys, we're all suffocating in here. Let's get this bugger parked up."

When finally, all the tanks were positioned and camouflaged, yet another day had passed.

Matti and Enrico were happy to be united once more, and not a single member of either crew misunderstood the bond that was between them, though they might not have known that this bond went back to childhood.


Once again training started, the only difference being that though they did not know their objectives, every last one of them knew that an objective was imminent. A country did not export hundreds of lumbering monsters without them being used. Gunnery practice, drill, inspections and general army bull were the norm. Days turned into weeks, the weather became cold and wintry, as the Siberian winds came down from the North early. The two tank crews had become very friendly towards one another, and it was generally thought that these two tanks should fight side by side when the time came, and it suited Enrico and Matti. Lieutenant Black was not quite the same character as Second Lieutenant Heap: he did not quite conjure the respect that Frank Heap did, and relied terribly heavily on Corporal Matthew Dumbridge. He was a slight man, and had a rather pasty and sickly pallor to him. Though he was twenty-four years of age, he did not have the same confidence as Matti who therefore tended to take command of 'Dawn'.

That first week, they spent their entire waking hours stripping the engine and rebuilding it with better engineering thanks to their Chief engineer, Simon Beale, improving an engine that had never been right from the beginning. Even though the entire mileage that this tank had done would work out to be a lot less than fifty, they discovered that the piston rings had all worn very badly, and that the whole engine was in need of a rebore. This was music to Simon Beale's ears, as he had worked on big tractor engines and understood fully the workings of the combustion engine. With the help of Richard Powers, the left brakeman, who in civilian life had also been an engineer, they thought they could build a better engine, with more power and more reliability.

Major Brookes was delighted with the way that these men were tackling what was obviously a faulty machine, and arranged for a tented workshop to be erected, which was also equipped with electricity for the running of lathes and drills. And after two weeks, there were several dozen tank crews organising engineering trips to the workshop. With new lagging around the exhaust, and a newly built engine which they kept ticking over for a whole day and night, so as to run it in, 'Dawn' was once again fit and ready to cut the mustard.

On the 7th November 1917, Major Brooks called all the tank commanders into the largest reception room of the Château d'Ohlain to inform them that on the morning of the 20th November, three hundred and sixty-five fighting tanks were going to line up against what was considered the weakest section along the Hindenburg line, with thirty-five support tanks which were the old original Mark I. These had had their guns removed, and were going to be used as supply vehicles for ammunition and fuel, or rescue tanks for saving injured men, and getting them quickly behind the lines; several had even been equipped with crane structures, so that damaged tanks could be salvaged from the battlefield. The idea was that the tanks would break a way through the German wire, with the infantry immediately behind them, and the cavalry waiting, further back in the rear for that famous breakthrough that only the cavalry could exploit. All the commanders were enthusiastic, and went back to their crews with high expectancy: that feeling that for once the top brass just *might* have got it right. For the next ten days, each crew would work on their specific plan within the battle; nothing was going to be left to chance. While all the time, the distant guns could be heard…

The morning of the 17th arrived: grey, windy and icy cold, but fortunately, no rain. The order had been given that each vehicle would move out to its designated jumping off spot, but they could only move on engine tick-over to reduce any noise that could alert the enemy to their arrival. It took two days for the tanks to reach the start line; each vehicle was restrained to eight hundred yards an hour, but the ploy worked: no enemy planes had been seen as Britain had complete mastery of the air, and the noise was kept to a minimum, along with the exhaust smoke. So the enemy had no idea of what was in store for them. As the night of the 19th fell around the battle field, the German soldiers were eating, drinking and generally believing that their posting was just about the cushiest one along any trench system. How wrong they were! The tanks had quietly moved into position all along the six miles battle front. Engines were switched off, no lights were showing, yet crews worked feverishly on final preparations to make sure that no tank was going to break down again, and especially not in the height of battle.

6.20 a.m., just before dawn appeared. A roar broke the silence of Cambrai as a thousand big guns of all calibres opened up onto the Hun lines. It was a complete surprise. Tired, aging German soldiers fell out of the beds, grabbing their guns as they made their way to the firing lines. Gas shells, smoke shells, fragmentation shells, high explosives and shrapnel shells; all were thrown by the British at a rate of fire that could only have been marvelled at during the first two years of the war. How perfect practice had made them! Though the enemy feared the guns, especially when gas was used, they never expected the fight to do anything other than falter, as it always did at the wire. And the wire on this stretch of trench was up to one hundred yards thick. There had never been such defences built before; why worry? Hold out against the shelling, and then return fire with machine guns when the typical onrush started. Those that were not killed or maimed by the Maxims would soon perish upon the wire. The defenders crouched and waited for the smoke and shelling to cease, then they would see those stupid Tommies coming, and then all hell would break loose.

As the guns opened up, the three hundred and sixty-five fighting MK IVs started up their engines and began to move forward. The move was led by 'Hilda', commanded by no less than General Elles. Most of the vehicles carried huge two ton bundles of wood called fascines. These would be taken right up to the trenches, and then dropped in so that other tanks could use them as bridges. Enrico and Matti's tanks had huge anchor-type claws, which as they passed over the barbed wire, could be lowered onto it, thus dragging the wire along, turning it into a huge ball. They would then move into a Y formation, dragging all the wire clear for the infantry, which followed in the shadow of the tanks, using them for cover. By the time the smoke cleared and the Germans then saw the enemy, they were terrified. Many ran back to the next trench system, others just put their hands in the air and waited for capture. Those that stood and fought lasted just a minute or two, as the machine guns and cannons of the tanks took great care to dispose of them quickly.

As 'Deborah' approached the wire, Lieutenant Frank Heap was directing everything around him well; he would scream to the brakemen and steerers to go this way or that, avoid this shell hole, mind not to break down, keep the gun firing at anything even if it was in many cases pointless; he never was even aware when the Germans started to fire back and red hot fragments of iron would splinter off the sides of the inside, sometimes hitting him, sometimes not; he was oblivious to anything, just keen to get the job done. "Lower the anchor, we are over the wire," he screamed at Enrico, who at first could not hear him, but soon guessed by the hand gestures that followed. Once the wire was hooked, noticing that 'Dawn' had done the same, he ordered his right brakeman to stop so that the left track would force the vehicle to go to the right. He was extremely pleased to see through a slit in the back part of the tank, that a huge bundle of wire was being pulled behind. 'Those poor bastards, after all those months it must have taken to lay down all that wire, and we have it up in a couple of minutes,' thought Frank Heap. With his swathe and also the chunk that had been removed by 'Dawn', there was now a vast avenue for the infantry to move through.

In the past the Germans had purposely left weak areas, so that the attacking troops would think this was a point of entry into the trenches, but always there was a crossfire of machine guns ready to cut the attackers to pieces. 'Deborah' and 'Dawn' had made straight for the strongest area, knowing that would almost certainly be the least defended. This was the case, and hundreds of British troops were now swarming through and into the first German forward trench. When Enrico had a chance to breathe, he looked out of his porthole to see how well 'Dawn' was doing. He need not have worried as Matti's tank was cruising along, gathering a huge harvest of barbed wire. He then looked back from whence they had come. There were plenty of armoured tanks still coming across no-man's-land, but he also noted that there were several blazing infernos from tanks that had obviously been hit by artillery fire. He looked on in horror at one tank, which he recognised as one commanded by Captain Fernbrook, who had been kind to him and Matti when they had both been injured during the High Wood offensive. He could see that someone was trying to crawl out through the now open door at the gun port of the vehicle's left side. 'Oh my God, the man is Fernbrook and he's on fire. They must have caught a shell that exploded inside causing the fire. Oh the poor sod, he must be dead soon, he's ablaze from head to toe!' thought Enrico. Though the Captain could not be heard by anybody, he was screaming in agony and flailing about wildly, and a passing infantry soldier took pity on him, aimed his rifle and put him out of his misery, before he carried on with his journey to the enemy trenches. A moment later the entire blazing vehicle blew up, as the ammunition and petrol ignited.

'Deborah' once again turned to the trenches; it had done its job with the wire and now would follow across the front forward trench to the first reserve trench. Enrico heard the clatter of machine gun bullets cracking against the side of their tank, and all of a sudden there was a small hole just above his left shoulder. He looked around to see if any damage had been done by the bullet that had obviously come through; nobody or nothing seemed to be out of the norm, so maybe they had got away with that one. They reached the reserve trench, dropped their fascine inside the trench and tried to cross it. Unfortunately the left track was too close to the edge of the fascine and the whole tank slid ever so slightly into the actual trench, leaving it balancing precariously, quite literally prepared to go which way…Enrico fell against the cannon as the tank lurched to its left side, and started to slide into the trench. He looked out of the porthole, to see if any German soldiers were around. Fortunately there was no one there to be seen. Frank Heap was shouting as loud as he could to the right hand steerer, and brakeman. "Pull us over, then I want you to try and reverse us out" The tank stopped sliding, lurched once more, this time to the right. "Stop! No more!" called out Enrico, "if you reverse now we will be down here for ever. You must go forward again, straighten up, and then reverse with both tracks." Veins were sticking out on his neck, and he was hoarse with shouting and worry. Lieutenant Heap looked at

Enrico, surged over to where he was standing, looked out of the porthole, realised that Enrico was right, and gave the order. The tank swayed again, but at least it straightened up with now both tracks pointing in the right direction.

Just as things started to go right again the engine stalled. "Christ, what next?" screamed Enrico to no one in particular. "My God," said Frank Heap, "we have run out of petrol. Wait, that's not possible, we should have plenty!" Then he smelt the air. "We have a leak somewhere." Enrico remembered the bullet that had come through, then went to the petrol tank and felt his way along the fuel pipe. Six inches from the engine intake, *there* was the trouble! The bullet had been pretty well spent by the time it hit the pipe, but it was enough to puncture a small hole and the petrol had just gently seeped out and away. At least it had not ignited inside the vehicle. With the smells of exhaust and cordite, it was perfectly understandable that the seeping fuel was not smelt or noticed. *Bang!* A clatter of fragments of a stick grenade clanged harmlessly on the side of the vehicle, but it was enough to bring Heap and the rest of the crew back to the reality of the battle.

Enrico once again looked through the porthole on his side of the tank; this time he was aware of a couple of German soldiers craning their heads around the corner of the trench that the tank was now stuck in. One of the soldiers pulled the pin on another grenade and lobbed it in the direction of the tank. *Bang!* More little pieces of metal rattled on the outside wall of the vehicle. Enrico pointed the cannon in the direction of where the defending Germans were, pulled the trigger and a six pound shell slammed right into the side of the trench, quite near to were the soldiers must have been standing; a piece of the trench wall collapsed into the bottom. This time a Hun warrior came out of hiding sporting a machine gun. *Rat-tat-tat!* Bullets pinged against the side, pieces of hot iron splintered off the inside and started hitting the crew. Enrico fired again, missed the machine gunner, but once more brought a section of the trench wall down. Now there was somewhere for the gunner to hide behind and keep up his rate of fire. Pieces of metal were getting bigger and were likely to cause damage to anyone or anything they hit. One bullet finally came through, and splattered into the opposite side of the tank. The crew were now starting to worry. Enrico took careful aim, fired and hit the machine gunner square on: very little was left to identify him as a member of the human race.

"Thank God you got him, a few more of their Maxim bullets and we would all be so much mincemeat," said a very relieved Lieutenant Heap, patting Enrico on the shoulder as he spoke.

"Give me some Mills bombs and I will take a look outside and see if we're in serious danger, and whether we can get out of here or not," said Enrico. He picked up a bag of six grenades and drew his service revolver, making sure that it had an entire chamber of bullets. He looked once again to see if any other Germans were around; the way seemed clear, so he opened the door just behind the gun on each side of the vehicle, waited a few seconds, threw it wide open and jumped out onto the muddy floor of the trench. His pistol was ready for any sudden moves, but nothing happened; it was as if the war was going on elsewhere, somewhere a long way away. It was Enrico, an iron monster and a trench, nothing else mattered. He ducked to a crouch and glanced around. The only movement came from the smoke that was rising from the remains of the German soldier that had been blown to pieces by Enrico's six pounder shell. He moved in the direction of the first corner, quietly and quickly, ready to shoot from the hip, or throw a Mills at whatever or whomever. He poked half a head around the corner, hoping upon hope that it would be empty of any enemy: luck was in. Then from the next corner he noticed movement, someone was coming; he stepped back right up against the fire step, just out of sight. He withdrew the pin on a Mills bomb, preparing to throw it at the rogue soldier who was there. 'Wow, it's one of us!' he carefully replaced the pin, and then called out, "Stop there and identify yourself!"

"Don't fire, I'm a friend, I saw your tank was in trouble and I made my way down to you to see if there was anything I could do?" said a rather frightened voice. "My name is Private Stephens, of the 51st Highlanders." He came round the trench and held out a hand for Enrico to shake. "Nice to meet you; where are you from, Sergeant?"

"I'm from Tranmere, just outside of Liverpool, Private. Thanks for coming."

They moved back to the tank to find the entire crew looking around. Private Peter Mitchell had been clever, he had raided the first aid box, withdrawn several plasters, wrapped them around the cracked fuel pipe, and proceeded to fill the petrol tank with the reserve fuel that they carried strapped to the top of the tank. Lieutenant Heap was examining the tracks, and wondering what they had to do to get out of this serious situation. Enrico climbed onto the fire step to look over and see what the rest of the world was doing. Then he was waving frantically. "What is it, Enrico?" called out Lieutenant Heap.

"It's Matti with 'Dawn', they are coming over. Maybe we can get a tow out of here?"

"Good idea, get the chain off the top, lads, we can hook up to 'Dawn' and get back on line, and back into the fray. I know you are all terribly eager for that!" said Frank Heap in a sarcastic tone of voice. A few seconds later, they heard the groaning sound of one wheezing engine, then 'Dawn' appeared at the top of the trench.

"Can we help?" came the distinctive sound of friend Matti.

"Hook us up, and then pull us out! Make it quick as there are enemy around somewhere!" said Enrico. The chain was soon hooked up to 'Dawn', then on the command 'Deborah's' engine was also placed into reverse. The struggle to get the stuck vehicle out of the trench was almost too much for both engines. Smoke, black as tar was pouring from their engines' exhaust and the gear boxes. On 'Dawn' everything was creaking and groaning, and just about ready to bust wide open, but bit by bit the machines moved backwards and out of the danger caused by the slip. Enrico looked around to see what had befallen Private Stephens. He caught sight of him just as he moved to the front of 'Deborah', as the monster was being towed out of the trench; something was just not right. It took him a second before he realised.

Once again Enrico jumped out of the door, this time pistol in hand, ready to do combat. He ran around the monster just in time to see Private Stephens pulling the pins on several stick grenades. Enrico didn't waste a second, and shot him straight through the head. He fell like a stone, stick grenades tumbling everywhere. "Duck…Grenades!" screamed Enrico. *Boom, bang!* Enrico had thrown himself sideways to avoid any blast, but he felt the hot air gush past him, and his helmet lifted on his head. He lay there, panting hard. He felt himself from top to toe: he was alright, not any wounds, though he knew he wouldn't have any, as he was immortal after all.

"What the hell was all that about?" exclaimed Lieutenant Heap, looking at the dent made in the front of his pride and joy. He then noticed bits of body stuck to the front of 'Deborah' and in the vicinity. "Hell, Enrico, what happened?"

"I saw him move around the front, and it was then seeing his back that I noticed that there were several bullet holes in his tunic, plus blood all over the back. I guess that he was an Anglo-German, or something, because his accent completely fooled me. But the blood gave him away and made me think that those clothes were not his: that made him a spy or saboteur!" Enrico stood up, shaking with excitement and adrenaline.

"Well, Enrico, you might just have saved the day for us. Well done! Now let's get the hell out of here, please!"

Enrico boarded 'Deborah' once again, manned his gun and wondered what was happening in this battle.

In fact, in many ways the battle of Cambrai was a great success. It proved that armour was obviously going to be the future of warfare, along with the aeroplane. The tank could finally break the stalemate that had held all the armies in trenches for the past three years. Finally, maybe, the cavalry could sweep through, chasing the Hun all the way back to Berlin.

Anyway, that was the dream. The tanks had smashed their way through the so-called impregnable Hindenburg line, and had pushed onto the town of Cambrai. There were two problems to be overcome; one was the Canal du Nord, which had just been built and was without water, thus making it almost an impossible barrier to cross. It was one hundred and fifty feet across and in some places, one hundred feet deep. The other obstacle was the Saint-Quentin Canal, which veered sharply from Crèvecoeur to Marcoing, making progress from the south difficult. So it became imperative that the attacking tanks should reach and take all the available bridges as soon as possible. As the battlefield area had never seriously been shelled over the last three years, the ground was still un-pockmarked and open easy country to traverse. Besides the natural rolling hills helped the attackers, as they gave cover from the guns, and those hills, unlike the flatness of Flanders, also meant the ground was firm, as water had always drained away easily.

On that first day of the attack, the tanks had made almost unprecedented inroads across the new battle terrain; they had secured crossings of the Saint-Quentin Canal at Masnières and Marcoing, and these crossings were now open for the 2nd and 5th Cavalry Divisions to exploit, taking a route around the town of Cambrai and attacking from the rear. Midway through the attack on the bridges, General Elles in his tank 'Hilda', had come to grief just around Ribecourt, and had to return, albeit at a slow faltering pace, to his original HQ, before the battle commenced.

So where were the Cavalry? Due to bad communications, the main body of horsemen was completely unaware of how the battle had progressed; in fact they had not even gone to their starting position, being a good seven miles back, behind the original lines. So, showing the usual incompetence, things had started to go from great beginnings to shambles. On that first day of battle, III Corps was achieving all its objectives. They had breached the Hindenburg Line in many places, capturing several thousand German troops, which were escorted back to the British lines. This first day was hailed as a great victory, and when news reached back along the lines of communication to London, for the first time since that fateful day in 1914, the bells of the country tolled.

Not all had been successful though; the 51st Highlanders had been caught by the Hun machine guns and had suffered great slaughter, hence the reason why the saboteur who had called himself Private Stephens had so easily managed to find a dead soldier's uniform that would fit him.

Time was passing; when it became dark the tanks were to find some sort of cover and make as best they could. Not easy in a huge battlefield, where enemy and friend alike were still all around you, but as darkness did approach this ploy was put into action.

Now that 'Deborah' had been released from the trench, from a fate that was almost certainly of her own making, they had yet to traverse it, but this time, a more careful approach was made, and the fascine that had been placed into the defensive line took their weight perfectly. 'Dawn' followed closely behind, and soon, they had passed over the complete trench system and were in open country. They came across a Mark I that had been turned into a supply vehicle, but this one was full of machine gun bullets, with six pounder shells of all sorts: shrapnel, gas and high explosive. When they approached, they realised that the tracks on the right hand side of the Mark I had been blown through, and a hole inside showed that a shell had burst, killing all the crew. It was time for 'Deborah' and 'Dawn' to rearm, while they could, and as quickly as possible, since smoke was billowing from the blown engine; with all that ammunition inside, it would make one hell of a mess! All the crew, except the gunners, had the task of transferring ammunition at the double, and each man took it in turn to urinate on the engine to help cool it down. Firing was going on all around them, but fortunately, nothing in their direction. Both the commanders and their crew were surprised to see just how many seriously damaged tanks there were. This meant that the Germans were fast learning how to deal with the metal monsters. Many dead were sprawled over the area, both Fritz and Tommy. Ammunition now loaded, and petrol tanks filled, it was time for the second objective, and that was Bourlon Wood, where their aim was to destroy any redoubts and machine gun nests.

Bourlon Wood was situated just south-west of Cambrai, but unbeknown to the Allies, it was saturated with the German reserve storm-troopers. They came up behind yet another burning tank, which was on the brow of a small hill, and as now darkness was beginning to descend, it seemed the ideal spot to take cover: as to any Hun, all they would see was the smoking hulk. A defensive picket was established around the two tanks, with spare Lewis guns in attendance. It was going to be a long, cold night, and just to make matters worse, it had begun to rain. It was obvious that German patrols were going around in the dark, mopping up any straggling tanks, and gunfire could be heard everywhere. But all through the night the sentries were not fired upon, so, as the wet, grey light of dawn of the 21st November crept above the horizon from the East, a scene of carnage of gigantic proportions was revealed: everywhere, were smouldering Mark IVs and as the battle began to resume, it became blatant that there were now somewhat less than half the numbers to carry on. The enemy had once again shown their adaptability in overcoming their initial fear of this weapon, and found strength in the fact that the Allied offensive could be dramatically slowed just by the use of armour piercing shells and bullets.

Lieutenant Heap gathered his crew together, and made ready for the next part of their particular role in this battle: that meant that 'Deborah' and 'Dawn' had to be fit enough to travel another three miles, and then engage the enemy at Bourlon Wood. Both engineers had worked feverishly all night over their machines to make sure that things would run smoothly and efficiently; the cracked fuel pipe had been successfully repaired and no longer gave cause for worry. The dents which now appeared all over both machines showed that enemy fire had certainly been in their direction, without causing serious damage so far; only 'Deborah' had been pierced with several bullets but even then, none of the crew had been injured. So, the feeling in both camps was buoyant and optimistic.

Engines were started up, crew boarded, and both of the iron beasts got under way. It was not quite sunrise yet when the first lurch forward occurred. Three miles approximately to go, before they knew they would come up against enemy fire, at least serious enemy fire, as in fact the Hun was all around, mopping up or being mopped up. The firing had been spasmodic but quite ferocious all night, with the occasional big bang as high explosives went up: this was either an ammunition dump blowing or a tank being hit and exploding.

At best it would take an hour of driving, but the terrain was now becoming pockmarked with shell holes; the rain coming down with some force was making the ground very slippery, and mud was starting to become a hindrance. Enrico spied through his porthole slit, searching for any signs of enemy movement, but as he looked, the tank would veer to one side or another, often throwing him right across to the engine, where he would land and burn himself trying to stand up again. Fritz was there, somewhere, as bullets were constantly pinging off the front and sides of the monster. The smoke inside was quickly becoming unbearable, and it was suggested by the right brakeman that the gun door should be left open, even if it was a risk. At least they could then breathe. Enrico looked at Frank Heap who nodded his approval, so the door was pushed open and left to swing this way and that, as the land ship plunged into shell holes and ditches, throwing everything and everybody this way and that. 'At this rate' thought Lieutenant Heap, 'it will be hours before we make our rendezvous!'

'Dawn' was not more than thirty yards behind 'Deborah', but like her male counterpart, she, too, was experiencing difficulties in keeping any sort of speed over the now rough ground. To make matters worse, the water was not draining away; instead it was starting to fill some of the deeper shell holes. 'Dawn' drove into one such shell hole which looked quite innocuous to the driver, but it was so deep that the water entered the crew compartment. There was a quick panic, nursing the engine as water rushed around the inside, in case they stalled; in fact she did not stall, but instead of climbing out the other side, started to slip this way and that. Matti looked on in horror, not knowing what the heck to do, but the lumbering beast eventually gripped enough to pull them out of that particular problem.

He looked out of his porthole, cocked his machine gun, and then fired over to the far left. Just a quick burst, no more than twenty rounds, but he felt sure that he was looking at a group of German troopers. Nothing happened, but he kept looking, knowing that it was better to be safe than sorry. Then a line of tracer bullets came zooming in his direction. Matti instinctively ducked, but the bullets cracked and spluttered as they hit the side of the tank. Pieces of hot metal whizzed around the inside, sometimes hitting members of the crew, but doing no serious harm, just being an annoyance. "You bastards, I knew you were there all the time!" Matti took more careful aim, then let a long burst go off in the direction of the enemy; something must have hit home as their tracer stopped abruptly, then he saw that 'Deborah' was taking action towards this little nest of vipers. She had stopped dead for a few seconds, time enough for Enrico to place a shrapnel shell at the machine gunners. It worked, as there was an explosion right in the shell hole that they had set up as their nest.

'Deborah' turned in that direction, deciding to make sure that it was completely out of action. It took two minutes to get over the rough ground to where the gunners were. There were three of them: one was obviously dead, as he seemed to be in several pieces, the other two were badly wounded, but quite capable of causing more mayhem to any future soldiers or tanks. They must have realised what was going to happen as the entire crew could hear the screams above the noise of gunfire and engine noise. The leviathan crashed into their small shell hole, crushing the two remaining Germans under the left track. The noise of the screaming and cracking of bones made everything else seem quiet. To make matters worse, one of the Germans got stuck to the track and was pulled over and over, leaving bits of himself everywhere, especially on the vehicle. This would certainly have to be removed by someone, if it didn't all fall off, of its own accord. Enrico went quite white, not for the first time in his military career, and looked for a moment or two as if he was going to be sick. A large piece of German torso was now hanging from the open door, blood dripping everywhere. "This always happens to me," he said to anyone who could hear, "if there are bodies and body parts around, I fall into them!"

One and a half hours later, there on the brow of the hill, was Bourlon Wood. 'Not as menacing as High Wood' thought Enrico. But he could see that there were plenty of gun emplacements, which indicated that the Hun was well dug in and ready. They could also see lots of water. Hopefully this would be just surface water, nothing deep? 'Well, we'll soon know how many enemy soldiers there are there!' thought Lieutenant Heap. "Enrico, look around you. How many tanks are following us?"

"Well, I can see Matti… wait, there are several coming over that last brow. I would guess that in about ten minutes there might be ten of us."

"The next question is… is it enough to do anything in that wood?"

"Frank, you are the Commander; I go where you point this blighter. But I will say, that having come this far, and after all, we haven't encountered too much in the way of opposition, I personally feel we should give it our best shot!"

"We will wait and see how many get here in the next few minutes. Keep your eyes peeled, and keep those engines turning over, we might want to get the hell out of here in a hurry!" This of course caused a lot of laughter, as it was meant to.

*435*

The information that had been passed onto the Bourlon Wood tank crews had been very vague. Nobody seemed to know anything about the wood, whether it would have defenders or be empty and easy to get a hold of. Not even the size had been given to them, and now just under the fire line of the wood, Lieutenant Heap's crew was waiting; surprised that it was at least a mile long, so what good would a dozen or more tanks do? Were there defenders there? Like Enrico, he had noticed several gun emplacements, which meant machine guns nests. But how many soldiers would there be? Then there was the problem of the water. If big shells had dropped, it might well be deep, or it might just be surface water, how could he tell?

The entire crew had been frantically peering from the various portholes, looking for any signs of enemy movement, while they waited for the straggling tanks to get close to them; they saw nothing that told them anything.

"Enrico, something is not right here. I am very nervous of us falling into a trap."

"Well, Frank, that's why you are the Commander. I don't want that sort of responsibility: it's too hard to get it right all the time. Speaking for myself though, I think we should bombard them from just a little higher up, and see what happens."

"That had crossed my mind too. I might go across and have a talk with Lieutenant Black; it's a hard one to call!"

Ten minutes later, he was back inside 'Deborah'; grinning from ear to ear he said to Enrico, "Lieutenant Black agrees with us: attack from here and see if we can get a response which will give us a clue as to how many of them there are."

Seven other MK IVs had appeared, and were waiting for orders as to what to do next; it seemed obvious that as 'Deborah' had been the first to get there, she should lead and Frank Heap would command overall. He went from vehicle to vehicle, and it was heartily agreed that they would get into a line not more than fifty yards from each other, drive to the buff of the hill that they now stood on, just high enough so that the guns could fire into the wood surround. Then if all seemed reasonably secure, they would move in and try and capture it. It took another ten minutes for the tanks to line up as if on parade; as each one's guns got high enough to clear the ground and hit the wood, they started to fire. Enrico fired into where he thought gun emplacements were. He hit something, as there was a huge explosion, but it was too big to just have been caused by his shell. He then saw several soldiers run into the wood for better cover. The tanks started to send in gas shells; this caused great panic, which seemed a positive result.

"We can do this thing, don't you agree, Enrico?"

"Yep, we can do this: they seem to be on the run."

The tank was put into gear once again, and reluctantly she moved off in the direction of Bourlon Wood. Looking behind, Enrico noticed that the rest seemed to be following. They got to where the water started, and it was obvious that it was only surface water, so 'Deborah' charged ahead. They were now only one hundred yards from the edge of the wood, when all of a sudden, the tank veered to the right and down into a deep shell hole, which sadly was brimming with black liquid mud. Into the tank the water flooded; it was soon up to the engine which spluttered and died.

There was no starting that engine again. Just as things began to look bad, they got worse. The hidden gun emplacements opened up on the tanks, thoroughly catching them, stranded in open country. The first tank to be hit was 'Deborah': a shell hit the left track, blowing it right off, so even if the engine could have started, it would be going nowhere. The next shell blasted a huge hole in the front, and fragments entered the crew compartment. The two steerers died immediately. Enrico screamed for help to load the gun. At least they could fire off whatever ammunition they had left at the gun emplacements: they might get lucky. *Bang, bang, bang... boom!* One of the 'Deborah' shells hit and penetrated a concrete emplacement; the lucky shot must have hit a pile of ammunition as the explosion was so big it even created a small tidal wave across the water that had trapped them. Enrico then noticed that 'Dawn' was very close by, firing round after round of machine gun bullets into anything that might be holding German troops.

"Frank, Frank, are you alright? We should evacuate to 'Dawn'," said Enrico in a high pitched voice.

"How far is she from us?"

"Not more than fifty or sixty yards."

"Come on then, all out, take the breeches from the guns and throw them in the mud. Let's get out of here!"

With that, Enrico threw open the door that he had closed after the tank had moved into battle. He stood in the frame of the door, hoping upon hope that Matti would quickly see them making a dash for it, and give covering fire. He jumped into the mire, and was, before he knew it, up to his waist in gluey muddy water. He struggled, but made very little headway. Bullets started to ping all around him, and to make matters worse, the water was so cold it took his breath away. Onward he pushed; he looked behind to see two of the crew struggling to follow him. Steam was coming from exhausted mouths, as they panted and heaved to get onto drier, higher ground. The mud would not give up its grasp; it wanted to keep them all there. Again he looked behind him to see the last figure of Lieutenant Frank Heap jump clear of 'Deborah', just as she was hit with yet another shell.

This time it set her alight, albeit briefly; it must have been some ammunition exploding, but Enrico was too tired and too exhausted from the concentration required to get out of the bog to be able to hear anything. Anyway, with all the crashing and banging, what was another explosion among friends? He got behind 'Dawn', out of harm's way; no bullets could get him now, though mortars were also dropping around, so better get inside. He banged hard and long on the back entrance, and eventually the

438

door was opened and he crawled inside panting heavily, his lungs and heart fit to burst.

"Thanks, you get back. I will help the others to get in."

After what seemed an eternity Frank Heap and two other men appeared at the door and were helped inside.

"There is no one else, we have four dead, two blown up inside, two gunned down on the way over. Let's get this beast out of here, they have us cold," said Lieutenant Heap to Enrico who was still gasping badly.

Lieutenant Black, the commander of 'Dawn' grabbed the moment in both hands. Get out of here! That was all he needed to hear. The engine roared, 'Dawn' turned as on a sixpence, and moved in the direction that she had come from, all the time firing at anything and everything in the vicinity of Bourlon Wood.

Only 'Dawn' and two other tanks made it from that field of fire. The five other tanks had all been destroyed by armour piercing shells, and were completely engulfed in flames. 'Deborah' was gradually sinking in the water and mud, maybe only to be discovered many years after the event. Even the last three vehicles were somewhat damaged: all showed the scars of battle. It took four hours for 'Dawn' just to get back to the starting line. They would regroup there, rearm, refuel, and wait for further orders.

Once again, British forces had failed to exploit their breakthrough into open country. But this time, it was obviously the fault of poor communications. After three days of tank battle, having had the Hun firmly on the run, the attackers relaxed just long enough, for the enemy to reform, regroup, and counterattack. After a great deal of fighting, all of which was very bitter, the British were driven back to almost the starting point once again. The difference this time was that everyone now knew that there was no such thing as an impregnable line; any trench or fortification could be overrun with the right sort of equipment, and in this case it was the tank, clumsy, awkward, vulnerable, slow and underpowered, underarmed, but without doubt the future.

The battle had started on the 20th November, and it stuttered on until 6th December, but for 'Dawn' and all the crews that had just scraped through by the skin of their teeth, that was the end of the battle.

Out of nearly four hundred tanks that took part, just forty tanks remained for further use. At least another fifty were left on the battlefield, then captured and later used by the Germans, against the Allies. Quite some irony there somewhere! Forty thousand soldiers were killed or seriously injured in the battle with a comparable number for the Germans too. Bourlon Wood was again attacked, but by the Bantam Division, a band of little men, all under five foot three inches in height. With the help of the Welsh Bantam Division the Allies managed to take the wood, but the taking of it had cost the lives of over four thousand men, and for what! To be driven out again some days later.

As for Enrico and Matti, having the VC gave them status, so much so that when they both realised that there was not going to be another tank charge, they decided to ask for a transfer back to the London Northern Rifle Brigade who were still stationed in the Ypres salient.

# XII

Christmas was coming, and life in the trenches had its normal routine of lice, rats, frostbite, colds and influenza, but worst of all, trenchfoot. Trenchfoot was a cousin to leprosy; men had to endure standing in shell holes up to their waist in icy water, and often this routine could last seventy-two hours. Little wonder that the skin could not take this sort of punishment, and would often die on the bone, and peel off. Men could go into the trenches for up to a week, perfectly healthy as they entered, but on returning to the rear, would find that part of their legs were literally rotting away. It became standard practice that a junior officer would inspect the men's feet on a daily basis, and each man had to rub whale oil into his metatarsals. Whether this really had any beneficial effect, nobody was sure, but it made the soldiers feel more at ease.

So Matti and Enrico, having been allowed to transfer back yet again, made it to the Ypres salient on the 18th December. Yet another new Colonel was in charge, a Colonel Sir Allenbrie-Brooker, recently of the Scots Guards. Both Enrico and Matti stood patiently to attention, awaiting their Colonel's pleasure; VCs meant nothing to Allenbrie-Brooker, all he saw were a lowly Sergeant and an extremely lowly Corporal, one that was bordering on being plump, which indicated to the Colonel no discipline or self control. Having kept them standing there for ten minutes, he finally looked up to acknowledge them both.

"I have your records in front of me, couple of would-be heroes, eh? Think you're going to win the war single-handed? Well, you're back in your old Brigade, and that means playing as a team!"

He sat back in the chair and twirled his moustache with his left hand, drew a deep breath, and continued: "You will do tours of duty in the trenches like everybody else; you'll get no special favours from me. I see, Dumbridge, that you have requested leave, well no one gets leave until I say so! We'll see how things go, and maybe some leave can be given towards the end of January. I will expect you both to work diligently, and always present yourself in the best military tradition."

Not once did the Colonel allow the duo to ask any questions, and he concluded the meeting by saying: "I want you both to go and present yourselves to Lieutenant Kelly, who will give you your duties." On hearing this name, both the lads' hearts lifted with joy. "Dismissed!" Both saluted smartly, turned on their heels, and left through the same dugout door that they had on many occasions before. Despite the obnoxious attitude of the Colonel, both Enrico and Matti were elated to be in something they thought of as home.

Walking carefully once more down a trench system that was more than familiar to both of them, having to dodge to this side or that to avoid busy soldiers who were carrying supplies to the front line, they went on their search for Lieutenant Kelly; as they walked, there was the spasmodic shelling in the background, sending greetings of death and destruction from one side to the other. Turning into one remembered deep trench, they recognised that they had reached the area that was for the Junior Officers and NCOs; there, in front of them was the entrance to one particular dugout, one that would almost certainly be holding their friend. Enrico rapped hard on the wooden frame that held the dark cloth cover which was there for protection against the shells that might land in the vicinity. Cloth was going to make all the difference against flying shell fragments, unlike the Colonel's dugout which had a steel door and frame! Juniors and NCOs were two a penny, so the top brass could not worry about them or afford the cost of real protection.

"Yes, who's there? Come in, come in."

That was a very familiar voice, and Enrico looked at Matti and grinned from ear to ear. They marched in, jumped to attention, saluted smartly, and said:

"Sergeant Caruso and Corporal Dumbridge reporting for duty, *Sir!*"

"You couple of arse holes," said Kelly, who immediately burst into laughter at seeing his friends again. "What is all this bullshit then?"

The duo relaxed and also laughed. Enrico went forward, threw his arms around 'Spider' Kelly, and then kissed him firmly on both cheeks.

"Enough of that sort of stuff, you will have us all prosecuted for being Nine Bob notes. My God, have I missed you two lads! If I hadn't known you were coming back I might have asked for a transfer to the Tank Brigade myself! So how was it? I heard you were at Cambrai, is that true?"

Enrico sat on the edge of the table while Matti sat on the other chair. Enrico then spent the next ten minutes giving a detailed account of what had happened in the battle. But the last sentence was the most poignant for friend Kelly to hear...

"Tanks are without doubt the way that wars will be fought. They will be bigger, faster, better armed, but they will stop any trench jamming. Trench warfare will be a thing of the past. I can foresee a time when battles will be fought between huge armies of armoured vehicles; very few men will be needed, just iron and steel."

"I believe you! Many other soldiers are saying much the same as you."

"So what is it about this new Colonel? He seemed more than a little uncaring about anybody, at least that was my first impression," said Matti.

"Don't worry about him, he won't be here long enough to give anybody grief. He's a career officer, and has come to us from the Scots Guards. But he's oblivious to danger, and often stands on the firing line looking out at the German lines. Sooner or later, a sniper will score a few points with him. Frankly I'm quite surprised that he has lived this long. But, beware; he's a nasty piece of stuff, so I feel there will be few mourners at his wake." With that, Michael 'Spider' Kelly rose from his chair and said, "Let's get some grub!"

"But just before we go, tell me about you becoming a Lieutenant, and congratulations for making it!" said Enrico, with Matti nodding in agreement.

"It was just in the line of progression: in the battle for High Wood, all the other junior officers were either killed or wounded, and they needed someone with experience. There were no heroics, just as I have said, natural progression."

"Well, I can't think of anybody more suited, so I agree with Enrico: congratulations!" exclaimed Matti.

Once more they resumed the familiar routine of two days in the front line trench, often manning a Lewis gun, two days in the reserve trench organising supplies, and two days off, which meant sometimes a trip to Poperinge, but more often than not, drill, inspections and general army bull.

Christmas came and went. For Enrico, this meant nothing, but to Matti, this was awful as he so wanted to be with his Dawn. She was still nursing in Calais, and wrote to him almost every day, which meant he got a bundle of letters every now and again. He wrote back almost on a daily basis too, and was pining terribly for his beloved. Their love had grown more and more intense; it became almost unbearable for both of them. Matti had to stop her from venturing to the front line so as to be near him, and it was obvious to one and all that as soon as this war ended, the first thing on their agenda was a trip to see a Vicar, and arrange the first available date for a wedding. It is strange that with two old adages, either can apply. 'Out of sight, out of mind' – 'Absence makes the heart grow fonder.' Well, it was perfectly clear which one applied to Matti and Dawn. Now every penny that was being earned was saved by the both of them, and Matti had now changed his will to make Dawn a beneficiary; his family would understand.

Enrico loved his friend, and was happy that he was happy. He was not quite sure that the wedding would ever happen, as Matti had never come clean about the age gap, and though neither of them thought much about the past now, there was the problem of one dead policeman to contend with. 'Still, time will tell for all things,' thought Enrico.

Things were starting to change on the Western Front. The U.S.A. had declared war on Germany and its friends; this gave the potential of at least three million more armed soldiers to fight for the Allied cause. America had been brought into the conflict because Germany had gone onto the offensive with its U-boats, sinking anything and everything that might have something to do with the Allies. Then, as if to make matters worse, the Germans had tried to encourage the Mexicans to fight the U.S.A., so as to regain the lost provinces of New Mexico and Texas. That failed miserably, and America had no choice but to come into the war on the side of the Allies. This was a huge bonus to Britain, as the U.S. had unlimited resources, which could be completely reshaped for war purposes.

Germany was doomed, everyone knew it. Prisoners that crossed over from the enemy trenches were glad to be out of the fighting. They were hungry and at the end of their tether, and the German new recruits were getting ever more juvenile, as school leavers were encouraged to enlist immediately. The civilians within the German borders were starting to starve as the British blockade was taking serious effect. The only point in the Kaiser's favour was the disappearance of Russia. Russia had been beaten into complete submission; it had brought down the Tsar, who was murdered along with his entire family. Communism was the new religion, under the leadership of a Marxist called Lenin. The German government had allowed his safe passage from Switzerland back to Russia, where he soon took control, then made peace with the Germans, much to the chagrin of the British and French.

But what this did for the Germans was to release another million men. They could be transferred from the Eastern Front to the Western Front. A million extra men could maybe swing the cause for the Germans; they knew that it was probably now impossible to win the war, but a victory might just win a good concession in the peace negotiations. So Kaiser Bill, along with Generals Paul von Hindenburg and Erich von Ludendorff, devised a last ditch battle which, like in 1914, in the Schlieffen Plan, would overrun the Allies along the Belgian coast and drive the British back to the French ports and across to England, and then pursuing the French they would take Paris, and make the Allies come to a settlement. This new battle was to take place on 21st March 1918; this would be before the great build-up of American troops had taken place. There were now many thousands of Yankee soldiers in France; some had even fought in battles, including Ypres Salient, Verdun and elsewhere on the front. But the majority were untrained and not ready to fight; this was what the German top brass was banking on. A quick bloody nose, then come to the table to talk peace. But the British and French Commanders had learned a thing or two over the last four years of bitter fighting; they knew that the Germans had to slog it out before the hordes of American troops arrived. They also realised that now that Russia and Romania were out of the picture, there would be plenty of extra Hun fighters coming to do battle. It was just a matter of where and when.

On March 17th, Enrico had to do a tour of duty at the front, which included the manning of a Lewis Gun position, along with three other soldiers, a long way into no-man's-land. It started to rain very hard. After several hours of continuous downpour, the shell hole that they manned was beginning to fill with water. It was extremely cold, and all four of them were shivering badly and trying desperately hard to keep warm and dry.

"Use your helmets to throw out the water," exclaimed Enrico. But that meant your head got wet and cold. Soon all four of them were soaked to the skin, and there seemed very little chance that this weather was going

446

to improve. The rain had set in, and that was going to be that. They could not, under any circumstances leave their post, so it was a matter of just holding in there.

The whole of the first night it rained and rained; they covered themselves as best they could with oilskin capes that were standard issue for winter in Flanders. But that could not stop the rain entering their shell hole. More water started to fill the hole; again Enrico had them all bailing out. At one thirty in the morning, just after a German star shell had fallen to earth, he noticed that Jonnie Miller had gone completely white, was no longer shivering and was starting to nod off to sleep.

"Jonnie, wake up, you can't go to sleep, you will never wake up if you do! Wake up and bail, that's an order."

There was no response; no matter how hard he hit him or shouted in his ear, he would not react. Enrico knew it was just a matter of time, but still he kept shaking him and pinching, rubbing his arms and legs. Nothing worked, and Jonnie was now breathing very slowly. 'What the hell do I do? If I try and take him back to our lines, I might get court-martialled for abandoning my post; if I don't take him back right now, he's dead in the next few minutes. Come on, you little bugger, wake up.' It was a hopeless task, and Enrico knew it. A few minutes later Jonnie Miller, who was probably no older than sixteen, died of exposure. The other two lads, all younger than Enrico, looked at him in abject horror, as if this had all been of his making.

"Well, you two, see what happens if you let yourselves go. Now keep this hole clear of water, keep yourselves as dry as possible, and keep awake. I will allow some sleep when the light comes bringing a little daytime heat. Until then, keep alert! We're looking that way, Private Lynch! That's the way the enemy are, not behind you! Start bailing or face a charge when we get back to our own lines. Private Tyler, keep that Lewis Gun dry and prepared for any action. And stay awake! I will get rid of Private Miller; he's going over the edge, that way we get more room."

It was a long night, and on many occasions Enrico had to scream at the other two to make sure that they stayed awake. There were times that he too felt as if it would be easier and better to let go, and drift off this mortal coil and see what the next world had to offer. But he was a stubborn blighter, and why give in to death? He knew he had not started to live yet. Dawn eventually came, but an eternity had passed; it was as the rain started to abate that he realised that he had made a bad error of judgement. He should never have dumped the body over the edge. The Germans could now clearly see it. He knew it was going to bring fire in their direction, and at eight forty five that morning, mortar shells started to explode in and around the area of their shell hole.

"Keep your heads down. They will only waste so many mortars if we don't retaliate. They might just think that the body was of a patrol that lost a member in some way. Oh Christ, I don't know, just keep down!"

The shells and mortars dropped for about seven minutes, before the firers gave up, returning to whatever they had been doing before the order to fire had been given. Enrico knew that snipers would be keeping a special watch on this area, so no more bailing and splashing water everywhere, at least not in daylight. It therefore meant that to keep dry and warm was going to be hard. They ate some dry rations, not that anyone knew what dry rations really consisted of, probably a mixture of oats, wheat, some dried meat and lard to bind it all together. It tasted awful, but no one gave a damn about such things as taste: fill your belly and keep your energy level high.

That day passed almost as slowly as the night. Enrico allowed the other two to sleep as best they could in two-hourly spells, then that afternoon, making sure that the others were now alert again, and keeping an eye on the German lines, he slept. A cold wind blew some surface water into his face, bringing him to consciousness once more; it was dark, and where were the other two? 'Bastards, where the hell are they?' He looked all around, but could see no one. 'Shit, those buggers are going to see me up against a firing post!' Just then he heard a slithering rustle informing him that someone was approaching. "Who goes there?" he waited, and then the answer came back.

"Sorry, Sergeant, I had to have a shit, it became desperate." It was Private Peter Lynch; he climbed back into the trench, looked around, then added, "Where is Tyler?"

"I was hoping you could tell me," answered Enrico with a slight tremble of fear in his voice.

"Shit, Sarge, I knew he was close to quitting, but I never thought he would do it. He could have only gone a few minutes, he was here when I went for my dump, and honestly, that could only have been... no more than ten minutes ago. He must be close by."

Enrico thought and pondered 'what should I do? I will call out, but if there's no response I'll have a good look around.' A German star shell went up, giving Lynch and Enrico a chance to check surreptitiously.

"What was that?" said Lynch, "just over there, about forty yards away to my left?"

"I'm going to have a look, stay here; if we go back and he has been taken by the Military Police, it will mean a court martial for both of us. If necessary I will kill him myself and claim he was shot by the Hun. Will you back me up?"

"Yes, Sergeant, I will. That bastard should not have buggered off. What will you do to him, if you get him back?"

"Let me catch him first, and then we'll see."

Enrico crawled out of the shell hole and slithered this way and that in the general direction of where Lynch had seen something. He was a past master of creeping around without being seen or heard, and he made his way quickly into the unknown.

He didn't have to go far. There, huddled into a foetus position and crying softly to himself was one Private Tyler.

"For fuck's sake, what the hell do you think you're doing here?"

Tyler drew his service pistol, and pointed it at Enrico. He was in a terrible state, and though Enrico was angry, he also felt really sorry for this young lad who really should be at home in the arms of his mother.

"I'm not coming back there with you, so stay away. If I'm going to die, then let the Germans do it with a shot. I'm freezing and soaking, I cannot take any more of this hell."

"Keep your voice down, anyone from either side can hear you; both will shoot if they believe anyone is here. So what d'you think you can do? There is nowhere you can run to. If the Germans catch you, they will shoot you. If you make it back to our lines, the MPs will take you, and for sure a court martial will put you up against a wall. Think of your mother and father, the disgrace they will have to endure. We only have the night to worry about, and then tomorrow morning we will be relieved. Come back, I shall forget all about it, we can overcome problems like this."

"Sergeant, I hate this army life," whimpered Tyler, a look of abject misery etched on his boyish face. "I don't want to kill Germans. Anyway I'm too young to even be here. I was told by the recruiting Sergeant…"

"To walk around the park and come back when you are eighteen?" interrupted Enrico.

"Is that how they got you?" his crying had stopped and he was clearly bucking up.

"Yes, that's how they got me! Will you come back with me now, please?"

"Everybody has told me you are a straight man… I'll come…"
*Crack, crack!*

Enrico looked on in horror as the still crouching figure of Private Tyler just fell forward with most of his head missing.

'A sniper and he must be close by, as I could easily hear the report of the silenced gun. I'll see if I can get him before he gets me, he must know I'm here.' Fortunately for Enrico, he had never risen from his crawling position so it was very unlikely that the sniper could see him. But he knew he was there, and he must know that Enrico knew roughly where he was. The hunt was on, both men knew that. Enrico very quietly withdrew his pistol, and then moved away to his left, not making any noise whatsoever. He had to get him and quickly. He moved another twenty or so yards when he turned sharp right, then another twenty yards and another sharp right; now he should be behind the sniper, if he hadn't moved. Quiet as a mouse, Enrico stalked this German sniper. He knew if he didn't get him, the sniper might find the machine gun nest that was really quite close by, and then Private Lynch and Enrico would not stand a chance. Another couple of yards, move sideways, just a little to the rim of a shell hole.

There, in the bottom, facing the other way was the darkened figure of a German sniper, gun ready and pointing in the direction that Enrico had started from. He quietly drew his knife, easing himself onto the rim. A star shell burst with the glow of daylight, showing the world and his brother that Enrico was just about to leap. No time to think, he lunged into the hole, not worrying about noise now, and plunged his knife deep into the back of the now aware sniper. Too late for him: as the blade thrust deep, a scream that must have woken the Kaiser himself, burst forth from the shuddering Hun. He wriggled and writhed while Enrico held that knife inside him. All the time the soldier screamed, Enrico knew his own chances of getting out alive were diminishing. He pushed his free right hand under the neck of the still slithering warrior and pulled his head up quickly. There was a loud crack, and the screaming turned for a moment into a gurgle, then all was quiet. He withdrew the knife, cleaned the blade on the German's tunic, and turned onto his back. Tears were streaming from his eyes and he could not stop shaking.

He heard something that made him forget his nerves for a moment; he quietly pulled his revolver out again and cocked it. Another person was close by. He waited, hardly daring to breathe. Another pebble moved to his right, he knew now it must be another sniper: of course, they always hunt in pairs. A dark shape appeared over the rim, no sound was made, but a black cold feeling had come over Enrico: it must be number two. He took a breath, pointed his pistol and fired, *bang, bang, bang!* Then a last *bang!* again. The dark shape was dead for sure, he didn't need to look. But he also knew that every German this side of Berlin would have heard all that firing. 'Got to get back to the Lewis Gun and Lynch, and real quick.' Without thinking of the probability of being seen, he rose to his feet and ran like hell. "Coming in, don't shoot!" Just as he made it back into the hole where a trembling Private Lynch was waiting, a star shell went up along with several Very lights from the British trenches. All hell then broke loose. Guns, big and small, blazed away. Enrico and Lynch crouched in their crater, not daring to move or even talk. Terror gripped them both. Gradually, both the lads drifted into a fearful exhausted sleep, a sleep that neither expected to awaken from. Later, the firing stopped, but sleep had overtaken them in such a way that nothing was going to disturb it. When Enrico finally awoke, Private Lynch was manning the gun and the sun was once again shining.

"You let me sleep!"

"You needed it! Anyway I fell asleep too, don't tell on me and I won't tell on you!" he looked at his Sergeant and smiled warmly. "Sergeant, that was one hell of a tour of duty; d'you mind if I refuse to go next time?"

They both gave a nervous laugh, but they both knew that their luck had been close to running out.

At eight o'clock sharp that morning, along crept the relief.

"Thank God, are we both glad to see you!"

But when they got back to the line, Enrico had to write his report. He made sure that Private Tyler got a good section, explaining that the both of them had crept out to get the snipers who they knew were there. Sadly Tyler bought one and went west. Enrico was not sure that anyone believed his report, but Lynch did back him, as promised, and there was nothing for it but to accept it and carry on. Only Lieutenant Kelly knew, or at least guessed what really had happened, but he said nothing.

Sergeant Caruso and Private Lynch had both been very shaken by their ordeal, and even Colonel Allenbrie-Brooker realised that both men needed a good rest; instead of the normal bull, a week's recuperation in Poperinge would be granted. It was fortunate for Enrico that two days after he was there, Matti was also allowed a two day break; so they would meet on the 19th at Talbot House. The first thing that Enrico did was to delouse at the old slaughter house in Ypres; the water was so hot that he actually felt as if he had been slightly broiled like a lobster when climbing out, but any heat discomfort was far more preferable to the permanent itching from the lice. All his clothes had been steam cleaned, so for a short time he felt like a new man. He had his seven day pass in his pocket, and set off for Poperinge. Talbot House was full, but he had managed to secure a small attic room above an estaminet in the main square. That evening, it was going to be akin to a visit to heaven, for he was going to spend quite a bit of money on the good sweet, dark Belgian beer, and masses of eggs, ham and chips. What more could a young Sergeant want? While eating his succulent fare, an old war horse soldier from the mining division that he had got to know and like, appeared, and after greetings had been exchanged, and the pair had par-taken of a few beers, Enrico asked the now Sergeant Francis Thompson what news of the old mining brigade.

"Well, I don't know how much you know, Enrico," said Francis, as he slurped yet another beer, managing to spill most of it on the table; brushing the little puddle onto the floor with his left arm, he continued, "I suppose you heard that one of the tunnels your corporal friend and you were involved in was used to explode under the Messines Ridge."

"I heard about the battle of Messines and I guessed that would be the case, but tell me, I haven't heard of 'Empire Jack' for a long time…"

"Well, the rumour is that the top brass knew that Rumania would be kicked out of the war, and Norton Griffiths, as far as I understand, was sent there on a secret mission, to set fire to all the oil wells to stop the Germans getting their hands on the fuel. I don't know how true this is, but the word is that he was nearly taken at every turn by the Germans, but managed to stay just that one jump ahead. Anyway, the oil wells were rendered useless, but I've seen neither hide nor hair of him for a long time now. If he's got any sense, he's back in Blighty. Strange man, but you could not help but like him. I hope he survives the war."

A few more beers were consumed, and finally Enrico admitted defeat. With his bladder almost bursting, he excused himself and went to the toilet; he then decided to give in to a bed with a mattress and blankets. His last thoughts were 'If I die tonight, this is heaven!'

He awoke late to the smell of roasting coffee and freshly baked bread. He then realised that it was nine thirty, and he had slept for nearly ten hours. He arose, did his ablutions, dressed and had breakfast. He was going to spend the day catching up on some of the newspapers that were lying around; some of these papers were up to a month old, but when you don't get news, it does not matter that what news you *do* read is late. He ate a light lunch, had another siesta in the afternoon, and then decided that it might be fun to have a little action in the evening. He made his way to the southern part of town, where he knew of an estaminet that sported a few likely girls. On arriving he discovered the place was almost full to overflowing with French, Belgian, English and Commonwealth troops, and all the soldiers there were looking for the same sort of relief as Enrico, just a chance to spend an hour or two with a woman. Men were struggling to reach the bar to buy that obligatory drink. Enrico stood at the door, and realised there were two lines: one for the bar, and one for the little anteroom that held all the girls. 'Oh, blimey! Can I really be bothered? If I have sex with any of the girls here, she'll already be overflowing!' So wincing in disgust, he turned on his heels to go out, and at that moment a bright young French girl bumped into him, as she was trying to get in. His automatic reaction was to apologise, as if he was the one guilty of bumping. She smiled, and as she started to go past him, he touched her arm to stop her.

"Mademoiselle, are you going to be working here?"

A shy nod of the head was his answer. "Then can I take you out to dinner, and I will pay you to spend the night with me."

She looked at him and said: "What is your name, soldier?" and Enrico was surprised at how good her English was.

"My name is Enrico, Enrico Caruso, and before you ask, yes, I was named after the opera singer!"

"Well, Enrico Caruso, how could I ever refuse anybody with such a beautiful voice? But it will cost you a meal, a bottle of wine, and ten shillings if I'm to spend the night with you."

"Done!" Enrico rested her hand in the crook of his arm, and they both walked off to where Enrico was staying. The meal was ordered by the young girl, who had introduced herself as Odile, and this, much to Enrico's delight consisted of braised rabbit, cooked in beer and goat's cheese, with lashings of boiled potatoes, accompanied by a bottle of the best house wine. Both ate heartily, leaving nothing to be thrown away; the rabbit's life had not been in vain. This was followed by two lots of cheeses: a nice runny Camembert, which surprised Enrico, as he thought he would hate it, and some more of that goat's cheese. The meal was rounded off with a heavenly tarte aux pommes. The only downside of the meal was the coffee, which tasted more of roasted acorns than any coffee beans that may have been floating in it. Odile suggested that they go for a promenade around the town square, but after ten minutes of walking, his concentration had enlarged to other things, so with a smile on her face, she asked gently if he would like them both to retire to his boudoir. This was hastily agreed, and he almost ran back with the anticipation of what was to come.

The next morning was a surprise to everyone, as the sun had come up and warmth once again penetrated the ground. Spring was in the air, and a warm sunny day felt nice on the skin, giving that glowing feeling of rebirth; days like those made a soul come back to life. The two of them had a hearty breakfast of eggs and bacon, English style, along with lots of strong sweet tea. Enrico looked at Odile and smiled in a warm friendly way at her. He knew what she was, but she had come to him with grace and warmth, making him believe that she really cared. He appreciated her for her efforts, for making him feel special. When it was time to part, she looked at him and waited for a show of appreciation, which was given when the ten shillings he promised turned into two pound notes. Odile took them gratefully, thanked him with a full kiss on the lips, then said her goodbyes and walked out of his life. The moment she walked out of the estaminet, Enrico felt lonely. 'I am alone: there is no one in my life. I have just a few friends; 'Spider' and Matti are the closest, and Matti will almost certainly marry his Dawn, then she won't want me around. Maybe it's time I got a proper girlfriend, someone to love, just like Matti and Dawn.' He sat there at the table nursing his now cold tea, pondering why he felt so low.

The waitress approached to take his cold tea away. "Would you like some more tea?" she asked in an almost perfect accent. She was a very slight, dark haired beauty of not more than sixteen years of age; she most certainly did not look like any French or Belgian girls he had ever met. "Er, no thank you…but I will have a brandy, if you don't mind."

"Well, it is a little early, but why not!" she laughed lightly, and showed a beautiful row of white teeth. Enrico was already captivated by her looks and mannerisms.

"Where do you come from?" he asked.

"Well, that is a hard one," she answered with another little laugh, "I was born here in Belgium, in Ostend, but my father is from Poland and my mother from England, though her English is a little rusty these days."

"My God, that is fantastic, where d'you think I was born?"

"By your accent, I would say somewhere in the North of

England?"

"Well, you would be out by many hundreds of miles. I was born in Warsaw, Poland. So what d'you think of that?" They both laughed and enjoyed the banter between them. Enrico never did get his brandy; he got something much better…hope for the future. This was the first time in his life that he had ever looked at a girl and thought about something other than being nursed, served or sexually relieved. It was a warm glowing feeling, just like the day outside.

"What is your name?" he enquired in a quiet gentle voice.

"Sheila, Sheila Georgiou. And yours?"

"Enrico Caruso Lokowski. And before you ask, yes after the Italian opera singer!" "Which opera singer is that?" she retorted in a deadpan way that completely threw Enrico. Then the penny dropped, she had been teasing him, and again they both laughed. At this point Enrico was very glad that Sheila had not spied Odile coming or going. 'This is crazy, why should I worry about anything, we have only just met. Am I going mad or something?'

"Sheila, I'm here for several days; would it be possible for me to take you out for a meal or something, anytime or anywhere, just to suit you?"

"Well, I would love to do something with you, but you will have to ask my mother first. My father is in the Belgian army, and we have not heard anything from him since 1915; we don't know if he is alive or dead, though I have a very strong feeling he is still alive and fighting somewhere."

She went on to tell him most of her life story there and then, then after bringing some more acorn coffee, this time for both of them, she sat listening to Enrico telling his own story, about how they got stuck in England, his mother dying, his father's drinking then dying, his school life and especially about his dearest friend Matti. They laughed and joked for a great deal of the morning until the owner came in looking for her, and gave her a serious dressing down for not doing any work. Enrico took the blame upon himself, and promised not to hold her back anymore. He took her hand gently, kissed it in a friendly way that gave no offence, promised to meet her after her shift had finished at seven o'clock that night and escort her to her home. He very nearly danced out of the estaminet with delight; he felt so light and happy, after being so low earlier. 'How quickly things can change!' he thought, as he made his way towards Talbot House and friend Matti. 'Boy, have I got things to tell him!' He didn't have to wait, as Matti was there to greet him.

"What have you been up to? You have an expression of delight on your mug that I've never witnessed before. Have you been a dirty sly dog?" asked Matti, and then looked around to make sure that no 'Tubby' Clayton was overhearing their conversation.

"Well, yes, I have been up to no good, which I now regret, because I have met the girl of my dreams!"

"Are you serious? Who is she?" Matti looked on his friend with a new sense of wonderment, being an incurable romantic. He could already envision a double wedding and the four of them living happily ever after together. Matti could hope and dream with the best of them!

Enrico ordered two teas, and then proceeded to tell his friend all the latest news. They both sat at the table, talked and were happy. It didn't take much to brighten their days, simple pleasures were enough.

"Well, you realise I'll have to vet this young lady for suitability," joked Matti.

"I promised to escort her home after work, so I suppose, if you really feel you must tag along, I won't stop you. Maybe you will then think I've lost my marbles?"

"Listen," interrupted Matti, cupping a hand to his ear, "the guns seem to have got more intense, don't you think so?"

"They are German guns; you can hear whiz bangs amongst that lot. I wouldn't want to be in the trenches right now, that is starting to sound serious. Wait... can you hear that... that's British sixty pounders answering back. Blimey, what's going on there then?"

Indeed the guns had opened up on both sides: there was a definite duel going on, not the spasmodic bursts that were there to keep both sides on their toes.

"I'm glad we're on leave."

"Enrico, look who has just come through the door, it's the little Jew! So the bugger has survived so far."

"Maurice, over here!" called Enrico. Maurice looked around to see who was calling over to him. When he saw who it was, his sun-browned face lit up into a beaming golden colour, and he almost ran to his old friends.

"The Lord Jehovah, why aren't you both gone bleedin' west then?"

Enrico stood and hugged the little Jew, and very nearly smacked a kiss on his cheeks, but thought better of it at the last moment.

"My God, it's good to see you, let me give the blighter a hug too!" exclaimed Matti, as he pushed Enrico out of the way. "Lieutenant Kelly said you have volunteered to join the runners, and you seem to have come through alright then?"

"It's true, nothing was quite the same after High Wood: all the old Brigade were like the song says, 'anging on the old barbed wire. There was no one that I knew or liked left. I thought of trying to follow you two, but as you were obviously a right couple of poofs, I didn't like to get between you…in more ways than one. So I became a runner. To tell the truth, most of my work 'as been far behind the lines, and that's 'ow I likes it. I've 'ad enough of this 'ere bleedin' shootin' nonsense, people get 'urt."

"My goodness, it was always hard to understand what the hell you were talking about, but now, it seems ten times worse," laughed Enrico. "Sit down and let me buy you a cup of splodge."

"Boy, it's a treat for me 'umble pies to see you two tossers again."

"Such a delicate turn of phrase you have there, Maurice old pal! It's a fair treat to my ears to hear such eloquence spoken in the King's

English. What university was it again?" jibed Enrico, knowing darn well Maurice wouldn't have a clue as to what he was talking about; in fact the only remark that came back, along with a blank expression was "*ehhhhh?*"

The three of them were united again like the three musketeers, yet with three entirely different personalities, showing that anyone can gel and mix during times of conflict. In Civvy Street, they wouldn't even have looked at one another, but in the army, mutual preservation became the rule of thumb. War made strange bedfellows.

"Tell me, Maurice, don't you think the guns have got more intense?" asked Matti, straining an ear again.

"I 'aves to say I fink so. I fink Fritz is spoiling for fight, especially now they knocked the Ruskies out of the game."

"Enrico, what and who is calling out?"

It was true; someone from the street was calling for all troops to come out. Gradually Talbot House cleared of soldiers, everyone milling towards the town square. There, standing on a large cart in the centre was a Regimental Sergeant Major from the Irish Guards; next to him was a Lieutenant Colonel from the same regiment. The Sergeant was asking for quiet, though he made much more noise than the entire crowd put together.

"Quiet, you men, this is important, let the Officer speak!" screamed the Sergeant Major. Protecting his ears from the pain of being screamed next to, the Colonel quickly climbed onto the wagon to talk to the men present.

"Men, we believe that the Germans are going to attack, if they haven't already. Orders have come through that everyone, except the wounded, must return to their units immediately: that means right now. Get your rifles and all your gear then back you go. Sorry, I am sure that you all deserve your leave, but the war won't wait for you. God's speed to you all."

"Shit, I knew something was wrong. Now I'll have to postpone my little rendezvous with Sheila, I'm going to run over and tell her right away. Anyway, I'll have to pick up my gear from the estaminet. Meet you back here in ten minutes; see if you can get us transport, I can't really say I fancy the walk back!"

Enrico gave a quick hug to Maurice, "and where d'you have to report to?"

"Well, Sergeant, seeing as you is twisting me arm, and threatening me with physical violence, until I get orders to the contrary, I guess I'll be coming back with you two 'erberts!"

"That's great! Then go with Matti, steal a rifle, and get us all some transport."

Enrico ran out of the door; looking back he shouted one last thing: "Ten minutes, that's all!"

He ran across the other side of the square, and down the road to where his estaminet was. He looked for Sheila, but did not immediately see her. He ran up the stairs, grabbed his rifle, packed his gear and went to find the patron to pay his bill.

"Can I have a quick word with Sheila?"

"I'm supposed to look after her; she is working here, not socialising!" but when he noticed that Enrico's face had turned from a polite expression to an extremely angry glare, he backed off, saying: "I'll just go and get her, but don't keep her long!"

Two minutes later, when she appeared, Enrico took both her hands in his, "Sheila, I know we don't know one another, and I think your mother might be unhappy you are talking so seriously to a British soldier, but from the moment your face came into view, I've had a feeling I've never experienced before. As you probably realised, the guns have become more intense, and now we've just had orders to return to our unit, so I cannot escort you home tonight. Just tell me that I can come and see you next time I get leave, and that will be a good enough reason for me to stay alive."

She smiled graciously at him, squeezed his hand gently, and said: "I like you too" immediately, "and of course, I'll look forward to meeting you again." With that Enrico leant forward, and kissed her gently on her forehead, picked up his things, and went to the door, looked back, and smiled one last time.

Matti had managed to flag down an empty ambulance.

"Where are you going, Private?"

"We've been ordered to go to Essex Farm; for some reason they're going to evacuate the wounded there."

"Right, you're going to take three of us that way. You can drop us off at the crossroads to Essex Farm, and we'll make our way into Wipers. We're just waiting for the Sergeant." As he spoke Enrico was already walking around the corner towards them.

As it turned out, there were so many soldiers going back into the salient that it might have been just as quick to walk, and what should have taken no more than twenty minutes took more than two hours. At the crossroads they said goodbye and good luck to the driver, and very quickly made for the trench system that would take them into the town centre where they made their way across to the Lille gate, and into the section that housed their brigade. Enrico was amazed to see how quickly the top brass had organised the resupplying of ammunition, and everybody from the lowest squaddie to a top officer was made to carry in boxes of bullets, Mills bombs, or Stokes mortars. They were determined not to be caught with their pants down. The lads decided to bypass the Colonel, and find 'Spider', who most certainly would be organising the men into position. Finally, after an hour of searching, there he was, on the floor of a dugout, with at least half a dozen Sergeants hovering over him, studying a map of the trench system. The Sergeants were dismissed to do his bidding, and it was then that Lieutenant Kelly became aware of Matti, Enrico, and the little Jew.

"Enrico, Matti, Bechstein, I'm glad to see you got back here.

Trouble is brewing. In the last hour, we've lost at least thirty soldiers from the shelling, and spotter planes have come back, informing us of a huge build-up of Hun troops over a fifty mile range of ground, mainly British sectors."

At this he turned to Maurice: "It's good to see you here. But why are you here? Have you been ordered back?"

"I'm on leave, too, Sir, so as there is no unit per se for me to go to, I fought it would be nice to be back with friendly, familiar faces."

Kelly smiled, as he acknowledged the statement. "Well, you realise I won't be able to save you, when they put you up against the wall for abandoning your position, but don't worry too much, as you'll already be dead from the Germans!"

"Charming!" said Maurice. "So I'll be shot if I do, and shot if I don't!"

At this they all laughed.

Michael Kelly then turned to Enrico: "Would you object to taking a band of twenty or thirty machine gunners and bombers, and take a very forward point in no-man's-land? Dig in well, and hold the position if there is an attack, until you've almost run out of ammunition, and then run a strategic retreat. I want to make sure that Fritz is made well aware that it is not going to be a pushover to take our lines, even if we are outnumbered and outgunned. Once the battle starts, we will use rockets for communication; yellow means keep your bloody heads down, red means let them have it with everything, and blue means get the hell out of there as quick as possible! You can take Matti and Bechstein with you if you so wish. But what I suggest you do, is to get half a dozen of the men you would like to put in charge of small squads, and decide your positioning in the shell holes. As far as I understand it, every area in the Salient is doing the same, so you won't be alone out there in no-man's-land."

"Sir, I'll be very happy to do this, but I would like to ask Matti and Maurice if they would like to come, not order them." And as he looked back, he knew he'd already wasted his breath: they were not going to leave him. Enrico was quickly introduced to the rest of the happy band of marauders. He selected five other men who looked as if they would not panic under close fire, then divided the rest of the men into various squads. He then addressed them, telling them exactly what was expected of them, and ordered the men to gather all the ammunition and bombs they could carry. They weren't going to go out until it was dark, which would give them plenty of time to find suitable shell holes, and dig in and prepare. But prepare for what? Did Enrico or anyone else really know or understand the workings of the German military mind, what was going to happen, and more importantly when?

It was a cool but clear bright day, and Enrico and Matti had prepared everything they could think of for the journey back into no-man's-land; again, nerves were taut but their courage could not be questioned. It seemed to take an eternity for the sun to go down and darkness to envelop the battlefield. At first, long shadows gave a very eerie aspect to the landscape, and no one could have got ten yards past the wire without being seen, but just before eleven o'clock that night heavy duty clouds crossed over the sky and gave them the sort of darkness that they desired.

"Does everybody have everything they need? I know you have all got plenty of ammunition and bombs, but what about rations, and water? Water is the most important, make sure you have all filled your canteens, and make sure you can steal or borrow one or two more for yourselves, you cannot have too many. When we're out there, nobody is to fire off any shots unless it's to save yourself from attack, or if you hear me blow this whistle three times…How many times must I blow it?"

A chorus of, "three times, Sergeant!" was the reply that he wanted and got.

"Right then, we might be out there hours or maybe days or weeks, though personally I hope it's for just hours. You now all know where you're going and who's in charge; follow your orders and make every bullet count.

Good luck, and stay alive."

Gradually, group by group they moved out into the unknown, and what ever fate had in store for them. Enrico was the last to leave; he turned to make sure that everyone was geared up, and then looked up and down the trench, just in time to see 'Spider' Kelly come around the bend and hail him.

"Oh, thank goodness I found you before you went. Good luck, kill as many as possible, stay alive and come back safe. Short and to the point, that's me for you."

Kelly held out his hand for Enrico to take. They shook hands and looked at one another.

"Take care of yourself, Michael, make sure you stay alive. Matti and me, we will survive, we're immortal, and you know that!"

He smiled, turned, climbed the wire and waited for his own squad to follow, and then they all disappeared into the gloom of the darkness, away from the British front line trench.

'God, they were quiet. I taught them well. Please, God, bring them back safely.'

The shelling had slowed in all sectors, which meant that it was very quiet out in no-man's-land, but the lads had been well trained in being quiet, and all made it to their respective shell holes without incident. They immediately set up their machine guns, positioned all their weapons in preparation for the forthcoming battle, and then started to dig into the shell holes to make them safer and better strongholds against the Hun, if and when they decided to attack. By first light, everyone had managed to complete their work and they were all well hidden from the enemy. As light swept long shadows once again over the cratered landscape, Enrico turned to Matti, who was on the verge of closing his eyes and trying to sleep, and said, "The light plays incredible tricks on one's eyes this time in the morning, but how beautiful it all looks with these orange and yellowish brown colours; any good painter could have a field day here."

"I wish they would: any painter can have my place any day," retorted Matti. He then closed his eyes and before Enrico could say another word was gently snoring, almost to the rhythm of the guns. He smiled to himself and could only think of his friend in a caring protective way. If Matti needed to sleep, then let him. Once more the guns started to pick up in ferocity and then some even started to drop in their sector. Matti woke up when he heard the familiar whining of a whiz bang drop quite close by. "Has it started?" he asked, as he grabbed for his rifle.

"I cannot be sure; I've been looking through the periscope, but can see no serious movement from the Hun trench." At just that moment a machine gun started firing from the German line, a machine gun nest that they knew nothing about.

"Where the heck did he spring from?" enquired Enrico, but knew he would get no answer from any of his men. Looking frantically from side to side, he was searching for that first sight of men jumping up out of their trench. He then heard another machine gun open up from behind the British lines. 'Maybe it's just a duel between the two of them,' he thought. Mortars started to drop around their sector again, all the time getting closer to the various shell holes housing the machine gunners and bombers. There was a huge explosion, off to Enrico's right, followed by a single scream. One of his team had been knocked out, for the explosion was from a mortar hitting the bombs, maybe setting one or two off. There was nothing that Enrico could do; if there were any survivors they would have to make the best of it and try and make their own way back to some sort of safety. This became the pattern for the day, shelling at random, machine gunning to provoke some sort of response, and mortars to weed out groups like his, which were going to make a stand in no-man's-land. All they could do was keep their heads down, and pray to whatever God would be looking out for them. The day wore on slowly for Matti and Enrico; nothing much was said; they just lay on the crater floor, huddled up together, waiting for that shell that would take them away from this hell hole. That shell never came for them, and as night once again started to close in around them, they knew that they were of course immortal.

When the sun sank over the horizon, on this night of the 20th March there was no moon, just extremely angry dark clouds that threatened rain, but never gave it; Enrico realised this was the right time to crawl from shell hole to shell hole and make sure that everyone was once again fine and dandy. A star shell went up from the Hun side then two from the British. Each time that happened, Enrico would freeze in whatever position he found himself. Each time he approached a refuge he was challenged, but of course gave the right countersign. It was not until he reached the far right shell hole, at the end of their sector that he found where the explosion had occurred. Still smouldering were the remains of the six men who had been sent there, all very badly burnt and blown apart. Once again, Enrico felt nausea swell up from the pit of his stomach, and once again managed to swallow it back down. Well, there was nothing to do here, better to get back to his own hole in the ground; anyway, he was feeling extremely cold and tired from the tension of crawling out across this ravaged land.

It was then that he noticed two things that made him start. The first was the four huge rats already eating the remains of his friends in the hole. They were so big and tame, that they paid no heed at all to Enrico, probably thinking he might well be the next meal to dine on. Then from the corner of his eye, he noticed some movement. He froze, but quietly managed to draw his service revolver. It was a German sniper, obviously coming to find out what had happened in this area. Enrico played dead as the Hun soldier crawled up to the lip of the crater. The German froze too, as he heard a rustling sound coming from within the hole. He relaxed a little when he heard the scurrying of what could only be rats. He took another move nearer. Enrico looked squarely at him knowing he probably couldn't be seen in return, as he was slightly obscured by debris of shelling. 'What is he looking for?' thought Enrico. The German started to move

467

around the crater, coming closer to where Enrico was hiding. 'He must see my legs soon.' He did, but mistook them for just that, legs lying in the collection of body parts. Enrico didn't breathe, just stayed as still as the grave. He could now hear the sound of the German breathing heavily; he was not more than two feet away. Enrico's pistol was almost at his head, what should he do?

He didn't know what the next move should be. The German was just lying there, right in front of him, but luck being what it was, the sniper was looking down into the crater floor. He moved again, this time he slipped into the hole. Enrico heard the sound of clothing being moved. 'The bastard is searching for something in the bodies.' He then heard what could only have been a can being opened, then the gurgle of water being drunk from a bottle. 'The bugger is hungry and thirsty; he's stealing the dead men's rations.' Then a scratching sound came up, a small light appeared then immediately disappeared again, followed by an exhaling of breath. Enrico watched as a small cloud of smoke lazily went skywards. Then he heard the rustle of papers. 'He must be looking for clues or something about these men. I'll have to stop him. But let the sod have his last cigarette.' Enrico quietly withdrew his knife, but kept his gun handy too. After what seemed a lifetime, but was only another five minutes, Enrico heard the obvious sound of the soldier putting out his cigarette: this was his moment. He raised himself into a crouching position and sprang over the rim onto the luckless German. His knife went this way and that, making sure that his throat was well and truly cut to stop any scream from launching out. He must have stuck that blade into the Hun twenty times; which probably were nineteen too many, as the man was quite dead from the throat slash. Enrico was panting furiously, his heart pounding like a jazz drummer doing his solo. 'Time to get out of here before his friends start coming over!'

On his way back he informed each group of what had happened, and advised them to keep a vigilant watch for any movement... no sleep tonight!

Four o'clock in the morning of the 21st March 1918; Enrico was once again woken from a fitful sleep by the changing sound of the big guns. All the squad were wide awake and listening intently. At first it seemed that the guns were just picking up in intensity again, but then it became obvious that the sound was getting louder and it looked as if it was coming from the south. What had happened was that the German guns had started their bombardment from the area of Arras, and that was then the signal for all the guns to intensify their bombardment of the British lines. The noise was terrible; nothing had ever prepared Enrico, Matti or any of the others for such a terrifying attack of shells. Everywhere shells were exploding, sometimes gas was used, but fortunately not in Enrico's sector. Detonations blasted all around them, and there was nothing that one could do, but put one's head into the honest earth and hope and pray for the best.

Enrico and Matti, with Maurice Bechstein close at hand, were lying face down, shaking and trembling in such an intense way that an older, less fit person would have had a heart attack or stroke and perished there and then. Enrico thought of his father and mother, Matti thought of Dawn, Maurice thought of London. All three were expecting to die at any minute. A shell burst, not more than three feet away from their left side of the crater rim. They were nearly buried alive from the dirt thrown from the explosion; they all scrambled to get on top of the soil that had been blasted into their hole. Enrico knew that tears were welling up in his eyes, and fear gripped his stomach so badly that he thought he was about to lose control of his bowels. Indeed he just kept passing the worst wind he had ever known, not that anyone gave it a thought or even cared enough to complain; truth be known they were all doing the same thing. Matti was screaming loudly, but not as loud as the shells were singing their songs overhead. Maurice had gone into Orthodox mode, and lay in the hole, reciting lamentations that he didn't even know he knew, again lying there just rocking his head backwards and forwards. The same was happening in some way or another to all the men out there in no-man's-land, and in the trenches.

The firing seemed to go on forever. Many men were killed from the shelling or the gas, many went quite mad. Some even got up in the trenches and ran around screaming wildly, until fragments from a shell took them west. It was something these men had never experienced before, though even if they had, one never got used to this sort of treatment. Bits of soldiers, past and present, were being thrown this way and that. Bits of men were hanging out on the wire, until another shell took those pieces and threw them somewhere else. Enrico knew that he had now died and gone to hell. He felt almost calm with that thought: after all the traumas, he turned out to be mortal after all. 'Anyway, if this is hell, then at least it cannot get any worse.' Matti was so dry and so hungry that all he thought about now was the raging thirst in his throat, and the hunger pangs in his stomach. Getting some respite from these feelings was far more urgent than worrying if he was going to be blown up. He stretched his hand out to where his canteen should be. 'Got it, but where's the water?' A jagged hole could clearly be seen in the side: it was a shell fragment that had emptied it. He stretched again, and found a full one this time. He drank and drank until the canteen was almost completely devoid of liquid. Then he remembered the hunger. Again he stretched out his hand to find a large tin of bully beef. He withdrew his bayonet, and started to cut the can open. He grabbed at the contents and pushed as much as he could into his mouth, hardly taking time to chew, just swallowing then biting at more. Maurice lay there now, just nodding; he was a quivering mess, he wasn't thinking of anything any more, just lay there and nodded.

In the front line trenches, men were being splattered with the remains of the comrades who had been next to them. Sometimes a shell piece would kill all in a section, other times the explosion might just kill one who was standing in the middle of a group, leaving the others wounded or even unhurt. But at least now, they knew when the attack was going to happen: after the shelling stopped.

Over a fifty mile stretch of British trench systems, the bombardment harried the troops, killing, maiming and driving men mad. But at five thirty that morning the bombardment changed yet again. Now the guns had lowered, flattening no-man's-land and it became obvious to all that this was now the start of a creeping barrage, which meant the soldiers were going to be close behind.

Enrico and Matti understood this too. Enrico peered over the rim, having lost the periscope under a pile of debris.

"Shit, lads, keep down, here comes a creeping barrage!" Shells soon burst in front of them, all around them, then behind them. Once again they were unhurt, having come through yet another terrifying ordeal. Matti looked at Enrico, and fairly exclaimed in amazement, "Enrico, you have gone completely white! You've lost your black hair."

"Matti, get your gun ready, don't worry about the colour of my hair; at least I still have hair on a head, and a head on shoulders. Sometimes you're a bloody idiot! Look, it's ash and dirt... black underneath?"

"Oh yes; sorry."

Then all of a sudden, a terrifyingly loud scream was heard from the German trenches: they were coming. "Ready, men? Get those Mills bombs primed, fix another belt ready for the Lewis gun. Prepare yourselves; we've just a moment or two before they know we're here. Where is that bloody whistle?" He looked around but could not remember where he had put it. He was too scared really to care; he knew that all the groups would start firing in a second or two. The attackers were in their thousands; Enrico had never seen such a charge up to now; counterattacks he had known before, but never anything like this.

The first Hun soldiers were now no more than twenty yards away when Enrico heard himself give the order to fire. It was him that said the words, it was even him that took a Mills bomb and started throwing, but he wasn't in the body that was doing these things; his mind was in two places: one fighting the Hun, the other looking on as if nothing meant anything to him anymore; this persona was just going through the motions. The Lewis gun took its toll. Germans were rushing headlong into a solid wall of lead. Men just fell forward, one after another. Again, Enrico knew he was throwing bombs, but he was also just casually looking on this scene of carnage as if looking at a painting. Another belt was placed into the gun, and then it seized up.

"Enrico!" screamed Matti, "The fucking gun has jammed, what shall we do?"

"Piss on it, throw water over the barrel... Come on, lads you know what to do!"

Who was that talking? It sounded like Enrico, it came from his mouth, but his doppelgänger had hardly understood what or how things were getting done. Another wave of attackers came over; now they were spilling over their own dead to get forward. Stick grenades started to bang around the shell hole. Enrico threw a Mills at where he thought they were coming from... *Bang!* his other self watched as a German soldier left the ground for what seemed a long slow climb, but in reality was up about two feet, and down into the ground inside of a second. *Splut, splut!* bullets were starting to ping all around them. It was now obvious to the Germans where they were, and it was going to get a lot tougher from now on. The gun started to work again. Another box of Mills bombs was opened. A small squeal came from the far side of the shell hole, and the other Enrico noticed that Charles Collins had bought one, and slumped forward onto his own rucksack. Enrico reached over and grabbed his rifle. He was still wondering who was going to fire it when he realised that he was looking down the barrel and sighting on running enemy. Enrico shouted orders to Matti to wheel the Lewis over to the left, as some Germans seemed to be bypassing them, and he knew if they were surrounded it would all be up quite quickly.

The other Enrico just looked on in wonderment. A huge blast sent

472

him reeling back: a stick grenade had landed on the edge of their crater. He was alright, just winded. He picked up the rifle and again started firing into onrushing Germans. In some places the death rate of the attackers had been so bad that men had fallen onto other men, pinning them to the ground, and they were gradually covered and suffocated by more and more falling men. Maurice was feeding the belts into the Lewis gun, and out of the barrel were spurting hard, hot lumps of death. There were so many attackers, Matti didn't have to aim, just fire; he was sure to be bringing more and more down, but one thing was certain at this moment, no Germans had passed yet. Enrico asked Matti, "How many more belts of bullets do we have left?"

"Maybe a box full, but then we are in trouble, and that box is under the pile of dirt that tried hard to cover us! Can you find it?"

"One jump ahead of you. Here it is… need something though to open it."

"Wake up, Enrico, use your bayonet! Are you here with us?" Matti looked at Enrico closely, wondering what was going on in his mind.

Enrico opened the last box; he knew this ammunition would last no more than ten minutes at this rate of firing. There were probably no more than thirty Mills bombs left, which would not even last a few minutes at the speed that they were being thrown. They all still had their rifles and service revolvers, and then it would mean throwing sticks and stones. Not quite what Lieutenant Kelly had in mind for them! The enemy had made a temporary withdrawal; this gave what was left of the squad time to regroup. Then it was another onslaught, with even more Hun chasing across this ravaged moonscape of Flanders, to kill and expel the British, once and for all. Once the battle had started, in many parts the attackers had completely overrun the Allies. In many instances, entire Brigades had been completely wiped off the face of the earth. Thousands and thousands of men from both sides had been killed or wounded. This was indeed the start of the Kaiser's last battle, the "Kaiserschlacht". They were finally going to sweep the British back. It was a desperate gamble, made by desperate men, army Officers who knew that this was indeed the last throw of the dice; double sixes had to appear on every throw.

More than one million men on the German side initially swept the British reeling at Amiens and St. Quentin. The shock was extremely great all along the fifty mile front. This even entailed a tank-to-tank battle, which was the very first ever. The Germans had captured and used many British MK IVs and MK Vs. They had also developed an extreme vehicle of their own which was called an "A7V Sturmpanzerwagen". It was a huge lumbering beast that had a crew of eighteen, armed with 57mm guns, but like its British counterpart, was overweight, being a little over thirty tons, and underpowered. It was high and easily blown up, or knocked over by a shell hitting the side. As it was so tall and clumsy, any severe incline might just topple it over as well. There had been twenty A7V tanks produced; none of them survived the battle.

Enrico and Matti knew the end was closing in on them, when the next wave of Germans attacked. Again the Lewis gun jammed through overheating. Again, their precious water was used to cool it down. Gradually the Germans crept closer, now finally using snipers behind their wall of dead troops. Enrico knew that any minute now they must make a run for it, and he explained that it would be every man for himself, if anyone fell for whatever reason; it was the duty of the others to leave him behind. These were the orders given to him, and he didn't like them, but he would make sure that they would be carried out. The last Mills bombs were thrown, the last belt was used. They exchanged rifle fire with the Hun, while Matti smashed the Lewis gun so that it could not be used by the enemy.

"Ready, lads? We have to make a run for it and now… Look, there are now Germans a little way behind us, we'll have to try and dodge them. Good luck, see you all back at our line… Go!"

They had fixed bayonets and had to now run the gauntlet. Enrico noticed that there was a German soldier lining up his rifle to fire at one of them, so it was his duty to get rid of him first. He fired from the hip on the run. Missed, but the German fired and caught Private Nigel Tagging, who dropped like a stone, just a couple of yards from the crater which had been home for the last couple of days. Enrico, now in charge of his own senses, ran as fast as he could and caught the German who just stood there trying to reload; he thrust his bayonet into the man whose mouth fell open with the shock of the attack; he didn't scream or shout, just grabbed at the bayonet as it pushed into his stomach, then looked on in horror as his fingers left his hand as the bayonet was pulled out again. He remained standing, not in pain, merely in shock, then a shot from the British front line trench entered his chest and he fell forward and died. In the time the German had taken to hit the ground, Enrico was already close to the front line wire, trying not to run in a straight line. But he realised too late that he had taken the wrong route, and had to run to his left while trying once again to find the opening. But where was the opening? The wire had been blown this way and that by the bombardment. Enrico decided, as he noticed that Matti and Maurice were having the same problem, just to try and crawl through what was in front of him. By this time his rifle was of no further use to him, so he threw it away, and went on all fours to crawl under the wire. He was soon caught up on the barbs quite badly, and started to feel panic coming on.

The other Enrico appeared again, completely out of his body, not understanding what was happening or why; with all the crashing and banging going on all around him, why didn't he feel fear? No fear, just muddleheadedness. He felt something hit him, his other self looked on, felt no pain; but Enrico on the ground knew that pain: he had been shot in the leg again. But it could not be serious as he could still move forward. He untangled himself, and not for the first time from the wire, and moved onwards again. Now he could clearly see friendly faces, not that any soldier on the firing line could take time to notice him; he was on his own. Three more yards of wire. Lift this piece, crawl, lift that piece, and crawl again. Then the wire sprung once more. He looked the way he had come to see a dead German who had made it to the wire, and crashed into it in his death throws. One more effort, there, was the lip of the trench. Bullets were whistling all around again. But he had made it. He fell into the trench as if it was heaven, he almost kissed the ground. He felt his doppelgänger enter the reality of the situation and promptly fainted.

The next day he awoke to find that he was in a field dressing station with his left foot sticking up in the air with a huge dressing on it. It was not a serious wound, but it hurt like hell. He would be out of action again for a week or two, at least that's what he hoped. But what of Matti and Maurice? He looked around but could see no faces that he recognised. When he tried to get some attention, he was sharply told by an orderly to keep his trap shut, they were not there for his pleasure. So he shut his trap.

The shelling and firing were fierce indeed, not for a moment did anything let up. The Hun had now already pushed another forty miles past St. Quentin, well on their way to doing what they had set out to do. The trouble was that soon, the front line Germans had completely outrun their supplies; this meant that when the attackers found a British food store, the German Officers could not stop the ordinary soldiers from pilfering the hoard of stores that the British had. Germany was starving, the soldiers had the worst foodstuff of any fighting army; little wonder that they thought they had entered paradise when confronting the riches of a British food dump. Wine and spirits were flowing like water; men were in a state of total anarchy: all that was on their minds was how could they win against men that were being fed this well.

Soon, the tide turned once more, and the attackers became defenders once again, and were pushed more or less back to their starting line. The battle was called off on the 25th April 1918. Nearly two hundred thousand Germans had been killed or wounded, which more or less equalled the British and Commonwealth casualties. General Gough was made the scapegoat for the near defeat of the Allies, and sacked.

As for the Ypres Salient, the Germans never entered the town, the nearest they got was about half a mile from the centre, on the Menin Road. No German made it into the town unless as a prisoner.

Enrico was discharged from the dressing station after just four days, and was sent back to the front line, though he had now obtained a nasty limp from the wound on his leg. It was going to trouble him for a month or more, but apart from yet another scar, he would be relatively unscathed. Matti had made it safely through the wire, along with the little Jew; but none of the others made it back, though several were taken prisoners, and eventually made their way into Germany, but not in the way they would have wished! Matti had not been able to visit Enrico, as no one was being allowed to leave the trenches. General Douglas Haig had sent out an edict stating that… "No man should leave his post, unless wounded or dead. This was going to be to the last man and the last bullet…!"

Enrico, to his great joy, found Matti and Michael 'Spider' Kelly straight away, in the trench where they had jumped off from, just those few days ago.

"Bugger me, Matti, look what bad penny has turned up! Can't you stay dead for just once in your life?" said Kelly as he turned and saw his friend standing there. Matti went wild with happiness, threw his arms around his pal, and then nearly put him straight back in hospital as he lunged into his bad leg.

"Christ, man, I wanted to come over but they wouldn't let me… Duck, here comes a whiz bang!" *Zinnnnng, crack!* But it was further down the trench that it did its nasty work. "I thought I would be sent to hospital, but after only four days, here I am again. 'Spider', I need a holiday by the warm sea, could you arrange that for me for maybe tomorrow?"

"Not a chance, sunshine: we need everybody here; they have driven us back, but they haven't broken through, and we're not going to let them. I need you more now than I have ever needed you. Are you going to be up to it?"

"Of course I'm here for you two; I won't let you down, though I have to tell you that being out there was the scariest thing I have ever had to do. But one good thing came out of it… I didn't fall into any slimy body parts this time."

A chuckle came from the other two, but it was quickly back to business.

"With that leg injured again, I guess carrying ammunition is out for you for a while, but you can still man a Lewis gun or mortar?"

"No problem, just lead me there and give me the tools; I'll shoot the swine as they come near."

"Oh, they'll come near again, that you can be sure of! Have you eaten lately?"

"No, to be honest I could use a good feed up right now."

"Right, get some tins of whatever, and bring them with you back here. There is a food store literally round the next corner, right next to the shit hole."

"Oh, well thought out! Right next to the shit hole. Good thinking that! What has happened to our Colonel?"

"He bought it almost right at the outset. Silly arse stood proud on the fire step, lasted all of ten seconds. He was hit by at least five bullets; he died as he would have wanted to." Then Kelly shrugged his shoulders and added: "Missed by no one."

Life back in the front line trenches was now more dangerous than anyone had ever experienced before. The Hun troops kept up a constant attack, either with stormtroops or just the continued shelling. Relentless shelling; there was no safe area, and in the front line soldiers were only expecting to live hours, not even days. There was no sleep, and precious little hot food reaching those men; this was partly due to the fact that the cooks had been drafted into becoming riflemen too. Even the musicians, who in time of battle became stretcher bearers, were now expected to tote a rifle and use it on the enemy. No one was exempt from the labours of the battle, even the wounded like Enrico had to go back to the line and continue doing their duty.

But Fritz never broke that line completely, and by the 1st April 1918, everyone knew that the Kaiser's troops were broken, and that now it was the turn of the Allies to start the long push back. All that waste of life, and for what? Like most of the battles of the Great War, it became attrition. After the 1st April it became very clear that once again, Wipers had held out. Now was the time for the politicians; maybe Germany and the Austro Hungarian Empire could be dealt the final killer blow at the conference table?

# XIII

Life after the 1st April started to become a little more relaxed within the front line trenches. The Germans were a beaten army, yet it didn't mean that they were finished: they still had a sting in their tails, but everyone, including the Hun themselves, knew they could not win this war. At best, by fighting on, they could hopefully make a satisfactory peace.

Finally, after the 5th April, the fighting stopped, though the big guns went back to the normal harassing that had been the norm since 1914, when the first signs of stalemate appeared. Hot food made it down to the front line again. Men were now getting relieved from their arduous duties; this meant that they could bathe, delouse, change clothes, get minor ailments looked at by some sort of medical orderly. Army bull remained as intense as ever, and the soldiers were almost grateful for seeing Officers that they once again saluted, Sergeants that gave them hell, Corporals that bossed everyone around; life was indeed good!

Matti was given leave, a proper seven days' leave, time enough to go to Calais where he could see his beloved Dawn. It was strange for Enrico, but Matti was indeed becoming independent; at first he felt sad and slightly resentful, but those feelings quickly passed as he understood and accepted that his closest friend was so happy. Anyway, with luck, Enrico might be going down the same road: he was so looking forward to meeting Sheila again, and this time, getting to take her home and meet her mother, and then who knows what?

Maurice had been in trouble with a German who made it into the front line trench. Much to the little Jew's horror, just as the Hun soldier jumped down into the trench, Maurice's gun jammed. So while the soldier was trying to organise a thrust with his bayonet, Maurice hit him in the mouth with his fist. Down the German went, but as he fell, his rifle came up and hit the cockney sparrow in the teeth, knocking most of his top row out. The German should have been grateful, because that punch saved his life: he became a prisoner, but the little Jew, who was never a handsome man, now looked awful, and when he grinned it was almost too much to bear by anyone but the bravest. But what was left of the broken teeth started to give cause for alarm, so he was escorted back to a field dressing station, and the rest were removed… without any anaesthetic!

The 15th April came; this was the big day for Enrico, for once again, he could now try and finish his leave in Poperinge and finally meet Sheila, and her family. He had written to her on several occasions, addressing his letters to the estaminet where they had first met. She wrote one letter back, saying how much she looked forward to their meeting. She also said that her father was now home, and looked forward to speaking Polish again. Her father had been captured by the Germans and given hard labour, but a couple of months ago he had escaped into Holland then made his way back; while crossing the border, a Dutch guard had shot him in the leg, which eventually turned gangrenous and had to be cut off. When he had recovered sufficiently, he was discharged from the service and allowed to go home.

So, dressed in his best bib and tucker, sporting his two medals for all to see, Enrico presented himself to his lovely young Sheila. As they met in Poperinge, in the estaminet, he took her hand like the gentleman he would have wanted to be and kissed it very gently, all the time looking into her large beautiful deep brown eyes.

He approved of her parents, and they liked him. Enrico was very soon head over heels in love with Sheila. He did not try to seduce her; he now knew the road he must take, while wooing her. His Polish was very rusty, but it helped win over her father. They spent all the time together that they could, before Enrico was called back to do his duty at the end of his leave. Matti too, had had a wonderful time with Dawn; they were so committed to one another that they had agreed to marry, either a couple of weeks after the war ended, now that it looked as if there was finally going to be a conclusion to all the suffering and mayhem, or on his next leave whatever was the closest. Nothing had been thought out about what would happen after the war, what job he would do, where they would live, just the fact that they would marry. Secretly, Matti thought that the army might be a good career move — there will always be wars — and he knew that no one believed the newspapers' rhetoric about this being the war to end all wars. Though Matti loved his place in the army, he had no real respect for authority, and despised all politicians whoever they were, but he could handle himself well now, and he knew how to make things work, in this man's fighting force.

The friends met up again in the trenches; the big guns still fired at random, but most infantry troops knew the score well now, and it wasn't difficult for an experienced soldier to tell where a shell was going to land, or what sort of shell it was, being either shrapnel, fragmentation, high explosive or gas. Fewer and fewer casualties were accruing, which for the ordinary Tommy was a blessed relief, but for some reason the top brass thought it much better if everyone was still blasting away at one another. A state of 'live and let live' existed within the opposing armies. In some systems of trenches, the ones that were generally closest to one another, often Fritz would call over, warning the Tommies that they had been ordered to fire, or that there would be some shelling going to occur at such and such a time. Just outside of Loos, both forces used the same well, and the Germans would use it in the morning, the British in the afternoon. This state of mutual preservation was only ended when a Brigadier who was serving in Loos heard about this and ordered a raiding party to waylay the Germans one morning, but a Tommy had warned them beforehand of the forthcoming ambush. No one got shot. But the Brigadier just ruffled his feathers, and grunted like his ancestors before him.

Enrico greeted Matti with a hug, but there was a distance between them now as things had changed. They were of course glad to see one another, as old friendships like theirs would survive, albeit slightly differently.

The spring of 1918 was a warm and pleasant one; the wild flowers bloomed in no-man's-land, just like they always had. Nature takes care of its own: nothing man did was going to change the seasons, and that meant flowers growing, birds singing, foxes, voles and all wildlife recolonising the battlefields; all of nature was returning to life again. Fieldmice used human skulls for their nests, and why not, they were just the right size and shape. Birds nested in the broken trees as if they still stood tall and straight. Foxes scavenged here and there, often setting off the odd bomb or two by mistake, thinking it an object to play with. In all of this nature, how could men continue this nonsense? But they did!

Spring turned to summer, and summer into autumn. The troops knew that peace talks were in progress; it was now just a matter of time until peace was declared. Enrico was talking to Matti about his plans for life after the war: he had decided that if Sheila's parents would allow him to marry their daughter, he would help rebuild a house in their area, and maybe buy into some sort of business. He fancied the idea of an estaminet, or a small hotel; after all there was his father's money which was still in Tranmere, waiting for him.

"Matti, I've been thinking, I know we're going to survive, that was obvious from the start, but why should we worry about being wounded again? It may be safer, but it's still not safe in the trenches, and I'm sure we could wrangle another transfer. What d'you think?"

"Mmmm, maybe. I saw Maurice about a week ago, and he has a real cushy number, running about delivering messages, and generally staying behind the lines. What about us two becoming runners?"

"Let's talk with 'Spider' and see what he says, agreed?"

"Agreed!"

They wandered around the trench system, keeping out of any Officers' way: they were not looking for work to do! They made their way right up to the front line, and there, was Lieutenant Michael 'Spider' Kelly, shouting orders to some raw young lads, who had only appeared in the trench a couple of days ago; these were not recruits, these were conscripts, called up to do their duty.

"Sir!" Enrico stamped to attention, and tried to salute their friend.

"What the hell do you two want? Can't you see I'm busy? I'm trying to save these young lads' lives. Would you believe I caught them standing on the firing line smoking cigarettes and chatting with their heads at least ten inches above the rim of the trench, in full view of the Hun? When I challenged them, what d'you think they said? It's alright, Sir… *Alright, Sir!!*" shouted Kelly in a rage. "They bloody well think this is a game. Everyone knows the war is nearly over, they said…*Over*, they said! Are they fucking mad, or has someone forgot to tell me something?" Kelly was now in full flow. "You stupid little cretins, if the bloody Hun doesn't shoot you, I will. There is no peace until I tell you there is. Keep your heads down, that's why we have periscopes. I have just saved your lives, Fritz doesn't know about peace either, so when I know, I will tell those shits across the way there, then I will tell you." He was now pointing in the direction of the German front line. "Is that clear, do you all have that imbedded in your brains, because that is better than a bullet imbedded there? Well, what do you all have to say?"

"Sorry, Sir, it won't happen again."

"No, it *won't*, like I said; if I see any of you again doing something dumb, I will shoot you before the bloody Germans do! Now get back up there and keep a sharp look out." He turned, walked towards Matti and Enrico, winking.

"Fancy a cuppa, lads?"

The agreed date for a transfer to the Runners was to be the 1st September. Sergeant Enrico Caruso and Corporal Matthew Dumbridge were to report direct to Headquarters of the General Staff at St. Omer. From there they would be delivering messages across the country, but now behind the lines. A safe job for them to have: they were more likely to be struck by lightning than shot or blown west, by enemy fire.

The time soon came for the two lads to part company at least for a while with their friends, especially one 'Spider' Kelly. The night before they left for St. Omer, Kelly threw an intimate party in his dugout, just for the three of them. Much to the amazement of both the lads, Michael had procured three bottles of very good pre-war champagne. "Crikey, Mike, you never stop amazing me! Where the heck did you get this batch from?" asked an astounded Enrico.

"Well, that would be telling, but as you are leaving this haven of tranquillity tomorrow, for the hustle and bustle of running around fancy top brass, pretending that you give a damn, I will tell you!" He coughed, stood erect with his left hand stuck into his tunic, just like Napoléon. Then in a solemn, deep tone, he continued. "I, Lieutenant Michael Kelly known to his friends and not friends, as 'Spider', though I have never understood why…"

"Get on with it!" chided Matti, showing absolutely no reverence for this solemn occasion, with a huge grin on his face.

"I shall continue after that very rude interruption. As I was saying… no, I have forgotten now; what the hell was I saying? Oh yes, as I was saying, I found these 'ere bottles from a cellar in the town of Wipers about six months ago. I just happened to be resting in the shelled remains of someone's home, when the floor gave way, showing me, like a light from heaven, a set of stairs going down. Well, you know me, lads, duty first before all else; I had to go down these steps; after all, the entire German army might have been down there waiting for me to get out of the way!"

"Is this going to take all night, I'm thirsty?" cried Enrico with false tears.

"Don't you two realise how important this statement is? I might have been taking on the whole German army including Uncle Bill himself? It takes a hero to face that prospect!"

"Well, was Kaiser Bill down there?" asked Matti.

"Well, actually no, but three bottles were, so I attacked them and took them as prisoners!"

The two lads clapped enthusiastically at the long drawn-out tale of woe. Then Enrico cracked open one of the bottles, and poured the contents.

The three of them indulged themselves with the three champagne bottles, and before two hours had elapsed the bottles were empty. They did not feel intoxicated, and the conversation had long petered out, leaving a heavy silence in its place. Enrico covered his mouth with his hand and coughed deliberately, as if to break the spell.

"I think I speak for Matti, as well as myself, when I say that you've been real special to us! If it had not been for you, we would never have survived this war, but would be just numbers, like all the other poor buggers, lying out there in no-man's-land or on the wire. We both know we owe you a lot. The three of us are friends, let it stay that way. Keep in touch, at least after this fiasco has ended. Matti is talking about staying in the army, if they will have him. I'm probably going to stay here in Belgium, either as an hotelier or an owner of a good estaminet. Whatever, but both of you will always be welcome, and no money will ever be exchanged between us. Anyway, everyone knows what a tightfisted bastard you are! Thanks for everything, once again. And stop blabbing, you're not a child!"

"I agree with everything that Enrico has said. We've never been heroes, you know it, and we know it too. But we have survived, and that is down to your strictness from day one: you showed us how to become men, and we are grateful."

"Well, what can I say? You have both become friends, despite the fact that you are just NCOs and not Officers like what I is! But joking apart, you have done well, and I do wish us all to meet after the war ends. But, and this is a but, remember, it hasn't ended yet. Keep yourselves safe; all this nonsense about being immortal, that's just so much hogwash; you have both been extremely lucky, and deservedly so. Stay that way, take no chances, and keep alive. Now bugger off, I have work to do!"

With that, both the lads stood to attention and saluted Kelly. They then turned and walked out of his dugout and maybe his life, whilst all the while Kelly was pretending to blow his nose on an extremely dirty hand-kerchief.

The next morning, at the crack of dawn, they were both waiting on the side of the road at Belgian Battery Corner for the lorry to take them to St. Omer. Neither said a word, what was to say anyway? Life moves on; this was going to be a new chapter for both of them.

They reached St. Omer just in time to stop and have some cooked eggs and bacon. Two strong cups of tea for each of them later, and they were ready to face their new existence. The house that held the British Headquarters was a severe 18th century, castle-like town house. It must have had at least twenty bedrooms, all now housing the top British brass. There were guards everywhere; the lads needed twenty minutes just to get past the first sentry, as they had no letters of authority with them, because they had never been issued. So it took some sorting out, before they finally got in to meet Lieutenant Swift, who would be their liaison Officer. He quickly showed them around, telling them a brief history of the building; it turned out that Swift was an Architect in civilian life. The place was of great historical interest to him; to Matti and Enrico, it was just a rather cold, gloomy building that maybe once had seen better days.

They were shown where to store their packs and to lay their bunks: a hard wooden floor, but luxury for them both after the trenches. He also showed them their bathroom, reserved for NCOs, and there was a bath as well! A bath, sheer luxury, they could finally get rid of their lice! Lieutenant

487

Swift looked at them both closely, "Always present yourselves in a clean and well dressed mode. The brass will not tolerate any slackers, or any tardiness; I suggest you both get a haircut right away. Clean up your clothes, and generally smarten up. You are free until tomorrow, so get to it. There is a barber, two streets away, a Frenchman, but forgetting that, he is quite good. One last thing, you have agreed to be runners; it can be dangerous, though most of your work will be behind the lines. Always go direct to wherever and whomever, never tally on the way. And *never*, and I emphasise never, talk to strangers about what you do or where you do it, and never show the messages which are always top secret. Your lives might depend on you doing as you are told!" Swift looked at them sternly, and then ended with: "Right, see you at six o'clock tomorrow morning, you are both dismissed."

For Enrico and Matti the work became fun. They were now behind the lines, doing something that didn't include killing people or falling into dead bodies. They were eating well, sleeping well, and generally having a good time. Most of the journeys, they did together, as it was always safer in pairs. They went to the French Headquarters at Cassel; there they were allowed to eat some very good French food, though Matti drew the line at snails. And the canteen always had good French wine to try, not the paint stripper that had become the norm for them. Sometimes they had to go to Hazebrouck; this would be to give special orders to various Generals. At Hazebrouck, they relived their times when they were training for trench duty; not that the training had shown any authenticity as to what it was really going to be like.

Matti managed to go quite regularly to see Dawn in Calais; it was on the second visit that Dawn dropped the bombshell: "Matti darling, I must tell you that I have now missed two periods, and I know in myself that I am pregnant!"

"Pregnant…Are you sure? Of course you are sure. Well, maybe it's a little early, but I'm over the moon with joy. Me a Father! I shall be a much better one than my Dad was to me, that I promise."

When he told Enrico, who was shaken but happy for him, his friend asked, "Has she told or seen a doctor yet?"

"No, not yet; if she tells them now, she will be sent home in disgrace. We will marry in a month or six weeks' time hopefully. Anyway, that's the plan."

Dawn managed to keep it a secret until the end of September, when one day she had morning sickness there, in front of a doctor. He was shaken, she was mortified. Two days later Dawn was on a ferry back to England where she would live with her parents until Matti came to marry her.

Matti was extremely unhappy to find that in the 20th century, women were still castigated for doing what came naturally, but he would soon do the right thing and marry her, making Dawn a wife and giving their child a father.

Enrico got to see Sheila on several occasions, staying in the family home. It had been agreed that Enrico could court her, and after the war was won, they could get married. Enrico too, was full to overflowing with love, which spilled into his feelings for his fellow man. Though the guns were never out of earshot, somehow they became part of another world: his was now peaceful, the sun always shone, it was never cold, and there was no such thing as lice or death. Rats had disappeared from their thoughts; in fact God had changed his mind altogether about rats, and they had been dispatched from the planet completely. This was a time of joy and plenty, nothing was going to change things ever again for the two friends.

October the 20th came, and the lads were ordered in to see Lieutenant Swift.

"I have a task for you both, one that entails a little danger. You have to deliver several letters to various commanders, all the way up the line into the Somme region. These special orders are to tell the commanders to make some advances, as things need to be moved along."

"Lieutenant, you cannot be serious? Everyone knows that an

armistice is imminent. Why spoil it by trying to make advances into enemy-held territory?"

"That is the reason we need to advance. Everyone knows that an armistice is imminent, yes, true! Everyone and Kaiser Bill know that if we just hold out, then it will just peter out. Well, the way that things seem to be going at the conference table, shows that Fritz still hasn't learnt that he has lost. We need to push on to show him that simple fact. We need to get the best terms, *our* terms, not to be dictated to by that jumped-up, withered-armed little freak that has caused all this trouble."

"I hear you, and I can see what you are saying might have some bearing on how things are eventually sorted out. But, why allow men to die unnecessarily; hasn't there been enough death in this war to satisfy the top brass?"

"Sergeant, you have no right to say these things. You could be court-martialled for saying much less, it is almost treason!"

"Sir, we have got to know one another quite well over the last few weeks; I respect you, but you have never been in the front line trenches, we have, we know what it's like. Your life is worthless if a bullet has your name on it," said Enrico now showing some passion, with his fists resting on the Lieutenant's table. Swift was becoming nervous, and wished he had never said anything to the two NCOs; they would have just delivered their messages and orders without even asking. He took a deep breath and tried one last time.

"Sergeant Caruso, I have given you orders; are you going to carry them out, or shall I call the MPs?"

"Lieutenant Swift, there is no need for that. Enrico was only mouthing off what everyone knows or thinks. We are on our way," protested Matti, in defence of his lifelong friend. "Enrico, let's be on our way. We cannot stay here chatting to the Officer all day, work to be done."

They retreated outside into the courtyard. Matti gave a huge sigh of relief. "You nearly got us into serious hot water then. If that idiot hadn't been such a coward, we might be facing something more deadly than the Hun. Get that motorcycle, you can drive. But please keep it slow. It is one thing to be shot by the enemy, but to have an accident with you steering, that would be too much for body and soul to bear. Twenty miles an hour or I will tell on you! Then you can be shot on your own."

Enrico smiled, but didn't laugh; what the hell was there to laugh about anyway?

The runs to the Somme became a regular occurrence. There had been no incidents that were a danger to them, but they knew they were always bringing orders that would send other men to their deaths, unnecessarily.

The 1st of November came, and it was confirmed that an armistice would be signed for the eleventh hour of the eleventh day of the eleventh month. Ten days from then. So why were the armies still pushing one another? Why not live and let live? How strange it now seems, that governments knew the date of an armistice, yet allowed the Generals to waste human life so easily. Fighting was still going on all over the world. In the air, planes were doing mortal combat with one another; at sea the U-boat threat, though now not as dangerous as it had been, still existed: they were still sinking ships and drowning sailors, and on the battlefields, it was just the same: machine gunners had plenty of belts of ammunition that they could still fire off; there was always someone ready to fire yet another shot: 'I want to be the last one to throw the last Mills bomb.' Every soldier from both sides wanted to be the one to fire the last shot. The sickness that had gripped the armies didn't seem to have abated much over the last four years. Let's kill one last Hun, let's make one more widow or one more grieving parent. Why stop a good thing?

On that 1st November, a cold blustery day, Enrico and Matti were once again ordered up to the Somme area with yet new orders of destruction. It was hard going for them as either the ground was wet and muddy, which made them slip and slide, or in other areas it was extremely bumpy from being frozen solid, which made very slow going; whatever happened, they must deliver these orders. Their first port of call was at Beaumont Hamel.

They didn't get there until quite late that afternoon, and they were given permission to stay over for the night, because the weather was closing in and a storm was brewing. The next morning was very frosty, but the storm which had threatened had not appeared, and now the ground was solid. They had breakfast, and moved off at around nine o'clock; the light was low in the winter sky, and the surface was dangerous for the motorcycle, but they must press on to their next port of call, at Fricourt. It was just approximately ten miles further along the trenches, and should have taken not more than an hour, but on the 2nd November it took nearly four hours, which meant they didn't arrive until afternoon. The orders were once again delivered; once again the weather was closing in, which meant they would stay yet one more night. They dined well that evening with some very friendly NCOs, who had taken a shine to them both, or maybe it was the fact that there was now just nine more days to survive this madness. Where the Sergeants got a huge chicken from, let alone cooked it on the front line, was anyone's guess, but they had got one, along with potatoes, peas and bread and jam. And better still, was the fact that they were quite prepared to share their luck with Enrico and Matti.

The next morning being the 3rd November, all shook hands and said their farewells. Enrico and Matti had one more delivery that should have been delivered on the first day; it was to the Commanding Officer at Maricourt. The Officer in question was a Colonel Waters; he should have been a sailor, but he had one problem: he actually could not stand to be at sea, getting very sea sick. He loved ships, and was always in awe at the grandeur of the British Navy; he loved all vessels, any size, he just did not want to be in them. His father had been a Rear Admiral, but was pleased enough when his son got his first commission in the army; he worked his way up very rapidly. His men loved him, and all would risk their necks for anything he wanted of them. Enrico and Matti both had that feeling that they were in the presence of a special person. He asked them to hang on for a while, have some food and rest up, which they gladly did.

"Yesterday I sent out a runner to a forward position, one commanded by Lieutenant Owen; the man should have been back, but we have no word whatsoever, and tomorrow, Lieutenant Owen must push forward. Now I can only ask you if you would volunteer, I cannot make you do it, as you are not attached to my company, but would you hang on till first light, and if the other runner has not arrived back, I think we must assume that he is either dead or wounded. So would you two try again for us, as I have no men to spare?"

Enrico looked at Matti, and Matti commented: "Looks like here we go again!" So Enrico turned back to Colonel Waters, and said, in a not terribly enthusiastic voice: "Of course, Sir, we'll go for you."

That night, both Enrico and Matti were in a reflective mood. How quickly they had fallen back into the old routines! Unable to sleep, Enrico stood on the firestep watching the heavy clouds rushing by, and then admiring the myriads of stars making an appearance between the gaps. He absent-mindedly scratched himself before he realised the lice had made yet another unwelcome visit.

They had always had a dull ache in the pit of their stomachs before going on a dangerous mission, but this time it seemed worse: they had got used to being out of the killing fields, and the thought of going back did not exactly fill them with the joys of spring. Just before dawn, they were offered something to eat and drink, before being taken to Colonel Waters.

"Thank you, lads, but you are our only hope for getting this order through." He then shook both their hands, and sent them on their way.

It was the 4th November 1918, seven days before armistice. The wind whistled, with a shrill, icy chill. Though the temperature was only minus one, it was the sort of cold that ate into your bones. There was no trench system to follow; they must make their way from shell hole to shell hole, but they had studied the map well, and knew exactly where to go. They fixed the bayonets on their rifles in preparation, and were given half a dozen Mills bombs each to carry, just in case; but they were not looking for trouble, and they were going to be very careful on this particular journey. Their objective was one of the many forward machine gun nests that were manned by the Manchester Company, and they were positioned for defence against any attacks from the Germans who held the other side of the Oise-Sambre canal. Enrico and Matti crouched in the first gloom of dawn, on the edge of the front line trench. They had to traverse the best part of a mile across open country before reaching Lieutenant Owen's dugout.

"Well, Matti, now we know why we're called runners! We're going to have to run from shell hole to shell hole; so, do you feel fit?"

"About fit to burst."

"Then, sunshine, let's go!"

They both leapt up and zigzagged like crazy hares being chased by whippets. The first big shell hole was a good hundred yards, and when they jumped into it, they were relieved that as yet, they had drawn no fire. Enrico looked over the rim, carefully, and saw that the next biggest was no more than twenty yards away to their left, so up they got and ran to that. Again, no fire, but the shell hole was full of decaying corpses, mainly German, and the smell of corruption, once again brought back all the terrible things that had happened to them over the past years. The next big crater was about fifty yards in front of them, and they decided to make yet another charge, still zigzagging. They leapt into the hole, panting furiously, and Matti said, gasping: "Enrico, I've got to stop eating this bully beef!"

So far they had been very lucky, but it was still very gloomy, and hopefully the Hun was tucked up in bed. There were a series of large craters all around them, indicating that a furious battle had taken place, and there were many dead, lying all over the place, from both sides.

"Right, Matti, follow what I do; we'll literally jump from one hole to another. We're doing well." Up he sprang again, with Matti following. One hole here, a crater there, another there, and so on, each time getting closer to their objective. They were now more than half way, and if the weather had been clearer, they would have been able to see their destination.

"Matti, I want us to make for the one on the left, there," he pointed to where you could see the big earth mound blown up by a huge shell. Once again, they ran zig-zagging to the hole, and leapt into it, more or less simultaneously. They crawled around to the opposite rim, disturbing several rats which were quietly having breakfast on some previous tenants that had gone west. As they looked over the rim for their next haven, they were disturbed by a little movement and a low groaning sound. Matti turned and grabbed Enrico in a fright, "What the fuck was that?" he asked, hardly daring to turn his face backwards. But Enrico had been fazed by the groan, too, and had he not had his tin helmet on, Matti would have noticed that his hair was standing on end. Together they turned their head slowly backwards towards the noise, and they noticed that it was another Tommy, who they had assumed was one of the corpses. They moved back, to see if they could be of assistance, and turned him over onto his back so they could see his face. Horror struck them both at the same time:

"Oh, my God! Maurice! This is not you! You were meant to survive! You were like us two, immortal!" but Maurice could hardly hear or see them. He had been shot through the lung, and had taken nearly two days to drown in his own blood. It was obvious that he was in the last throes of dying. Matti removed his helmet, and brushed the mud and hair from his face. He was looking at them, and mouthing something; they could not be sure of what he was trying to say. Matti cradled Maurice close to him, to give him some comfort, and his breathing was short and shallow. Matti put his ear close to Maurice's mouth, and he thought he heard the whispering sound of: "Fuck me, I have seen God," but he could not be sure, as Maurice gave a small sigh, and Enrico and Matti knew that the little Jew had gone for ever. Enrico looked at Matti, whose mouth had fallen open, and for once Enrico could not control himself; for the first time in many years, he openly burst into tears. The two friends hugged one another for several minutes, until they felt they were composed again. They went back to the other side of the rim to continue their trek. Enrico glanced back at Maurice Bechstein for one last time.

"So *he* was the runner for Colonel Waters!"

He then turned back, now fixed and determined. "Matti, let's keep running! There's a mist that should hide us from the Germans. I'm sick of all this jumping about. Let's get it over and done with!"

Up they jumped, and ran, and ran; after about three hundred yards, they temporarily stopped behind the broken wall of a derelict building. Both were bending over, panting frantically. Enrico handed Matti his canteen of water.

They were now just a matter of another hundred yards before they reached the dugout, with its connecting trenches. Once more they ran, and just as they were ready to jump in, they heard a shout that sounded like 'Englisher!' and a stream of tracer bullets came in their general direction, but they had been lucky and got into the trench, unscathed. An astonished Private, holding a mug of tea, looked at them both and said, in a very strong cockney accent: " 'Oo the 'ell are you two?" and "Where the 'ell 'ave you come from then?" Enrico looked at him, took the mug of tea, saying: "Where the 'ell 'ave you come from, *Sergeant?*" He drank half the tea and gave the rest to Matti, who then returned the empty mug.

"Right, Private, where will I find Lieutenant Owen? I have important orders from Colonel Waters."

"Sorry, Sergeant, it's just that it's been quiet, here. With all that firing out of the blue and you two leaping down into the trench, fair put the fear of Almighty in me! Lieutenant Owen, you say? If you go down the trench on the left, 'ere, after about two 'undred yards, you'll see a couple of Lewis guns mounted, facing the canal. Well, there's a dugout in there, where the officer sits, usually writing all that 'ere poetry that he likes so much."

They made their way to the dugout, and there, sitting on a couple of ammunition crates, was the slight figure of Lieutenant Wilfred Owen. He was not wearing his helmet, and sported a well groomed crop of black hair, parted very neatly down the middle. He had a small moustache, which was so sparse as to make him look like an adolescent. Though his clothes were clean, he looked unkempt in them; his complexion had an olive tinge, giving him a somewhat Mediterranean appearance. This may have had something to do with the fact that when the Spanish Armada was wrecked off the Irish and Welsh coasts, many of the surviving Spaniards eventually intermarried with the Welsh women, thus giving a lineage of swarthy descendants. His pencil was busily writing in a small notebook, until he realised that two NCOs were standing to attention in front of him. Enrico saluted, and said: "Sir, we have brought you special orders from Colonel Waters." He then handed a sealed envelope, which Owen casually opened. His jaw dropped, as he read the contents.

"Oh, hell! Whoever came up with this nonsense? It says here that I am to cross the canal, and immediately engage the enemy. This sounds like insanity!" At the top of his voice he screamed for Corporal Allen, who duly came.

"Corporal, call all the NCOs in. It seems we have a battle to conduct."

Enrico and Matti stepped back, wondering what was going to happen next. This was not their fight, their job was done. They could leave, and get back to their own lives again, the lives that did not include death and destruction. Yet, they were mesmerised into standing back, and watching, as soldiers ran here and there, like ants after their nest has been disturbed. NCOs came and went, all preparing the men for the charge that was going to take place. All they had to do was get across this canal. Though it had water in it, the water was probably no more than a foot to two foot deep. Just as Wilfred was ready to mount the ladder, and call the charge, he looked around for his own Sergeant, whom he had not seen since the onset of this panic.

"Where is Sergeant Higgins?" he asked, and a voice came back, saying: "He's been in the latrine, Sir, he's coming now."

'Higgins? Higgins? I have not heard that name for a long time' thought Enrico. He looked towards Matti, and noticed that his friend was staring, wild-eyed, and the hairs on the back of his neck bristled for all to see.

There was a gurgling scream erupting from the back of Matti's throat, a sound that stopped everybody, and they all looked towards him. His right hand rose, with his index finger pointing, and that gurgling sound turned into: "Higgins…Angus fucking Higgins! You're not dead!" On hearing his name being called, Sergeant Higgins stopped in his tracks and looked in bewilderment at the two men glaring at him. Then the penny started to drop; recognition came from the dark recesses of his brain. "*Oh, yes!* I remember you two! You knocked me senseless! And if I had not been in trouble with my superiors myself, I would have had you two banged up for what you did!" Enrico was frozen rigid, but Matti still pointing, kept rasping the sound: "Dead…dead…You've wrecked our fucking lives! You should be dead!" and gradually his hand came down. He ponderously took his rifle which was slung over his shoulder.

Lieutenant Owen had climbed the ladder, service revolver in hand, and was now standing above the firing line, prepared to call the charge. But instead, he was interrupted by the terrible sounds coming from his dugout. He looked back into the trench and shouted: "What the hell is going on, here?" Then turning back towards the canal, he blew his whistle and shouted: "Come on, me…" A burst of Maxim fire erupted from the opposite bank, and Lieutenant Wilfred Owen, one of Britain's Great War poets fell dead. All of this went unheeded by Matti and Enrico. Matti had now raised his rifle, with its bayonet pointing towards Angus Higgins, and he staggered like a drunken man towards him, shouting the words: "Dead, dead, you're dead!"

But Sergeant Higgins was quick, and he speedily withdrew his revolver, aimed it at Matti and fired. The hot lead tore through Corporal

498

Matthew Dumbridge's throat, and he fell forward onto his knees, still clutching his rifle, looking wild-eyed, yet managing to gurgle, blood gushing from the gaping wound, splashing all around him. But Angus Higgins did not stop there, and emptied the entire chamber into Matti's body. Matti fell forward onto his face, his left hand and leg trembling for a while before becoming still. For five or six seconds, there was absolute silence, and then Higgins with horror deeply etched on his features, glanced at Enrico. The latter looked at Matti, came out of his trance, and a huge gust of emotion swept through his body. He knew what he must do: as the tears flowed freely down his cheeks, he calmly withdrew a Mills bomb from his pocket, pulled the pin, and casually walked over to Higgins. All this time Higgins was fumbling, trying to reload his revolver, but before he could do so, Enrico had gone to him, grabbed the back of his hair, pulling his head backwards. He jammed the grenade deep into the Sergeant's mouth. The explosion gave a muffled roar, and Higgins, now reduced to a standing torso, slumped to the ground, taking the body of Enrico with him.

The Germans had not been asleep when all this commotion was going on, and the field guns had been alerted to the exact position. Round after round of shells rained into the trench system; those who were not blown to pieces were buried alive. After what seemed like an eternity of shelling, it stopped as suddenly as it started. The wind could be heard whistling again, as silence once more reigned supreme over the Oise-Sambre canal. Troops further along the trench now rushed to where the mêlée had taken place with a view to rescuing any survivors left.

The war raged on for another week; death and his scythe reaped their human harvest until the last minute. It was as if in the minds of the generals, from both sides, the stockpiles of shells and bullets should not be wasted, and should be used up before that clock struck eleven times. In the very last hour, the cavalry were charging through German-held territory, killing as many of the Boche as they could. It had even been suggested that the German Navy should go to sea one last time, and shell the British in a blaze of glory. In the air, mad risks were taken by pilots on both sides, to drop their last bomb, and empty their last magazine from their machine gun. On virtually every continent in the world, the same scene was played out, and it has been estimated that in the last hour, more than ten thousand soldiers, sailors, or airmen died in a last blaze of glory. Every artillery piece from both sides wanted to fire the last shell, so the last explosion was a huge one. Then, silence...the silence was eerie at first. Men were warned not to leave the trenches, and not to fraternise with the Germans, but after an hour had gone by, and the smoke had cleared, men ignored their officers' orders, at first by standing on the parapet, then by wandering into no-man's-land. Nobody broke that cease-fire, and gradually, as per the agreement of the armistice, the German army, carrying only its light arms, after four and a quarter years of fighting, melted away and left the field of battle.

On that first day of peace, there was great celebration throughout the world. The great 14-18 war to end all wars was finally over. Soon the burial parties carefully searched the battlefields to finally lay to rest fallen comrades. It was on the 12th November, with a flurry of snow in the air, that a burial party of men came upon the trench system at the Oise-Sambre canal. The first body that was recognised was that of Lieutenant Wilfred Owen, and in a dugout behind, only one surviving soldier was found, and he was badly mutilated. How he had managed to survive, God only knows. The other soldiers had been decimated by numerous shells. Everything was completely unrecognisable. They could not even establish how many bodies were in there, so like many other places, the dugout was filled in, and a small cross was erected. On that cross, were the sombre, melancholy words:

**"Soldiers of the Great War**
**Known unto God"**

500

# Epilogue

The 11th November 1918 came and went. War had ended, peace had returned, but was it a *just* peace? Probably not. Germany was still blockaded by English warships; people were starving in the streets. The Kaiser had abdicated, and was exiled in the Netherlands. He, who had once been Queen Victoria's favourite grandson, died, a broken and spent man in his mansion near Arnhem in 1941. The German fleet had been ordered to anchor at Scapa Flow to be decommissioned; but in 1919, still with nothing resolved, the sailors stranded there decided to scuttle their ships from sheer frustration.

All of Germany's heavy guns and aircraft were confiscated; it was agreed by the Allies that reparation should be paid by Germany, as it had started the conflict. But as the country was economically crippled anyway, the debt was completely unrealistic. The Deutsche Mark became worthless, and it was not long before men in employment were being paid with paper money by the wheelbarrow load. A billion Deutsche Marks meant nothing. Anarchy started to take the place of organised government. Communism had risen on the one hand, and extreme nationalism on the other. Shortly after the war ended a sorry little Austrian corporal, who had fought on occasions quite heroically in Langemark around the Ypres salient, rose to power through treachery and deceit, gradually taking control of an extreme right organisation, which was to become known as the Nazi Party.

It was easy for this young Adolf Hitler, whose only real talent was one of oration, to use the cruel terms of the peace treaty, and exploit the need for Germany to break free of the stranglehold of the reparation payments, to make his party gradually gain power.

In Britain, Winston Churchill claimed that the returning soldiers would come home to a land fit for heroes. Instead they came home to Depression. All industry had been manufacturing arms for war. How can you turn that into goods for peace? Poverty was still gripping the common man, a poverty they had fought to get rid of, for good and all. Industry had to be kick-started again, and that was going to be a long, slow process. In the meantime, people did not starve, but they went hungry.

Britain, France and America changed the map in the Middle East for ever; allowing the Arabs to think that fighting along the side of the Allies would procure them independence with self-rule, turned out to be a barefaced lie, and the French and British governments reneged on all promises that had been profferred. Palestine was split into two by the British, giving the Jews a toehold, which was eventually to become Israel. In Africa, past German colonies were divided up by the British, French and Belgians. In the Far East, German-held territories were taken over once again by the French and British, and also the Japanese. America, which had always fought against colonialism, decided it was time to get in on the act and annexed some of the Pacific islands.

Northern France was devastated, and much of the fine growing land had been so injected with heavy metals and gas, that it made the ground unfit for cultivation, as the produce would be rendered toxic for many generations to come. Some of the best regions for champagne had been laid waste by the continuous shelling. Whole villages and towns had to be completely rebuilt, and the city of Verdun, with its famous forts, like its Belgian counterpart, Ypres, was just one big pile of rubble.

Belgium had been almost completely decimated. Many villages and towns had been totally wiped off the face of any map. After some of the battles, even aerial photographs could not show up any recognisable features of any past human civilisation.

Winston Churchill wanted to make the town of Ypres into one big open memorial for the million British and Commonwealth troops that had died in and around it, but fortunately, the Belgian people had other ideas, and started to move back and rebuild. As complete town plans had been saved, in the early 1920s a replica in every detail was started in the rebuilding of the old medieval town. It is estimated that a million tons of ordnance never exploded on the various battlefields, and on the Ypres salient alone, more than two hundred tons of live ammunition has resurfaced each year in the fields to be disposed of. Much of it includes mustard and chlorine gas, which are very difficult to get rid of, and there are probably enough gas shells remaining to keep the bomb disposal units busy for the next two hundred years.

Many mines which had been dug and laid with high explosives, ready to blow up the German lines, also got lost. Tunnels caved in, entrances were forgotten. On one occasion in the 1950s, one of these mines exploded when lightning struck the ground. Fortunately, no one was killed or injured, but a few cows stopped giving milk for a while.

It is thought that in excess of thirty million soldiers died from all corners of the globe, and all of this the result of feuding between Kings, Kaisers, Tsars and Emperors, and silly little disputes over honour. Once started, it had become unstoppable, but was it worth it?

Dawn was to be informed, in early December, that Corporal Matthew Dumbridge, VC had gone missing on 4th November, and was now assumed to be dead. She gave birth prematurely to a son, who was also called Matthew. He survived, and in 1944, was killed on June 6th on the D-day landings in World War II. He never knew his father or his mother, as Dawn became a statistic of the thirty-eight million dead of the Spanish flu in 1919.

Sheila, like Dawn, was informed in December 1918, of the disappearance, and presumed fatality of one Sergeant Enrico Caruso, VC, MM. Three years later, the legacy that had been left by Enrico's father finally and unexpectedly found its way to Belgium. There was enough money to set the whole family in business. Sheila was to marry an ex-Belgian soldier, in 1928, and their first son was named Enrico.

Lieutenant Michael 'Spider' Kelly survived the Great War, and was broken-hearted when he discovered the news of the demise of his good friend, Matthew Dumbridge. But not hearing the fate of Enrico made him eagerly search the wounded list to see if his name appeared anywhere.

Six months had passed, when in the spring of 1919 Enrico Caruso's name came to light; he was now residing as a permanent patient in Queen Mary's Roehampton. He had lost one arm, one leg and had been blinded and horrifically burnt on his face, but he had lived. Michael Kelly had decided that he would spend all the time he could with his old friend, and it was through these long visits that Kelly had discovered the full story of the two lads. It had been Enrico's wish that Sheila should get all the money, but the legalities of transferring those sums had taken three years, and he was adamant with 'Spider' that Sheila should never know that he was still alive. Enrico survived until Queen Elizabeth II was to be crowned, but died as the Coronation procession entered Westminster.

As for 'Spider', he carried on in the army, and finally distinguished himself as a Brigadier in World War II, fighting with General Bernard Montgomery at El Alamein in North Africa. He never married: his family had always been the army. He loved his men, and in some cases, they reciprocated in kind when they understood that he being a bastard was for their own good. He died, a contented old man, albeit frowning at the thought of a woman Prime Minister. His last words were: "What has this country come to?"

# Circle of Pens Publications Ltd.

## would like to present the next exciting novel by Peter Georgiadis:

# "Quite A Pleasant Little Journey"

Set in the period of the Great War, it explores the problems the police had trying to investigate serial murders when, more than likely, a soldier was involved.

The book depicts the events taking place around the 1918 raid on the German controlled Belgian harbours of Zeebrugge and Ostend, where the British attempt to obstruct the U-Boats' haven.

Follow the police as they try to capture the perpetrator when being blocked at all turns by the bureaucracy of the War Office.

It has more twists than a short magazine Lee-Enfield 303 calibre rifle!!!